Piece it all Back Together

By

Feind Gottes

A HellBound Books Publishing LLC Book
Austin TX

Dedication

I would like to dedicate this book to my mother who inspired my love of reading and to Dawn for all her support and being my heart.

Lastly, I want to dedicate this, my first book, to my father, may he rest in peace, who would never have read it, but would have been proud as hell of his son for the accomplishment.

I'm not done making you proud, Dad!

Piece it all Back Together

Chapter One: Kingdom of Sorrow

1: June 27, 1983

To live in this world is to dwell in the kingdom of sorrow; either you're coping with your own or delivering it to your fellow man.

The words of his father had never felt more poignant as Aleksander Kaczmarek mentally prepared for his ride into the kingdom. He patiently watched for the arrival of his partners in crime, Piotr and Jakub, to join them in raining down sorrow upon a couple none of them had ever even met. The Boss had given them the order they were to send a message that would be loud, clear, and messy. Aleksander almost felt bad for the unwitting couple, but The Boss wanted it made clear that talking to the boys in blue came with dire consequences. He and his pals were simply messengers; at least that's how they would justify their depravity when the subject came up later. Anyone thinking of becoming a rat after this would have to be extremely brave or extraordinarily stupid.

After what had seemed hours of waiting, Piotr Paprota pulled up out front. Piotr didn't need to bump the horn on the faded purple Cadillac, Aleksander was already halfway down the walk before the car came to a complete stop. Aleksander hopped in the backseat without any cordial exchange of pleasantries. All three were in a grim mood knowing the wetwork that lie ahead of them. It had been Piotr's idea to do the deed in the light of day, telling his pals everyone expected this kind of thing in the dead of night. Only men with real balls would do such a thing in broad daylight. Piotr wasn't concerned by the depths of depravity they would sink to, his only concern was increasing their reputation for brutality. He wanted any mention of them to incite fear; neither Aleksander nor Jakub could argue with his logic. In their world fear equaled money.

"Bump?" Jakub wagged a baggie of white powder over the seat at Aleksander.

Aleksander simply grabbed the baggie without reply, getting it out of sight before any passersby decided to be an upstanding citizen. He didn't care about hiding the drugs, however they didn't need any unwanted attention delaying their bad intentions. The Boss certainly wouldn't tolerate it. The cocaine may not improve his mood, though it would turn his nerves to steel while supplying enough energy for a marathon. He dug his pinky into the powder, scooping up enough on his uncut nail to give a lesser man a heart attack. He snorted it up his right nostril hard, then the left. Aleksander repeated the process again before sitting back, enjoying his face numbing and his heart beating an insane rhythm.

"Why aren't we taking a boost? We'll be there long enough for the 'Purple Tornado' to be noticed, y'know, Piotr?" The words flew from Aleksander's drug fueled lips.

"Last thing I need is some pig walking the beat writin' parking tickets to run the plates on a stolen car. No, it ain't worth the risk. We'll park a couple blocks away, we'll be fine." If it was even possible, Piotr's low growl made him sound ten times meaner.

"Good enough for ya mum?" Jakub added in with his high pitch laugh from the passenger seat.

"No, but yours was last night, Jake." Aleksander sneered and flicked the finger at Jakub.

When the car stopped for a red light, Jakub howled and dove halfway into the back seat, going for Aleksander's throat. Both men landed a few light-hearted blows before Piotr brought the ruckus to a screeching halt.

"Knock it off!" Piotr's voice boomed like a shotgun blast, instantly freezing both men. "We get nicked 'cuz the two of you are screwing around an' I'll save ya the trouble of explaining it to The Boss, 'cuz I'll shoot ya both in the face and leave your asses right here on the pavement."

"Chill, Piotr. We was just gettin' a little tension out," Jakub whined.

"We're on the job. If you two clowns wanna fuck it up, I'll get a new crew to do it. This job is the most important thing we've ever done, you two jackasses! After this—The Boss will love us, no one will dare fuck with us, and we're gonna shower in fucking green. Got it? Now act like you know what the fuck you're doing or get the fuck out of my car!"

"We get it, Piotr. Just blowin' off some steam, nothing to get riled about." Aleksander was always the voice of reason. "Game faces on, we know what today means. Okay?"

Piotr eyed up both members of his crew, saying nothing. He hadn't become the alpha leader with kindness, though he trusted these two men more than anyone in his entire family. With murder in his eyes, he looked from Jakub to Aleksander, punching the accelerator without glancing up when the light finally turned green.

A few blocks from their destination, Piotr parallel parked the "Purple Tornado" on a side street. Before getting out of the vehicle, they sat around, passing the baggie of coke. Piotr grabbed a duffel bag from the trunk and shoved it into Jakub's chest, handing another smaller bag to Aleksander, then slammed it closed. The trio tried to act nonchalant as they walked down the street feeling power course through their veins. Cocaine, apprehension and excitement filled them, expecting the day to forever change their lives and end two others. They had no sympathy in their minds; this was just another job, nothing more. If they had any worry at all, it was for the unexpected that could get them busted. They'd all served time before, with no desire to repeat the experience—especially knowing this job would mean life at a minimum.

An excited Jakub nearly burst out laughing in anticipation when Piotr pushed the doorbell.

The house itself was a typical Buffalo style, single family ranch house. Red brick rose two or three feet off the foundation before giving way to white siding. Fresh wild flowers were planted along the front of the house, and the smell of tulips from flower boxes filled their nostrils with a sickly sweet scent. Most found it wonderful, while this motley crew thought it repugnant in the heat of a late June afternoon.

Listening to the doorbell echo inside, Piotr reached out to ring it a second time when the door opened. The smile on the tall, thin man's face faded instantly seeing who his visitors were. He immediately turned to run like a fool, and his three visitors were on him before his foot landed its second step.

"Welcome to hell, snitch!" Piotr whispered in his ear while Aleksander closed the door behind them. "Now where's your sweet little lady bird? You wouldn't want her to miss all the fun, now would you?"

2: *Present Day*

With smiles plastered across their faces, Karen and David walked out of the theater hand in hand. The film they had just seen would soon be forgotten, but they had fun, and that was the whole point.

Once upon a time they would've sat in the back of the theater making out, barely aware a movie was playing at all. Now, in their mid-thirties, the thought of wasting money kept their eyes on the screen, saving the adult fun until after. As they exited the theater, adult fun was all they had in mind, (a few words about the movie were prudent at the moment, lest it be money wasted after all) longing to get home to their pillow-top queen size bed.

"Thanks, honey. I needed a good belly laugh." Karen let go of her husband's hand to squeeze his arm tight for the short walk to their car.

"So did I. Glad it wasn't a stinker like that last one. I thought I was gonna pee my pants a couple times, I was laughing so hard."

"Umm, honey? I think you did."

David quickly glanced down at this crotch.

"Ha! Made ya look!"

"I was…umm…damn, okay you got me!" They both broke out in laughter, approaching their vehicle.

David slipped the keys from his pocket and clicked the unlock button, scowling at the silence. He tried again and heard the locks pop open. "Remind me to pick up a new battery for this dang thing when we're out tomorrow. I keep forgetting."

"Making a mental note of it. Now take me home and make me forget it!"

"Yes, ma'am!"

Their "date nights" always made them feel like teenagers all over again. These nights out kept their relationship from becoming stale, stagnant and complacent like everyone else they knew.

David looked to his wife with genuine affection in his eyes, and saw the same reflected back at him. Knowing she still had the same spark for him after all these years, made him as happy as the day he met her. They filled the ride home with small talk, though eager for the intimacy to come.

Finally he reached their street.

Karen laid a hand on her husband's thigh and leaned in to suck his earlobe, knowing it drove him absolutely insane.

"Do hurry, sweetie, so I can thank you properly for such a wonderful evening." She dug her fingernails into his thigh, accentuating the thought.

"You're such a bad girl. Perhaps a spanking is in order?" With a playful smile, David raised his eyebrows.

"Maybe I'll spank you!" Karen laughed and played along.

"Careful now, you're making me lightheaded. I just might crash. We wouldn't want that with our bed so close!" He turned in the driveway. "Excuse me, beautiful." David reached into the glove box for the garage opener, sliding his hand slowly down her thigh, making her quiver.

The door opened agonizingly slow. He pulled in quickly, slamming the car into park and opened his door before the car had even come to a complete stop. Karen followed suit, racing around the front of the car to get her hands on her husband.

As they made their way to the bedroom they were oblivious to their surroundings, too busy kissing with hands working frantically at each other's clothes. Like hormone-charged teenagers they were locked onto each other. The world fell away, the house didn't exist, the outside world was just background noise to their story. The entire universe became the reflections of each other in their eyes.

A moment later they were in the bedroom at the edge of the bed, losing the remainder of their clothing without a care in the world. They were lovers, doing what lovers do.

Karen and David were so lost in the throes of passion they didn't bother turning on any lights, knowing their way through their own home in the dark. Neither did they suspect that they were not alone.

He watched and waited, hidden inside the bedroom closet a few feet from the foot of the bed. He was content to observe, enjoying the show until he deemed the time was right. Any other man, a normal man, would be turned on by the passionate couple. He simply stared out from the slats in the closet door at the lovers bathed in the dim light from the street lamp outside. He stood completely still, controlling his heartbeat, waiting for the right moment. He closed his eyes and listened to the couple on the bed in front of him, breathing deep to slow his heart in preparation of the task ahead. He inhaled slow and deep, dropping his pulse below a normal resting rate while waiting for the couple to near climax, his moment. It didn't take long for their breathing to quicken, telling him it was nearly time.

While the lovers' moans grew louder, he slowly opened the closet door, careful not to make a sound, inching his way to the bed.

He paused, tightening his grip on the sharpened steel rod in his right hand, inching his way to the bed until he was no more than a foot behind the couple in missionary position. A few seconds passed before David's breathing reached a fevered pitch and his body tensed in orgasm. Fast as a scorpion's sting and with deadly accuracy, the man leapt up on the bed, straddling the undulating couple and thrust the spear down through David's lower back, straight through his kidney. The long narrow weapon slid through David with ease, penetrating into the woman beneath him.

She looked up in horror as he put his left hand atop the shaft of the spear leaning forward and driving it quickly through her abdomen, deep into the bed with all his weight behind it.

The shock was sudden, yet the endorphins released in the ecstasy of orgasm numbed them to the pain momentarily. Euphoria held their screams at bay for a few seconds.

The reflections of love they had seen in each other's eyes slowly contorted to shock and pain while the wave of orgasm still rippled through their bodies, momentarily freezing the screams that should have come.

The intruder jumped off the bed, pulling the curved blade of a long kukri style machete from a sheath on his back. He raised the downward curved blade over his head and brought it down with force and surgical precision.

Karen could only watch in horror as the blade sliced perfectly through the fourth and fifth cervical vertebrae. Warm blood gushed over her face as David's severed head fell to the bed beside her. A scream was finally at her lips, only to be cut short, when the same blade slashed down also removing her head.

The musky scent of sex hung in the air, but quickly faded as it mixed with the coppery fresh blood. The pungent stench of death turned the room into a slaughterhouse.

The intruder towered over the couple, drinking in the smell of blood and sex before it was gone completely. He had often mused to himself that he should bottle that scent and call it "Lovely Death." He figured he could sell it to uptight, rich twats for a thousand dollars an ounce. Realizing that he knew exactly what "fucking death" smelled like, he almost doubled over in laughter. He savored one last deep breath of it before it changed to the choking putrescence of death.

After the momentary pause to satisfy his olfactory nerve and morbid sense of humor, it was time to get to work. He collected the couple's heads, placing them in a garbage bag to carry into the master bath. He pushed the shower curtain rod to the center of the tub and set about removing the heads. From a small bag strapped across his back, he retrieved a short length of rope that he tied around Karen's head like a headband. He repeated the procedure on David's head with the other end. He then hung the rope over the rod letting them drain, before returning to the bedroom to deal with the bodies.

Though he worked quickly, he knew no one was about to come knocking at the door at this hour.

He placed the bodies in the tub to cut up into smaller pieces, then bagged up the plastic sheeting he had placed under the mattress. The sheeting hadn't caught much blood but it was one less stain to clean up. He made quick work dissecting the bodies into manageable portions that he placed in thick black garbage bags. Knowing his day job would allow him to retrieve them in plain sight, unnoticed in the morning, for the sake of expediency, he hid the bags under some brush behind the attached garage, to dispose of later. With that done, he set about cleaning up as much of the mess as possible.

The room only needed to stand up to a cursory peek through the window and nothing more. He wasn't concerned with hiding the fact that the couple were dead, he only wanted to delay it until the police came to investigate—which could be a few days or a few weeks, it didn't matter to him.

Once he completed the slight cleanup, he flipped the mattress and made the bed, ready to collect the drained heads hanging over the tub. He placed each head in a separate black plastic bag to take with him. Bleach and hot water made quick work of the mess in the tub. Though the master bedroom and bath would withstand a casual glance inside, the putrid stench of death hung in the air like a fog.

He hid the bags from the cleanup next to the others behind the garage, then returned for the heads. He smiled thinking about his next step before locking up on his way out.

3

The night lit up in swirls of flashing red light from Officer Eddie Washington's cruiser. He wanted to be home in bed with his lovely wife instead of heading toward a railroad underpass on a wild goose chase for a supposed dead body, likely to be either some junkie's hallucination or some blacked out junkie. Eddie knew compassion was what he should feel for these downtrodden souls, yet he was content to forget them like every other citizen in the city of Buffalo, or any other city. Which was exactly what they wanted. He wasn't fond of the thought of getting himself stabbed or shot chasing down some junkie's delusion. These were the type of calls every cop wished to ignore or pass off to some rookie but Officer Eddie Washington had drawn the short straw tonight.

Eddie parked his cruiser close to the opening of the old stone underpass hoping the flashing light bar would scare off any miscreants. All he wanted was to not find a dead body so he could go home and crawl in bed next to his wife, he had no interest in arresting any of the inhabitants on minor drug charges. He kept his right hand on the butt of his service revolver, shining his flashlight from side to side hoping to see nothing other than the garbage left in heaps everywhere. He walked forward slowly and methodically, and for the first several feet he saw nothing but the garbage and a few scampering rats. A little further in, alongside the tracks in a patch of softer ground, he saw a poor homeless man covered in a cardboard blanket bedded down for the night. He knew the man just wanted to be left alone to sleep, yet Eddie saw him as his chance to get out of here quickly.

He approached the sleeping man cautiously, not wanting to scare him as he shook him awake. "Sir?" The homeless man rolled over shielding his eyes from the light. "I'm very sorry to disturb you, sir, but may I speak to you a moment?"

The man seemed quite old with white scraggily hair and an equally unkempt long beard, though Eddie knew age was sometimes difficult to determine in people with long histories of drug or alcohol abuse. The man looked at him with perturbed bewilderment and sat up, rubbing his eyes. An empty fifth of cheap vodka fell to the ground as he shifted to face the officer.

"Again, I am sorry to bother you, sir. We received a call that someone saw a body down here. Have you seen anything?" Eddie kept his voice calm, hoping to quell any anger from waking the man in the first place.

The man rubbed his head and pondered the question, before answering in a dry, scratchy voice. "Marge, I think Marge said she seen somethin' up there." He pointed into the underpass.

"Did she say it was a body, sir? I'm not looking to disturb any of ya down here for nothing."

"Didn't say much a'tall. Say you got a nip, maybe?"

"Get me outta here quickly and I'll bring you a whole bottle of your favorite. Just tell me what this Marge told you. Was it a body she saw? Where was it?" Eddie was eager, but still trying to remain patient.

The man's yellowing eyes lit up at the prospect of liquor. "Bring me a bottle and I'll lead you to any damn body you want!"

"Do it now or you get jack shit." Eddie grabbed the man by the shoulders, and instantly regretted stirring up the stench of body odor and booze that seemed to ooze from him.

"Alright. Alright. You ain't gotta get all *goose-stop-o* on me. Marge said she saw an arm stickin' out a pile just up there a short ways. She done let out yelling something 'bout a monster on the loose. Marge sees Bigfoot every damn place. That enough to get me some hooch?"

"When did she tell you that?"

"I ain't got no damn watch!"

Eddie squeezed the man's shoulders uncomfortably hard, expressing his urgency. "When?"

"Hey! Ya ain't gotta beat it outta me!"

"Don't be a smart ass. When?"

"Fine. I dunno exactly. I took my last nip and was 'bout to bed down when she came a screamin' and yellin' that Bigfoot was after her. I tried to avoid the crazy bitch but she spotted me. Said somethin' bout Bigfoot on a kill crazy rampage. I smacked her a good one, y'know, to get her to stop makin' such a racket. Then she says she seen a dead body up there. I axed her what the hell she was gettin' on about 'cause she was all 'sterical and she says there was an arm stickin' outta some pile up there. That was it. She ran off screamin' as far as I could hear. It couldn't aben too long ago seein' as how it was dark then and it still be dark now. Now how's 'bout you go get me that bottle o' hooch?"

"Did you go look?"

"No. I thought maybe tomorrow if I 'membered when I come to, y'know? Didn't seem to make much sense bangin' 'roun' in the dark. Bigfoot may be bullshit, but there's worse things down here. Curiosity killed the cat, ya know! I dun good now, so some hooch would really hit the spot, if ya know what I mean?" The man looked at Officer Washington with hopeful desperation.

"Tell ya what. If I find that body, I'll put a meal in that belly for ya to go with the hooch." Eddie released the man's shoulders and stood up.

"You can do whatever ya damn well please long as you follow it up with that hooch!" He gave a wide toothless grin.

"We have a deal."

Further into the darkness of the underpass, Eddie walked away from the old homeless man, searching for what he was now excited might actually be a dead body and not some junkie's hallucination. Everyone in the department was well aware of bodies turning up all over the city over the last several years. They all had one thing in common—they had all been decapitated. If he found the body that would lead them to this serial killer he knew it would be a giant leap toward him making detective—something he desperately wanted. Although he didn't want to miss anything, Eddie walked with less caution, eager to find the body.

The bright beam of his flashlight danced along the piles of refuse lining the dirty cement walls. Eddie held his eyes wide as saucers scouring every inch exposed in his flashlight's arc of light. The seconds crawled like hours while Eddie's eyes began to burn from not blinking. He was too afraid that he'd miss something if he did. Anxiety formed a lump in his throat as he began to think there was nothing here at all. The light danced along crumpled cans, broken shards of colored glass from discarded liquor bottles, discarded pallets used for firewood and other various brick a brac until finally his light flickered across something peculiar. He froze holding his breath while he forced his eyes to focus.

Eddie moved in to take a closer look. The last thing he wanted was to look like a fool for calling out a detective for a store mannequin. He inched closer to what certainly looked to him like a person's arm sticking out of a garbage heap. He was aware it could easily be some passed out or possibly dead indigent resident and not the discovery to jumpstart his career. The closer he crept, the more it appeared to be too clean to belong to a homeless person sleeping in filth. The arm was exposed from wrist to bicep, while the remainder was completely covered by refuse. It looked like a woman's arm to Eddie though he couldn't say for certain. He reached forward poking the arm gently with his flashlight; no reaction. He jabbed the light slightly harder; still nothing. He yelled out, yet still there was no reaction. Eddie poked the arm, making sure it was real flesh versus the plastic of a discarded mannequin. His fingers pressed into cold, hard flesh. Officer Eddie Washington had discovered a dead body.

Eddie recoiled and nearly tripped over the train rail behind him in the process. He had reacted to his first corpse the same as any other person in the world, despite his police training. He took a deep breath, calming his nerves before approaching the body again. He knew better than to disturb a potential crime scene but he had to verify that it was indeed a crime scene and not a drug overdose or a drunk passed out in his own vomit. He cautiously leaned forward like he were about to poke a coiled snake ready to strike at any instant. He slowly lifted the piece of cardboard cluttered with loose garbage that covered the body from the shoulder up. Eddie about jumped out of his skin when a cockroach darted into the filth, attempting to escape the light. He let out a nervous laugh for letting a bug startle him before continuing to lift the dirty cardboard.

Eddie stared, unable to understand what he was seeing for a long moment. As a few more cockroaches scurried out of sight, his mind tried to tell him it must be a can turned on its side and stuffed with dirty, greasy rags or something.

A millennia seemed to pass before the horrible recognition flooded into his mind. His jaw dropped, realizing it wasn't an overturned can—he was looking into a person's neck because the body was missing its head.

He recoiled, dropping the cardboard blanket in a cloud of dust and proceeded to land hard on his ass as he tripped over the rail he had avoided a moment ago. Only his quick reflexes saved him from a concussion by catching himself before his head smashed into the adjoining steel rail. He burst out laughing at the thought of his wife seeing him right now. She'd likely point and laugh, calling him a "scaredy cat" or a pussy if she really felt ornery. He was glad none of his fellow officers were on scene or he'd likely be the butt of jokes until he retired.

"You may be a pussy, Eddie Washington, but damn if you didn't just stumble on a promotion." He smiled thinking of what this gruesome discovery may mean for his career.

Eddie found it amazing that no one had leaked any word to the press over the years. Commissioners—past and present—didn't want it known there may be a serial killer loose in the city while average schmoes like Eddie didn't want to think about it and knew to keep their mouths shut. For years, the Buffalo Police Department had dubbed the killer "The Executioner" for leaving headless bodies around the city. Though he didn't know if it was true or not, Eddie had heard rumors that sometimes the hands would be missing also. He didn't know exactly how many bodies had been found, but was guessing it was at least a dozen over the last decade or so. No one wanted to believe that, perhaps, the most prolific serial killer in history lurked somewhere in "The City of Good Neighbors." People in authority weren't talking about it—not with knowing they could forget about reelection if it came out. Eddie tingled with excitement at the thought of this body possibly leading to The Executioner finally being caught. As far as he knew, The Executioner had yet to leave behind any forensic evidence.

There's a first time for everything, he thought. While heading back toward his cruiser to retrieve a roll of caution tape to cordon off the area, Eddie pushed his delusions of grandeur aside and called in his grim discovery.

"Body or Bigfoot?" The old homeless man asked as Eddie raced past.

"A body for me and a bottle and a burger for you."

"Make it a big bottle, son!"

"You got it!"

Eddie popped the trunk and pulled out a large roll of yellow caution tape and a handful of flares, to lead a trail to the body.

He stopped himself from skipping his way back knowing he shouldn't be this happy that someone had been murdered.

He raced past the homeless man—possibly the only person happier than he was right now—suddenly thinking of his wife home alone waiting for him. Naturally, she would worry because he was already late.

He pulled out his phone to call her and was reminded of the words his father told him were the true meaning of life: happy wife, happy life. Eddie had always laughed at his father when he'd repeat the old adage—but now that he was married, realized the advice really hit the nail on the head.

Eddie set flares in an arc perimeter at the mouth of the underpass, then dropped one about every ten feet leading to the body. He made another perimeter of flares around the body. Working his way, he dropped flares to the far end, where he made a makeshift barricade with wooden pallets and wrapped them in police tape. He was nearly finished when he saw flashing lights approaching. Eddie ran back to the other side, directing his comrades to form a barricade with their cruisers.

The homeless man sat watching the commotion, growing impatient for his promised bottle of liquor even though he did find it all vaguely entertaining. Sleep was likely out of the question unless he moved off somewhere, and he wasn't going to do that until he got his bottle of hooch.

"You're the one that called in the body?" Detective Stephen Barker sounded gruff as he offered his hand to Eddie.

"Officer Eddie Washington, yes sir." Eddie failed at trying not to sound too proud as he took the proffered hand. "I hope I'm not speaking out of turn, but do you think it could be…" Eddie looked around dropping his voice to a whisper, "…the work of The Executioner?"

Detective Barker pulled back, looking Eddie in the eye. "Headless?"

Eddie nodded.

"Officially there's no such person. If I see a word of it in your report I'll personally make sure you're picking up dog shit along the canal until you pray for death to take you off the force."

Eddie hung his head thinking he had overstepped his bounds, but then the detective pulled him close.

"Unofficially, if it is, and you just helped catch the son of a bitch, both of our futures could be very bright. Show me you can keep your mouth shut and your eyes and ears open, okay?" Detective Barker smiled. "Well Officer Washington, how about you lead me to the poor unfortunate soul you found. And keep your eyes peeled for possible evidence."

"Yes, sir. About fifty feet in, right at the bend." With a slight bounce in his step, Eddie led the detective into the underpass.

Chapter Two: Chasing Demons

1

There are sounds in this world everyone hates; nails scraped on a chalkboard, a baby crying on a long international flight, the screeching of brakes right before a crash. Though, perhaps, the most universally hated sound of all is the ring of an alarm clock.

Jamie Windstein swatted at her blaring alarm like a drunken blind man until she finally smacked the right spot, silencing the damned thing.

She flopped her head to see the glowing red numbers, trying to gauge how much time she had before actually getting out of bed. It was only half past six in the morning, or in her sleep addled mind's estimation, a minimum of two slaps on the ol' snooze button before facing the inevitable.

She *hated* waking up, *hated* mornings, and most of all, she *hated* having no choice in the matter. Plus it was Monday, everyone's favorite day of the week. *If only I could kill the sun, I'd be one happy woman,* she said to herself.

A world of darkness sounded wonderful, though she was sure to find something to hate about that too—but a girl could dream.

Another late night, accompanied by heavy drinking compounded her exhaustion with a splitting headache. She laid still, and with tremendous difficulty willed her eyes to open more than tiny slits. Imagining eviscerating whoever had invented mornings with her bare hands brought a smile to her lips until finally they cooperated. Whoever the bastard was certainly deserved a slow painful death, she thought.

A minute before her wretched alarm sounded again, she rolled over with a grunt and smacked it to the off position. She tossed her thin legs over the edge of her bed and instinctively reached down for the bottle she kept by her feet. She unscrewed the top and took a large gulp of the cheap vodka trying to hold her hangover at bay for the moment.

"Hair of the dog and top of the fucking morning! Ugh." She grimaced, catching a glimpse of herself in the mirrored closet door. A haggard, disheveled woman with dead eyes stared back at her. "Well fuck you too, bitch!"

She set the bottle down and then zombie walked her way to the bathroom, trying not to bump into anything or trip over her own feet. Though the swallow of liquor had helped slightly, her head pounded a painful rhythm that threatened to split her cranium in two. Throwing back the shower curtain, she twisted the knob to boiling before stepping under the stream. She wished it would melt her right away and down the drain. Instead it slowly breathed new life into her aching body, guaranteeing she'd have to face another day.

"Fuck, I hate mornings!" she screamed at the ceiling. The impulsive release felt great but the sound vibrated in her head with a painful backlash. "Okay, okay. Damn! No more screaming, I got it."

She finished the rest of her shower in silence and exited the bathroom, feeling somewhat like a real person rather than a reanimated corpse. The pounding in her head—while subsiding—remained and she washed down some aspirin with a mouthful of vodka, hoping to kill it completely. If history repeated itself, she could bank on it being gone by the time she reached her office.

"Fuck! Seven thirty! Really?! Jamie get your ass in gear, bitch!" She was rarely on time no matter how often she berated herself, and being the boss didn't make it any better.

Jamie raced down the stairs, letting out a huge sigh of relief once hitting the bottom step. A pot of coffee was ready, something that was pretty hit and miss due to her near nightly binges. She snagged her travel mug, slamming it down next to the fresh pot. Sloppily, she filled it with the hot brown juice of life, nearly burning her hand in the process. She cursed, but she had her caffeine fix so the pain was mostly worth it. She splashed in a little pick me up from her kitchen bottle of vodka along with a few heaping spoonfuls of sugar. *Breakfast of champions*, she thought as she dashed out the side door and into the garage.

In her morning rush, Jamie mistook the buzzing noise outside as just her hangover.

She jumped in her car and backed up before the garage door fully opened, revealing Leon hard at work mowing her front lawn. Leon was a staple of the neighborhood, mowing nearly every lawn in a ten or fifteen block radius. He was a little slow mentally, with a kind and gentle soul. Despite his size, over six and a half feet in Jamie's estimation, Leon was harmless as a teddy bear. He wore his usual uniform, a plain green t-shirt under a pair of well-worn and faded denim overalls. Jamie suspected the overalls were all he owned—she had never seen him wear anything else. A large trucker style baseball cap with streaks of grease and grass crisscrossing a bright yellow smiley face and bold black letters proclaiming, "HAVE A NICE DAY!" sat askew on his head. His cap matched his personality perfectly.

Most of the uptight pricks in the neighborhood looked down on him even though he didn't ask for any payment for all the work he did. They saw him as inferior rather than the kind hearted gentle giant that he was. Jamie didn't care for her neighbors—or people in general—to begin with and she hated those who looked down their nose at Leon. She also took note of anyone she saw mistreat him.

Leon smiled like a happy child seeing his favorite person. Jamie was one of the few people who was nice to him in the whole neighborhood. He shut the mower off when he saw her wave out of her car window.

"Leon, sweetie, I'm so sorry. I'm in a hurry this morning. I don't have any cash on me. Is it okay if I catch you tomorrow?"

"O'course, Miz Jamie. You catch Leon later, is okay." Leon's grin grew even wider.

"Thanks, Leon, I'll make sure to give you a little extra for your trouble. My fridge ain't loaded but you know where the spare key's at, so you go in and grab a sandwich or a drink. You hear me?"

"Thank ya kindly, Miz Jamie, yous too kind. Leon gots his own sammich. PB & J like always, Miz Jamie. You have good day, 'kay?"

"You too, Leon. I'll find you tomorrow, I promise. Now I really gotta hustle my butt to the office."

"Bye, Miz Jamie!" Leon waved goodbye vigorously.

Jamie sped to her office, sipping her doctored coffee along the way.

She didn't care about beating Carrie, her secretary, to the office. She had only managed that a few times. Today she had an early client and since clients were a little sparse at the moment, she couldn't afford to lose one by being late… again.

She pulled into the parking garage next to her office and hustled to beat the potential client through the door. She burst in, praying she wasn't too late and let out a sigh of relief seeing only Carrie at the front desk.

"Morning, Ms. Windstein." The secretary's greeting was louder than usual and she gently tilted her head toward Jamie's open office door.

"Morning, Mrs. Washington." *Shit,* Jamie mouthed to Carrie, taking her hint.

"Ah, Mr. Combs insisted on waiting in your office." She scrunched her face up apologetically.

Jamie leaned over the counter in front of Carrie. "Shit. How long?" she whispered.

Carrie lowered her voice. "Only about a minute. Sorry, boss, he insisted."

Jamie rolled her eyes and stood up straight. "I need the Kipswitch file ASAP, and please call DA Roberts and confirm our lunch for today." Everything Jamie just said was bullshit to cover her lateness and make her sound more important. They smiled at each other conspiratorially.

"Yes, right away, Ms. Windstein." Carrie winked, trying not to laugh.

Jamie pushed her office door open with purpose, attempting to look extremely more busy than she actually was. "My apologies for the wait, Mr. Combs. Damn incompetent bureaucrats in this city! You want something done right, you gotta do it yourself! Idiots couldn't be bothered to courier over urgent filings—so in the courthouse I go this morning for two pieces of paper I needed yesterday! Again, I apologize for my tardiness." She shut the door behind her, silently praying he bought her bullshit.

Mr. Combs, a dark haired middle aged man, stood extending his hand in greeting. His attractiveness surprised her since the majority of her clients were older men and women seeking to confirm what they already knew—their spouse was a lying and/or cheating SOB.

She returned his warm smile taking his extended hand. "Good morning, Mr. Combs. Thank you so much for your patience. Would you like some coffee?" Jamie moved around behind her desk and took her seat.

"No need to apologize," he said. "I only just arrived a moment ago. I hope you don't mind me violating your personal space. I really hate waiting rooms with the inevitable small talk that goes along with them. And no thanks on the coffee, your secretary Ms. uh… Washington already offered."

"No problem. We're of the same mind on small talk. I mean, come on, we can all see what the damn weather is like," she feigned groaning. "You seem a bit anxious, so how can I help you, Mr. Combs? My secretary said you were light on details when you called."

Jamie expected the usual, a client seeking her assistance in catching their adulterous spouse in the act. She knew how common adultery cases would be when she opened her own private investigation office, but damn was she bored to death of them. One sad sap after another came through her door with the same basic sob story seeking to confirm what they already knew, then getting mad at her when she confirmed it with photos or video. She learned quick to get the bulk of her fees up front since most used their anger as an excuse to try ducking out of the bill. This man seated before her didn't look any different, aside from being quite handsome. Most of her clients shuffled in ashamed to be there, slamming the door on the way out after she delivered the bad news… and it was always bad news.

"I need your help finding someone, Ms. Windstein. I've tried tracking this person down myself but I've come to a dead end. I hope you can help me."

"When did she leave you, Mr. Combs? Fair warning, I refuse to help you find a woman who left because you abused her. If that's what you're looking for, you've come…"

Mr. Combs cut her off. "No, no nothing like that, I assure you. It's a man I'm looking for and before you ask, no, I'm not gay, either. You see, Ms. Windstein…"

"Please, just Jamie, if you would," she took a deep breath. Abusers came knocking at her door far too often and if that had been the case, she wanted to nip it in the bud sooner rather than later. "I apologize if I offended you."

"No apology necessary. You see," he continued," when I was young I spent some time in a group home—or what used to be called an orphanage. I met a young boy, slightly older than myself, while I was there. I'd prefer not go into details, suffice it to say, this young man saved my life. The Head Mistress was, let's just say, a particularly cruel woman, and well…I was never able to thank or repay this young man. I got adopted right after he stepped in to save me. They took him away for the offense and I never saw him again. I'd like to find him and thank him. I'm dying, Ms. Windstein—excuse me—Jamie." Mr. Combs hung his head though his desperation came through loud and clear. "Will you help me?"

Jamie stared blankly at her new client for a long moment without answering. She had learned to be suspicious of everyone who walked through her door. First, the man didn't look like he was about to drop dead any time soon, not that looks couldn't be deceiving.

Second, she was shocked a real case, a fairly noble case, had walked into her tiny office. She had worked missing person cases before, though they were definitely a rarity. She was taken aback and delighted by her sudden fortune to have a case requiring more than snapping photos of another cheating asshole.

"I'd certainly like to help, Mr. Combs. Obviously, I'll need more information," she began. "For starters, what was the name of the orphanage? When were you there? When did you last see this boy? Do you know where he was taken? Was he adopted? Did he runaway? Most importantly though, what is his name?"

Mr. Combs handed her a folder a couple inches thick. "Everything I've found up to today is in this folder. His name was James Reimse. He'd be between forty-five and fifty years old now. Unfortunately, I wasn't able to find his birth date in my own searches, so I can't be more exact. The trail went completely cold after I left *The Mormont Home for Children*, right after he saved me. I haven't been able to find any record of him at all. No record of him at the home. No record of transfer. Other than my memory, I can't prove he ever existed." He fell silent, tears welling up in his eyes. "Please help me, Jamie. I'm desperate."

"I'll do everything in my power, Mr. Combs," Jamie said sincerely. "No guarantees, you understand, though every effort will be made to find your friend." She cleared her throat, visibly uncomfortable. "I hate to do this, but before I begin, there is the matter of my retainer…"

Mr. Combs cut her off again. "Money is no object. Would ten thousand get you started?"

Jamie tried and failed not to be shocked by the amount. "Th-That's more than ample, Mr. Combs, and extremely generous. I doubt I'll require so much."

"This is extremely important to me, and time is of the essence."

"Can I ask you just one more thing, Mr. Combs?"

Mr. Combs smiled knowingly. "Why you?"

"Well, frankly yes. After all, I'm pretty small time. To be honest, I'm used to chasing down cheaters or the occasional bail jumper. So yeah, why me?"

"I'll be honest also," he took a breath. "I wanted someone I knew would and could dedicate themselves, one hundred percent, to this case. Sure a bigger firm has more resources, more manpower, but as long as we're being honest, they wouldn't really care. They'd see a cash cow and milk me for every possible dollar until they ultimately told me they couldn't find anything—or worse, sending me on a wild goose chase to justify their exorbitant fees. You, on the other hand, I'm positive will do everything to find Jimmy quickly. Plus, you came highly recommended from an acquaintance. I assume you remember Jack Killian."

Jamie hadn't thought of that name in a long time. Jack Killian also came to her with a missing person case. She was surprised Killian would recommend her to his worst enemy, let alone a friend, with how tumultuous his case ended. Killian hired her to find his missing step son—which she had. Unfortunately, when she discovered the young man, he was dead and what was even worse, Killian's own wife had murdered him. Thanks to Windstein Investigations, the woman still sat in Sing Sing Correctional Facility, serving life without parole. It was quite a salacious and scandalous affair, making Killian's recommendation shocking to put it mildly.

"Killian? Seriously? You'll have to excuse me if I find that more than a little hard to believe, Mr. Combs."

"I'm aware of the scandal but all you did was uncover it. He told me you did exactly what he requested—solving the case in a matter of days. The end result, tragic though it may be, wasn't your doing. You should know he holds no animosity toward you for it. He recommended you because, he said, you were fast, professional and wouldn't hide the truth just to spare my feelings. I take it you're surprised he holds you in very high regard?"

"You take it correctly. Glad to know, I guess, just unexpected. I think I have enough to get me started here, unless there's something else pertinent. I'm sure my secretary has it, but since you're here, could I trouble you for your number? I suspect I'll have some quick questions once I start diving in, that is if you don't mind?"

"Here's my card, Ms. Windstein, my personal cell number is on the back. Feel free to contact me anytime with any questions, day or night. I'll be in town until we've concluded our business. Finding Jimmy is all I care about right now." He looked at her imploringly. "You will be discreet? My health is no real secret but, as you can imagine, some would not be keen on me finding Jimmy. I'm a very wealthy man, so I'm sure you realize how crazy people get if they think their inheritance is at stake."

"You can trust my lips to stay sealed, other than to you, about this case or anything else. Your money and what you choose to do with it is your business not mine, Mr. Combs. All I care about is finding this Jimmy for you, anything after that is none of my concern. Unless you plan to kill him then I am obligated to report a crime." Jamie laughed, clearly joking.

"Do I look stupid enough to tell you such a thing? I hope not!" He joked right along with her. "Jimmy will be safe, you on the other hand..." He gave her a wink.

"Fair enough, sir, fair enough, though you may wanna think twice about messing with me. I'm ten gallons of whoop ass in a tiny little shot glass!" She gave him a wide smile. "Now, I trust you remember the way out—so scoot so I can get started."

"I pray you have more luck than I did, Ms. Windstein. Happy hunting!" Mr. Combs stood and extended his hand.

"Thank you for coming in, Mr. Combs. I'll be in touch soon."

2

He took one last look around for prying eyes before slipping his key into the lock on the back door. He remained overly cautious despite being invisible to the world. His caution was warranted, due to being where he wasn't supposed to be, entering a place that wasn't his own. He went into the garage, closing the door quickly and quietly behind him. He knew there was nobody home, but he could never be too careful.

He knew this homeowner kept odd hours, but he only needed a few minutes and he had given himself plenty of time.

He moved through the garage silent as a mouse, careful not to disturb anything on his way to the house entrance. He inserted the key he'd made for the door and gave it a twist. Turning the knob, he opened the door wide, and left it that way on the off chance he'd need to make a hasty exit.

He set the two black plastic bags that were draped over his shoulder down on top of the kitchen counter, just inside the door. Even though the closed curtains of the front window shielded him from any passersby, he kept his eyes peeled while he unfastened the twist ties holding the bags shut. He pulled a gift for the homeowner from each bag, enjoying their weight in his hands, before setting them carefully on the counter. He wanted them to be the first thing the homeowner saw upon arriving home and so he took extra care to line them up directly with the side door he'd left standing open. He imagined the look of shock his gifts would bring—widened eyes, jaw practically hitting the floor, and hopefully an ear piercing scream if he were lucky. It was the reaction he was excited for even though he wouldn't be here to see it up close. Any normal person would faint, or vomit, or run away screaming at the site of his gifts. He wanted to know what kind of person the homeowner would be; screamer, fainter or puker. He hoped for a reaction altogether different, something more, something… special.

For the most important addition to his gifts, he removed a black marker from his pocket. He had spent years thinking, plotting and planning this—and yet, now he hesitated. Once he walked out the door there would be no going back, he'd have to see this through to the end no matter what. This would change everything, along with the reaction it brought. He would be anxiously watching. Whatever the reaction was would determine how his plan proceeded. He scrawled his message, half on one gruesome gift and half on the other. He knew the message would not be understood at first, understanding would take time. *All good things come to those who wait, or so they say,* he thought to himself. Patience had brought him this far and now he had to trust it to carry him across the finish line.

Now that they bore his first message he readjusted his gifts to their proper positions. Whatever happened next was out of his hands now. He couldn't rule out the police being called in, though he felt confident they wouldn't. He had imagined a million scenarios and a call to 9-1-1 was at the bottom of the list. He wouldn't be able to avoid the boys in blue for the entire duration of his plan—they were part of it—but they'd come in later, of that he was quite certain. He was also certain they'd have less of a clue about what was happening, once they became involved, than the intended reader of his message. This one liked mysteries—and he had just set up the mystery of a lifetime.

3

Jamie Windstein sat in her office pondering the task given her by a dying man. She hadn't worked anything other than the usual crop of liars and cheaters in months. She had been dying for a real case, though one that wasn't so damn cold would have been nice. All she had to do was find a kid who'd been missing for like thirty years—and all before her client died.

No problem at all, she laughed to herself. If she managed to solve this one, she figured she'd have to change the name on the door to "Windstein Miracles" rather than "Investigations."

Jamie twirled Combs' business card between her thumb and forefinger, zoning out while trying to get her head in the game. She could empathize with her new client, who wouldn't want to find someone so consequential in their life? What she couldn't figure out was, if this Jimmy was so important, why did he wait until the Grim Reaper put a hand on his shoulder to start looking? Yes, people procrastinate, even important things. Hell, she was doing it now—but there was something off here that she couldn't put her finger on yet. She leaned forward to get started since, apparently, the answer wasn't going to magically appear in front of her.

Life had taught Jamie Windstein one thing: trust no one. With her motto in mind, first things first, she needed to find out everything possible about her supposedly dying client, Thomas Combs. She had access to all sorts of search engines unavailable to the public, however, the best place to begin a search on anyone was plain old Google. A quick search of "Thomas Combs Industries" brought up numerous articles, giving her a snapshot of her new client.

Thomas Combs made his fortune from the development of computer technologies after arriving in Silicon Valley in the mid-nineties. His real breakthrough was some sort of fancy computer chip, described in technical journals only tech geeks understood and that *she* didn't need to understand. He progressed steadily from that first chip until his hardware and some software were contained in about ninety percent of electronics sold today. He wasn't Bill Gates or Steve Jobs wealthy, but he wasn't far behind either. Interesting as all that may be, it had zero use to her investigation other than confirming Thomas Combs was far richer than he had let on. She found zilch that told her anything about the man, only how he had racked in billions on technology she'd never understand. She was glad he hadn't turned out to be some crime kingpin, yet everything she found was worthless where her investigation was concerned.

The basic information she found troubled her, however. Thomas Combs was wealthy enough to hire any detective in the world, or even an army of investigators, if he liked, and all far more skilled and experienced. Yet he chose her, a virtual unknown. Aside from the Killian case, she had never worked anything very high profile. She had no elite client list and still he chose her anyway. The word "why" shot to the front of her brain like a lightning strike. Thomas Combs could afford to have teams of investigators turning over every rock from coast to coast looking for this Jimmy Reimse, still he came to her. Even if she was the greatest detective since Sherlock Holmes, why hire one unknown woman when he could afford hundreds? Based off the reference of Jack Killian alone? An old bastard she couldn't believe would refer her to a cockroach after that debacle of a case. She couldn't make it add up. Thomas Combs was hiding something from her, maybe many things, and she was letting it get under her skin.

Stop looking a gift horse in the mouth, ya damn dummy, she said to herself, yet still the doubt remained.

She kept searching for information, and to her surprise, found Thomas Combs was considered one of the most eligible bachelors in the world. She noticed he wasn't wearing a wedding band but had assumed a genuinely handsome man with more money than God was likely in a relationship of some kind. She imagined the gold digging crazies came out of the woodwork at every turn for him. She sat back taking in what she knew so far; Thomas Combs was single, uber-rich, an entrepreneur, and an orphan looking for a child (now a man) who had saved his life or, at least, from a severe beating at the hands of an overzealous head mistress about thirty years ago. Most rich fucking people problems were a waiter serving them white wine instead of red or getting a speck of dust in their eye—making Thomas Combs an oddity. Still the question of "why her" burned away at her brain like an eternal flame.

She sighed, doing her best to push that question to the back of her mind so she could tackle the task at hand. Where in the world was James Reimse?

The majority of the information contained in the folder he had given her was completely or, at best, mostly useless. There were numerous pictures of the orphanage itself, blurry photos of children playing outside on the small playground—possibly, the only helpful photo in the batch. Jamie held up a group photo of all the children at the Mormont Home standing with the grim head mistress off to the right. "Wicked stepmother" sprung to mind, but definitely one mean bitch. She imagined the woman in the photo ruling over the children with an iron fist, which was, unfortunately, probably not uncommon in orphanages.

The record of abuse at homes like Mormont, who were tasked with the care of children, elderly or the mentally ill, was extraordinarily long. Jamie knew finding one without a history of abuse was the exception and not the rule. She found it amazing, or perhaps *appalling* was a better word, how little had really changed since Dickens' wrote the classic *Oliver Twist* over a hundred and fifty years ago. The abuses in these places made Oliver Twist look like a Saturday morning cartoon by comparison. Then out of the blue Jamie almost burst out laughing. Head Mistress Eva DeLong was a dead ringer for Cloris Leachman playing Nurse Diesel in the old Mel Brooks' film *High Anxiety*. The image brought a flood of memories rushing into her mind, forcing her to tear up remembering watching old Mel Brooks movies with her grandfather. Tears of loss morphed to tears of laughter when the image of another Leachman character, this time Frau Blücher from *Young Frankenstein*, popped into her mind's eye. Why couldn't all kids have a loving grandfather to show them the finer things in life, like Mel Brooks movies? Instead of love, these kids had memories of abandonment, neglect and, for too many, pain and suffering.

Don't dwell on things you can't change, she thought to herself. She had a job to do, although exacting some long overdue justice might not be so bad either.

Jamie pushed her old memories away, getting on with the investigation. She doubted searching "James Reimse" would turn up anything but you never knew until you tried, she thought. No hits as she expected. She tried to gather all the information she could about Jimmy, the school and anything related to them. She found little to nothing, which pretty much, was what she expected. If Jimmy had been easy to find, then Combs wouldn't have come to her in the first place.

Jamie wasn't surprised by the lack of digital information available. She had suspected to find very little about an orphanage that had closed before there was any such thing as the internet. Before Combs left her office she knew this case would likely involve her scanning through dusty, yellowing old files out in the real world. She assumed there had to be some kind of a transfer order or some other document on Jimmy. She didn't want to think of the alternative any more than Combs had, that little Jimmy was taken out into the middle of nowhere and buried. She hoped that even if that were the case, having someone know about it would be comfort. She prided herself on her knack for finding difficult to acquire information from those reluctant to aide her inquiry. Law enforcement may not approve of her methods, but she wasn't exactly asking for their permission.

Jamie figured there was no better place to begin than the source. Luckily the address for the Mormont Home for Children was one of the few useful pieces of information included in Combs' file. She clicked on to Google Maps to make sure the building was still standing after all these years. It was indeed still there, looking like it had been vacant since the day it closed its doors for good. She wondered why, though? Abandoned buildings littered the city of Buffalo like beer cans after a street fair, but it wasn't in a terrible area and appeared to be in relatively good shape, so why had it never been sold? The building didn't appear to have suffered a fire or anything to make it an eyesore in need demolition—it was simply another abandoned building, like so many others in the Rust Belt of the eastern United States. The windows were all smashed out, which was typical— usually by bored teenagers with a handful of rocks and nothing better to do. She knew buildings like this were generally a haven for the homeless, alcoholics and drug addicted—making it risky to enter after dark. Sometimes it felt like there were more safe refuges for rats and the downtrodden than decent homes for the hard working anymore.

Jamie's curiosity over the fate of the Mormont Home pushed her to continue. She needed to know what happened to it now. The story of the home was the story of its founder, A.H. Mormont, who was born around the turn of the twentieth century. She found that The Mormont Home for Children opened as the dream of a millionaire, A.H. Mormont, who had been orphaned at age three. Mormont's parents died in an unspecified accident and placed in the care of his Aunt and Uncle, Julia and Robert Baisley. The couple were apparently extremely abusive, though the exact nature of the abuse was omitted. The state removed him from their home and placed him in a state run orphanage where he faced more abuse. Jamie read that, despite all he suffered, A.H. Mormont had dedicated himself to getting an education. His efforts earned him a full scholarship to Harvard Business School where he excelled—catching the attention of the Rockefeller's, one of the richest families in the world at the time. After interning at one of the Rockefeller's businesses, Mormont started his own business in conjunction with the railroad, where he amassed his own fortune. He was also more charitable than most of his new social status.

In 1925 Mormont commissioned the building of The Mormont Home for Children. It was to be a safe haven for orphans, free from abuse of any kind. He wanted orphaned children to be well cared for and thoroughly educated so, like him, they could know a rich life. Jamie began to admire A.H. Mormont for what he accomplished and what he tried to leave as his legacy.

Then she discovered why the property had never been sold. A.H. Mormont himself, had stipulated in his will that the property must remain a home and/or school for orphan children. It could not be sold or used for any other purpose. He had set up a trust fund to run the orphanage, which had been large enough to run the home off of the interest alone, in perpetuity. This information brought Jamie another big fat question: if there had been plenty of money to operate the home, why had it ever closed? Did the trust somehow run dry? She knew it was more likely that someone embezzled the funds, but how—if it was locked in a trust?

She hadn't even been on the case a day and already this was looking complicated. Jamie loved a good mystery to sink her teeth into, yet this one was already bordering on ridiculous territory.

"Jamie, do you need anything before I head out?" Carrie interrupted her thoughts as she entered the office.

She jumped, as Carrie's voice caught her by surprise. "Damn! Don't be sneakin' up on a bitch! Especially one with a conceal carry permit!" Jamie laughed, and hand to her chest. "Is it that late already?"

"Sorry, Jams." Carrie smiled when Jamie grimaced—she'd hated the nickname, but for some reason, it had stuck. "Yeah, it's almost six, hun. Can I help you with anything?" Carrie then laughed. "And remember my hubby is a cop, so go ahead and try shooting me. You'll be in cuffs before the smoke clears."

"Oh, Eddie's already had me in those cuffs, honey. He just might pay me to bump you off so he can be with a real woman!" Jamie collapsed into giggles.

"Hey, those words will earn ya a big ol' bitch slap! I'm all the woman that poor man can handle and then some! You'd kill him!" They both laughed, needing a little comic relief to end the day. "Seriously, you need anything other than my husband, just ask. But that man is all mine!"

"Will do. The time got away from me while I accomplished all of Jack and Shit! Now go on home and suck that man dry before I do!" She licked her lips and gave Carrie a wicked smile.

"Aren't you just one dirty bitch tonight?! I just might though!" Carrie blushed as she walked away. "G'night boss!"

Jamie heard her giggling all the way to the office door. "Goodnight? You're fired, bitch, so don't come back!"

"You couldn't live without me, bitch, and ya know it!" Carrie laughed closing the office door behind her.

Jamie turned back to her computer screen once the other woman left. She wanted to learn as much about The Mormont Home for Children as she could. She tended to obsess when she had sunk her teeth into a case—and there was the extra benefit of this one paying extremely well. She figured the fee warranted a little overtime though, if she was honest with herself, she couldn't stop now if she wanted. Jamie loved a good mystery even more than she loved sex.

Chapter Three: With Unspoken Words

1: Sometime in the '80s

The tile of the hallway floor felt like ice on his tiny little feet. He knew he wasn't supposed to be out of his bed after "lights out" but curiosity and a burning desire to escape had gotten the better of him. A little prodding from his new partner in crime and sole friend in this place hadn't hurt either. The other boys spoke of escape with words like "impossible" or "miracle" yet he knew there had to be a way. They weren't murderers and this wasn't a maximum-security prison with armed guards, bloodhounds or gun turrets.

Tommy hated every single second of every single minute since walking through the doors of The Mormont Home for Children only three days ago. Instantly he felt his new home was cold, unfriendly, uninviting and the staff… even worse. His initial impression proved correct in the first few days and then worsened as time went on. He had found a friend in Jimmy, yet even that hadn't improved his instant hatred for The Mormont Home. He was filled with an overpowering dread when Jimmy told him about the staff and his experiences with them.

Tommy's focus since stepping through the doors was on escape. He wanted to run as far and as fast as he could from this place and everyone in it. He quickly learned that his new friend, Jimmy, had the same idea.

Jimmy had been at Mormont for a couple of years. He was older than Tommy by close to 2 years. He knew the ins and outs of the home—yet, after a few early failed attempts, he knew he needed help to escape successfully. The courage of companionship gave him the confidence to try again. Jimmy was a planner. He had plotted an escape route in his mind for months, going over and over it while he laid in bed at night. He prayed for freedom from this cold place and its cruel staff. He fixated on escape, though occasionally, his young mind strayed in a darker direction.

The boys became friends the instant Tommy heard Jimmy mutter, "Bloody cunt," under his breath after Head Mistress DeLong exited the common/play room after his introduction to the other children upon his arrival. Jimmy's whispered curse matched his own impression of his new ward, bringing a smile to his face. It was obvious to him from the moment he walked in that they were all afraid of the Head Mistress. Their weakness depressed him until he heard Jimmy, the only one with the balls to say what they were all thinking— even if it *was* only in a whisper. Tommy shot Jimmy a knowing smile and they were instant best friends. Tommy experienced little that could be called good luck to that point in his life and yet Lady Luck stood beside him in that moment. Jimmy had not only become his only friend in the world, but was also to be his new roommate. It was the only happy moment of his entire stay at The Mormont Home for Children.

The boys had peeked cautiously out of their bedroom door to find the hallway clear. Prior to Tommy's arrival, Jimmy had noted the times of the counselors' nightly rounds for months. He found little variation in the times, with only a minute or two difference, at most, from night to night. Mormont employees, aside from Head Mistress DeLong, were called "counselors" though the only counseling they ever provided was with an open or closed hand while they listened to the children's moans or, sometimes, screams.

Counselor Bob was on duty, the one the kids hated most for being short on words and quick with a hand (usually a backhand). Jimmy had informed Tommy of the painful consequences if they were caught, though his desire to escape outweighed the fear of a possible punishment. Counselor Bob took night duty a majority of the time, making him impossible to avoid—even though they knew if they were caught it didn't really matter who was on duty. Their fate would be in Head Mistress DeLong's hands if it came to that, making Counselor Bob the least of their worry for now. Immature impatience drove them to attempt an escape, regardless of the consequences of failure.

Jimmy assured Tommy they could make it safely to the kitchen and then slip out the side door that was used for deliveries, to their freedom. Tommy hated The Mormont Home so much after only three days, that he was willing to escape at any cost. He figured the punishment for failure was something he'd worry about if they got caught, but he was confident they wouldn't. Jimmy told him what could happen, but Tommy's desire to get away was too strong to give it much thought. Tommy had no frame of reference for punishments doled out at Mormont, while Jimmy simply decided it couldn't get any worse. Tommy merely hated The Mormont Home at this point, while Jimmy absolutely loathed the place for reasons he hoped his new friend never had to experience.

While praying the door didn't squeak as they shut it behind them, they saw no one as they took their first steps out onto the cold tile of the hallway. They each carried a pillowcase filled with the few possessions they were allowed to keep, and their shoes. Tommy was impressed that Jimmy had thought of everything, even the off chance of a high pitch squeak echoing off the tile. Jimmy led the way, staying a few steps ahead of Tommy. They were both on high alert, their heads swiveling back and forth like a pair of drug dealer's watching for cops on a street corner. Tommy could taste his freedom the instant they stepped into the hallway, despite his heart racing in his chest from the adrenaline rushing through his veins. He knew they had a long way to go even though they were free for the moment. Tommy kept his eyes peeled the way Jimmy told him to. They knew Counselor Bob's routine, although they didn't know if any other parts of the home were secured at night.

The two boys crept down the hallway cautiously quick, their immaturity pushing the pace while desperately trying to remain silent. They rounded the first corner of the journey, passing by the closed doors of their sleeping companions. A twinge of guilt rippled down Tommy's spine for leaving them behind, knowing they were all too scared to join anyway. *So far so good*, he thought, *so far not a creature stirring, especially Counselor Bob*.

They made a right turn and rounded the final corner with a sigh of relief, seeing the coast clear all the way to their destination. The kitchen door stood at the far end of the hall, while the bright red door of the broom closet— the door every child at Mormont feared—stood at the other. From Jimmy's stories, Tommy knew of the secret room behind the broom closet where the real horrors of

Mormont took place. Jimmy froze for a moment at the site.

"Almost there, Tommy, keep your eyes peeled."

Tommy nodded in response, doing as he was told, though for a moment, his eyes fixed on the bright red door too. The door led straight to hell, if Jimmy's stories were true—something Tommy never doubted. If they were caught, they both knew it was through that door they'd be taken for their severe punishment.

Tommy's feet froze in place on the icy tile like Jimmy's had a second ago. Images of being tortured filled his young mind and held him stiff with a fear like he'd never felt before. Unaware that Tommy had stopped, Jimmy continued moving forward eager to get through the kitchen and away. Jimmy was nearly at the door when he realized Tommy wasn't close behind him. Jimmy's heart leapt into his throat, faced with the decision to wait for Tommy or obey his brain that screaming at him to run for it and never look back.

"Tommy! Come on!" Jimmy urged his friend, fearing he had been too loud.

It worked—the hushed words snapped Tommy out of his temporary stupor. He stepped toward his friend, only to have his eyes bulge in their sockets while his jaw dropped to the floor. The terror on Tommy's face meant only one thing.

Jimmy spun around to face their worst nightmare, Head Mistress DeLong exiting through the kitchen door toward them. Their fear spiked as their hearts sank. Their hope of escape died instantly. Jimmy and Tommy looked at each other knowing there was only one thing they could do.

Jimmy gave voice to their only option. "Run!"

The chase ended in world record time. Head Mistress DeLong had the police whistle she wore around her neck to her lips before Jimmy's shout stopped echoing in the corridor. Jimmy and Tommy ran side by side away from DeLong until Counselor Bob bounded around the corner, boxing them in. They halted dead in their tracks, conceding defeat. Head Mistress DeLong grasped Jimmy by the back of his shirt collar and yanked him back hard, while Counselor Bob put Tommy in a bone crushing bear hug. The chase, if it could be called a chase, was at an end quicker than it had begun.

"Well, just what are two nasty little boys doing out of their rooms after lights out? Do we allow children to run the hallways at night, Counselor Bob?" The Head Mistress' sarcasm was lost on no one. Tommy thought she sounded exactly like the bitch she appeared to be with her annoying nasally voice.

"No, Head Mistress, I don't believe we do." Bob smirked, looking like a mentally challenged clown.

"Kindly escort these two miscreants back to their room and lock the door, Counselor Bob." Head Mistress DeLong paused to let her next words resonate. "Then meet me in my chambers to discuss their punishment." She over-emphasized her final word, looking down at the boys with a devilish smirk that sent a chill down their tiny spines.

"Yes, Head Mistress. Shall I wake any other counselors to consult on the matter?"

"Counselor Tony, I should think. I would greatly appreciate his input."

The boys gave each other an "Oh shit" look even though they knew the consequences before stepping into the hall. Fear replaced hope the second DeLong exited the kitchen a few seconds ago. Counselor Tony, like Bob, was feared and hated by the children. The two by themselves were mean, but together they were cruelty incarnate. The children called the pair "The Goon Squad" though other counselors sometimes shared the name. Head Mistress DeLong wielded them like her own custom made whip. Tommy had yet to learn what to expect from the coming punishment, despite Jimmy's tales, while Jimmy knew that death—for one or both of them—wasn't out of the question. Jimmy had seen how no one seemed to notice when the occupancy of The Mormont Home for Children was reduced by one or two.

"Excellent, Head Mistress! We'll meet you in two shakes." Counselor Bob stood with a stupid grin on his face and stared down at the boys looking like a little kid on Christmas day.

Bob took hold of the wannabe escapees by their hair, dragging them down the hall to their room. He kicked open the door, literally throwing them inside.

"Don't you little bastards go anywhere. If you make it to tomorrow, you'll remember tonight for the rest of your lives." Counselor Bob cracked his knuckles with a smile, then slammed the door.

Tommy gulped at the lump in his throat when he heard the sharp click of the lock.

2: Present Day

Jamie Windstein finally pulled into her garage to end her day. It was well after midnight. Her eyes burned from staring at the computer screen ever since her new client walked out of the office over twelve hours ago. Curiosity was gnawing away at her brain, however, breaking into an old building this late would be foolish. The homeless had likely taken up residency for the night, making it unsafe. She wasn't afraid of them—she could handle herself—but poking around in the middle of the night where you weren't likely to receive a friendly greeting wasn't exactly the best idea either. She decided it best to wait for daylight after the nightly occupants vacated in search of their daily fix. Daylight may also send the rats scurrying for cover. She sat there a moment with the engine still idling trying to calm her racing mind. She had no reason to rush since no one was waiting inside her empty house except her good ol' trusty friend vodka. She loved the bottle's company more than any real person and it wasn't going anywhere.

Jamie sat zoning out for several minutes until her need for alcohol tugged her back to life. She hadn't had anything all day since the nip in her morning coffee. She rarely had a bottle of vodka out of arm's reach, except at the office, if she could help it. Jamie wasn't stupid, she knew she shouldn't drink so much, however, she didn't give a shit either. She was obsessed on getting a drink now that the thought had entered her mind. Alcohol addiction and obsession on the new case fought for dominance. Both had her mind racing worse than a meth addict picking at invisible spiders after a weeklong bender. She didn't merely want her icy cold glass of "I no longer give a fuck," she needed it. She pulled the keys from the ignition, trying to stop herself from sprinting to the bottle that was waiting inside. "I have it under control." She told herself, the same as every addict in the history of addicts has done a million times. She wanted to believe it was true but knew deep down it wasn't. She had it under control the same way a driver has control of a car with no steering wheel.

Jamie walked through the side door, from her garage into the kitchen, not bothering to turn on any lights. She was more concerned with getting a drink immediately. She'd know her way around blindfolded or drunk, at least usually she did.

She dropped her purse on the counter with a plop, reaching for a glass in the overhead cupboard before the purse's strap hit the surface. She pivoted and pulled open the left-hand door to her freezer, snatching the familiar clear bottle—the freezer's sole occupant aside from ice cubes.

She held the bottle up in the refrigerator's light. "Shit!" She breathed out a curse seeing the bottle nearly empty. There was barely enough in it to get her started. She knew there was a partial bottle next to the coffee pot and another next to her bed and likely another dropped at random somewhere but wasn't sure if another full bottle lurked in the cupboard. She really didn't feel like heading back out on a liquor store run at this hour. She poured the last of the chilled vodka into her glass and dropped in a couple of ice cubes tossing the empty bottle into the trash with a bang.

Jamie threw back half the contents of the liquid salvation then set the glass down to rummage through her cupboards for another bottle. She let out a big sigh of relief when she struck gold, finding a full bottle. It stood in the usual spot, which meant nothing when one day blurred into the next. She never remembered if she had resupplied or not since she was often inebriated at the point of sale. They knew her by name at the nearest liquor store—only a couple blocks away—due to her sometimes daily visits. It wasn't the trip she dreaded, it was having to make small talk with whatever idiot was working the night shift. Jamie wanted to relax and shut off her brain for the night, something unlikely to happen.

"A toast to small miracles. Cheers!" Jamie gulped down the rest of the glass, refilled and then tossed the fresh bottle in the freezer, wondering if it'd even get cold before she drained it.

Jamie walked into her makeshift home office, what anyone else would call a family or living room, trying her best not to stub a toe in the dark. She had very little furniture, since she positively loathed company. No one would accuse Jamie Windstein of being a good interior decorator—she arranged her few things to suite her needs, not caring what anyone thought of it. If no one liked it, too bad. She had only ever invited Carrie, and that was only once. She could still recall Carrie telling her that she had the decorating skills of a bulldozer. She couldn't argue with the sentiment, nor did she really care.

She had papers scattered all about, empty vodka bottles piled in and around the little waste basket beside her desk, an empty pizza box or two along with a few discarded Styrofoam containers that had once held chicken wings. In effect, it looked like a mini tornado had traveled through the space at some point. Her bedroom usually looked similar. She glanced at the mess and was uninspired to clean up, although ordering some late night snack wasn't out of the question. It was Buffalo, after all, the birth place of the chicken wing and the only place in the world to get them done right—a fact every Buffalonian knew well.

She plopped herself down on the very worn and uncomfortable couch and nearly spilled her drink in the process, not that she cared. She was far from a neat freak. She sat back and sipped her vodka slowly, letting the bottle chill and allow her mind to wander to the new case. A mountain of unanswerable questions began to pile up in her head.

Newspaper headlines about the home's sudden closure were nowhere to be found, telling her someone powerful must have kept it silent. But who and why? What happened to the trust fund money intended to run the place in perpetuity? If there had been some tragic incident or salacious allegation, why no mention of it anywhere? If someone embezzled the money, how was that not a headline? Jamie made a mental note to herself to follow the money. She found no answers so far, only more questions—and those were just about the home itself. She found zero on James Reimse, though she suspected to find nothing on him. Her main focus was on finding Jimmy, though her brain told her his fate and the fate of the home were connected. Where did Jimmy go after his disappearance from The Mormont Home for Children? She knew his name likely changed, but to what? Was he even still alive? The question confounding her the most was why Jimmy had been taken away in the first place. What did he do that was so egregious they would have possibly killed him for it? Thomas Combs hadn't provided a whole lot of details— if he was so desperate then why hold back? While she sipped her vodka in the dark, an evil smirk formed on her lips at the thought of extracting details from him with a pair of pliers.

The longer Jamie sat drinking in the dark, the more frustrated she became. She hated having so many questions without a single answer—or even a decent guess. The questions spun in her head like matter around a black hole while she sipped away at her drink, staring into the dark. She simply sat there staring off into space like a mental patient pumped full of Thorazine, until a few tiny remnants of ice still hit her lips. She hopped up as though she had received an electric shock. Time for a refill.

"Jesus, how long have I been sitting here in the dark? Hope I wasn't talking to myself." She laughed wryly, aware of the irony.

Jamie reached up to flick the switch of the small end table lamp, deciding she had sat in the dark long enough. It clicked, yet refused to spring to life. She frowned, irritated that the bulb had burned out. She cursed herself when she remembered it had been burnt out for weeks— or was it a month?

Annoyed by her forgetfulness, she struggled to get up from the confines of the well-worn sofa and let out a deep sigh when she finally managed to stand. She absently flicked on the kitchen light when she made it to the freezer for a refill. She whipped the door open and grabbed the bottle without looking, a muscle memory built from a thousand such trips likely, even in her sleep. The bottle was surprisingly chilled, a telling sign that she had stared off into the dark much longer than she thought. She twisted the top, refilled her glass and then took a long pull straight from the bottle before returning it to its temporary home. She laughed at herself again, taking a swallow from the glass so she could squeeze in an ice cube without spilling any.

When she turned around, she nearly dropped the glass—shattering it to pieces on the tiled floor. Luckily, she didn't startle easily, if ever.

She stood stiff as the dead as she stared at sight on the kitchen's center island. Two severed heads—one male, one female—sat leaning gently against one another.

She didn't panic, nor did she scream or reach for her phone to call 9-1-1. She just stood there staring at them for a good long moment.

Her initial shock passed, recognition replacing it. She was almost positive she recognized the pair. She thought they looked like a couple from a few streets over. It wasn't the familiarity, nor the fact that two severed heads were sitting on her kitchen counter that grabbed her attention though. What captivated her were the words written across the foreheads of the pair.

She read the message over and over, trying to make any sense of it. She had no idea what the words meant, what they were supposed to mean or why they had been left here for her. *Exactly what I need right now*, she thought, *another damn mystery!*

Scrawled across the foreheads, in what looked like a child's handwriting, were the words: *Blood Remembers*.

Blood on the male and *Remembers* on the female. She had absolutely no idea what the cryptic message could possibly mean.

"Blood remembers." Jamie Windstein stood mystified in her empty kitchen with a full glass of vodka in her hand, whispering the words.

3

They watched the scene unfold on the monitor in front of them. Impatience nearly got the better of them, thinking she wasn't going to discover her little gift until the morning. Their eyes reddened and burned staring at the monitor, while Jamie just sat there in the dark occasionally appearing to mumble to herself. Boredom made them want to kick themselves for not installing microphones along with the cameras. It seemed a waste of time and money since she was always alone. Her only regular visitor was the mailman. They sat silently, watching her stare at nothing. If not for their excited anticipation of her discovery, they would have called it a night since they needed ESP to know what was going on in her head.

When she finally stood up, they slid to the edge of their seats in anticipation. Their eagerness only grew when she flicked on the light with her back to the gifts waiting on the counter behind her. They became agitated in those few moments, waiting for her to turn around while she refilled her glass, ignorant of what awaited her. A seven year old on the eve of his birthday showed more patience than they felt watching her. Time moved in slow motion as they impotently willed her to turn around. They wanted to see how she would react so badly they were compelled to scream out, but all they could do was watch helplessly.

They leaned forward, afraid to breathe when Jamie finally turned around, freezing stiff at the sight of the heads. They sat, ram-rod stiff as well, waiting to see what she would do. Would she drop her glass? Would she scream? Would she call the police? They had contemplated all the possible scenarios except for one; her actual reaction. She didn't drop her glass. She didn't scream like women always did in the movies. She didn't speed dial 911. They watched, waiting, while she simply stood there staring. They assumed she was in shock, though she seemed to be virtually unfazed by the gruesome sight. The two men looked at each other smiling, seeing there was more to Jamie Windstein than met the eye or their imaginations. She wasn't trembling in fear, running for help or fainting to the floor like most normal people would likely do. They thought they knew her well—yet in their wildest dream, they never anticipated her stoic, almost clinical reaction. They were already surprised then she blew their minds completely.

"What the?"

"Shhhh."

She stunned her watchers into silence by picking up the heads, one at a time, thoroughly examining each one. They watched, dying to know what was going through her mind. Did she understand the message? It wasn't likely just yet, but anything was possible. Perhaps she wondered where all the blood went? Did she really think she'd find any evidence left behind? She was an investigator, but they hoped she didn't think they were that stupid.

The taller of the pair stared intently through the screen, watching Jamie examine his gift to her. He would give anything to crawl straight into her head in order to find out what she thought. How long would it take her to understand his message? He knew there was the possibility she never would. While he pondered the fruitlessness of this entire endeavor, Jamie Windstein shocked him even more.

Apparently finished with her initial examination, Jamie picked up both heads, swiped her bottle from the freezer, and swiftly exited the kitchen into the garage. The astonishing thing was she didn't get into her car.

"Where are you going, my little darling?" The taller man smiled, realizing Jamie didn't just enjoy solving mysteries, she was one.

They continued watching in silent amazement, unable to stop smiling at this pleasantly unexpected development. Their astonishment only grew when she carefully slid a shelf aside, revealing a hidden door leading down to some secret basement room. They stared wide eyed until she disappeared from their sight.

"You sneaky little minx." The smaller of the men smirked.

They wanted to kick themselves for not inspecting her home more carefully to find the hidden door though, in fairness, they didn't expect her to have one. They felt stupid now. They knew she had secrets, of course, but not one this big. Both men maintained their own hidden places, but neither one suspected Jamie did as well. Intrigued they waited patiently until she reemerged, about an hour later, without the heads. They gazed at the monitor in disbelief, watching her refill her glass, switch the light off, and return to the couch where she resumed her intense staring off into the dark.

"Just what's going through that little head of yours, Jamie Windstein?" The taller man scratched his chin, puzzling over a woman he thought he knew so well.

Chapter Four: Along The Path To Ruin

1

Nothing matches the hustle and bustle of a northern city at the beginning of the summer season. Those hailing from the south and west have no idea what it's like to actually appreciate warm days and sunshine. When it's nice out ninety percent of the time, nice weather gets taken for granted. This is *not* the case in a city like Buffalo. When you only get a couple months of warm days and bright sunshine, you take advantage of every single day before the cold winds of winter come back again. Buffalonians in mid-June are like bears emerging from hibernation, ready to get busy living while it lasted. Winter in Buffalo could linger well into May yet by mid-June it was a bad memory, happily shoved out of mind until after Labor Day. It was now the season of street fairs and festivals—some already underway. Every weekend multiple events were held until the north winds blew across The Great Lakes, bringing it crashing to an end. Summer was alive and well in Buffalo long before the calendar marked the official start of it.

Thomas Combs sat outside Spot Coffee in downtown Buffalo, enjoying his cappuccino and what local men often referred to as "skirt season"—not summer. The warm temperatures brought freshly unpacked short skirts and shorter shorts for the young ladies. Thomas sat back, enjoying the view, like all other heterosexual males this time of year, getting his morning caffeine fix. Thomas noted that here in the heart of downtown Buffalo there wasn't much of a view, neither the skyline nor Lake Erie could be seen from here, so young ladies in short skirts or shorts would have to suffice. If nothing else, the sunshine and bare legs put him in a good mood.

"Thomas?" A nasally voice broke his daydreaming instantly.

Recognizing the voice, Thomas was unstartled. "Please, have a seat, or do you need to grab yourself a beverage first?"

"I'm fine for now, thank you. Coffee makes me jittery and my nerves are shot already."

"Relax, my friend. Sit down, there's much to discuss."

Reluctantly the short balding man pulled out the chair opposite Thomas and plopped himself down. Despite the early hour, he was disheveled, like a man at the end of a long, dreary day. The faint scent of aftershave emanated from his freshly shaved cheeks, the only sign he was just beginning his day. The short man adjusted his tie, perpetually crooked no matter how many times he did so, waiting for Thomas Combs to begin. Visibly nervous, the newcomer looked as if a cardiac failure was imminent. Thomas made him wait, reveling in how uncomfortable the man appeared regardless of him being a friend for decades. He thought the fresh air and sunshine would do his old friend some good.

The man let out a loud sigh. "Well? Why am I here, Thomas? A rich man like you can sit around here all day. Me? I have a job to get to—so how about you get on with it already."

Thomas stared down at the man a moment, silently conveying he was in no rush. "Very well then. I am glad to see you, though the feeling doesn't seem to be reciprocated." Thomas raised his eyebrows sarcastically.

"My apologies, Thomas. I mean, no offense, nor do I wish to be rude. Hearing from you brought up... memories. Memories I buried a long time ago. Sorry, I'm not unhappy to see you after all these years, it's just... well… that damn place! I just want to forget all about it. I thought I had, then you call and, *Wham*! Nightmares all fucking night. Understand? Don't you want to forget the whole mess?" The man's nasally voice made the whole diatribe sound like he was whining.

"I do understand and I am sincerely sorry it still has that effect on you after all these years. I didn't come here to cause you any trouble, honest. However, I need a favor. All you need to do is have a meeting. That's it, just a meeting. Nothing illegal, no blood on your hands, I promise. A couple little white lies then you return to your life trying to forget. It doesn't appear that's working very well for you though. Unfortunately, old friend, this is not a request. You're going to do this." Thomas looked the man dead in his eyes which said loud and clear, *do not argue.*

The man shifted anxiously in his chair and wished he were anywhere else. "A meeting with who, and about what? I work in a law office. I'm not about to do anything illegal, not for you, not for anyone." He tried to look stern but only managed to look like a petulant child.

"I promised, didn't I?"

Thomas doled out instructions to his friend while the morning hustle and bustle on the sidewalk slowed to practically nothing. When he had finished, the rush hour had waned completely—other than a few random passersby—until the street clogged for the lunch hour crowd. Thomas made sure his short, balding companion understood his directions before letting him go on his way to work. He returned to his morning paper while the other man shuffled off, out of sight, as he intended to do momentarily.

Thomas continued reading the paper outside Spot Coffee, enjoying the sun. He was in no hurry to get moving. He drained the remains of his cappuccino, intermittently admiring the silky smooth, bare legs of a lovely young blonde passing by. She appeared to be admiring him right back.

Unfortunately, his phone rang before he decided whether to approach her or not. His sudden frown turned into a smile, seeing it was Jamie Windstein calling. The young beauty was no match for someone both beautiful and intriguing.

"Good morning Jamie! Don't tell me you found something already?"

"No, nothing to report yet. I wondered if you could make time to meet with me today? I thought of a few questions I need to ask before I go looking for answers." Jamie's voice was scratchy and a little haggard.

"I'm actually free right now. I'm at Spot Coffee on Delaware, do you know it?"

"Yeah, I know the place. Twenty minutes?"

"I've just been admiring the umm…scenery down here. Sure. What's your poison? I can have something waiting for you."

"Double espresso—unless they have a triple." She chuckled slightly. "Ah, the scenery? Are you going to let one of our local ladies take the most eligible bachelor off the market?" Jamie tried to sound lighthearted though wasn't able to put much feeling behind it.

"That depends, will you marry me Jamie Windstein?" Thomas smiled hearing Jamie choke—obviously, the question caught her by surprise. "I assume that's a yes? You women are such a mystery to me." He laughed.

"Sorry, Thomas, but hell and no! However, if it makes you feel better, you can leave me all your money. I promise not to complain. See you in twenty, and that espresso better be piping hot and strong as hell!" Their friendly banter had somewhat lightened her mood.

"You've crushed my heart along with my hopes and dreams, Ms. Windstein! I'll make sure the espresso is perfect. Who knows? Maybe I'll change your mind while I'm here. See you soon."

Thomas smiled, returning to his paper in better mood than he had known in weeks, due to the beautiful morning combined with the unexpected call. A few days ago he dreaded this trip. He had vowed never to return to Buffalo after leaving the Mormont Home. Now, it appeared breaking that vow may be worth it in the end.

The thought of the petite, raven haired Jamie Windstein as his blushing bride flashed in his mind for only a brief moment, yet it widened his smile. The idea lingered until his ringing phone interrupted his daydream. The screen said "unknown" but he knew exactly who was calling.

2

Kirk Scheidt hated his job—the same as almost everybody else in the world. He realized it was pretty much a certainty, unless you happened to be a rock star or something equally awesome. Everyone who saw him thought he should be a professional football or basketball player because of his size, despite the fact that he had been born with two left feet. He was only slightly more athletic than a quadriplegic with multiple sclerosis. All anyone saw was a six foot seven giant with dark skin, and they all assumed he was lacking in the intelligence department. He was never free of a fresh bruise or two, mainly on his shins or forehead from bumping into pretty much everything in his general vicinity—a rather large vicinity. He ran into at least one doorway on a daily basis, and at the same time, his shins took a beating from endless obstacles he couldn't always see. This was his life and he rarely complained about it.

Kirk hated nearly everything about Lake View Manor Nursing Home; from the drab yellow walls of the building, to the elderly patients it housed—though he hated the smell the most. He found nothing more putrid than the smell of a nursing home. The place reeked with the combination of bleach, soiled adult diapers and death. Death hung in the air like smoke rising from an eternal fire. It came for us all eventually, of course, though having it hover all around him every shift made him want to come to work even less than normal.

Kirk despised coming to work but he had taken the job at this facility for a specific purpose. He had become a certified nursing assistant for a reason—even if almost everyone mistook him for a security guard. He couldn't blame them, though it did get tiresome. He wasn't proud of it but, deep down, he enjoyed that the patients feared him. He didn't need all of them afraid yet, but overall, it was a good thing. It certainly made his job much easier when they were too intimidated to ask him for anything unless absolutely necessary. The patients —clients, as they were referred to—didn't like talking to him and it was a feeling he reciprocated.

Kirk Scheidt was anti-social, preferring to keep to himself, though he could fake a smile and be polite. He was forced into introversion after years of the same dumb sayings like, "How's the weather up there?" He found it beyond difficult to be around people when they were so damn annoying. The banality made him want to scream or bash their heads in. Knowing he actually could didn't help the feeling. He never resorted to violence, he simply smiled—returning their stupidity with something equally stupid or a chuckle, as if it didn't put murder in his mind. He had taken this job on purpose, for one patient. He made sure she was his first visit every single shift, without fail.

"Good morning, Ma'am! And how's my favoritest patient in the whole wide world today?" Kirk made sure to be loud and overly joyful, knowing how much it annoyed her.

"Terrible, like every other damn morning. Now put me in my chair, Darky. I want my breakfast, you fat lummox!" The old woman spit hate back at him.

"Now don't go getting all uppity this morning! You wouldn't want me getting out those restraints again, would you?" He lowered his voice. "You aren't dead yet, unfortunately." He beamed from the doorway enjoying the way she cringed at the sound of his voice.

"Fuck you, darky," she mumbled under her breath.

"What was that, honey? I didn't catch it. If we're cranky already, it could be a *very* long day, indeed!" Kirk grinned ear to ear with every word.

"Nothing," she said begrudgingly. "Now get me in my chair! I want my breakfast."

"Okey dokey, old folky!" He approached her bedside and let down the rail, barely able to stop himself from bursting out laughing. He knew she absolutely loathed his jovial morning sarcasm.

The elderly woman could only grunt her dissatisfaction. She preferred death to this daily banter with the intolerable brute who came here just to torment her. She ground her teeth when he lifted her out of the bed, gentle as an angel, holding her a few inches over the wheelchair before dropping her like a rock. The drop wasn't enough to cause any real harm, just pain. She knew the big bastard would love to toss her like a football out the window, but because she was a paying customer, that would probably cause unwanted attention. Instead, she was forced to suffer his daily efforts to make her life completely miserable.

Kirk smiled like a loon, hoping the little drop had sent a shock wave of pain up the old bitch's spine. He knew it made no difference what he did, she deserved far worse than he could dole out now. He always made sure not to do any permanent damage. He planned to torment as many of her waking hours as humanly possible until the day she finally fucking died—hopefully in enormous pain. The last thing he wanted was to get fired, making him unable to torture the old woman to her last breath. The sad truth was that his only real joy in life came from the looks of anguish he put on her face.

"Oh, I'm sooo sorry, Ma'am! It appears you slipped a little there. You aren't hurt are you?" He then bent down to her ear. "You know it can be way worse, so if I were you, I'd just keep my fucking mouth shut, you old cunt." Kirk loved these tender moments they shared.

"I'm perfectly fine, boy." Her voice lacked all its former authority, so the scorn she had attempted fell flat. The first of the day's many tears traced a line down her wrinkled face.

"Oh goody, dear. I want to see you live to a ripe old age. In fact, I insist on staying right by your side the whole time—holding the hand of my favoritest patient ever!" Kirk made sure he spoke loud enough for his coworkers to hear.

He pushed her chair down the hallway to the dining hall—a large open room used at meal times and for other activities when they arose. His coworkers smiled at him as he passed by, and a few even greeted him a good morning, although he knew none of them actually liked him. He was nothing to them other than the big, dumb galoot he wanted them to see. He couldn't be invisible at his size, so he played the role he needed his coworkers to see. His size always made people stare. Police paid less attention to criminals, making him feel like an exhibit in a museum no matter where he went or what he did. The advantage, he found, came from his incredible size being a natural distraction from anything he might be doing. His cruel reign over his favorite patient went unhindered as long as he kept bruises to a minimum. He dreamed of twisting her wrinkled old head right off her scrawny neck, kicking it soccer style to the moon—however, he did relish making her life a living hell every day.

Kirk Scheidt wasn't normally a mean or cruel man by nature. He had been called a gentle giant since childhood, and rightly so. In fact, prior to working at Lake View Manor, he had never intentionally hurt anyone in his life. His size made unintentional accidents happen on occasion, it was the inevitable consequence of being abnormally large. He laid the blame on others more than himself since you had to be blind not to see him coming. When he was in primary school he had earned the nickname "Kirk the Killer" after accidentally squishing an escaped lab rat when it had the misfortune to run in front of his oversized feet. He had cried when he realized he had killed a living creature, even though his classmates believed it was from the embarrassment of everyone pointing and laughing at him. Their teasing afterwards didn't cease until the end of the school year. A lifetime of introversion began that day, at the young age of ten.

Kirk remembered hating his nickname at the time, but he delighted in telling it to his favorite patient on his first day on the job. He thought, wrongly, that she would recognize him immediately. Unfortunately, the years let the memory of him slip away before he reminded her. He also let her know he took this job to make her life a living hell until she burned for eternity in the real one. He told her how he was going to volunteer to work on his weekends off, trade shifts with other staff and anything else he needed to do in order to be by her side every day possible. He took an unnatural amount of pleasure in seeing the look on her face every time he appeared in her doorway on his day off.

Kirk's favorite patient in the whole world was the one and only Eva DeLong, former Head Mistress at The Mormont Home for Children. Kirk had been her ward for an unforgettable moment in his youth, a time he never forgot. He remembered the suffering she had rained down on him and dozens, maybe hundreds, of children—even if the world saw only a frail, wrinkled old woman today. Kirk knew the woman was pure evil, despite age stealing her former strength. He could do anything to her now and it would never make up for all the pain she brought upon others over her long years on this Earth.

Kirk detested DeLong to her marrow and so he reminded the old bitch of her many sins every chance he got. His only regret was that he couldn't be the thorn poking her in the side twenty four hours a day. Initially he took the job at Lake View Manor simply to watch her slowly wither away to nothing. Once he saw her, he couldn't resist taking her under his "care." It only took a few days for him to become addicted to making her every waking moment pure hell. Former Head Mistress Eva DeLong was the only person in the world Kirk held so much animosity toward. He needed to see the Reaper come calling just so he would know she was definitely dead. Perhaps on that day, he thought, the nightmares would finally leave him alone.

3

Steam rose from the top of the double espresso waiting for Jamie Windstein when she arrived at Spot Coffee. Thomas was still seated at the same outside table where his old acquaintance met with him a short time ago. After his phone call, he'd just enough time to order Jamie's espresso before she arrived. He greeted her with a friendly smile, pulling the chair out across from him.

"Good morning!" He stretched his arm to her.

"It's certainly morning." She shook his hand out of courtesy.

"Not a morning person, Ms. Windstein? Sorry, Jamie. Everything alright?"

"Long night. Probably a longer day." She was all business.

"Understood. I won't pry. What can I do for you this fine Buffalo morning? Was the information I gave you any help at all?" he said, attempting to lighten her mood.

"Maybe. I'm not really sure yet." She tried not to sound too annoyed. "I was hoping you could shed some light on the incident leading to your friend's disappearance. You said he saved your life, but you didn't give me any details. Could you tell me a little more about it and the Mormont Home in general?" Jamie didn't have time for any pleasantries.

"Well, that's straight to the point."

"Excuse me if I'm a little cranky this morning. I didn't exactly sleep very well. Please don't take it personally." She sighed. "You already noticed I'm not really a morning person or a people person—if I'm being totally honest. My secretary tells me I'm too blunt, so fair warning."

"It's alright, Ms. Windstein—damn—Jamie, sorry. I'm not sure where to begin."

"The beginning is usually a good place." She shot him a small smile, hoping she hadn't come off too harsh.

"Well, you did warn me." He shrugged with a chuckle. "James Reimse and I became friends almost instantly. I was scared shitless entering that home for the first time and I had only just lost my parents. Today I'd say, it all felt a little surreal. Head Mistress Delong didn't exactly exude warmth. You saw the pictures of her, right?"

"Yes, I saw. Old battle axe is the name it brought to mind."

"We called her a lot worse, trust me. Anyway that's how Jimmy and I became instant best friends. You see, when I arrived at Mormont, the Head Mistress took me directly to the common room, where the children spent most of their time during the day, and introduced me to everyone. It wasn't much of an introduction, something like 'Everyone this is Thomas, Thomas this is everyone.' Needless to say, my first impression wasn't exactly pleasant. Before she left she said, I'll never forget this, she said 'This is Tommy, he's one of us now.' One of us, seriously?" he asked, incredulous. "Anyway, as she walked away I heard Jimmy mutter under his breath, 'bloody cunt.' I almost fell down laughing. We just looked at each other and just knew we were friends already. Being friends with Jimmy was the only joy I found there. We couldn't have been happier when we learned we were going to be roommates.

"When I arrived at Mormont I felt nothing but grief for my parents and hated the entire world. Did they offer any help with that? No, instead I got cruel Head Mistress DeLong and her damn Goon Squad. That's what we called the two main counselors, Bob and Tony. A few days later Jimmy and I made our first escape attempt together. He'd tried before I got there a few times. All I remember was wanting to run away, far and fast, from everything and everyone. My world had crashed and burned, Jamie. I was a lost soul if ever there was one." He paused for a moment. "We got caught, of course. The punishment we received…well…can I just say it was severe and leave it at that? Some things are best forgotten, Jamie. It was my first punishment but it was just another one for Jimmy. He'd been there for about two years before I arrived and had already lost count of the beatings he'd endured. Knowing what we went through together, I don't know how he survived. I arrived at Mormont at twelve, Jimmy told me he was fourteen."

"Hold up. Sorry to interrupt you but it's been bugging me all night. I assumed the home shut down for the abuse you talk about, but do you have any clue why it never got mentioned in the local papers? You would think what happened should have been a pretty big scandal." Jamie doubted he knew but maybe he could steer her in the right direction.

"Honestly, I don't know. The Combs adopted me, praise the heavens, shortly before it got shut down and I didn't even look for info about it. I just assumed, like you did, that the abuse leaked out and the home quietly closed to prevent a public scandal. I guess I never gave it much thought really. It is weird, now that you mention it, because it was a private home not a state owned one. I didn't discover any political associations, but then I wasn't looking for any. I would assume there had to be a powerful one to keep it hushed up completely. There was no mention at all?"

"None." Even though she'd hoped he knew something more, she wasn't pleased with his answer.

"How about telling me how Jimmy saved your life? Please forgive me if I'm being rude. I'm just a little frustrated over the lack of information. I imagine you are as well." Jamie chose her words carefully. She didn't completely trust the man yet.

Before Thomas could respond, they were interrupted by his cell phone. "Pardon me just a moment?" He held up his index finger while he answered. "Hello…Sorry, I'm in a meeting right now, how can I help you?...Can I call you back in say…" Thomas looked to Jamie. "…forty-five minutes?" Jamie gave a positive nod. "Two hours? Why so long?...I see. Well, if that's the best you can do then…Okay, I will. Thank you, Mr. Iohs." Thomas slid the phone back into his pocket and turned back to Jamie. "My apologies. No, you're not being rude. I've never really talked about this time in my life before. Honestly, I wanted to forget it ever happened. However, if you can glean anything useful from it I'll try my best to give you an accurate account." Thomas dropped his head unable to look her in the eye. "Jimmy and I attempted escaping again and got caught again, of course. I think you can guess we tried to escape a few times and so for several months they watched us like hawks. We waited. We plotted and planned the whole time. They would lock us in our room at night even though that was illegal in case of a fire. We knew a night escape would be impossible because of that, so we needed to try another way. We did our best to lull them to sleep by staying on our best behavior—following every rule and not so much as looking at DeLong or her goons cross-eyed. We bided our time, watching for them to drop their guard. We waited for the exact right moment when their eyes were off of us for just long enough. Finally our window of opportunity came. Sorry, am I going too slow?"

"You're doing fine. Please, continue," she urged him on.

"We found a blind spot on the playground where we could sneak through the fence unseen and get far away before anyone noticed. Once they took their eyes off us, we made a break for it. Jamie, it couldn't have been more perfect. I held up a loose part of the fence for Jimmy to go under, then he held it for me. I was halfway out when DeLong came around the corner of the building by a stroke of really bad luck. She wasn't looking for us, but she caught us in the act. A few more seconds, that's all we needed—but no, that fucking cunt, excuse my language, came at that precise second. We were busted. Jimmy faced a choice, drop the fence with me halfway through and make a run for it, or wait for me, knowing we wouldn't make it. Honestly, his choice probably didn't matter, but he didn't run. DeLong grabbed my legs. She was blowing her damn police whistle like a woman possessed and pulling me back inside the fence at the same time. It brought her goons running and all hope was lost. DeLong's Goon Squad is what we all called them, but I think I told you that already." Jamie nodded her head. "Jimmy could have turned tail and run, Jamie, and I wouldn't have been mad. Instead he crawled back under the fence to attack DeLong, screaming at her to let go of me. Anyone else would have run for the hills, but not Jimmy. He came back for me knowing full well that attacking DeLong would have severe consequences. I can still see him punching away at her. It may have been a comical sight, but we both knew what it meant." He chuckled to himself. "You should have seen it. He flew through that fence and pushed her square in the...pardon me." Thomas leaned in, lowering his voice. "He pushed her right in the tits. It all happened so fast. DeLong let go of me and the fists started flying. Jimmy managed to get in a couple good ones until The Goon Squad showed up. It ended abruptly, as you can imagine. Jimmy and I both knew he was done for. The goons pulled Jimmy off DeLong, then they separated us. I didn't know it at the time, but that was the last I would ever see of him." Tears threatened as he hung his head. "A few hours later I heard the lock on my door click and DeLong came in. The evil I saw in her face at that moment, I've never seen the likes of since—not even in a horror movie. She grinned at me and then told me she hadn't forgotten about me. She told me my punishment would be something I'd never forget and that I should forget about Jimmy. I have no idea what they did to him, Jamie. Honestly, I don't." His voice cracked. "Maybe they killed him or maybe they did something even worse. Kids disappeared from Mormont sometimes—Jimmy wasn't the first. DeLong informed me my punishment would have to wait until after lights out the next night and then she locked me in to think about what was coming. I didn't believe in luck or fate, not after what I'd been through, but the very next morning Mr. & Mrs. Combs came to Mormont, requesting me." He couldn't hold back his tears any longer. "If they hadn't showed up, I may have learned what happened to Jimmy the hard way. I didn't want to leave Jimmy behind, but I knew I couldn't stay either. Later I confessed to my new family what happened to me at Mormont. Unfortunately, by that time, it was too late. They inquired about Jimmy, but got stonewalled. A short time after that, Mormont closed its doors for good—putting an end to the matter. That's all I know, Jamie. I don't know if my new family asking questions had anything to do with the closing, and I really don't think it did. I do remember we celebrated it! Nancy, my new mom, made a cake and we never spoke of The Mormont Home for Children ever again." Thomas wiped his eyes once he finished.

Jamie sat silent, letting him compose himself before making any comment. "I'm very sorry, Thomas. I'm also sorry for making you dredge up those dark memories. I do appreciate your honesty though." She paused giving him a moment before getting back to their business. "So before you began trying to find Jimmy, you never looked into the home itself?" Thomas shook his head no. "I found out the home was supposed to run practically forever thanks to a trust set up by A.H. Mormont. I will be trying to find out what happened to the money, since it could be connected somehow or lead me in a roundabout way to what happened to your friend. Do you remember seeing anything about the trust money at all? I don't believe in coincidence, Mr. Combs, and both the money and Jimmy disappeared about the same time." Jamie still had the feeling her client was withholding information for some reason she couldn't see.

"Thank you, but you have nothing to be sorry about, Jamie. Please, call me Tom." He smiled. "I only focused on Jimmy, so I'm sorry, I didn't look into the home itself. As you can see, I didn't find much of anything. Maybe the money is still being held in the trust? If the home closed because the abuse was discovered then maybe it's still sitting there or had to be used to settle a lawsuit. I never even thought to look into it. I'm no detective, I didn't see the fate of the home and Jimmy being connected in any way."

"I doubt the money is just sitting in a trust. I'd guess someone made off with it. It might be nothing, but any detective will tell you to always follow the money. Now, I have just one last thing, if it's alright?"

"Go ahead, Jamie."

"Do you know if or which members of the staff are still alive? Unless I find some paper trail, though I'd say that's unlikely, I'll need to question them. I doubt I'll be able to find out what happened to Jimmy any other way. One of them knows something, which will tell us the most important part, is Jimmy alive to be found at all?"

"Honestly, I assume one or more of them are alive. I didn't dare confront them. I'd like to shoot each of them in the face, so I was a little afraid of actually meeting up with them. I've dreamed about killing them all—especially that fucking cunt, DeLong, pardon my French. The Goon Squad was Robert Keane and Anthony Rollins. There were other counselors but those two were her left and right hand, and both were there when Jimmy disappeared. If anyone knows anything, it'll be those three. I hope they're all alive for you, but at the same time I also hope they all have some horribly painful cancer or something. I doubt they'll be difficult to find, provided they are alive." Any remorse he felt for Jimmy was clearly wiped away by his hatred of DeLong and her thugs.

"If they're alive, Thomas, I promise I'll find them and they will not enjoy the visit. I hold child abusing scum in the lowest regard. If they fail to supply answers they will regret it." She shot him a sly smile.

"They deserve the worst. If you do need to—let's just say—forcibly extract information, please, tell them Tommy Basnett says hello." He returned a wicked grin of his own.

"Absolutely!"

Jamie pushed herself away from the table, standing up to make her exit. She shook Thomas' hand, wishing him a good day and then walked away from the impromptu meeting back to her vehicle. She hadn't really learned anything that would help her locate Jimmy, however, she knew Thomas was holding back on her. She didn't believe for a second that he never looked to see if DeLong and her Goon Squad were around. They were the last people to see Jimmy alive, so far as she could tell, and she was supposed to believe Thomas didn't bother to see where they were now? It made no sense. You didn't have to be Sherlock Holmes to know those three people had the information you needed.

Thinking about the entire conversation, she still wondered why he hired her. She knew he had some secret agenda, one she needed to figure out soon. He was playing some sort of game and she needed to know why. She had told Thomas she didn't believe in coincidences. And it was no coincidence that her little surprise and Thomas Combs just happened to show up on the same day.

Then, more vexing, what in the hell did "Blood Remembers" mean? If any of the last twenty-four hours was coincidence she'd eat her own shorts, she thought.

4

Everything comes in threes, good or bad, or so the saying goes. If you're actually paying attention though, you find things rarely actually happen that way. Eddie Washington couldn't be happier at the moment, since his grim discovery. Good thing number two was leading him to his third good thing. The first good thing was taking the call from dispatch about a possible dead body. The second good thing, for him, was discovering the body, which may be a victim of the rumored serial killer, The Executioner. Now, Detective Stephen Barker called. He was asked to come to the medical examiner's office to examine the body with the detective and Erie County's Head Medical Examiner, Dr. Clive Ketchum. The unexpected call definitely made his day, already. He had never actually seen a dead body, outside of a peacefully embalmed family member resting in the padded comfort of a casket, let alone take part in the examination of one for evidence or clues about the killer. Detective Barker, in his always gruff tone, told him the autopsy had been performed, and he would like him to be there to go over the report and look the body over further. Eddie wasn't able to say yes fast enough.

Eddie pulled into the parking lot behind the Medical Examiner's office and saw Detective Barker waiting with his arms crossed, leaning against his car's fender, looking every bit his usual grumpy self. Eddie smiled, noticing that Detective Barker was a dead ringer for Peter Faulk, who played the disheveled TV detective, Columbo. Like his TV doppelganger, the detective was fairly short—Eddie guessed about five and a half feet— and slightly hunched over. Furthering the comparison, the detective sported dark unkempt hair, which looked like he ran a comb through it once and called it good enough. He also kept a permanent five o'clock shadow, completing his slovenly appearance. Eddie noted the only thing the detective lacked to complete the Columbo comparison, was the weather-worn overcoat the TV detective always wore. Eddie had grown up watching the show which made the whole situation too ironic to him.

Eddie opened his car door and took a deep breath. He nodded at Detective Barker, trying not to look like a beaming idiot. "Good morning, sir!"

"I ain't your Captain, so drop the 'sir' crap. It's just Barker. When you on duty next?"

"Not for a few hours. How long ya think this will take? Should I call Captain Hitchcock?"

"No, no. Look, Officer Washington, you're not officially here, okay? You did a good job the other night. You're only here to observe, so keep your mouth shut and your eyes open unless you can say something useful and then don't. Prove to me I didn't make a colossal mistake bringing you here, and we'll consider this experiment a success. Fuck this up and good luck making detective before retirement, understood?"

"I got it. I won't disappoint you, sir. I'm grateful for the opportunity." Eddie hung his head, feeling like a kid in the principal's office.

"If I thought you were an idiot, you wouldn't be here, so let's see if either of us being here even matters."

The two men walked silently side by side into the Office of the Medical Examiner. Eddie walked tall, proud to even be there. He wanted to believe the detective was testing him to see if he could keep his mouth shut, and he was anxious to prove that it wasn't a difficult test for him to pass. Eddie followed, with no clue where they were going since he had never been here. The only time he had seen Dr. Ketchum was on the local news a few times, otherwise he didn't know the man. The doctor had always struck him as a strict clinical professional, which was exactly what he thought a medical examiner should be. Eddie was pleasantly surprised that the building didn't smell like a hospital. It didn't really appear different from any other government office. The air reeked of pine and arrogance, though most would say power. Eddie made a mental note to keep his mouth shut, eyes open, and—somewhere deep in his gut—to never ever enter politics.

Unlike Eddie, Detective Barker knew exactly where to go. Every homicide investigation began with this trip, so he lost count of his visits down to the morgue for autopsy observations or reports. He hated coming here, but it was a necessary evil—unless he transferred to a different division, which wasn't going to happen.

Barker's first trip here had almost been his last, due to losing his breakfast, turning his head just in time to not contaminate a body. He wondered how Eddie would fare on his first visit. Failing to vomit was actually quite rare for any first timer. Now, he found it routine. He thought about warning Eddie, but talked himself out of it—everyone must experience it their own way. Dr. Ketchum's preliminary findings and how Eddie would react peaked his curiosity in equal measure. Sadly, he knew there was little chance he'd learn much—if anything—from the report, yet a slim chance was better than nothing.

"Isn't this where we're meeting Dr. Ketchum?" Confusion overtook Eddie as they passed Ketchum's office.

"Nope." Detective Barker hid a smile and continued on down the hall.

Eddie shrugged it off, figuring Barker knew his way around. They continued on to the bank of elevators at the end of being asked along in the first place and now, venturing into the unknown. He felt like a child on his first visit to the zoo—everything was new and exciting. He earned the nickname "Steady Eddie" at a young age for always keeping his cool, a nickname that annoyed him back then. Now, heading to examine a dead body with his stomach in knots, he was glad for that ability to remain calm no matter what life threw at him. He assumed everything was a test, including his ability to keep a strong stomach once the body was rolled out. He managed to control himself when he found the body—at least keeping his stomach contents down—so he expected he would again. The last thing he wanted was to embarrass himself in front of Detective Barker, a possible career killing embarrassment.

The shiny, stainless steel doors opened at the basement floor, ending the uncomfortable silence that always accompanies an elevator ride. Immediately two things struck Eddie; the building was ten or fifteen degrees cooler down here, and a wave of chemical-soaked air threatened to drown him. The stench of bleach mixed with other industrial cleaners filled his nostrils and nearly made him gag. Eddie involuntarily recoiled while his new mentor marched forward, seemingly unfazed. Eddie thought he'd rather walk through a barn than this hyper-sanitized hall that was burning his nose and eyes. However, he knew if he wished to work in homicide alongside Barker, he'd have to get used to it—or find something else to do. Detective Barker guided him down the hallway, turning left, then right, pausing at a pair of heavy double doors. Beside the doors hung a warning sign that read in big red letters:

Authorized Personnel Only Beyond This Point. Unauthorized Access Will Be Prosecuted.

Barker looked Eddie dead in his eyes. "Remember what I told you. Eyes open, mouth shut."

Barker didn't wait for any response and turned back around, pushing through the doors. Eddie intended to do as Barker instructed, although he was overwhelmed by the whole experience already. Barker's brusque demeanor, coupled with the pressure of this being a make or break moment for his entire career, didn't exactly ease his tension. He knew the next few minutes may decide his fate for the next twenty years or more. He was *Steady Eddie*, yet right this second, he felt like he was on trial for his life. He took a deep, cleansing breath then did the only thing he could—observe.

Eddie trailed behind Barker, noticing the bank of refrigerated morgue drawers along the left wall in two rows of six shiny silver doors. Seven of the dozen doors bore a white information tag hanging from their handles, signifying a body inside. Eddie noticed a seal on each tagged door, a security measure not unlike the seal on a tractor trailer's door. Eddie kept pace, trying to take in everything, though his eyes kept returning to the three stainless steel autopsy tables directly in front of them. The last table looked to be the only one with a cadaver atop it, covered in a pale blue sheet. Opposite the cadaver drawers, along the right side of the room, sat two steel desks neatly organized with several file folders stacked neatly on one side with a computer monitor to the other side. At the far end, behind the occupied autopsy table, sat a much larger desk, clearly belonging to Head Medical Examiner, Dr. Clive Ketchum. It wasn't the most cluttered, disorganized desk Eddie had ever seen—a distinction belonging to his wife's best friend and boss, Jamie Windstein—though it wasn't far behind either. There was little else for Eddie to take notice of other than the assorted medical instruments arranged neatly atop green cloth on silver trays beside each autopsy table, along with a rolling surgical light.

Doctor Ketchum sat at his desk and took no notice of the two intruders, seemingly deep in thought as he stared at his computer screen. Eddie smiled. Seeing the doctor concentrating on his work until the world faded away humanized the man to him. Until that moment, Doctor Ketchum had only been someone Eddie had seen on TV and now, he was a real person. The slap of hard soles on linoleum eventually roused the doctor from his work. He pushed back from his garbage heap of a desk and broke into an instant smile seeing the detective approaching with Eddie in tow. He stood up, stretching his six foot frame by arching his back to relieve the stiffness of being seated too long, the bane of every office workers' existence.

"Stephen! Hello!" Dr. Ketchum's tone matched his smile. "And I see you've brought a... um... partner? Has the great Stephen Barker lowered himself to such a depth? Say it ain't so!"

"Hey, doc. Very funny." Detective Barker frowned. "Doc, this is Officer Eddie Washington." He turned back to Eddie. "Eddie, I assume you at least know who Dr. Ketchum is?"

"It's an honor, Dr. Ketchum. Pleased to meet you, sir." Eddie stretched his hand out to the doctor.

"A pleasure, Officer Washington. Please, forgive my feeble attempts at humor. My friend, Stephen, has a disdain for other human beings rivaling a rattlesnake." Dr. Ketchum winked at Barker who responded with another frown. "So are you married to his niece or some such thing?"

Barker glared at the doctor. "Officer Washington discovered the body. He didn't soil himself so I brought him along to observe."

"Well, Officer Washington, you must have left quite an impression to get such a glowing reference from Detective Rattlesnake." Dr. Ketchum seemed to revel in ribbing the detective, something Eddie would not have thought a healthy thing to do just a second ago.

"Oh, shut up, Clive!" Barker continued to frown. "Are we gonna take a look at this body or listen to your stand-up act all day?"

"Alright, alright don't get your knickers in a pinch. Geez! Officer Washington, you'll find the morgue is a pretty dreary place, so I try to bring some levity to its general doom and gloom, even if a sourpuss like Stephen insists on being a humorless twat." Dr. Ketchum smiled and winked at Eddie before ducking away from a backhanded swat from Barker.

"Just Eddie, please, doctor." Eddie tried to hold back a laugh.

"Edward it is then. You may call me Clive. Its grim enough in here without maintaining useless formalities. Now, if you gentlemen will step over here, we'll take a look at the victim. I'll show you what I've determined so far since none of the lab work is back yet." Dr. Ketchum led them over to his occupied autopsy table.

Dr. Ketchum gently pulled back the pale blue sheet covering the headless corpse, as if pulling the covers back on his own sleeping child. Eddie noticed that despite the head examiner's jovialness, he appeared to take his work quite seriously. Eddie kept Barker's words in mind, trying to take in every little bit of information possible. He made himself pause to take stock of what he'd observed already, while waiting for Ketchum to begin. Detective Barker looked like Columbo, had the grim seriousness of an accountant, and a complete disdain for company. Dr. Ketchum was tall and fit with slicked back blond hair, looking somewhat like a Swedish version of the actor Andy Garcia with gold rimmed glasses. The fact that Ketchum and Barker had obviously worked enough cases to have a personal relationship wasn't lost on him either. Last, and most important, he took in the headless body—the reason he was here. The uncovered naked male cadaver laid on the autopsy table with a Y-incision already sown back together, running from the waist all the way up to the chest and then spreading to each shoulder. Eddie first noticed the lack of any birthmarks or tattoos to identify the man, so if his fingerprints didn't turn up his name, he'd remain a John Doe possibly forever.

"So, Edward." Eddie snapped his head up, surprised to be addressed. "Since this is your first time, tell us what you see. Prove to my old grumpy friend that intelligent life exists outside of the two of us and that having a partner wouldn't be a cataclysmic, world ending event for him." Dr. Ketchum looked to Barker with a smile.

"You're a regular jackass, you know that?" Barker scowled.

"Yes actually, I do. My wife tells me so daily yet, over a dozen years on, she still can't get enough of me— and neither can you." Dr. Ketchum crossed his arms with a self-satisfied smile. "Please, Edward, ignore this grouch. Show him he brought in the right man today."

Eddie took a moment to gather his confidence, wanting more than anything to impress these two men. If he sounded like a blithering idiot now, it would be all over for him.

He took a deep breath then began. "Okay." He let out a sigh. "First, the victim doesn't appear to have any physical markings to indicate his identity. No birthmarks, no tattoos nor any obvious scars, so unless his fingerprints are on record, we're screwed, as far as identification is concerned. So onto the body's condition. Aside from the missing head, I don't see any signs of struggle. No bruises, no defensive wounds, no sign he struggled at all against whoever removed his head."

Barker shot a curious look at Dr. Ketchum. "Which tells us what?"

Eddie didn't hesitate. "It means he was unconscious—I'd guess drugged—or he was immobilized, though there are no ligature marks. Or he was already dead when his head was taken. Since the head is missing, we can't say he wasn't hit with something, though I'd say drugged is more likely. If he was, the drug could point us in the direction of his killer. How long does it usually take to get the toxicology report back, Dr. Ketchum?"

"I sent the sample already, so about a week from now—end of the week if we're extraordinarily lucky. I can run some tests here for traces of any anesthetic, barbiturates or some other common drug, but I don't have the equipment to find anything exotic. The full tox report will have specifics about what was used, and in what concentration—all I can really determine here is if some common drug was used or not." Dr. Ketchum paused and winked at Barker. "Very good, Edward! Tell me, why do you think our victim was drugged rather than knocked out with a bat or something?"

"There are no signs this guy struggled, not even a little bit. My guess is the killer was smaller or, at least, weaker than our victim. If that is the case, it makes sense that a smaller killer would drug the victim to incapacitate him to prevent being overpowered."

Ketchum shot Barker a giant grin. "See, Stephen? Not everyone in the world is an idiot. Looks like you brought the right man, alright."

Barker shifted uncomfortably. "Nice work, kid. All pretty simple stuff though, so don't let it go to your head. And you, wise ass…" He turned to Ketchum. "If you can tear your lips from Officer Washington's ass for a minute, did you run his damn prints yet? I'm betting you have an ID already, but wanted to play your little game first." Barker raised his eyebrows to show his impatience.

"You know I did." Dr. Ketchum smiled sarcastically. "I thought the purpose, Stephen, was to give Edward a chance to impress and you know damn well he did, no matter how much you try to downplay it. So before I get to the print report, perhaps Edward can impress us again. Hell, maybe he can even wow us!" Ketchum smirked at Barker and then turned to Eddie. "Edward, please, indulge me a moment, if you will. Let's see if you can charm Detective Rattlesnake with your intuitiveness. Look at the neck, where this poor fellow's head used to be, and tell us what you see. Take your time, this isn't a test. I'm actually curious about what you think."

Eddie took another deep breath to slow his heart that was threatening to burst through his chest. He had already pleasantly surprised himself by not tripping over his own tongue, expressing his initial thoughts so hopefully lightning would strike twice today. Barker was correct that his observations weren't astounding, but impressing Ketchum felt good. He liked the doctor almost instantly. Barker, on the other hand, was a tough nut to crack. He seemed like the type of guy you could be acquainted with for decades and never know much more than his favorite beer. He also seemed to be a guy who could see you lift a building with your little finger and look completely unimpressed. Eddie wheeled the surgical light around to the head of the table or, in this case, the headless end. He adjusted the light to illuminate the victim's neck, then bent down to take a good, hard look. He wasn't sure what the doctor expected, so he tried to heed Barker's words and simply observe.

After a minute Barker grew impatient. "Well?"

Dr. Ketchum smacked him lightly on the shoulder. "Would you relax? Give Edward a chance, for crying out loud!"

"It's alright, Dr. Ketchum." Eddie stood up, facing his superiors. "I'm not sure what you're expecting me to see here but here goes…the cut appears fairly straight, though it looks rough. I don't believe this is the work of a blade, at least not any blade I know of. It doesn't look to me like some garden variety saw, like a hacksaw or power saw or a circular saw either. Do you have an approximate time of death? When I found the body, I assumed it had laid there a couple of days, minimum."

Dr. Ketchum couldn't help smiling. "I put time of death at approximately seventy two to eighty four hours ago, difficult to be much more accurate than that without more information. What makes you ask?" Dr. Ketchum was anxious to know what Eddie thought.

"Well, because the skin along the cut is jagged—not smooth like if a sharp blade had been used. That made me curious if that's from normal decomposition, or from whatever was used to remove the head."

"Excellent, Edward!" Dr. Ketchum nearly jumped with excitement. "Now, pick up the magnifying glass on the tray there. Take a look at the spine itself, and tell me what you see." Dr. Ketchum looked over at Barker, giddy as a school girl who was waiting to find out if her crush likes her back.

Eddie plucked the magnifying glass from the tray, holding it over the spine like Dr. Ketchum instructed. He stared, bewildered by what Ketchum expected him to see. At first, he didn't notice anything out of the ordinary, though none of this was ordinary for him. Then he thought he realized what the doctor wanted him to see.

Eddie didn't think he could bear the disappointment in Ketchum's face, so he squatted down out of sight. "Are these burn marks? The striations across the bone look like burns."

Dr. Ketchum clapped loudly, surprising both Barker and Eddie with the sudden noise that echoed in the empty morgue. "Exactly! Fantastic, Edward!" Eddie stood up with a smile. "I don't know what instrument the killer used, either. However, like you said, it wasn't a sharp blade, like a machete or sword, and it wasn't any saw I've ever seen. A power saw—like a circular or reciprocating saw—can create enough heat to mare the bone in that way, but it looks much different. Those markings look like friction burns rather than a hot blade, charring the bone as it cut through. Plus power saws tend to tear the skin, rather than cut it, so I'd expect the skin to look much more jagged or chewed up than it is there. So, this is where I've hit the proverbial wall." Dr. Ketchum rubbed his chin, perplexed.

Silence filled the morgue as all three men contemplated what possible weapon their killer used. Barker stood with his arms folded over his chest, Dr. Ketchum rubbed his chin staring at the ceiling, and

Eddie stood looking down into the gaping neck on the table. Eddie desperately wanted to come up with the weapon to impress his superiors. A virtual gallery of weapons flipped through his mind, but nothing fit. He thought for several minutes before his mind landed on something, though he was afraid of sounding stupid after doing so well thus far. He swallowed hard, deciding to take a stab in the dark.

"What about a band saw? Aren't those used at meat packing plants to cut through frozen meat?" Eddie hoped that didn't sound as dumb as it felt.

Dr. Ketchum considered the idea for a moment before responding. "Good thought, but I don't think so. Like other power saws, the bone would nearly blacken like a burn, and with a band saw, the skin would be fairly smooth—similar to being cut with a blade, unless it was old and worn. The marks on the vertebrae of our victim are too striated to be a band saw, they're in a more circular pattern. Keep thinking though, that was good."

"Chainsaw?" Barker tossed out.

"Oh no, Stephen, not at all. A chainsaw tears up the skin terribly. The skin would look like a dog chewed up the edges."

Silence returned while they kept thinking. Eddie tried to think of anything that would cut through bone slower than a sword, while generating less heat than any powered saw and cut through flesh somewhat smoothly at the same time. He wracked his brain, desperate to come up with the answer before anyone else. He impressed Ketchum, though Barker seemed underwhelmed to this point. Eddie knew he was running out of time. He flipped through a mental gallery of sharp objects like someone skimming through a mugshot book back at the station, but still, no weapon matched the details.

Barker broke the silence when his patience had ended. "Well, Clive,   I think I'm ready for the fingerprint report—unless we receive some divine intervention. So who's the vic?"

"Sadly, it appears the wall still stands, even with three of us smacking into it. Oh well, maybe later." Dr. Ketchum let out a heavy sigh and stepped to his desk. He patted Eddie on the shoulder as he passed by, leaning in so only Eddie could hear him. "Don't let him discourage you, Edward. You're doing great."

Eddie smiled like a child who had just been handed a lollipop as big as his own head. He couldn't help it, despite the fact he was standing over a headless corpse in the city morgue that stunk from decades of death thoroughly sunken into the walls. He stared at his feet, unable to look at Barker regardless of Dr. Ketchum's encouraging words. Whether Barker's apathy was genuine or fake mattered very little, the effect it had was disheartening. He closed his eyes, continuing to search his brain for any weapon, even something odd. He desperately wanted to impress Detective Barker and this might be his only chance.

"Michael Snyder." Dr. Ketchum's voice broke Eddie's concentration. "Forty-three, no police record of note, just a few traffic tickets and one domestic complaint, nothing violent. Recently divorced from his wife, Jessie Snyder, maiden name Anderson."

"How recent?"

Dr. Ketchum traced a finger down the page. "Let's see…final in March. March the twenty-second to be exact."

Barker pulled out his notepad. "Attorney's name? Wife's too, if it's listed."

"Let's see here… yes, here it is. Sean Barnes represented him and the ex… oh, shit! Sandra Largulis—Sandy the Shark—represented the ex."

"Everyone knows Sandy. Well that's a big fat dead end. She won't turn over a post-it note without a warrant." Barker threw up his hands, dejected.

Contrarily, Eddie lit up at the mention of Largulis, though he kept his enthusiasm in check. He hadn't come up with the decapitating method, so he thought this might be his last chance to impress the detective. "I may know a way to swim around the shark."

Barker stared with a quizzical look on his face. "What are you on about, Washington?"

"No guarantees but I may know a way around Largulis. The only information Sandy the Shark will give us is that she represented the ex, something we already know. However, my wife works for a local private investigator who does work for Largulis quite often. I doubt I can get the dirty details, but maybe I can get something. Anything at all is more than we'll get from Sandy." Eddie killed a grin while waiting for Barker's response.

"Do you have time to stop in before your shift starts?"

Eddie checked his watch, "Probably not, though I doubt Jamie is in the office. I'll call my wife on the way out to set up a time since I'll probably need to talk to Jamie directly."

"Jamie?"

"Jamie Windstein, my wife is her secretary, but they're also close friends. Why, you know her?"

"I think I've met her in passing once or twice at the courthouse so, yes and no. She digs up dirt for Largulis?"

"Obviously, I don't know about this case, but yeah. I think Sandy is their biggest client, since my wife mentions her all the time. When Largulis needs dirt, Jamie is definitely who she goes to for it." Eddie let out a sigh, seeing he finally impressed Barker, at least, a little.

"Well, Edward, it looks like you've taken the rattle out of the rattlesnake! Will wonders never cease?" Dr. Ketchum patted Eddie on the back and laughed at Barker.

"Oh, would you just shut it, Clive!" Barker's half-hearted rebuke fooled no one. "If he comes up with whatever tool took off the vic's head then I'll be impressed!"

A light bulb went off in Eddie's brain, like a lightning strike. Barker's use of the word "tool" instead of weapon made the connection in his brain. His wife, Carrie, enjoyed watching veterinarian shows on Animal Planet all the time. They bored him to tears and so he usually worked on a crossword puzzle or simply zoned out—though he watched with her occasionally. Last Saturday had been one of those occasions and now he could kiss her for watching that crap.

"Dr. Ketchum?"

"Yes, Edward?" Dr. Ketchum eyed him with enthusiastic curiosity.

"What about a wire saw?"

"Wire saw? What the hell is that, Washington?" Barker looked confused.

"My wife, Carrie, she likes to watch these veterinarian shows on that Animal Planet Channel or whatever. I find it boring so I'm usually not paying attention, but last Saturday I watched one with her for a little while. Anyway, the vet needed to remove the horns from a goat or bull—I forget what it was, not that it matters. They used a wire saw to do it. It's just a piece of steel wire attached to two handles that you pull back and forth. A kid could make one. There's enough friction that the horns smoke while the vet does it, but not enough heat to actually char the bone like a power saw would. What do you think, Dr. Ketchum?" Eddie held his breath, desperate to be right.

Dr. Ketchum stood silent for a moment and rubbed his chin again, making Eddie sweat while he waited for his answer. After a few seconds, Dr. Ketchum turned to Barker and looked him square in the eye. "You said you'd be impressed, so get impressed." Dr. Ketchum turned to Eddie with a huge smile plastered across his face. "Is the rattlesnake smiling or is he still picking his jaw up off the floor?" Dr. Ketchum winked at Eddie.

"How in the fuck did you come up with that, Washington?" Barker was clearly dumbfounded.

"It was actually you, sir." Eddie smiled. "When you said tool a moment ago, instead of weapon, it popped right in my head."

"You know I hate to say I told you so, but I do believe I told you so!" Ketchum turned his smile back to Barker. "This young man just wowed you, Stephen. You should learn a little patience. My dad—God rest his soul—once told me, 'Clive, they say patience is a virtue and, perhaps that's true, but what I know for a fact is that impatience will put you straight on the path to ruin.' Edward, in a matter of minutes, just put us on the right path. I think we can fill him in on what we've gotten him into now, don't you think?"

Barker dropped his head in defeat. "I don't think we have any other choice." Barker looked Eddie in the eye, even more serious than he had been. "We'd like you like to join our team, Officer Washington. We've been tasked with hunting down a serial killer who has plagued this city for well over a decade. The rumor that we call him *The Executioner* is true. You're looking at the whole team here, it's just Dr. Ketchum and I. Want to join us?"

Eddie's eyes nearly bulged out of their sockets. "Absolutely! Yes!"

5

He entered the garage a few seconds after the overhead door closed behind her little Honda Civic. Curiosity ate away at him like a cancer. He needed to know what Jamie Windstein hid behind her secret door like an addict needs a fix. He hated surprises, especially after carefully planning this all out for years. He knew everything else hinged on her initial reaction, though he didn't expect her to shock him with it. Little Jamie Windstein had certainly accomplished that a few hours ago. Now he had to know her secret so that he could adjust accordingly. He was used to being stoic, the perfect picture of calm, but now he fought against the excitement pulsing through his veins. He closed his eyes, breathing deep to regain his calm before he made an unnecessary mistake. He didn't make mistakes. He silently chanted a mantra of "be careful" in his head slowing his heart and mind.

He wanted to kick himself for letting her secret door slip by him. It was a mistake, but not a fatal one, thankfully. He hoped he could bypass whatever security she had installed. He knew he could crack almost anything, but he didn't like unknowns any more than surprises. He wore disposable paper overalls and a ski mask in case she installed hidden cameras in her secret place. He never took Jamie for a dummy, and he would have massive security if this were his secret space. His heart began to race with anticipation again, approaching the shelves he had watched her slide out of the way only a few hours ago.

He stood in front of the shelves, admiring her handiwork. He knew the shelves hid a secret entrance, yet standing in front of it now he still couldn't see any hint of it. The doorway seemed completely invisible without so much as a scuff on the floor from the door opening or the shelves being moved. He was impressed. If he hadn't seen her reveal the secret door, he still wouldn't know it was there at all.

He slid the shelves to the side like he watched her do a few hours ago, yet he didn't know what to do afterward. He searched for an agonizing few minutes, unable to find the handle or lock. Finally his fingers stumbled upon a cutout that slid to the side, revealing the locking mechanism. He silently thanked Jamie Windstein for installing a simple key lock rather than some hi-tech electronic keypad. His hacking skills were considerable but it was a time consuming operation. Jamie might be gone the whole day, though it wasn't something he could count on. He planned to be quick—take a look at what she was hiding then get out. His curiosity was killing him. He knew he'd find two severed heads inside, but what else was little Jamie Windstein hiding in there?

Luckily, his lock picking skills made quick work of the simple lock, yet that in itself gave him pause. Obviously, Jamie had a massive secret to hide, so why make the door nearly impossible to find then install a lock that a child could pick? It was odd and it made him nervous for the real security. He heard the lock click open after only a few seconds of working on it, bringing a nervous smile to his lips under the mask. The moment of truth, he thought. He ground his teeth as he waited for an alarm to start blaring. He pushed the door open slowly, only a few millimeters at a time, hearing no alarm. The thought of a silent alarm flashed through his mind, though he found no indication of anything along the door or its frame. Again the easy entry made him pause nervously—she had to have more security of some kind. He silently chastised her carelessness, although he knew there had to be more.

The door opened onto a staircase leading into the dark. He cautiously stepped down, expecting possibly a pressure sensor alarm, still nothing happened. He moved on carefully, unable to believe Jamie didn't install some kind of security down here. He knew she wasn't a fool, so there had to be something he hadn't found yet. He tried not to go too fast, though he needed to get back outside before anyone got suspicious.

His fingers rubbed across a light switch when he hit the bottom stair, though he didn't dare use it. He pulled a flashlight from his inside pocket and clicked it to life. The stairs ended at nothing. He stood at the bottom, staring into a plain, flat wall no more than two or three feet from the bottom stair. He knew that it couldn't be a dead end, which meant, hidden on the wall somewhere, he had another lock to find. He doubted it would be as simple as the one above. He shined the flashlight slowly across the smooth grey wall, seeing nothing. He saw no seam of any kind hiding the lock, which meant nothing. He pushed on the wall to test it. It seemed solid as steel. The first lock had been well hidden, and this one seemed downright invisible. He stared at the wall—both dumbfounded and impressed in equal measure—looking for the slightest sign of the lock and grew frustrated. After several minutes, his eyes finally noticed a faint square outline, larger than on the first door. The small outline refused to slide to the side, so he pushed against it lightly. It made a hushed click, making him shudder and grit his teeth, expecting a siren to start blaring. His relieved smile faded to a frown when he lifted the little cutout to reveal an electronic keypad. The sudden elation of finding the lock disappeared, while his heart sank to his feet. He had the equipment to break her code, but he needed time—lots of it. His need to know Jamie's secret burned in his veins, though caution warned him of the danger involved. Breaking the keycode could take hours—hours in which Jamie could return home or someone would notice he was missing. He bit his lip weighing his options.

He pulled his cell phone from another pocket, heading back up the stairs. Standing in the empty garage, he dialed his partner on his burner phone. He positively loathed talking on the phone, yet it was a necessary evil under the circumstances.

He tapped his foot impatiently while waiting for an answer, which came on the second ring. "How long do I have?...'kay. I need all the time you can give me…Keypad…Ring me the second you're done."

He stood there, thinking for a moment after hanging up. He figured he had two hours minimum. He knew he likely had all day if need be, but he couldn't bet on it. Plus he needed to get back to where he was supposed to be soon. He cursed himself for not finding the secret door earlier, then grabbed his tool bag and headed back to Jamie's secret room. The anticipation of discovering Jamie's secret was the only thing holding his frustration in check. They say curiosity killed the cat, however at this very moment, he'd kill almost anything to know Jamie Windstein's dirty little secret.

Chapter Five: Begging For The Truth

1

Jamie Windstein left her meeting with Thomas Combs almost completely dissatisfied with not one real answer and the distinct feeling he held back important information for some unknown reason. The man made no logical sense. If he hadn't looked into any of the staff members still being alive, she'd eat her own shoe. Tracking down Delong and her main goons was a no-brainer and her top priority when she got to the office. The thought of the office reminded her to check in with Carrie. *She's probably assumed I'm not coming in by now*, Jamie thought. Carrie could handle things, and should be used to her boss being late—or failing to show up—but the woman was her friend and a worrier.

"Hey, Carrie, sorry I didn't call earlier. I met with Mr. Combs first thing this morning…if you could please mark it on his billing sheet? I planned on heading over to that abandoned children's home now, unless I've missed something of dire importance." Jamie gritted her teeth, expecting Carrie to curse her out for not calling sooner. "I doubt I'll find anything other than some bums, rats, and probably some vomit. I'll come in when I'm done, hopefully no more than a couple of hours. It shouldn't take me too long."

"Wow! Sounds like fun...Not! Better late than never Jams! I don't' start to worry about you until at least noon." Carrie giggled, though they both knew that was a lie. "Pretty quiet morning, though a Mister...umm...Al Jourgensen called to set up a meeting. My guess is a photo job, though he wouldn't say. Said he would only talk to you. Otherwise, it's been quiet. You alright, hun? You sound a little agitated."

"Agitated would be putting it mildly, but I'll live. Want me to pick anything up for you on my way back?"

"I don't think I need anything. Just call me when you're done. I ain't gonna sit here worrying that you got beaten, raped and murdered just because you lost track of damn time. You don't pay me enough for that! And yes, that's a request for a raise!" Carrie laughed.

"You worry too much! And why would I give you a raise when Eddie and I already decided to bump you off and abscond to the Caribbean? Bye." Jamie laughed, then hung up before Carrie scolded her.

Jamie's grim mood finally began to lift—their banter always made her feel better. She actually wore a smile as she made her way over to the abandoned home. The lighter feeling faded quickly with her thoughts returning to her surprise discovery. She still had no clue what the message meant, or why anyone would leave it in that manner for her. The mystery of "What in the world happened to Jimmy Reimse?" already had her head spinning, so she didn't need the distraction. All the questions spun on a demented carousel in her mind now that her meeting with Combs had only raised more questions.

The lack of any clues whatsoever wasn't merely making her angry, it pissed her off. Jamie Windstein was not a woman you wanted to piss off.

She cranked the stereo, hoping to drown out the noise in her head, with no such luck. A good song was like a cop, she thought, never one around when you need one. Buffalo only had a couple rock stations that were any good and, thanks to Murphy's Law, both were on a commercial break. She believed that should be illegal. The frustration wasn't improving her sour mood much. Finally, after an unbearable few minutes, music began blasting from the speakers. Surprisingly, it wasn't a completely terrible song either, so perhaps her luck was changing. She began singing—if you could call it that— along, shoving all the questions to the back of her mind for the moment.

Jamie was still irritated as she pulled up to her destination. She felt like a coiled spring ready to snap at any second. Clenching her fists, she wished she could punch something without hurting herself, in order let go of all her tension. Deep breaths didn't do anything for her at the moment, and she needed to focus. She couldn't relax so she tried channeling her anger at the abandoned building itself, the former Mormont Home for Children.

Jamie thought it better not to park directly in front of the abandoned building in broad daylight. She didn't think it was a good idea to attract any attention, even though entering an abandoned building was merely a misdemeanor. However, she preferred to go about her business unnoticed, if possible.

It wasn't the worst neighborhood, though no one would call it a good one either. The street saw little traffic, which could emboldened the desperate if they saw a woman enter alone. She decided it best to pull up closer to the intersection at the end of the block, where there would be more traffic. She shut off the engine and exited, wary of any prying eyes.

Jamie did her best not to attract attention, circling around to approach the building from the backside and out of sight. She hoped her calculations were correct, that during the day anyone who took shelter in the building at night would be gone. She crossed her fingers and hoped it wasn't a naïve thought. She knew homeless people, generally were harmless—it was the addicts looking for a fix she had to beware of. A desperate addict could be unpredictable and dangerous. They'd rob and rape their own mothers if it got them their fix. She may be fearless, but she saw no sense in being foolish, making now the best time there would be to check this place out. She walked along, trying not to look too conspicuous, though she doubted anyone cared or noticed. Regardless of her defensive capabilities, she knew overly cautious was better than dead.

Jamie approached, hoping to find the section of fence Thomas Combs told her about, the section he and Jimmy attempted to escape through. She knew it was now a likely point of entry for night residents—if the fence still stood at all. She came to the chain link fence, though no one would call it that anymore. All the metal poles, along with the chain link they once held up, were toppled over and barely visible now, under a blanket of weeds. Jagged pieces of rusty metal poked up in a few places and served as the only indication a fence had ever been there. It had been trampled almost completely flat, though what Jamie found stunning was that no one had taken it to sell for scrap yet. She looked around, trying to approximate the spot where Jimmy and Thomas tried to escape. It wasn't difficult to find. There was an ell in the building exactly like Thomas had described. It was the only spot where they could have possibly slipped out unseen.

The playground area was actually larger than Jamie expected. She saw the rusted remnants of a jungle gym, some swings, and what remained of a merry-go-round. She paused, trying to picture the two boys attempting to slip out unnoticed while the other children played. She could feel their desperation to escape the abuse. The hair on her arms stood on end, picturing DeLong catching them in the act. In her mind, she screamed for them to run knowing it was already too late. The fear they must have felt filled her mind and slowly turned to anger with the knowledge of what came next for them. She never understood the mind of an abuser. She thought lording power over the weak had to be one of mankind's worst traits, and our sadistic tendencies made it even worse. Man is the only animal capable of such a thing, despite how sophisticated we think we are. Standing outside the Mormont Home for Children, she could feel the pain of every child with the misfortune to come under the care of Head Mistress DeLong. It weighed on her like a mountain and it made her more determined than ever to track down DeLong and her Goon Squad. She fixated on bringing them to long overdue justice—her justice, for all the suffering they had wrought.

Jamie pushed all that aside for the moment, approaching the entry that faced the playground, where no doubt, the children went in and out. An old, badly rusted steel door hung on its hinges like someone clinging for dear life on a cliff by one weary, shaking finger. She didn't know how it managed to stay upright, hanging there so precariously. She pulled it, expecting it to fall to the ground. It screeched loudly like a thousand cats yowling in unison, a truly horrible sound. She cringed at the noise, though she hoped it scared off any rats hiding inside—she really hated rats. She pulled on a thin pair of gloves before stepping inside. She wasn't worried about leaving fingerprints—no one cared if she was here—and she wasn't a germophobe but she despised running her hands through dust, likely to be thick, and she didn't care to visit the hospital for a tetanus shot either.

Jamie stepped into the Mormont Home cautiously, on the lookout for any potential inhabitants—thankfully, seeing none. Plenty of natural light poured in through the broken windows, though she carried a small flashlight in her back pocket in case she needed it later. She sneered at the dust particles. They danced like snowflakes in the rays of sun beaming into the filthy space. Debris from fallen ceiling tiles littered the floor, along with a plethora of assorted garbage. Shards of green, brown, and clear glass glinted in the sun everywhere. Countless bottles of liquor had been smashed to pieces through the years, mixing with shards from the broken windows—definitely not a place to walk around barefoot. Jamie carefully wound her way quickly across a room that, by her client's description, had once been a playroom. In Buffalo the weather didn't permit going outside for at least half the year.

She headed for the doorway at the opposite end of the room, trying to avoid the broken glass.

Jamie assumed another steel door once hung at the entrance, making her wonder why a scraper took this one but left the outside door. *People were weird*, she thought.

The doorway led into a long hallway with rooms on either side—living quarters for the children. Wooden doors hung precariously on some, though most were missing. The hall darkened the further she went, so she pulled out her flashlight and clicked it to life. The first few rooms she passed by weren't bedrooms but appeared to be classrooms, though the desks were gone. She walked on, occasionally peering into one of the bedrooms to see if anything useful had been left behind.

Each room held two single beds with room for a nightstand or dresser between them, just the way Thomas Combs had described. The rooms appeared to be approximately twice the size of a standard prison cell—an appropriate comparison given the treatment provided—and only slightly more comfortable than one.

Jamie took in the dilapidated state of the home as she made her way down the hall. She was happy no child would ever be abused here again, yet she also felt a sadness that another salvageable building was going to rot in her city. The building seemed structurally sound, while the aesthetics certainly needed improvement. The walls were littered with bare patches where the paint had peeled off, leaving what remained looking like dried up crepe paper. It had the effect of turning the Mormont Home into a dull, grey decomposing corpse. Walking through, she couldn't help thinking the only thing the building lacked were steel bars to make it a functional prison. Ironically the children living here when the home closed probably thought of it as exactly that, their prison. She found the dull grey of decay—seen everywhere—to be the true face of the Mormont Home, at least, during its years under DeLong and her Goon Squad.

Jamie rounded the corner at the end of the hall, finding herself at what looked like the main office. There was a first-aid or nurse's office directly across the hall, denoted by a white square with a red cross in the center of it, hanging over the doorway. She stepped into the office first, hoping to find some files or records left behind, yet expecting nothing. Her instincts were, unfortunately, correct. A few blank or faded papers littered the floor, otherwise the office had been emptied out. Both the desk and filing cabinets were empty—without so much as an empty folder left behind. Anything useful had either been moved somewhere else or used to get a fire started during cold Buffalo nights. It didn't matter where the files went, the point was they weren't here.

Jamie poked her head into the nurse's office, finding it equally empty. *Well, so far this was a wasted trip,* she thought. She continued on. The further she went, hope of finding anything waned more and more. She couldn't help thinking what a cold heartless place Mormont seemed to be. A.H. Mormont must be spinning in his grave over what his dream of a better life for orphans had turned into in the end. He built the home to be a safe place, free from abuse, free from even the fear of abuse—and still it devolved into his worst nightmares by the end. The thought made a chill run up her spine and raised goosebumps on her arms, despite the warmth of the day. She felt every ounce of the sadness and pain this home had seen seeping straight out of the walls. Mormont intended the home to turn sadness to happiness and joy, but DeLong and her Goon Squad destroyed his dream. The home was nothing more than a cold, stale, dead space now. The very air made most turn and leave, yet that feeling fueled Jamie's desire to find out why and how it went so wrong. She intended to find the truth no matter what it took.

With the air threatening to choke her, Jamie continued on until she came to a tee at the end of the hall. The hall ended at an open door to her right, which looked like the cafeteria, while to the left a short hall dead-ended at a strange, bright red door. The door's color, while out of place, also appeared odd due to its apparent pristine condition. Even if she wasn't drawn to the strange red door, there was little, if anything, to be gleaned from the cafeteria and kitchen. She found herself compelled to approach the door, despite red being the universal color for danger. Moving toward it felt like floating in a dream, she seemed to have no choice in the matter. Her feet moved forward of their own accord, bringing her body along for the ride.

Jamie stood in front of the red door, awed by the oddity. The door was solid wood—oak she thought—making the fact it had been left behind even stranger. It would've made some homeless resident a great warm fire, yet it was untouched. Odder still, the paint had not faded, chipped or peeled away. It looked practically brand new, aside from needing a good cleaning. She couldn't figure out why it hadn't been used for a fire when nearly everything else burnable had been. She had to admit there was something off-putting about it, perhaps no one had been brave enough to remove it. It was certainly strange, she thought. She lifted her hand to the golden doorknob, hesitating for a moment.

"Just open the damn thing, you silly bitch. It's just a damn door!" The echo of her own voice nearly made her leap out of her skin. "Christ's sake, Jamie! You're an idiot." She laughed at herself.

Still, Jamie stood stiff, staring at the red door unable to make her hand turn the knob. She shook her head at her own foolishness, inhaled a deep breath and then braced herself as she finally turned the knob. She pulled the door open slowly, shining her flashlight inside. A blur of movement shot toward her making her jump back like she just unleashed a horde of the undead. A scream stopped dead in her throat when a wooden broom handle struck the floor with a sharp bang. The scream turned to laughter that echoed through the entire building.

"Jamie Windstein, you are one stupid cunt!"

Jamie took a second to catch her breath then looked inside. The big, scary red door opened on nothing other than a tiny broom closet. A small grey utility sink hung from the wall to the left of the door with a shelf above it at about shoulder level. Directly in front of her was a row of metal hooks where brooms, mops and such once hung, and then to the right stood metal shelving, presumably for cleaning supplies. It seemed nothing scary or nefarious hid behind the red door. It was a tiny space, maybe six square feet, barely enough room for a janitor to turn around. She laughed at herself for getting so spooked.

"Some big, tough PI you are, Jamie Windstein!" She shook her head deciding she had wasted enough time finding nothing.

Jamie decided to cut her loses, but before she turned to leave she froze stiff. Something caught her eye on the back wall in front of her. She squinted, shining her flashlight between the utility sink and the metal hooks. There seemed to be a seam that shouldn't be there. She pushed against the wall but it didn't budge. She kicked it, which only accomplished hurting her foot and sent a few curse words flying from her lips.

"Open says me." She smiled knowing nothing would happen. "Oh well, it was worth a shot."

Jamie stared, knowing the seam didn't belong where it was—only an inch or two from the corner. It has to be some hidden opening, she told herself. She stupidly kicked the wall again, sending another sharp pain shooting up her leg. She hopped on one foot for a second, putting herself off balance. Instinctively, she reached out to steady herself, looking up as she did. She grabbed ahold of one of the hooks, preventing her from going down in a heap. As Jamie put her sore foot down to regain her balance, her eye caught a spot near the ceiling. It looked like a smudge from a dirty finger.

"Hmm, now how did you get way up there?"

Without hesitation, Jamie reached up. Her finger easily found a soft spot right above the mark. She pressed it and heard a click come from behind the wall, then it slid inward. She pushed it as far as it would go, into the darkness behind it. She snatched up the flashlight she had set on the utility sink, anxiously flicking it back to life. The light illuminated a much larger room than she had expected. She didn't know why a children's home needed a secret room, though she knew no one hid anything good—aside from treasure and no one at Mormont had ever been a pirate.

Jamie couldn't believe her eyes as she shined her light around the room. It looked like some S&M room straight out of a movie. She never doubted that Head Mistress DeLong was a sadist but she didn't expect this. Rusted chains hung from the wall on her right with leather bindings on their ends. The sight turned her stomach when she noticed that the chains weren't high enough for an adult.

A table at the back of the room held assorted dusty whips, paddles and other tools used to beat the children unfortunate enough to end up in here. She turned her head, suddenly nauseated by the images racing through her mind. Her eyes welled up thinking about what happened here. She hunched over gagging and expected her morning coffee to splatter to the floor any second. She managed not to vomit, though it took her a few minutes to compose herself.

Jamie kept her back to the chains and the table, not wishing to see them again, while trying to see if the room held anything actually useful to her. The rest of the room was pretty sparse, with the exception of one item. She sucked in a deep breath as a smile spreading across her lips. In the far corner sat a single filing cabinet. Instantly excited, the hairs on her arms stood on end. She tried not to get her hopes too high in case it was yet another dead-end. She couldn't help herself though—if she didn't get an answer or two soon, she was definitely going to kill someone.

Jamie pulled the top drawer, making it squeal like a stuck pig. She peeked inside—empty. She tried the next drawer, again nothing. She licked her lips and fought off her growing anger, reaching down to the last drawer. She gripped the handle until her knuckles turned white, afraid to find her last chance end in nothing too. She pulled back hard and fast with her eyes closed, needing some damn answers right fucking now! She held her eyes shut afraid to look inside.

"Please, please, please let me find something!" Jamie held her breath, not wanting to be disappointed again.

She took one long, deep breath and blew it out while opening her eyelids slightly. She nearly screamed in delight like she had just won the Mega-Lotto Jackpot. Sitting inside the drawer was one small stack of manila folders. It could still be nothing, but at this moment it was the cherry on top of the cherry on the most delicious sundae ever made for Jamie Windstein.

Jamie couldn't snatch up the folders fast enough, though she didn't bother—nor dare—to look inside them yet. Right now, she couldn't take another disappointment if they contained nothing useful. Her need to beat it out of this creepy building outweighed her desire to see if the files held any answers. She held the files in a death lock under her arm, shining the light around one last time to make sure she didn't miss anything else of importance. She saw nothing and then ducked back out of the secret room, closing the door on this room forever, she hoped. She moved quickly, unable to exit fast enough. The place was making her skin crawl, and she wanted out. Jamie nearly broke into a sprint to get through the door and back outside. She sucked in fresh air, squeezing the files under her arm with a smile.

2

Esther Jablonski looked over at the young man who had pulled up to a stop alongside her at a red light. She held a burst of laughter in check, since her mother taught her from a young age to always be polite. The young man wasn't hurting anyone—after all, he was merely oblivious to the world around him at the moment. She may be a month from her eightieth birthday, yet she still remembered the joy of youth on a beautifully sunny day such as this. She had to put a hand to her mouth to prevent her own laughter, not wishing to interrupt the man's joy. She found his happiness infectious whether he realized she was there or not. She admired him from afar, happy that he had unwittingly brightened an old lady's day. A tinge of sadness hit her when the light turned green, and he sped off, taking all his joyfulness with him.

Eddie Washington was on cloud nine, leaving County Medical building. He could only remember feeling this good twice in his life—the day he lost his virginity and the day he married his wife, Carrie Fairfax. He didn't even notice Esther Jablonski, the little, old white-haired lady, stopped next to him at the red light. He was too busy singing loudly along with the radio and tapping the steering wheel to the beat, until the light finally turned green. He felt as though he might burst with excitement any second. He fought to maintain his calm demeanor while Detective Barker and Dr. Clive Ketchum briefed him on what they knew so far about Buffalo's most notorious and unknown serial killer, The Executioner.

They informed Eddie that the murders went back at least fifteen years, possibly longer. Eddie had only heard whispers with no idea The Executioner was so prolific. Dr. Ketchum did the majority of the talking since Barker wasn't exactly a "Chatty Kathy" by anyone's standards. He listened, trying to keep his composure so he didn't come across like an idiot. Dr. Ketchum told him they knew of twenty-four victims—minimum—who could positively be attributed to The Executioner and five others they believed listed as probable victims. The biggest shock came when they told him the twenty-four confirmed victims were likely only the tip of the iceberg. They believed, based on unsolved missing person cases fitting the parameters of the known victims, the actual number of victims could be double or triple the current confirmed amount.

Dr. Ketchum also informed Eddie the only attribute consistent with all the confirmed victims was that they were all over age thirty. The majority of victims were male, though only by a small margin, making gender a non-factor in how The Executioner chose his victims. Most, like the most recent victim, were divorced or separated within the last year of their lives, yet not all victims had been. Approximately half the known victims' hands were removed, along with the head, making identification difficult though not impossible. The Executioner was intelligent enough to know that and so the significance of removing the hands was unknown. The only consistent facts on The Executioner were all his victims being thirty years of age or older and all were decapitated. Barker and Ketchum had found no other connections or similarities. Also, not one single head had ever been recovered—something that irritated Dr. Ketchum to no end—coupled with the lack of any real forensic evidence. Two dozen victims, yet so far, not a single hair, partial fingerprint, single microscopic fiber nor any trace of DNA had been discovered. Dr. Ketchum called *The Executioner* a ghost, swooping in to decapitate his victims then disappearing again without a trace. The only proof *The Executioner* even existed, Barker added, were the victims he left, nothing more.

Barker also chimed in, telling Eddie several different weapons were used for the beheadings. Some of the decapitations appeared to be accomplished with a blade or even a sword, some with an axe, some with various power tools and at least one—aside from this most recent victim—appeared to have been done with a wire saw. The headless bodies seemed to turn up once or twice a year with no corresponding events like a full moon, or anything seemingly connecting them. The bodies turned up at various points, both inside and outside the city, so even the dump sites weren't connected. Barker reluctantly admitted to Eddie they hadn't turned up a single credible suspect so far. Each individual victim certainly had potential enemies, Barker had continued, yet no common thread connected more than two of the victims to each other—let alone all twenty-four. Barker looked dejected as he admitted being beyond perplexed by *The Executioner*. The fact that *The Executioner* was a sociopath served as the only fact they knew about him. They also told Eddie, *The Executioner* may go down as the most prolific serial killer in history—once they managed to catch him.

Eddie sat in stunned fascination while Detective Barker and Dr. Ketchum laid out all they knew about *The Executioner*. He found it astonishing that this serial killer lurked in his city for so long without making a single mistake nor making any headlines. The only comparison Eddie could think of was the infamous Ed Gein, who went unsuspected and undiscovered until the very end. The thought of Gein did give Eddie hope though, because they all made a mistake at some point, leading to their capture. The information Barker and Ketchum relayed was enough on its own to give Eddie a heart attack then they asked him to join their little team or task force. Barker surprised Eddie further by informing him that he had already spoken to his captain,

Captain Hitchcock, about the reassignment. There wasn't a chance in hell Eddie would turn down such an offer, but Barker nearly brought on a real heart attack when he informed Eddie he arranged the transfer before calling him to meet at the medical examiner's office.

"Ol' Grumpy Gus here is one ornery bastard, but when it comes to who he can trust, Edward, it's like he has a sixth sense." Dr. Ketchum smiled broadly. "Welcome to the team."

Eddie blushed three shades of red and couldn't stop smiling. His first thought was telling Carrie the good news—she'd be so proud she just might explode. Also, it would make asking her for info on their victim seem less intrusive. Barker, returning to form as a dream crusher, informed Eddie not to get too excited because all he really had to look forward to was uncountable hours of grunt work. Eddie didn't care in the slightest. The offer put his head in the clouds and he knew this was huge for his career. Ketchum warned him of the long days of frustration to come if they ever managed to catch *The Executioner*. They also swore him to secrecy. Ketchum warned Eddie that he was to tell no one what he was working on. Barker, of course, took it further, warning Eddie that if one word of this case leaked to the press he'd be back in his dress blues walking the beat until his feet wore down to the bone. Ketchum assured Eddie they weren't hiding the investigation, they were merely trying to prevent public panic since so far, they had no clues and no suspects about a serial killer walking Buffalo streets for well over a decade. Eddie agreed with them one hundred percent on the issue.

Eddie knew well how public outcry and panic can have terrible consequences. A couple decades ago, a serial rapist had plagued Buffalo. Public panic led to political pressure which led to a premature arrest. Unfortunately, the wrong man was arrested for the crimes. A wrong man who rotted in prison for nearly twenty years until, finally, DNA evidence exonerated him. Eddie didn't want a fiasco like that any more than Barker or Ketchum did. Eddie knew it made all cops look bad, despite the fault lying with political figures who wanted to use the high profile arrest in campaign ads. It made him sick to his stomach. Eddie assured Barker and Ketchum they could count on him a thousand percent.

Eddie arrived at the parking lot closest to Jamie Windstein's office. He couldn't help feeling like the proverbial dog having his day today. He didn't expect Jamie to be in, so he could have simply called Carrie. But he wanted to see her beautiful face light up when she heard his news—not to mention, he had a double agenda; first, to share his good news and then, to get any information on Michael Snyder that he could. He knew getting Carrie to hand him any information was a long shot—she'd likely defer the decision to Jamie—but it seemed to be his lucky day so it was worth a shot.

While Eddie was there, Barker headed to see Sandy "the Shark" Largulis, so he'd likely be even grumpier this afternoon.

Eddie had energy to burn and he bounced up the steps, foregoing the elevator. He opened the dark wooden door with "Jamie Windstein, Private Investigator" written in gold on the wavy glass window—the kind of opaque glass that only let light and shadows through. He calmed himself before turning the knob so his face didn't give away the good news before his mouth did. He put on his best serious police officer face and then opened the door.

"Eddie!" Carrie burst out, happy to see her husband unexpectedly. "To what do I owe this pleasant surprise? What did you do?" She gave him a stern look.

Her reaction instantly wiped away his serious face. "Can a guy stop in to see his pretty wife on a beautiful morning without something being wrong?" He winked at her.

"Sure, however, when was the last time you stopped here unannounced for a good reason?" Carrie raised a suspicious eyebrow at her husband. "I'll answer for you. Never—the answer is never."

"I'm afraid you've got me, honey, I've come for Jamie. We're running off together. You were supposed to be out running errands or something. I'm sorry you have to hear it this way." He hung his head in shame sarcastically, trying to sell the lie.

"Well, it looks like you're the world's worst planner—not to mention husband—since she's not even here. Some cop you are! Oh, and you better start sucking up to me quick, mister!" She scowled.

"In that case, how about a little office hanky panky before the boss gets back." He winked again and she blushed.

"How about you bring that sweet face over here and give me a kiss, or you can get used to our lumpy couch for the next month! Just be glad we don't have a dog!"

Eddie kissed his wife long and hard, holding her tight, taking advantage of the empty office. He thought about telling her he'd only been half joking about having sex right there on her desk to celebrate. He squeezed her tight after their lips finally separated, enjoying the way she felt against him and the sweet scent of her perfume.

"Now, are you gonna tell me why you stopped by or am I gonna have to beat it out of you?"

"You can beat me if you want to." He moved his eyebrows up and down suggestively and she smacked him on the shoulder.

"What's got you all feisty this morning? Come on, spill it!"

"Well…" Eddie began. "Remember how I got in very late the other night?"

"Of course, our bed was awfully lonely. But I know I married a cop." She smiled.

"I told you I was late because I found a body down by the old rail station, beneath the underpass."

"Don't tell me you lied, Eddie Washington. I'll be damn pissed, surprise visit or not."

"Don't worry, I'm not here because I lied to you. The detective who met me at the scene called me right after you left this morning. He asked me to meet him at the County Medical Examiner's office for the examination of the body."

Carrie shoved him playfully. "Get out!"

"It's true! Long story short I've been reassigned. It's not quite a promotion but… sorta. This detective—Barker's his name—and the Head Medical Examiner, Dr. Ketchum, want me to join them to track down the killer."

"Oh my God, Eddie! Fantastic!" Carrie practically leapt into her husband's arms, kissing him all over.

"I know! It's crazy, right? I'll still need to take the sergeant's exam, but for now, I'm essentially Barker's partner on this. This case could make or break me." He paused. "One mistake and my career could be over before it begins," Eddie said nervously.

"Don't you dare hang your head! Detective Washington always gets his man!"

"All I can really tell you is that this case is huge and I won't be able to discuss much of it with you. I hate to say that, especially since I came here to tell you my good news and…"

Carrie cut him off, knowing her husband better than he knew himself. "You need something from me? Or Jamie?"

"Well, yeah. I know you won't be able to share much, but anything is better than nothing. I need your help if you're able." He met her eyes. "The body I found was identified as Michael Snyder. He recently divorced his wife, and her attorney was Sandy the Shark. I wondered if Jamie worked the case. Honestly, we have nothing right now so anything you can share will help."

"I'm not sure how much help I or Jamie can be, everything is confidential."

"I know that. I don't need the case file, just maybe if Jamie may know if he had any enemies or something along those lines. Confirming Jamie even worked the case is more than I have right now. This Barker is one grumpy SOB, so anything will help."

"I'm not breaking any laws confirming if we worked the case, anything more you'll have to get from Jamie though."

"I knew that before I walked in, honey. I can't say much either, so we're in the same boat. This goes beyond just the body of Snyder though."

"Ooh, serial killer big?" Excitement overtook her. Despite her cookie cutter image, Carrie had a morbid fascination with mass murderers and serial killers.

Eddie realized he already said too much. "I can neither confirm nor deny that, ma'am."

"You son of a B! I'm right?" Carrie nearly jumped out of her skin. "My own husband—chasing the first serial killer in Buffalo history. Well color me blown out of the water!"

"Technically, dear, not the first. There was the Bike Path Killer/Rapist and the .22 Caliber Killer in the eighties, remember?"

"Yeah, but neither of those were a traditional serial killer, Eddie. The Bike Path guy was primarily a rapist and the other one was mainly a racist asshole who shot random black people over the course of a few days—or was it a couple weeks?" She was talking faster, hardly taking a breath between sentences. "I'm talking about the complete package, a total psychopathic sociopath, a wolf in sheep's clothing kind, who hides in plain sight able to act normal in public but is really a complete freakin' whacko! You know, like Bundy or Gacy or Dahmer!" Carrie's eyes went wide with excitement.

"I get what you're saying, honey. I already told you too much, so please don't say a word—not even to Jamie, okay? If a single word leaks about this, my career as a cop is over. Not a word to anyone, Carrie, I'm serious." He held her gaze, imploring her to understand the importance. "Any idea when Jamie will get back, by the way?"

"Any minute now, actually. Don't worry, honey, I won't say a word and you know it. Jamie might be able to help though, she *is* an investigator after all."

"Barker would never agree to that. I think Dr. Ketchum had to talk him into even bringing me into the loop. Barker is one grumpy SOB. I can't read him to save my life. Dr. Ketchum seemed to really like me almost instantly though. They don't want to start a public panic when we honestly have nothing to go on, Carebear. Whoever this guy is, he's damn good."

"I understand, honey, I just get excited. You know me. You'll catch him and become famous!" Carrie smiled and opened a file drawer, rummaging inside for the right file. "You said Snyder, right?"

"Yes. Michael."

"Okay, got it! Well, I can confirm Jamie worked the case. It was a divorce case sent over by the Shark. Anything more than that you'll have to get straight from the horse's mouth." Carrie chuckled. "Don't tell Jamie I just called her a horse."

"We knew Sandy was the wife's lawyer, but if Jamie can tell me anything, it'll be more than I have now. Wanna celebrate over lunch or do you need to wait for Jamie?"

Carrie stuck out her bottom lip in a mock pout. "I probably should wait for her. Shouldn't be long, honey bunny, so why don't you come over here and give momma some more sugar."

Eddie raced around the counter to his wife like a love struck teenager. He grabbed Carrie around the waist, dipping her over dramatically, and nearly tumbling them over. He managed to catch himself in time and swung his wife back up, holding her tight while they laughed over the near debacle. The couple enjoyed a long passionate kiss.

Eddie was just about to go in for another kiss when his cell phone rang, followed a second later by the office phone ringing, ruining the moment and forcing their embrace to end. Eddie and Carrie frowned at each other then parted to handle their business.

Eddie swiped answer, assuming his professional face, while Carrie answered the office line. He immediately grabbed the notepad and pen from his back pocket and hastily scribbled down information. Beside him, Carrie joked with Jamie, calling to say she was on her way.

When both calls ended, Carrie's smile left her lips as she noticed the look on her husband's face.

"Gotta go, don't you?" she pouted.

"Unfortunately, yes. Please tell Jamie I'd like to speak to her ASAP about Snyder. Set it up for tomorrow if you can. We'll celebrate tonight, I promise." He gave his wife an apologetic smile, though he knew she wasn't really upset with him. "Why don't you make reservations somewhere nice? I'll call you later for the deets."

"It'll cost ya, mister! Now scoot! You've got a serial killer to catch!" She leaned over to give him a goodbye kiss. "I'm so proud of you."

"Thank you, Missus Washington. I'll make sure you're very proud later." Eddie winked at his wife as he headed toward the door.

Eddie raced down the stairs to meet up with Barker at a potential crime scene. Barker had called with the address of a couple who appeared to be missing. The address seemed familiar, though he couldn't quite place the street in his mind. Once back in his car, he punched the address into his GPS. The missing couple lived only a few blocks away from Jamie Windstein's house, which was probably why he recognized it.

An ironic coincidence, but cops didn't get paid for coincidences. Eddie honestly didn't see any reason for it to be anything more than that though. The girl may be a little odd sometimes, and a loner all the time—but Eddie couldn't see little Jamie Windstein being a serial killer.

He knew her well, and she was too small, he thought. He laughed at the thought, quickly putting it out of mind.

First, Barker and Ketchum asking him to join their hunt for a serial killer and now, he was off to investigate a potential crime scene. Eddie pulled onto the street even more excited than when he arrived.

3

A triple beep pierced the air, followed by the hushed click of the lock after an agonizing wait that felt like hours. His curiosity had grown to mammoth proportions while seconds crawled by like days. Hearing the click made him want to jump to the moon with excitement. Despite time seeming to stand still, a quick glance at his watch showed him only an hour had passed. His phone remained silent, telling him he still had plenty of time. The possibility of someone wondering where he was remained, though he doubted anyone really cared, even if they had noticed his absence this morning

His anticipation to see what Jamie was hiding became unbearable while he waited for his tool to do all the work. All he could do was sit on the stairs in the dark, impatiently waiting to hear the triple beeps and the click of the lock. He held his breath, clicked his flashlight back to life, and stood up, stretching his legs and more than ready to see Jamie's dirty little secret. Questions spun out of control in his brain like, why did she need this space? If she needed to hide sensitive case information wouldn't a safe be sufficient? Why did she need a room so secret and secure? He pulled the door open, loudly blowing out his held breath. He closed his eyes a moment, suddenly afraid he would find nothing special, making the whole morning a waste of time.

He opened his eyes quickly, like ripping off a Band-Aid, and his jaw hit the floor. Now, he could see why his little gifts hadn't alarmed Jamie Windstein in the slightest. The reason she didn't panic or call the police glowed in the light from his flashlight. He saw clearly, the last people Jamie Windstein wanted poking around her home were the police. If anyone other than himself ever discovered this room, Jamie would have some major explaining to do—to put it mildly. Until this moment he didn't think anything could shock him. He was wrong, very, very wrong.

He stood frozen in the open doorway, overwhelmed by what he saw. He was simply astonished at the sight, wondering how in the world he didn't know or even suspect anything like this. At the far end of the room sat a lone leather recliner which looked like it could possibly be the most comfortable chair ever made. He imagined the soft brown leather holding Jamie like a baby cradled in its mother's arms. The room looked like it would be a cozy study in anyone else's home, made for curling up with a good book for hours uninterrupted—but this was Jamie's secret hideaway. There were a few assorted file folders on a little end table beside the recliner, though this room was not for her to work on cases. The room appeared to be Jamie's personal thinking room, her quiet place—though if so, she possessed some disturbingly dark thoughts.

It was the large wooden shelves to either side of the recliner that froze him in place. They reached from floor to ceiling, and in a normal room would likely be filled with books—but not in this room. At first he didn't want to believe what his eyes showed him. His mind said it had to be fake, yet he knew better. He hadn't expected Jamie to be such a kindred spirit.

There remained some space on the shelves, though they were quite full, which was even more amazing to him. Jamie had certainly been a busy bee, to build a collection so large, he thought. He wanted to smack himself for missing something this big after watching her for months. The fact he hadn't even had a clue boggled his mind. He stood in the doorway simply stunned by what he saw, until it dawned on him how long he was taking.

He couldn't get over how impressed he was by her collection. His entire plan would have been different if only he had known about this sooner. He knew there was no point wasting time thinking about the woulda, coulda, shouldas though. It took him another minute to stop staring in complete awe at Jamie's dark secrets on display before him. He spun around and around taking it all in. She had unexpectedly surprised him and he couldn't be happier about it.

He sat down in her soft leather chair trying to put himself inside her mind for a moment. He wondered how many times she sat in this very spot looking over her handiwork. Whether he turned his head right or left he was greeted by a vision of grim macabre. He breathed deep, trying to take in the full weight of his discovery. The shelves were filled with dozens upon dozens of severed heads, just like the gifts he left on her kitchen counter. The two heads with his message scrawled across them sat on the floor in front of the chair. A smile spread over his face from ear to ear.

He pictured her sitting in this exact spot last night staring at his message as she pondered its meaning. He wanted those words swirling around in her head. He wanted her to repeat them over and over hoping somehow she'd remember what they meant. He didn't know if his plan would work, if he could make her remember, until he'd discovered this room—her dirty little secret. Now he knew that she'd remember eventually, he could see she already had, she just didn't know it.

This discovery was definitely a game changer, and he couldn't wait to see the look on his partner's face when he told him about it. Jamie Windstein seemed to be far more than either of them imagined in their wildest dreams. He couldn't remember being this excited about anything since he had been a child, maybe ever. He loved a good mystery, just like Jamie did. Now he saw, she may be the biggest mystery of all time.

Chapter Six: Slaughtered In Their Dreams

1: Sometime in the 80s

"Now what to do with two nasty, naughty little boys? Are children allowed to run around the halls at night?" Head Mistress DeLong oozed venom with every word.

"No, Head Mistress." The Goon Squad smiled answering as one.

"Did you hear that boys? You're not allowed to run the halls in the middle of the night. What do you think should be your punishment, hmm?" DeLong looked from one boy to the other. "Lock you in your room for a week without food or water?" She spoke slowly and deliberately letting her words sink in. "Not to your liking? Perhaps just a warning? What say you, Counselors?" She delighted in building the boys' fear.

Robert turned to smirk at Anthony. "Whatever the Head Mistress thinks is best."

"How about you boys, what say you?" The glint of evil in DeLong's eyes could send a chill down a rattlesnake's spine.

Tommy turned his head to Jimmy, his eyes wide with fear. Tommy trembled, never feeling so frightened before, while Jimmy stood rock solid like a statue. Jimmy stood resolute, ready to face whatever came at him head-on. Jimmy refused to give Head Mistress DeLong and her Goon Squad the satisfaction of seeing the fear racing through his veins to plaster on his face. Jimmy stared at Tommy, trying to transfer his will with his eyes.

The look Jimmy gave Tommy acted as a stern reminder of the instructions he'd given his friend while they waited, locked in their room. "Say nothing. Push all your fear deep down in your gut. Never scream out, it only encourages them to do worse. Stay strong and give them nothing, Tommy."

Tommy repeated Jimmy's words in his head like a mantra as he stood before DeLong and the goons—though the courage he'd had back in their room waned as he faced punishment. The strength of Jimmy's words began to weaken while they were marched single file, to the red door and then through to the secret room. Head Mistress DeLong had led the way, wearing a tight black leather body suit and a black captain's hat—a captain leading lambs to the slaughter. Counselor Bob followed along so close that if DeLong suddenly stopped, he'd run straight up her ass. Counselor Tony brought up the rear with Jimmy and Tommy—heads down—sandwiched between the two goons. The boys marched in silence like the condemned heading to the gallows, while the Goon Squad beamed like four year olds on their way to the ice cream shop. Head Mistress DeLong never seemed happy, regardless of the circumstance despite the wicked smile she wore.

Tommy thought of DeLong as a Nazi and nearly giggled, which he knew would be a death sentence. All she lacked was a goosestep and swastika armband, he mused. He wished he could share the thought with Jimmy, knowing it wasn't possible. All jovial thoughts vanished once they entered the secret room. The goons stripped the boys naked then shackled them by both wrists and ankles facing the wall, their backs to DeLong and the Good Squad. Tommy now thought of them as the axis of evil about to hand down their vicious judgement.

Tommy felt like he might lose his bladder. His friend telling him what to expect didn't ease Tommy's first trip to the hidden torture chamber. A single tear spilled from the corner of Tommy's eye before he realized it. He was about to be savagely beaten. He stood shivering, naked in the dark knowing this.

Jimmy turned to Tommy, seeing the tear. "Don't you do it, Tommy! Damn it! Stay strong!"

Tommy tried his best to heed his friend's words. He hadn't seen their pure evil yet but Jimmy had. He shut his eyes, squeezing them tight, and balled his hands into fists until his knuckles turned white. He did his best to will himself the strength to face whatever came at him. Jimmy's words from earlier returned to his head, once more transporting him away from this wretched place, if only for a moment.

"No answer, boys?" They felt her sneer even if they couldn't see it. "Unfortunately, you leave me no choice then, I'll have to decide for you." Head Mistress DeLong let out a great sigh as though choosing was some great burden on her. She sauntered up behind them, giving their hair a light tussle like a mother does to a toddler—though there was no warmth in it. "Steel your spines, boys. Breaking little yearlings like you is *so* much fun!" She taunted, leaning in between them to smell their terror.

Tommy held his eyes shut so tight they ached, though he knew he'd lose his resolve if he saw her face.

Without looking, he could see the evil smirk spread across her blood red lips, and the spark of hell behind her eyes. DeLong's tight leather outfit creaked as she stretched back, hands on her hips, making both boys cringe. The sound sent a chill down his spine. If he lived to be a thousand years old, he didn't think he'd ever forget that sound or the sound of her stiletto heels clicking on the hall floor.

Her clicking heels came to a stop by a table in the back corner that had numerous whips and things set on top of it. He didn't recognize everything he saw on the table and he was sure he didn't want to find out.

Head Mistress DeLong swept her hand lightly over the assorted instruments, causing a few of the metallic objects to clank softly. "What to use? What to use?" she mused, purposely building more tension. "What punishment is appropriate for two extraordinarily naughty little boys?"

Another chill raced up Tommy's spine at the sound of DeLong's taunting and the light clanking of metal. He clenched his fists and eyes even tighter against his fear and desperately tried to heed Jimmy's words. A vision of his mother holding him tight to her breast burst into his mind's eye. She softly hummed a lullaby while rubbing his head and whispered everything would be alright. He fought to push the image from his mind before it sent tears cascading down his cheeks. It was in that moment, somewhere deep in his gut, Tommy found the dark heart of his resolve. Instantly, he felt calm wash over him like a warm bath.

Tommy had never heard the term "dig deep," yet here in this cold room, on the verge of unimaginable pain, he dug deeper than anyone ever had. He reached down deep to the very bottom of the abyss. There he found a black ball of hate forged from the loss of his parents, made of all the anger their loss brought him. He saw himself clutch the black ball, squeezing it with the strength of a thousand men. He gripped it tighter and tighter, adding to it all the hate he felt for The Mormont Home, the Goon Squad, and most of all, his hatred of Head Mistress DeLong. He heard his mother tell him to hold tight to the ball and never, ever let it go.

Tommy's anger and hate consumed him until they were all that was left. He didn't even feel the whip until it cracked against his back for the third time. It stung, though he barely felt it. Bob, The Goon swung the whip with reckless abandon, not caring which boy he hit with each swing, while DeLong and Counselor Tony applauded and laughed at each strike. Bob cracked the whip on their soft flesh, wanting to hear them scream, swinging harder when they didn't. Tommy knew he'd never forget the sound of the cracking whip followed by demented applause.

Tommy felt his flesh welt and split while blood began to trickle down his back. He didn't cry out, he only clutched his black ball even tighter. Tears streamed from his eyes—they were impossible to stop—while he added every strike to his ball. The harder he squeezed the more it felt like it was happening to someone else. He pictured himself standing in the corner, holding his black ball in a death grip, merely an observer to the atrocity being committed. He chanced a look over to Jimmy, his companion in hell. Jimmy was a rock, taking every strike like they were feathers blowing against him in the wind. Tears rolled from his eyes in a flood, the same as they did from Tommy's, yet they were the only sign something was wrong. Tommy realized now that Jimmy had been right. They must stay strong. They had to give them nothing.

Tommy knew for certain he'd never forget Jimmy's words before the goons came. "We can be beaten, and we will be. We can be slaughtered in their dreams, and we will be. Slaughtered in their sick, demented dreams—but I promise you, Tommy, one day we will slaughter them and it won't be in a fucking dream."

2: Present Day

Jamie entered her office feeling better than she had all day. She held the dusty files she found at Mormont Home tightly to her chest. She barged through her office door so excited she didn't even realize—or acknowledge—the presence of her lone friend and secretary until she spoke.

"Well, look what the cat finally dragged in!" Carrie beamed a smile from behind her desk.

Carrie's voice froze Jamie like a teenager trying to sneak in after curfew. "Oh hey, Carrie!" Her voice fell flat.

"Well hello to you too."

"Sorry, my mind is off in never, never land. Anything new?"

"Quite a lot for once, actually. Need any help with that?" Carrie pointed at the files Jamie had, clutched to her chest like they were the stone tablets Moses carried down from Mount Sinai.

"Sorry, but no. What do you mean by quite a lot?" Jamie was genuinely curious. "Don't be coy, spill woman!"

"Well, you really missed out. Maybe if you showed up on time, alas, you're too late." Carrie sarcastically scolded her boss.

"Well if you're displeased with my punctuality you can always quit, bitch." Jamie snarled.

"We both know you couldn't run a lemonade stand by yourself, so don't tempt me." Carrie winked.

"Are you gonna spill the beans or not?" Jamie stamped her foot on the ground like a petulant child.

"Fine, fine, don't go throwin' a hissy fit. Eddie stopped in to run off with you so you missed your one chance. Now, you'll die an old, bitter woman with a hundred cats or something." Carrie couldn't hold back her laughter.

"Well, when you see that man again, tell him to stop making booty calls at my place in the middle of the night. Every damn night! It's really getting ridiculous!" Jamie played back. "Seriously though, what did your sweet hunk of man meat want?"

Carrie tried to catch her breath from laughing so hard. "He stopped by with great news, though I suspect if he didn't need some information from us he'd have waited for me to get home." She frowned.

"Now you've got me curious. Go on!"

"Okay, the good news is Eddie basically got a promotion this morning. I didn't tell you, but Saturday night Eddie discovered a dead body. That's all I knew until he stopped in—you literally just missed him. Anyway, the important thing is the detective working the case asked Eddie to meet him at the County Medical Examiner's office this morning to look over the body and what not. Apparently, my man impressed the detective and head medical examiner so much they asked him to join some special task force assigned to the case. He wasn't allowed to say much else." Carrie glowed conveying the news about her husband.

"Wow! Fantastic news! Good for him. About time the BPD did something intelligent!" Jamie high fived Carrie. "You said he needed some info from us? What's that all about?"

"He needs to talk to you about it but he had to rush out for something related to the case. You only missed him by about five minutes. The body he found was Michael Snyder. Turns out he recently got divorced and the ex's lawyer was Sandy the Shark. Eddie knows

Sandy is a regular client of ours so he wanted to know if you worked the case. I guess it's their only lead. I looked it up for him and yeah, you did work the case. I told him any more info would have to come from you. He knows you can't tell him much, but he said anything is better than the nothing they have. He told me to set up an actual appointment whenever you're free, other than today, of course. I wanted to talk to you before I set it up, though." Carrie's eyes shone with pride for her husband.

Jamie stood silent, as if in deep thought for a moment. "Michael Snyder? Hmm, when did I work the case?"

Carrie hesitated a moment, looking down at the folder still on her desk. "Not long ago…let me see here…last November. You only logged about twenty-five hours during the second week of November. The divorce was final in April." Carrie looked back up at her boss.

"I'd need to refresh my memory on it. I think all I did was a couple of photoshoots. What was the ex's name? Sandy's actual client?" Jamie squinted her eyes, searching her memory.

"Jessie, Jessie Snyder. Ring any bells?"

"Maybe. Mind if I take the file to my office? I'll brush up on it before I meet with Eddie. I doubt I'll be much help, not much there. He say how the guy died or anything?"

"Here you go." Carrie handed over the file. "No, he couldn't give me any of the gory details. Although…" Carrie motioned Jamie to lean in as if an eavesdropper was nearby. "I think it's a serial killer! That stays between us or Eddie will get in trouble."

Jamie stared blankly, while her mind spun out of control. She knew nothing linked her to the body other than a few photos taken over six months ago. She remembered Michael Snyder well—the wife abusing piece of human filth. She knew she left no evidence behind, just like the others she had left for the police to find over the years. The shocking thing was Eddie finding the body and then getting assigned to the case. She contemplated whether that was good or bad, unable to decide. She'd think about it later, after she'd either located Jimmy Reimse for Thomas Combs or hit a dead end.

"Looks like you married Serpico. Damn girl!" Jamie smiled.

"No, honey. Serpico busted crooked cops. Eddie's more like a male Clarice Starling!" Carrie smiled proudly.

"Who?"

"You know, *Silence of the Lambs*? Jodie Foster's character, where she works with Hannibal the Cannibal to catch a serial killer?"

"Oh, the fava beans guy?"

"Yeah, geez!" Carrie sighed shaking her head.

"Whatever." Jamie waved off her lack of pop culture knowledge. "Anyway, it's great Eddie got such an awesome opportunity. I hope he gets the bastard, whoever did it. Now, I need to get to work. Let me know when you schedule Eddie for a meeting. I'll take him back to my office and give him information 'til it hurts! Rawr!" Jamie couldn't resist the jab, earning her a smack. "Owee!" She rubbed her shoulder sarcastically. "Seriously, I need to get back to work and I need you to do me a favor, okay?"

"You're the boss, your wish is my command!" Carrie did a mock bow. "Except defiling my husband—I'll cut a bitch." Carrie winked at Jamie.

"Just try it!" She joked, before sobering. "Seriously though, I need you to find a few people for me. Should be pretty easy, they're all old, probably in their 60s or 70s, maybe more."

"Hang on, let me grab a pen." Carrie snagged one from her Minions pen holder, along with a yellow legal pad. "Okay, shoot."

"Eva DeLong, D-e-capital L-o-n-g. Robert Keane, K-E-A-N-E, and Anthony Rollins, with two Ls. They were all employees at The Mormont Home when it closed. I need to know which ones are still alive and where they are now. If they're all dead, then this case probably is too."

"Okay, I'll get right on it. Just those three? No one else who worked there?"

"If you find anyone else who worked there at the time then add them to the list, I suppose. Those three are probably the only ones who know anything, so no need to dig deep on anyone else. If you need anything I'll be in my office the rest of the day, okay?" Jamie turned toward her office anxious to dig into the files she found.

Jamie dropped the files in the middle of her desk and took her seat, dying to dive in. She leaned back, letting out a big sigh of relief. She decided Eddie being assigned to the Snyder murder case was good news, even if it did surprise her. She tried to dump her bodies out of his jurisdiction, so he must have found Snyder by chance. It didn't worry her though. She always hoped to leave Eddie out of it, not win him a promotion, but such was life. She wasn't afraid of Eddie, or any other cop, tracing anything back to her. She left nothing to be traced anywhere. She knew some cop had to be searching for her, and the upside of it being Eddie was the possibility of getting information on the case. Eddie was a good cop, unlikely to tell her anything, however he would likely let things slip to Carrie—who couldn't keep a secret to save her life. She loved Carrie to bits, but knew Carrie would gossip, especially to her. She let loose another big sigh, recognizing it wasn't worth worrying about. Jamie had a mystery to solve—and the dusty folders in front of her just might hold an answer or two. She hoped.

3

After you've lived in a city long enough everything starts to look the same. Eddie suspected this to be true of any city, though Buffalo was a city he knew like the back of his hand. Some neighborhoods were certainly worse than others in their similarity, but drive through one residential neighborhood and you've basically seen them all. Most neighborhoods displayed one cookie-cutter home after another, though there were occasional standouts. He often wondered how anyone remembered which house they even lived in, since each house for several blocks all looked almost identical.

The thought lingered in Eddie's mind while he made his way to the potential crime scene. Most Buffalo homes were built in one of two eras: the turn of the century and post-WWII. It seemed over half the houses in the city were built between 1945 and 1955, mostly from GI Bill programs begun by Franklin Roosevelt after the war.

He made his way through Jamie's neighborhood noticing nothing special, very little distinguished it from any other in the city. The houses all blurred together, indistinguishable from one another, until he finally arrived at his destination, 786 Alaska Street. He made a bet with himself on the house color during the boring drive over, since most were blue or white. He chose blue so now he owed himself a dollar.

Eddie parked behind Detective Barker's unmarked dark blue sedan, unsurprised his new partner beat him there. The detective leaned against his car's fender waiting impatiently, exactly like he had been that morning. The look on Barker's face would've given a rookie a panic attack, however Eddie was learning quickly that Barker was just agitated. He imagined Barker rushing out of his car to lean on it, making it look like he had been waiting for hours. The thought nearly made him burst into laughter, though he knew doing so would bring the detective's ire.

"Hey, boss, hope I didn't keep you waiting long." Eddie knew he hadn't.

"Few minutes is all. Find anything out from your PI friend?"

"Jamie wasn't in, but my wife confirmed she worked the case. My wife is scheduling a meeting with Jamie, so hopefully I'll have something to go on tomorrow morning. Jamie's a friend. Hopefully, that'll make details a little easier to get. When we're done here I'll call to see what time the meeting is. I doubt we'll get much, but it's better than nothing." He paused." I'm guessing Sandy the Shark gave you all of jack and shit?"

"Not even that much. Damn lawyers! Buncha slimy snakes if you ask me. They practically made me get a warrant just to confirm The Shark represented the ex which is effing public information!" Barker threw up his arms in disgust.

Barker's rant shocked Eddie. "No real surprise, her reputation precedes her by miles." Eddie sympathized. "So why are we here? What's the connection to Snyder?"

"No Snyder connection, at least, none I know about. Probably a waste of our time. The neighbor reported the couple—Karen and David Osbourne—missing. She hasn't seen them for a few days. I checked both of their employers, they haven't been in, and they aren't on vacation. She's twenty-nine and he's thirty-one, married about 5 or 6 years. If nothing seems amiss we'll turn it over to missing persons, but something smells off to me. Like this morning—keep your eyes open, mouth shut and look for anything odd."

Eddie jotted down the couple's names in his notebook under the address Barker gave him. "Yes, sir."

"Quit with the sir crap. I ain't your father and we ain't in the military. It's Barker—just Barker. Now, come on." Barker didn't wait for a response turning to head up the walkway to the front door.

Eddie followed, staying a few steps behind to look around for anything out of place. Nothing obvious stood out. No stray toys in the yard, which probably meant the Osbournes didn't have any children. The home was an average house for the area, a simple ranch style with brick rising a foot or two from the foundation and then changing to dark blue vinyl siding. Eddie noticed four others just like it within eyesight of the front door, only differentiated by the color of the siding. Eddie also noticed the homes varied slightly in their layout. The differences were subtle, but slightly distinguishable from another.

While Barker knocked on the front door, Eddie saw an elderly woman—likely the neighbor who reported the couple missing—peeking out her curtain, clearly trying to keep an eye on them. Every neighborhood sported at least one nosy neighbor writing a book on everyone's comings and goings or anything else they found noteworthy. Eddie dreaded the future interview he'd have with her, knowing she was likely already on the phone gossiping with whoever she could.

Barker banged harder against the front door a second time, though both men knew they weren't going to receive an answer. Eddie cupped his hands around his eyes and tried unsuccessfully to peer through the window to the right of the door. What he did see appeared undisturbed, no sign of some knockdown, drag out fight or struggle. He felt a stab of disappointment at finding nothing to this point.

Barker tried the door knob just in case, though he knew it was locked. Perhaps, if the perps left in a hurry there'd be a chance they forgot to lock up. As he expected, it was locked.

He turned to tell Eddie to try the window, but found Eddie already there. He reached above the door and ran his hand along the top of the frame for a possible spare key, finding nothing other than dust. He knew it was a bit of an old fashioned hiding place for a spare key, but there were no potted plants or flower boxes or anywhere else to hide one.

"Why don't you circle around to the back," he pointed to the right, "while I go around the other way. I'll meet you at the back door. Keep your eyes peeled for one of those fake rock things or anything to hide a spare key in, and check for open windows as you go. I don't think this young couple suddenly decided to run away for no reason. Let's find a way in without wasting time on a warrant."

"Sure thing, Barker. I couldn't see much, but no signs of any struggle." Eddie trailed Barker down the steps.

"I know. I don't like it."

Eddie walked around the right side of the house and found nothing of interest. All the windows were locked and nothing appeared out of place. He saw nothing odd. It just looked like the couple simply were not home— nothing nefarious about that. The neighborhood was quiet, nothing odd about that. Schools were still in session and most adults would be at work at this hour. He enjoyed the peace and quiet, though given his profession, it usually meant something terrible was just around the corner.

Eddie waited patiently for Barker by the back door of the Osbourne home, unable to find a spare key hidden anywhere. He wasn't concerned. He'd sees a possible way in even if Barker found nothing. He tapped his foot, wondering where Barker could be. It shouldn't have taken him any longer than Eddie to reach the back door.

Suddenly, to Eddie's surprise, the door opened, nearly causing him to fall over his own feet.

"Careful, rookie." Barker winked, surprising Eddie further. "Found a spare key by the garage door. Both cars are still in it, by the way."

"Funny." Eddie frowned. "Glad you found a key, I thought we might have to wrangle the air conditioner out of the window around the corner."

Barker rubbed his not-so-six-pack abs. "I think I'm glad too."

"Wait, did you just make a joke? Hold on. I need to write this down. I'm sure Doctor Ketchum won't believe it!" Eddie smiled broadly.

"Oh, shut up and get in here, wise ass! I'll have you stuck behind a desk until your hemorrhoids have hemorrhoids."

"There's the Barker I know." Eddie entered the Osbourne's house, sidestepping a smack to the head by Barker.

They split up to search the house more quickly. It was a small house, though more than ample for a couple without children. Eddie again, saw nothing out of place indicating any sort of foul play. He saw no signs at all of this being a crime scene. The air lacked the scent of heavy cleaners, though over all, the house was neat and clean. Eddie made his way to the couple's bedroom and found nothing odd there at first glance. The curtains were drawn and the bed was neatly made. The dark made it difficult to see.

The smell of bleach knocked Eddie back with a nauseating force, burning his eyes and nostrils as he opened the door to the master bath. A cursory glance inside showed nothing else out of the ordinary, just the heavy smell of bleach or ammonia.

"Barker! I think I got something. Master bath."

Barker stood behind him within seconds. "What ya got, kid?"

"The smell of bleach in here about gagged me. The rest of the house seems normal so it's odd someone did a major clean up just in here."

Barker moved past Eddie into the master bathroom. He inspected the sink and tub, getting on his hands and knees to examine the tile along the edge of the tub. After several minutes he stood, looking frustrated, but that was nothing new—it was his natural look. Barker bumped into him, without apology, barging back into the bedroom. He flicked on the light to reveal why the curtains had been drawn. Instantly, Eddie could see dark spots on the dark brown carpet and dark streaks on the wall beside the headboard. The wall had obviously been cleaned, though not as thoroughly as the bathroom. He watched while Barker walked slowly around the bed, studying the carpet like an art expert examining the Mona Lisa. Barker stopped near the head of the bed opposite from where Eddie stood at the foot. Eddie simply observed as Barker carefully pulled the covers back, revealing a clean blue sheet beneath them. Barker looked unsatisfied as he tossed the pillows to the floor, pulling the fitted sheet from the mattress.

"Grab the other side, rook."

Eddie jumped forward, kicking himself for needing to be told. He moved to the head of the bed, pulling the sheet back in unison with Barker and dropping it to the floor with the pillows. Eddie stood, looking perplexed along with Barker, staring down at the clean, white mattress. The stains on the carpet coupled with the streaks on the walls screamed something terrible happened here but the mattress appeared untouched.

Barker remained silent a long moment staring down. "What's wrong with this mattress, rookie? Look at it."

Eddie felt stupid. "Well, it's clean. Fairly nice, nothing too expensive. Otherwise, I don't…wait—" The light finally clicked on in Eddie's head. "It's clean. Too clean."

"Now you got it, rook. You had me worried for a second." Barker caught himself before he smiled. "Stains on the floor," he pointed, "obviously cleaned, but not well. Same with the streaks on the wall. Not too hard to guess it's blood. Then there's the fact that the Osbournes weren't teenagers, so I assume they were sexually active. Now, unless they bought this mattress yesterday, it's too clean, no stains. Grab the end, let's flip it over."

Barker gave Eddie a nod then they carefully lifted the mattress, flipping it up. They paused with the mattress resting on its edge. Eddie turned to Barker, smiling— and then immediately catching himself, chastened himself. Smiling wasn't appropriate at the moment.

The other side of the mattress was one big, dark brown stain. They both knew it was blood, a lot of it.

"I think it's safe to call in forensics now." Barker grinned at Eddie surprising him.

4

Jamie Windstein sat and thumbed through the folders, unable to regain her focus. Her mind kept returning to the new development with Eddie Washington. What if she made a mistake? Didn't everyone eventually? She knew somewhere along the line she'd leave a fiber, a partial finger print, a single strand of hair or maybe she'd miss a pair of eyes hidden in the darkness. Worrying about it was new to her—she never had before. She tried tracing and retracing her steps in her mind, knowing Snyder's body was one hundred percent clean. Her desk may be a mess of organized chaos, but when her dark side came out, she was methodically tidy. She knew worrying was pointless and yet the thought kept coming back. She took a deep breath and pushed it all to the back of her mind, opening the top folder that sat in front of her. She needed her focus to be on the mysterious Jimmy Reimse, not off on some pointless tangent.

The folder contained general information sheets on several children once boarded at the Mormont Home. Some included a photo, others didn't. Jamie flipped through each page with her mind drifting back to the secret room behind the broom closet. She wondered how many of these children were beaten and tortured in that room. How many of these sad, little faces returned to their rooms crying a river of tears from the abuse doled out by Head Mistress DeLong and her Goon Squad? Each one screamed out to her—to anyone—to save them. She found herself unable to look at their faces after a few pages, concentrating instead on their names. James Reimse, so far, was nowhere to be found. Halfway into the first folder, Carrie Washington interrupted her by tapping on the door.

"It's open, hun." Jamie tried not to sound annoyed.

"Sorry to interrupt, Jams, but I'm starving. I was gonna run downstairs to Timmy Ho's real quick, want anything?" Carrie shot her boss a friendly smile, knowing no one in Buffalo ever turned down an offer of Tim Horton's coffee.

"Hmmm…an extra-large, triple cream, no sugar, sounds fantastic!" Jamie smiled back.

"That's a given." Carrie rolled her eyes. "I meant a sandwich or maybe a donut? Don't lie and tell me you ate something already because we both know you bloody well didn't. Men like a little meat on the bone, y'know!"

"Fine, Mom! Grab me a damn donut! You know what I like." Only then did Jamie realize she was famished, though she hated to admit it. "Do they make anything without damn honey mustard on it? I hate that crap."

"Umm…how about a panini? They're big, we can split it."

"Fine, fine. Now scoot! Momma's got work to do!"

"Yes, boss! Right away, boss!" Carrie gave a mock salute and then hurried away before Jamie hurled something at her.

Jamie just smiled, thankful she had such a good friend. Carrie may not know everything about her, but she knew enough, and that made Jamie's world a little less lonely. Jamie felt better momentarily, until thoughts of Carrie turned her mind back to Eddie. If some stranger discovered her dark secret it'd be an easy fix— she'd just kill him. Eddie represented a different problem if he were to discover what she did in her off hours, and she didn't want to think about it. She took another deep breath and put her focus back on the files. She desperately hoped James Reimse was in here somewhere or, at least, something was there to point her in the right direction.

Jamie flipped through the information sheets, still trying her hardest to avoid looking at the photos. She found no James Reimse, nor her client Thomas, and her frustration mounted with every page she turned. She saw the horrors of the hidden torture room in every innocent, little face passing through her fingertips, turning frustration to anger. She wanted to hunt down Head Mistress Eva DeLong and her goons and make them pay. The thought of DeLong screaming by her hand brought a smile back to her face. The twisted bitch would suffer badly.

"And they ain't never gonna find your body, you sick cunt!" She unconsciously spoke aloud to her empty office.

Jamie found herself so lost in the thought of five minutes alone with DeLong that she nearly jumped out of her skin when Carrie walked in with a smile, holding out Jamie's tall cup of coffee. On the desk, she placed half a panini and a strawberry filled donut on a paper plate.

"Fuck's sake, Carrie! Fattening me up for the slaughter? What the hell is a panini anyway?"

"Oh shut it, you! Your bony ass needs a lot more than this. A panini is basically a fancy way of saying grilled cheese sandwich or…a hot ham and cheese sandwich in this case. Shut up and eat it. You need some fattening up, November ain't far away and you know Eddie and I like to cook up one big, fat bird!" Carrie barely got the words out between giggles.

"Bite me, Mom! Christ, maybe I'll just eat you instead!"

"You wish! That's Eddie's job, and I'll have you know, he does a damn fine job of it too!" Carrie delighted in a little risqué humor when they were alone.

"You'd send him packing after one night with me, honey. I guarantee it!" Jamie licked her lips with a smile.

"Jamie Windstein! You're absolutely terrible! Glad you're in a better mood though."

"All you, sweetheart. Now, find me those three assholes and I may just be so thankful I'll give Eddie a run for his money on that little honeypot of yours!" Jamie shot Carrie a wicked smile.

Carrie blushed. "I'd say you deserve a spanking but you'd probably like it!"

"You're probably right," Jamie laughed.

Carrie turned to make her exit when Jamie—unable to resist—popped up from her desk to give her friend a hard slap on the backside.

"That's it! I'm calling HR! That's some sexual harassment right there! I'll sue your damn pants off!" Carrie mocked offense.

"You want my pants off, just ask, sugar!" Jamie laughed so hard she couldn't breathe. "Seriously though, find those three assholes and I'm deep in your debt."

"Well then, count on it!" Carrie left, closing the door behind her.

Jamie let out a long sigh to purge her laughter and returned to the grave matter in the folders sitting in front of her. An unwritten rule of the universe, Jamie thought, was an inability to focus when facing an important task that requires your undivided attention. The ease of sliding into frivolity made focus nearly impossible at those times. For instance, Jamie found her mind picturing Carrie's cute, tight ass right now, instead of looking through the files—even though she wasn't really into girls. She slapped herself hard across the cheek in an attempt to shed the ridiculous thought. It remained so she followed the slap by violently shaking her head until she was out of breath. She felt dizzy, but it worked and she was able to return to the children's information sheets. She took a bite of the panini, surprised by how good it was and followed it with a sip of coffee. Carrie really did know her well.

Jamie picked at her sandwich, trying to grasp why these files were hidden away. The faces, along with the confirmation of horrible abuse haunted her mind. Why hide the files of a few dozen children? She found no sense in it. The thought of the abuse these kids experienced sent a shiver down her spine. Jamie had always thought that adults who abused children were the lowest form of scum—right down there with wife beaters and rapists. Thieves and murderers could be redeemed, but there was a special place in the darkest bowels of hell for anyone who physically or sexually abused women and children. Jamie hoped Carrie's search had been more successful than the pile of nothing she found in her files.

Jamie poured through the files a second time and hoped she had missed something, even though she knew she hadn't. She found no James Reimse nor Thomas. Had he given Thomas a false name, she wondered. And if so, why? She could think of no reason for a thirteen or fourteen year old to give his best friend a made-up name. It didn't make any sense. If he wasn't in these files then her entire adventure into Mormont was a colossal waste of time. She despised dead ends.

Jamie refused to believe the files meant nothing. She convinced herself there must be something useful in them that she simply wasn't seeing. She went through them a third time, putting aside every boy named James to show Thomas. Maybe Jimmy had lied. Maybe, Reimse wasn't his name. She scanned the pages slowly, making sure none were stuck together and she didn't miss any. In all, she put aside fifteen children named James. Of those, only a third had a photo attached. Jamie wasn't a believer or the sort to pray, but she prayed now for Thomas to recognize one of the names or perhaps even a photo.

5

The big bushy tail bounced along the grass like a cat's toy pulled on a string. Mr. Whiskers waited patiently, hunkering down on his front paws while he waited for just the right moment to strike. He watched and waited, tracking the bushy fur tail that moved through the grass. He hid in the shadow of the porch steps, patiently biding his time. The bushy tail drew closer and headed straight at him. His muscles tensed like a runner waiting to steal second base in America's favorite pastime.

Mr. Whiskers' eyes widened as he stared down his approaching victim. He didn't know what people called the creature, he only knew it would soon be his. The furry thing drew closer while Mr. Whiskers wiggled his hind quarters back and forth, ready to strike. The furry critter was nearly in range—just a little closer. Finally the moment came and Mr. Whiskers sprung on the unsuspecting squirrel, quick as a flash. The rodent had no chance; Mr. Whiskers was a veteran feline serial killer.

Mr. Whiskers gripped his prey—a well-practiced maneuver—in a bear hug of paws with claws out, holding tight. The squirrel struggled, letting loose a terrible high-pitched scream until Mr. Whiskers' teeth found its throat and brought silence, with a sickening crunch.

The old man sat on his back porch, watching the whole scenario play out like a movie. It was the only entertainment left to him in his retirement. He rocked back and forth in his old chair, never believing for a second that the wily old Mr. Whiskers wouldn't be victorious. Sitting on a weather worn table next to him, condensed water dripped down the side of a glass filled with sweet tea, whiskey and ice. The fresh water ring would eventually add to the already large water stain where he always set his glass. He gently rocked himself, watching his vicious old cat stalk and kill vermin, a little envious of the feline. Mr. Whiskers remained an adept killer, unlike his elderly owner. The cat never made a meal of his victims, he killed viciously simply because he enjoyed the kill—much like his owner did once upon a time.

A few minutes later the old tomcat slinked up the porch steps with the squirrel's broken, bloody body hanging limp in his mouth. Mr. Whiskers didn't carry his prize with the puffed out chest of the conquering hero, rather like a weary meat packer coming home from the slaughterhouse, indifferent to the grisly nature of his work. The tom dragged the dead squirrel—his gift—to his master and then dropped his limp gift at his slippered feet.

The old man looked down at Mr. Whiskers with the same stern look he gave the cat every other time. "Good boy, Mr. Whiskers. Now git!" The old man kicked his foot out at the cat.

Mr. Whiskers was no stranger to their game—they played it every day—quickly scurrying off down the porch steps, unscathed. The old man cursed like a sailor and picked up the dead squirrel, flinging it off into the bushes where his manicured lawn ended—a scene they had repeated hundreds of times. Mr. Whiskers didn't care, he busied himself looking for his next kill.

The old man sat back in his chair, taking a sip of the heavy handed whiskey drink. He rocked back, cursing his old tomcat under his breath, and proud all the same. It reminded him how much pleasure he used to get from hurting things. He could never say it in polite company, but he missed that feeling like nothing else. He enjoyed watching his old tom stalk his prey, filled with envy as he killed one critter after another. He wished for one more kill, the way normal folk wish for a cold sweet tea on a hot day. He lamented the "good ol' days,"—all elderly do—though not many knew "good ol' days" like his. He didn't miss how good radio or television used to be, nor miss hearing his favorite band. No, those things held no appeal to him.

The old man's interests were of far darker things. He missed the scream of a child in the dark as his hands wrapped around its little neck. He ached to hear those screams one more time. Unfortunately, arthritis and the onset of dementia stole the thrill of ever hearing that again. Pain made doing much more than rocking in his chair unbearable. Here he sat, day after day, with the summer breeze bringing the disgusting stench of flowers or worse, the stink of manure spread on the fields surrounding him. He had been reduced to a nobody out in the middle of nowhere.

He hated the country, always had, even as a kid. He was a city boy, born and raised, and he missed the conveniences of urban life. He wanted a corner store within walking distance, quite the range in his younger days. He wanted food delivery—good luck getting a pizza delivered in the middle of fucking nowhere! He missed the hustle and bustle of ignorant masses everywhere. Most of all, he missed stalking prey and the ecstasy of a kill. He loathed being reduced to a lonely observer of his wicked, old black tomcat's stalking and killing. In short, he was a miserable old man on a slow march to the grave.

He rocked his last days away, yearning for a tiny neck to wrap his giant meat hooks around, until the tiny light went out in its eyes. Arthritis made it difficult not to drop his spiked sweet tea these days, let alone choke the life from anything. The pain of inflamed joints was nothing to the fear dementia brought. He moved to the middle of nowhere out of fear of inadvertently admitting his past crimes to random strangers. He knew remaining in the city was far too dangerous for him. He may be safe from that danger now, but he was bored out of his mind. However, it was better than spending the remainder of his days in a tiny prison cell, even though his new home acted as his prison anyway. Old Mr.

Whiskers did the killing now, dropping an endless supply of bloody, dead field mice, rats, chipmunks and squirrels at his feet. It did nothing to quell his own dark urges for the kill.

He took another sip of his drink, praying for death to finally take him away. He longed for death the way the ill longed for a cure. "Give me death or give me something young to wrap these damn hands around." There was no one within a mile to hear him vent his frustration. The old man sighed then took another sip.

6

Thomas Combs smiled as he looked at the caller ID on his cell phone. "Hello again, Ms. Windstein. Sorry—Jamie. Find something?"

"Maybe, maybe not." Jamie hesitated, not wanting to offend her client. "Any chance Jimmy lied to you about his name?"

"I guess it's possible, but why would he? We didn't have any secrets between each other. I'd say it would be highly unlikely. Did you find something?"

"Well, after our meeting this morning I went to the Mormont Home."

"Ugh, you didn't happen to drop a match before you left by chance, did you? I would love to see that place burn to the damn ground." Thomas feigned laughter but he wasn't joking.

"Sorry, no. I did find something you'd probably prefer I didn't though…the, um, room behind the broom closet." Jamie instantly regretted not waiting for a face to face meeting to reveal this so she could see his reaction. She could feel his shocked silence. "My apologies, Thomas. I can only imagine the memories that must conjure up."

"No, no it's alright, Jamie." Thomas paused a moment. "Now I know I hired the right person for the job. How on earth did you find it?"

"Dumb luck, honestly. It's not important. Inside I found a small batch of files containing general information on some of the children. I hoped they'd be helpful, but nothing on Jimmy nor you either. I know it'll be difficult but could you bring yourself to look at them for me? Maybe there's some common thread you'll recognize that I can't. They must have some significance to be hidden away like that." Jamie held her breath waiting for his response.

"I, well…sure. Can you swing by my hotel this evening? I have an errand to run now but maybe we can meet in the bar? Does nine work for you?"

"Nine works for me. I'm sure a couple stiff drinks are warranted for this. Wait, where are you staying?"

"The Adam's Mark, I trust you know it?"

"Yeah, I know it. The dining room bar or the little sports bar?"

"Dining room, it'll be the quieter one by then."

"Okay. See you then, Thomas." She ended the call without waiting for him to respond.

Jamie needed her meeting with Thomas to give her something to go on, she had nothing to this point. She tucked the files of all the boys named James together into one folder, placing the whole stack in a small satchel. She now found herself with a few hours to kill and nothing to do. She hoped Carrie might get a drink with her. She needed to distract her mind from dwelling on everything before she downed a bottle of vodka before her meeting with Thomas. She wanted a clear head when she talked to him to gauge his body language and facial expressions while they talked. She knew he still had more to tell. She kicked herself again for mentioning the hidden room over the phone, but it was too late now.

"Carrie?"

Carrie popped her head in. "Yeah, Jams?"

"Any luck with those three assholes? Maybe brighten a little girl's day?" Jamie batted her eyelashes, flashing a mock smile.

"Actually yes, I did. I've decided you can't have them though, bad little girls don't get presents."

"Well then I'm sorry, bitch, you're fired!"

"Always playing the same damn card! Well, you know what? Fuck it! I need a new job somewhere I'll be appreciated! Maybe Fellino and Carnes is hiring, I hear they have excellent benefits too. Dental, I hear! Got that? They have dental!" Carrie gave an Oscar worthy performance, though Jamie wasn't buying it.

Jamie plucked up her phone's receiver. "I'll put in a good word for you, right now. When do you want to begin your new career with those ambulance chasing sleaze bags? If I could make a suggestion? You'll want to trade those lovely heels in for a pair of barn boots—shit gets pretty deep over there!"

"You're just so mean!" Carrie wiped a fake tear from her eye then broke into a smile. "Here you go, boss. Your three, um…assholes, with current addresses. Now, since I've decided to stay and I do such a fantastic job, some might even say outstanding, I think we should discuss my raise and dental coverage!"

"How about a drink and my undying appreciation, buttercup?" Jamie batted her eyelashes again. "Whatcha say, dollface? Can I get you drunk and take advantage of that hot little body of yours?"

"Oh my! Stop! I do believe you're giving me the vapors!" Carrie gave her best southern belle impersonation while fanning herself.

"Damn! I hope there's a pill for that!" Jamie laughed. "If those three give me any answers you may just get that raise. Wanna grab a drink, though? I have a few hours to kill before I meet with Mr. Combs again."

"Sorry, wish I could but Eddie and I have a dinner date to celebrate his promotion."

"Oh, duh! Sorry—of course you do. Well, don't make my gorgeous man pay." Jamie winked. "Take some money from petty cash. My treat tonight and tell him congratulations for me."

"You sure? Eddie gets funny about charity." Carrie frowned.

"It isn't charity so tell him to get over it. Tell him it's his wife's raise! Seriously though, it's the least I can do for my only friends in this world. Tell him he'll accept it or he gets jack and shit about Snyder."

"Thanks, hun. You know how men are. They act like you castrated them if someone else picks up the tab. I'll tell him you wouldn't take no for an answer."

"Oh, wait." Jamie stopped her before she slipped away. "Would you grab me a twenty while you're in there. I need cash for Leon. I promised."

"The lawnmower guy?"

"That's the one."

"He's a sweetie. Back in a shake. Oh, and here's the info on those three." Carrie handed over a folder. "Two of them are fairly close by, the other is a bit further, about an hour or so south of the city. Robert Keane. The woman is in a nursing home and the other one—Rollins—has a house in the city, not a very good area on the south side. Can I ask why you're hunting down grandmas and grandpas?"

"It's alright, hun. It's for this Combs case. They may be the only ones with any useful info. At least, I hope so. If not—I'm fucked, complete dead end."

"Ah, I see. Well, good luck then and thank you again for dinner. Oh, that reminds me, when can he come see you? I'm sure he'll ask about it."

"Any time is fine with me. See what works for him, then call or text it to me—especially if he wants to meet in the morning." Jamie groaned. "If he can't make it tomorrow, you can wait until I get in."

"Will do. I'll be right back with Leon's money for you. Need any extra for your meeting tonight?"

"Nope, he can cover me. His case, his treat."

She glanced at the file Carrie handed her on DeLong, Keane and Rollins. Finally some good news, she thought. She was growing tired of the big nothing sandwich on James Reimse she'd turned up so far. One of the three, if not all, knew something useful. She relished the thought of extracting information from them, hoping they'd make the job difficult. She ached to show all three just what she thought of child abusing scum like them. DeLong being in a nursing home could be complicated, but she'd figure something out. Jamie wanted that bitch to suffer to the bitter end whether she talked or not. DeLong would talk though, they all talked eventually.

Chapter Seven: Deadly Business

1

He entered the room silently, appearing like a specter in the waning light drifting through the window blinds. He slipped around to the head of the bed, quiet as the dead, not wishing to alert the sleeping woman to his presence. He towered over her, looking down at her frail, withered body wondering how he ever considered her the scariest person in the entire world. She was but a shadow of the monster she had been once. The bane of his existence—who'd threatened to snuff out his existence completely—reduced to a meek mouse he could crush easier than a piece of paper. The irony of their swapped positions seemed funny to him now. Now, he was the monster and she the helpless one. His loathing for her never ceased, despite her being a fragile bag of bones now.

He loomed over the old woman, wanting badly to plunge a blade deep into her temple simply to watch her writhe in agony while she bled out. He had envisioned it thousands of times over the years. He couldn't though, a quick death was far too good for her. She needed great suffering all the way to her last breath and he'd be there laughing. The temptation to reach down and snap her neck like the frail twig overpowered him momentarily, taking all his strength to stop himself.

He visited her numerous times over the years, sometimes making himself known, other times content to watch her slowly wither away. He knew her death would bring joy to many, though for now she still had a purpose to serve. For now, he took immense pleasure in watching her painfully fade away. He couldn't wait for her to burn in hell, though he didn't believe any religious mumbo jumbo. He decided long ago to make her suffer for the duration of her life, in case there was no judgement in the next. The thought of her eternal torture may be the only truly happy thought he ever had.

He visited out of necessity tonight, having to put his fantasies on hold. He reached down and fought the urge to choke the life from her, once and for all. Her once raven black hair had turned the pure white of snow. *The only thing pure about her,* he thought. He clamped one gloved hand tight over her mouth, twisting her face toward him. She woke with a start, instinctively trying to pull his hand away. Her arms lacked the strength to fight off a child, let alone him, these days. Her eyes bugged out in her panic. He delighted in seeing her fear, the same she had seen in his eyes all those years ago. It took him decades to turn the tables on his former abuser, which now filled him with profound pleasure. He remembered thinking of suicide as his only means of escape back then. He wondered if she thought about suicide when she thought of him now. She'd never admit to it though he suspected she longed for death any way it came.

He grabbed a handful of her wispy white locks with all the care of a hawk plucking a mouse from a field. He pulled her head back, ensuring he had her full attention. He enjoyed watching her squirm so much he questioned why he didn't visit more often. He took a long whiff of her, enjoying the smell of fear oozing from every pore on her body while her eyes threatened to pop out of their shallow sockets. He looked her straight in the eye with a smile, enjoying her squirm in his grip.

Slowly he leaned down close to her ear, increasing his grip on her hair and squeezing the hand over her mouth even tighter. "Good evening, Head Mistress DeLong. Calm yourself, dear. I come the bearer of good news." He flashed her a sly smile. "Tomorrow or maybe the next day, you'll have a special visitor." DeLong's eyes grew larger, shaking her head. "Oh, my dear, don't fret. This visitor isn't coming to harm you. She comes only with questions. Questions you will not answer under any circumstance, understand?" DeLong nodded her head in the affirmative. "Good, Head Mistress. You can tell her some basic facts, nothing more. If you mention one word about me, back then or now, I will take you away from this place to one more deserving of a woman like yourself. Are we clear?" Again DeLong nodded her head. "Good, Head Mistress, very good. Now close those little peepers, they make me sick." DeLong closed her eyes as he commanded. "Good girl. Now sleep well, you fucking cunt. I have eyes on you, always. Remember that."

He twisted her head away from him and back to the position it had been in when he entered her dimly lit room at Lake View Manor Nursing Home. He resisted another sudden urge to bash her skull in with his bare fists and instead he turned to exit as the sun set completely, leaving her in darkness. The once mighty Head Mistress DeLong trembled uncontrollably beneath her thin blankets bringing a smile of pure joy to his lips. The years of abuse he suffered in his youth left him with little love for his fellow man, however, Eva Delong, former Head Mistress of The Mormont Home for Children sat atop the mountain of hate inside him.

He exited the room with a nod to his old friend, Kirk Scheidt, satisfied his message had been delivered effectively. The nod silently conveyed his thanks for granting him access to their old nemesis. He slid a folded hundred-dollar bill into Kirk's dark hand, knowing Kirk would gladly provide the service free of charge. The giant black man slid the bill in his pocket nonchalantly with a friendly nod to his old friend. The two men shared a bond of pain that, luckily, only a few others could comprehend. They were bonded forever by their experiences in youth and a burning hatred for the old woman still shaking under her covers.

"Make sure she remembers what I told her in the morning."

"My pleasure." Kirk grinned wickedly before his old friend turned to leave.

2

An old, beat up, unmarked rusty van was likely to raise more than a few eyebrows in a good neighborhood. Old ladies and mothers would speed dial 9-1-1 while children screamed out, "Stranger Danger!" Cliché or not, a van looking like this one was the universal symbol for child predators. In any normal neighborhood reaction would be swift, but not in this neighborhood. In a neighborhood lined with dilapidated, rundown homes, where half sat lifeless and abandoned and the other half should be condemned, in a neighborhood like this no one cared, or even noticed. Any vehicle that didn't backfire every few seconds or otherwise create a racket ,received no attention at all. The people living here knew they were the forgotten, the people no one cared about.

The poverty and conditions here could turn the Dalai Lama cynical and bitter. In this poverty-stricken neighborhood, a van—a pedophile's vehicle to most—went unnoticed, rolling to a stop in their neighborhood.

The van came to a stop in front of 1915 Ronkwe Drive, on the south side of the city, like it had almost every day for weeks now. The houses in the area weren't the only things rundown, everything stood in some stage of decomposition—the people not excluded. The skeletons of closed manufacturing plants lined the main route leading here. A neighborhood originally built for the sole purpose of housing the workers who once made a decent living working in those same factories. This neighborhood wasn't unique, ones exactly like it stretched from here to Cleveland to Chicago and beyond. The Northeastern United States wasn't called the rust belt for nothing. He didn't even think about it as he slide the gear shift into park, the sight was too common to notice any more.

He looked around for any prying eyes out of habit, knowing in this neighborhood, it wasn't necessary. People around here tended to mind their own business unless a bullet came whizzing through their window and even then they weren't likely to do more than yell a complaint. Either he or his partner drove down here so often over the last several weeks no one took any notice of the van at all now. The city ignored this entire neighborhood, making it virtually invisible, thus rendering their business here invisible too. He unlocked the van's rear doors hopping inside unnoticed.

He absolutely loathed this place, regardless of how satisfying the reason was for him being here. His hatred didn't stem from this being such a shitty neighborhood, although it didn't help. His hate came from his current actions, all he must do in order to create maximum shock later and maximum suffering now for one well deserving son of a bitch. He cursed, pulling on the disposable coveralls without ripping them. He wished he could've bought full hazardous materials; HazMat, suit but the purchase would draw unwanted attention. The house he'd come here to enter, stunk worse than a horde of skunks swimming in raw sewage. He was glad this was likely to be his final visit—he never wanted to come here again. The irony that this was his idea wasn't lost on him, though he appreciated the sick places his mind went. He wished the punishment he devised had been for DeLong, but her being in a nursing home made it impractical. He exited the van to enter the house at 1915 Ronkwe for the last time.

He tossed his gas mask onto a large box, one easily mistaken for produce or another food product, then bumped the van doors closed. He slipped inside the front door quickly after unlocking it. He slid the gas mask on once inside and out of sight. The smell hit him like a wall of water, despite the mask. It didn't filter the stench completely, though it was diminished below vomit inducing levels. The house looked more like the city dump than a home, and it stunk even worse. Hoarders at least, collected things of some value, but not this one. This one, apparently hoarded only garbage. The owner's apparent love of refuse had been what gave him the sick idea for the man's punishment. If he wanted to live in filth, then he'd have filth beyond his wildest dreams—or, in this case, nightmares.

He followed the well-worn footpaths through the mountains of trash to the rickety staircase leading to the second floor full of trash. He took care not to bump into anything which would cause an avalanche he'd never be able to dig through. He thought booby-trapped trails during the Vietnam war were likely easier to navigate than the narrow path winding through 1915 Ronkwe. He couldn't decide which would be worse, tripping a claymore mine that blew his legs off, or getting buried alive under a mountain of stinking garbage. He'd prefer the claymore about now, he thought. He cursed the owner, since these trips would take less than a minute if he didn't have to tiptoe the whole way. He reached the top of the stairs, relieved his journey was nearly over.

He let the door creak loudly open, loving how it made his victim shake with fear. He hated coming to this place, though tormenting this man made it all worth it. The dying light of the sun lit the room just enough to put its horrors on full display. He set the fresh box of "produce" down and raised the window shades. The sight revealed by the sun's light was enough to make a billy goat puke. The stench made him cringe even with his gas mask on. He smiled in spite of it all, thrilled by the wickedness of his cruelty.

He didn't have time to bask in his own accomplishment though. He had places to be, aside from his desire for a hasty retreat from this disgusting place forever. He returned to the box he lugged up the stairs, pulling out a thick, black garbage bag from inside. He loosened the twist tie, holding the bag closed, though his clumsy gloved fingers fought him. He grimaced seeing what his partner bagged up earlier in the afternoon for him, thankful for the gas mask. He held the opening of the bag as far away from him as possible pouring its contents out onto an already large reeking pile. The commotion sent a swarm of flies into the air, seemingly angry about being disturbed. He ignored them—they were a nuisance not harmful—stuffing the empty bag back in the box. He took a couple steps back toward the bedroom door and heaved the box to the back, raising another swarm of flies.

He heard the faint voice whining from the far side of the room, choosing to ignore it as he usually did. He often came here for this business, failing to acknowledge the man's presence the entire visit, another little torment he enjoyed. He would simply take care of his business and leave. This time however, could be his final opportunity to say his peace before the end to this whole fiasco. He sauntered over to his victim to gloat one final time. He reached the far wall, preparing to give his final benediction, and squatted down.

"Kill me." The man's voice was weak—barely audible above the din of flies.

"Sorry, that pleasure is for another, though I'd love to oblige. Soon, I promise. Maybe not soon enough for you, but soon." He tapped his finger against the man's forehead. "Guess you should have been a better man, Counselor Tony. But you weren't, so here we are. This is still better than you deserve, asshole."

Anthony Rollins closed his eyes. "Please, please just kill me."

He felt no mercy. "Soon you'll have a visitor, someone new to you. Maybe she'll take pity on you if you're lucky. I'm sorry though, there's no guarantee. Maybe if you beg, she'll find the mercy for you that I lack." He smiled and watched a tear roll from Anthony Rollins' eye. He leaned in closer. "There is only one guarantee for you, Tony. I do hope it puts your mind at ease. I guarantee, when you finally fucking die, the fires of hell will feel like a reward. Goodbye, Anthony Rollins."

The sound of the man sobbing made him smile all the way back to the van.

3

Jamie sat staring at her image in the mirror. Unrecognizable to herself, some other woman stared back at her. She detested looking at herself ever since she could remember. She pulled her long black hair back in a ponytail so she didn't have to fuss with it. The dark circles below her green eyes served as a reminder of her many late nights. Those same late nights accentuated the faint—though worsening—lines of crow's feet at the corner of each emerald eye. A weak and powerless stranger stared out of the mirror, reminding her just how exhausted she was—and the day wasn't even over yet. She needed a good night's sleep, which never came, and to vent her frustration in her own dark way—though she had no time for that either. She wondered why she tried to blend in with a society she despised, knowing the simple answer: necessity. The answer did little to improve her foul mood. She knew blending in made her invisible, which was necessary if she wanted to avoid the same fate as Bundy, Gacy, Dahmer, or a thousand others who shared a dark side.

While Jamie applied the few touches of makeup she could stomach, the questions began to swirl again. She stopped herself from smashing the mirror into a million pieces out of frustration at her lack of answers. The fact that she had been on the case for only about thirty-six hours alleviated none of her anger. She loved the gratification of solving a good mystery, not the frustration born from hitting one dead end after another. Making matters worse, she had to make herself presentable for a public appearance when she'd much rather sprint through a crowd wielding a chainsaw.

Jamie's mind began to slip down the rabbit hole of questions plaguing her over the case. The further she went, the more questions she found. She knew if the blanks didn't start filling in soon they would drive her mad. Of course, if anyone ever discovered her extracurricular activities, they'd think her mad already. If her private room was discovered, the men in little white coats wouldn't be far behind to haul her off to a padded room for the rest of her life. The thought didn't fill her with dread, even though it definitely wouldn't be her first choice.

Unable to sit in front of the damn mirror any longer, Jamie stood up, satisfied she looked presentable enough. She still had more time to kill, but she was bored. She wasn't a woman who needed three hours to get ready to leave the house—three minutes seemed too long to her. She couldn't sit around with her mind running wild, so her only option was to arrive early and try not to drink too much before Thomas Combs met her. She decided sitting around growing angry at her lack of answers was no option at all. She flew out the door to be on her way.

Jamie cursed herself for not waiting a few more minutes for the sun to set as she was blinded on her drive down Interstate 190, into the city. The sun sat fairly high in the sky with complete sunset more than an hour away, similar to her meeting with Thomas. Unfortunately for Jamie, the great ball of fire sat at eye level and she was driving head on into it. Her sunglasses and the car's sun visor were only slightly more effective than trying to carry water in a sieve. The ride wasn't all bad though—the combination of the blinding sun and blaring rock 'n' roll took her mind off everything else. She wanted to cheer when she reached her exit, dropping her off right beside The Adam's Mark, despite the much needed distraction of the drive. She pulled into the parking garage behind the hotel, wanting a drink more than a fat kid wants cake.

Jamie walked into the Adam's Mark, happy to see the majority of the dinner crowd gone. She made her way through the open dining area to the bar at the back and saw only a few lingering patrons yet to clear out. Though it was far from full only a few people sat at the bar. She headed for the emptier end and she took a seat on one of the padded stools, hoping to avoid bullshit, small talk and unwanted admirers. Oh great, she thought, more fucking mirrors! She'd forgotten, when speaking to Thomas, about the wall of mirrors behind the bar, lined with bottles of booze. She was in luck, as the lone bartender pushed her vodka on the rocks into her hand quickly.

While Jamie waited, she did her best to avoid eye contact with anyone in the mirrors, including herself. The last thing she wanted to deal with was some idiot hoping for a one-nighter because he happened to be away from his wife for more than twelve hours. She simply sat staring at her drink, desperate to have no human interaction aside from with the bartender. She ordered her third vodka, bored stiff with Thomas nowhere in sight. When Jamie was little, her grandmother used to say she had the patience of an angry rattlesnake—with an attitude to match. She really hadn't improved much. She tried killing time by attempting to decide which she hated more; waiting or unsolved mysteries. It turned out to be a virtual tie, which made her want to bolt from the bar and snap the neck of the first random stranger she happened upon.

"Bar keep?"

The young bartender looked down the bar at her vacantly. "Yeah?"

"Any chance a girl could bum a smoke?" Jamie quit smoking years ago, yet impatience and social intolerance mixed with alcohol stirred an insatiable craving.

"Sure." The young bartender reached under the bar and produced his pack, plucking one out for her. "Here ya go. One cancer stick, ma'am." He smiled.

"Ma'am?" She raised a disapproving eyebrow at him, not returning his smile. "I see someone doesn't like tips. Call me ma'am one more time, and no tip will be the least of your worries, umm…sorry, what's your name?"

The bartender's eyes widened, realizing his error. "Christian—everyone calls me Chris, though. I am sorry. It's just habit around here. Honestly, I meant no offense."

"I'll forgive you this time." She conceded, flashing a smile so he'd relax—although she did enjoy making him squirm. "My mother—God rest her soul—liked being called ma'am, Chris. However, I ain't that damn old yet, so just Jamie, if you please."

"In that case, I sincerely apologize, Jamie. I didn't think you were old, quite the opposite." He gave her a hundred watt smile.

"You're cute, but I ain't that young either, so cool your jets. Thanks for the cancer stick. Oh, matches?"

Chris flipped her a pack of matches bearing the hotel's logo. Jamie couldn't tell if he was flirting or trying to preserve his tip, though she suspected the latter. She tended bar while in college so she knew the tricks of the trade on both sides of the bar, very well.

"Thanks. You gonna make me settle my tab or will you trust me to come back?" She tossed in a flirty smile of her own for good measure.

"You look trustworthy, so don't get me in trouble unless you plan to punish me later." Chris winked and smiled, determined not to give up on the prettiest woman in the entire place right now.

Jamie sneered. "You couldn't handle this, believe me. Plus, I ain't goin' far from the alcohol." Jamie grabbed her handbag with a frown. "You can ensure I won't take off if you be a dear and set this behind the bar for me. Please?"

"Sure thing."

"Don't forget about me." She batted her eyes at him and sauntered away.

The warmth of mid-June was a refreshing change from the frigid air that had hung over Buffalo like death until only a few weeks ago. Jamie lit her cigarette, remembering immediately why she used to love to hate the little bastards so much—the terrible smell! Yet after not smoking for so long, the dizzy-headed high it gave her felt fantastic. It was the dragon that smokers chased, though when you smoked regularly you rarely got light headed. When her cigarette was about half gone, she saw Thomas walking up the sidewalk.

Jamie waved to get his attention and stubbed the cigarette into the sand on the outside ashtray. She stood away from the main entrance several feet, keeping her smoke away from the entrance while she had waited for him. It always annoyed her when smokers stood right next to the door, forcing everyone to pass through a wall of smoke—it was just rude. She despised idiot smokers or any other idiots, in general. She shook her head to get the internal tangent out as Thomas approached.

"Good evening, Mr. Combs, good to see you again."

"Good to see you too, Jamie. And please just, Thomas." He noticed the ashtray and frowned, disapprovingly. "I didn't know you smoked. Tsk tsk, Ms. Windstein." He smiled to take the teeth out his scolding.

"I'm really not. I got here early. A couple drinks mixed with impatience led me astray. I sneak one every now and again to remind me why I quit."

"I'm only teasing you. Everything in moderation, a good friend used to always tell me. I sneak a cigar occasionally myself, especially when drinks are involved." He shot her a knowing wink.

"Actually, I love the smell of a good cigar though I prefer walking through a cigar shop. Now, I hope you ate some brain food for dinner because I need some damn answers before I explode. So how about you buy the prettiest girl in Buffalo a drink or...a dozen?" Jamie batted her eyes at Thomas, taking his arm as he escorted her inside.

"Prettiest girl in Buffalo? Hmm, let's see." He rubbed his chin in thought, looking down at her.

Jamie smacked him. "I thought you were a wise man. Perhaps, I was mistaken. When a girl tells you she's the prettiest, you just nod your damn head in agreement and shut your mouth if you know what's good for you!"

"I don't know about wise but I can say you are certainly the most beautiful woman I've seen…in the last five minutes." He laughed while Jamie smacked him a second time. "Ouch! Gentle, Ms. Windstein, that's my check writing arm!"

Jamie immediately began massaging his arm where she hit him. "Well, we can't have any harm come to that one. Now, hows about you buy this girl a drink before she dies of thirst!"

"Very well, the bottom shelf awaits!" Thomas wailed and lead her toward the door.

Jamie mockingly smacked his cheek. "I'm a top shelf lady! Don't worry, you'll see when you pick up my tab. Also, you'll be paying dearly for that comment, Monsieur Combs. I may be little but this lady can throw back with the best." She squeezed his arm, genuinely enjoying the company for the first time in a long time.

"Oh my, I suppose you've earned it after this little discovery of yours I look forward to hearing about."

"Damn straight, I have! I'll tell you all about it once you buy me a drink."

The pair walked through the over-sized glass doors of the Adam's Mark with Jamie leading her client through the lobby and past the empty dining tables to the bar. Chris, the bartender, frowned seeing her sporting a man on her arm but he did have a fresh vodka on the rocks waiting. She caught a glimpse of herself in the mirrored glass behind the bar with Thomas Combs on her arm. It made her feel almost normal, an alien feeling. It also made her feel several years younger and that gave her a rush of energy. *We make quite a handsome couple,* she thought.

"I guess we should get down to business then? Chris? My bag, please. And the gentleman here will pick up my tab." Jamie smiled at Thomas, catching the disappointment on Chris' face out of the corner of her eye. It felt good to have the attention of two men. *I still got it,* she thought.

Chris set her satchel on the bar looking like a sad little puppy.

Thomas handed the young bartender a hundred dollar bill. "Keep the change, young man—unless my lady friend's tab is more than I think." He winked at Jamie as Chris' demeanor brightened considerably.

"Not that much. Damn! Chris here, deserves it." She smiled at her client before turning to Chris. "Thank you for the smoke and keeping this," she patted her satchel, "safe."

"It was no problem. You're very welcome and thanks to you, sir. You are far too generous."

"It appears all the thanks belong to you, but could I trouble you a little further?" Thomas leaned in as though about to query about something illegal. "Is it possible to get a couple bottles sent up to my suite, or will you get in trouble? The lady and I have some private business to discuss, and minibars kinda suck for entertaining." Thomas noticed a slight frown come to the young man's face. "Oh, don't fret young man, real business—nothing salacious. She may well return before she exits your lovely establishment."

Chris blushed a deep red. "I…uh, I didn't…I mean…umm, technically you're supposed to call room service but I'll hook you up, sir."

"I don't want you getting in trouble now."

Chris cleared his throat. "No trouble, though it'll be a bit pricey. I won't tell if you don't though."

Thomas pulled several bills from his pocket, placing them in Chris' hand without counting. "A bottle of Tanqueray 10, some sliced limes, a bucket of ice and whatever the lady was drinking. Suite 917, okay?"

Thomas and Jamie got off the elevator at the top floor, making their way to his suite. Jamie stayed locked on his arm until he slid his keycard through the lock and stepped aside for her to enter. Thomas' suite, likely the best in the city, looked nice, though she'd seen nicer ones in other cities. The suite opened into an oversized room with a small table and two chairs, a couple of lounge chairs and a long couch sat beyond it with the restroom to the immediate left of the entrance. A spiral staircase led up to a loft bedroom at the back of the room. Aside from the table and furniture in the back, a small bar with two stools stood along the left side, making the room large enough to host a small party. Jamie noted the layout, setting her satchel on the small table while they waited for their bar delivery.

"Well, this is cozy. I see you're really slumming it while you're here in Buffalo." Jamie teased him. "And just how is millionaire, Thomas Combs, enjoying our fine city thus far?" Jamie surprised herself at how comfortable she was around him already.

"If a hotel is gonna be my home while I'm here, it should be a nice home, no?" He winked. "Buffalo is much better than I remember, although, my first impression wasn't…well…pleasant. It's actually my first time back since the Combs adopted me."

Jamie could feel the sorrow in his voice. "I suspect it had to be hard returning here even after all these years. That kind of impression tends to stick with you." Jamie was truly sympathetic, though she also saw an opportunity to gain information while his guard was down. "Are your adoptive parents still alive?"

"Sadly, no. Mom passed away after a long battle with cervical cancer. My dad passed not long after. I think he couldn't fathom the thought of life without her. I like to think their souls knew they weren't meant to be apart." He paused and gave a sheepish smile. "I'm sure you probably think that's crazy."

"No, not crazy at all. I think it's beautiful. Two souls entwined for all eternity? Tell me, Mr. Combs, are you a hopeless romantic?" Jamie couldn't resist trying to lighten the mood while gaining some insight into her client.

"Thank you. I doubt anyone would call me a romantic, hopeless or otherwise. Don't believe me? I can put you in touch with some of my exes." He laughed. "All kidding aside, I'd like to believe we all have a soulmate out there somewhere, whether it ends up being a lover or just a close friend. I'd guess you're no romantic at all, hmmm, Madame Windstein?" He raised an accusing eyebrow.

Jamie laughed loudly. "Oh, I don't believe a single ounce of that love bullshit. I've learned life is shit and then we die, usually alone. A few seconds of happiness now and then may dot your timeline, a warm chocolate chip cookie fresh from the oven, a five second orgasm, or the smell when you first walk in a cigar shop. That's it, that's as good as it will ever get. Savor those little moments—those fractions of a second—because the rest of life is one big steaming bowl of shit stew. We have no choice, we have to eat it one giant, heaping spoonful at a time." Jamie held her head high, proud of her extreme pessimism.

"Wow! What a wonderful life philosophy you've got there." Sarcasm oozed from Thomas. "So, the beautiful Jamie Windstein has never been in love?"

"Me? In love?" She spit the words with venom. "Love is, without a doubt, the most overused and underfelt word in the English language. People say it ad nauseum and, yes, I'm sure on some rare occasions they actually feel it ,but only an infinitesimal number of the times they repeat it. People say that word—love—long after the feeling has died. They say 'I love you' one second and sign their divorce papers the next. It's all bullshit, Thomas, trust me. Love is, one hundred percent, complete and total, Grade-A bullshit. So no, to answer your question, Jamie Windstein has never nor will ever be in love."

"Geez, compared to you, I guess I am a hopeless romantic!" He chuckled to break the slight tension. "Who knows, maybe someday a knight in shining armor will appear and sweep you straight off your feet. I can see the headline now, *Jamie Windstein Finds Love, Hell Freezes Over All On The Same Day*!"

They both laughed while Jamie smacked him again. "Wise ass! You're lucky I like you or you'd be lying in a bloody heap on the floor after a comment like that." She shook her tiny fist at him. "All I can say is love is bullshit. Complete. Unadulterated. Bullshit. Knights in shining armor are right where they belong—in faery tales. The real world is bereft of love, save for a few miniscule moments."

"Ah, I think you're forgetting a mother's love, I think. Wouldn't you say that was real love?" He pressed.

Jamie immediately saw red and her voice raised. "You're talking to a woman left on the doorstep of strangers as a baby, sir. Fuck your mother's love. That's some bullshit too!" Her anger surprised even herself, forcing her to take a deep breath and calm down. "Sorry."

"No, I'm sorry, Jamie. I didn't know, honest. Please forgive me. I didn't intend to dredge up a horrible memory. I hired you to do that for me." He smiled kindly.

"It's okay. I shouldn't have gotten angry. See! Even the mention of love turns ugly." She laughed, slightly embarrassed by her outburst.

He gave her a wink. "Whatever. I guess we better get down to business before we waste the whole night like two teenagers on a first date."

Before Jamie could respond, there was a knock on the door.

"Thank goodness!" Jamie wanted a drink worse than the previous night after her grim discovery. The thought crossed her mind for a fraction of a second to tell Thomas about it before she pushed it far, far away. Don't even think it, she scolded herself. Luckily, she had no time to dwell on it with Thomas wheeling in the bar cart. She held herself back from sprinting to the bottle of vodka, popping the top, and draining it in one swallow. She knew back at home later may be an entirely different story.

"Aren't you a sight for sore eyes?" She addressed the bottle of vodka like an old friend.

Thomas grabbed two glasses from the bar.

"Make mine a double, Jeeves. Maybe a triple—no one's looking."

"Yes, ma'am!"

Thomas handed Jamie her glass of vodka, garnished with a slice of orange, before pouring himself a glass of gin—splash of tonic, a lime.

While Thomas played bartender, Jamie snagged her satchel and slapped it up on the bar to remove the files she brought. She decided some answers were long overdue, regardless of her enjoyment of the evening thus far. If Thomas didn't end her answer drought, she may just exit via the window. She downed the glass of vodka in one swallow and handed it back to Thomas for a refill before he'd even tasted his own drink.

Thomas grabbed the bottle of vodka and filled her glass, deciding it'd be best to set it on the bar next to her. "Damn! Guess I did upset you. Again, please accept my apology."

Jamie looked him dead in the eye. "Screw apologies, I need answers. Provide those and I'll accept a big fat check instead of an apology. Cheers!"

4

Part of Abigail Peterson loved the eyes that followed her when she exited the gym, while the other part of her wished for invisibility. She knew a young woman alone needed constant environmental awareness, or run the risk of becoming just another statistic. She wasn't vain—she worked out in case someone attacked her again. Victim was not a label she wished to wear. In college, she hadn't been fit, wasn't strong enough to fight off the attacker who came for her. Determination to never again be the victim, drove her workouts and her paranoia. She hit the button to unlock her car door, immediately sliding her thumb over the red panic button, ready if anything happened.

Abigail's legs twitched and trembled on the short drive home, having really pushed her limit on the treadmill. She dreamed of one day running one of the big marathons, like Boston or New York City, so every day she pushed herself to the brink of collapse. She knew the odds of winning one of the big races were slim, yet she still pictured herself sprinting across the finish line with the crowd cheering her name. Most got satisfaction from simply making it that far. They wanted to tell everyone they had done it, but Abigail wanted more. Mainly, she wanted to live free of fear, though her fear drove her—pushed her to do more, to be more. Abigail Peterson wanted the world to see her as a strong woman, a survivor, who would never be dominated by a man ever again.

Abigail kept her eyes peeled as she crept along the final block to her driveway, on the lookout for anything out of the ordinary. Staying hyper-vigilant had become second nature for her at this point—it wasn't something she thought about. "Never Again" wasn't just some inspirational phrase for Abigail, it was her daily mantra. She also had those words tattooed on the inside of her right forearm, to renew her resolve whenever needed. The words repeated in her mind all day long; while running on the treadmill, while she walked outside, or while sitting at her desk at work. She saw danger everywhere, just waiting for her to let her guard down for a split second.

Abigail pulled into her driveway, stopping a few inches from her garage door before hitting the button to open it. Before closing the door behind her, she always made sure the garage was empty, watchful for anyone lurking in the shadows or sneaking in behind her. Her friends laughed at her overly cautious habits but she didn't care. She refused to ever put herself in a vulnerable position again.

Abigail let out a long sigh when the garage door closed, finally releasing the breath she instinctively held. Each step into her home brought a wave of calm over her as her fear and anxiety faded a little more. She tossed her keys on the kitchen counter, moving through her home with confidence. She didn't turn on any lights, though, as that would only alert predators to her presence.

She entered her bedroom and tossed her gym bag onto the bed as her legs began to feel like Jell-O from her workout. She kicked off her shoes, stripping off her sweaty gym clothes as she headed to the master bath. Flicking on the light with her elbow—the room was windowless—she tossed her sweat soaked t-shirt into the hamper and pulled back the shower curtain. Public showers made her skin crawl, so she never showered at the gym unless she had absolutely no choice. A rarity, since she planned her days down to the most miniscule details, even planning her bathroom breaks in advance as much as possible. She craved her evenings alone in the safety of her own home the way junkie's crave getting their daily fix. All she wanted was a steaming hot shower, her soft cotton pajamas, maybe a glass of wine, and to relax on her couch with the new book she'd downloaded.

Abigail took a deep cleansing breath, relieved that she survived another day. "Never again," she proclaimed to the mirror as she stepped into the steam filled shower.

He broke into a giant smile the second he heard her get in the shower. *People are so stupid,* he thought. People hung their brain next to their coat the second they unlocked their own door and few seemed immune from it. He'd even seen cops let down their guard once entering their front doors—as though bad things magically disappeared when their shift was over. People took for granted that home was a safe place.

Abigail walked right by him without notice, simply because she didn't want to turn on a light. He'd watched her—he knew she showered every evening, so he sat in the dark and patiently waited for her to arrive. She took off all the armor she wore the instant the door closed behind her, exactly the way he knew she would. He didn't need to sneak around or even hide, though he sincerely doubted she would have noticed him—even with the lights on. It was disappointing to him. He thought a single woman living alone, who appeared so vigilant everywhere else, would be more cautious. She wasn't though. Abigail Peterson was just like everyone else—automatically assuming home equaled safe for no actual reason. He represented the fraction of a percent of the time that the home didn't mean safe.

He simply sat waiting, intently listening for the sound of the bathroom door clicking closed. He almost laughed when she didn't take that small precaution. He crept into her bedroom, careful to keep quiet even though he knew he could likely stomp and she wouldn't hear. She confirmed it when she began singing, though he didn't know the song. He paused a moment to listen to her pleasant singing voice. His business could wait a few seconds.

The familiarity of the scene about to happen wasn't lost on him. He crept into the master bath feeling like Norman Bates, sans black dress and wig. He held a butcher knife at his thigh rather than poised high overhead as Bates had done, however—it *was* only a movie after all. He moved forward quietly, yet quickly, hoping she'd take no notice of his shadow through the curtain. He pressed his back to the wall opposite the shower head, pushing his leg against the tub. He waited there a second until the thrill he got right before a kill had finished rippling through his veins in a wave. Gripping the shower curtain tight in his left hand, he tightened his grip on the butcher knife until the adrenaline surge faded.

While he stood against the tub, poised to strike, he played out everything he was about to do in his head. Finally ready, he raised the butcher knife, silently counting to three. One…Two…he slid the curtain back like a whip.

The beautifully fit and naked Abigail Peterson immediately spun around, her eyes shooting wide with fear. They stared at each other for a fraction of a second, neither making a move. He could see his dark reflection in her pupils, which were wide as dimes, then her mouth dropped as she readied herself to let loose a bloodcurdling scream. The scream never came.

He swung the shining steel blade forward with accuracy and force, halting the scream dead in her throat. He struck with the speed of a cobra strike and Abigail never stood a chance. He took great pride in his precision, unlike Norman Bates, who stabbed away with reckless abandon—he needed her dead, not mangled.

The point of the blade pierced her throat less than a hair's breadth below her gaping jaw. The force of the blow sunk the butcher knife in her neck up to the hilt, while the tip clinked gently on the porcelain tile behind her. It was all over in seconds and Abigail Peterson would never scream again. He wrapped his left arm around her waist. Like a lover he stared into her eyes, gently allowing her to slide down. He kissed her softly on the lips as her last goodbye.

"I'm sorry, sweet Abigail," he said as he gently brushed her dark hair behind her ear. "I'm here on business, not pleasure, dear. You are quite beautiful—I wish time permitted us to get acquainted over weeks instead of mere seconds. If only we had met for another reason, at another time—but I need you to do something for me now. You're going to deliver a message to someone very special to me." He noticed the tattoo on her forearm. He nodded in agreement. "Never Again? Yes, sweet Abigail, no one will ever hurt you again."

He laid her down flat and then reached up to turn off the water. He pulled the knife from her neck, watching her blood flow down the drain. He was anxious to deliver his next message to the lovely Jamie Windstein, since her first reaction surprised him so much. Standing up, he looked at the peacefully still body one final time then retrieved his small tool bag from where he had put it under her bed.

Returning to the tub, he made quick work of removing young Abigail's head with a hacksaw. Her blood flowed straight into the drain while he watched intently, until the flow slowed to drips. He then went to work removing her arms, slightly below the shoulder, taking care to even out her legs, sawing them off about six inches below her waist. He pulled a stainless steel hook—normally used to hang sides of beef—from his bag, stepping onto the tub's edge to screw it into the ceiling. Once it was secure, he hung Abigail's torso to finish draining. In the meantime he cut her limbs into pieces to make it easier for disposal.

He bagged up the bloody chunks of meat with the same care he would have given to litter on the side of the road. Before starting his cleanup, he set Abigail's slender hands to the side for another purpose. He thanked whatever invisible entity watched over him that the kill had taken place in the shower. It made the cleanup a breeze, keeping splatter to a minimum, both in the initial kill and his sawing her into chunks. He gently toweled off the damp torso, now fully drained. Pulling a small knife from its sheath on his belt, he began to carve his message into her tender flesh. A few drops of blood trickled from the wounds he made, which he left there to dry. He found the lines of blood made his words—carved in her flesh just below her small, yet perfect breasts—more aesthetically pleasing. Finished, he lifted the torso off the hook and slide it into a black bag for transport, then removed the hook from the ceiling. He rinsed everything else down the drain with bleach and hot water. He wasn't worried about being overly thorough as he toweled off the side wall and then used Abigail's hands for his final touch.

5

Some restaurants you frequent for their good cheap food, some simply to be seen in, and then there are the restaurants you frequent on special occasions to celebrate. The latter may be a little pricey, made worth it by combining great food with great atmosphere. An establishment thoroughly embedded in the final category for them, Carrie and Edward Washington entered the Blue Bayou Café to celebrate Eddie's good fortune. Since Jamie offered to pick up the tab, they could've gone anywhere in the city—but this was their favorite for special occasions. Also, Carrie hadn't mentioned their date night was on Jamie's dime as of yet. Neither of them cared for the other, fancier restaurants they could've chosen—they found those places uncomfortable, mostly filled with snobs who looked down their noses at "common folk" like them. Also a meal for two tended to be larger than a mortgage payment, which made them uncomfortable, even if the meal *was* on Jamie. She wanted a special evening with her husband, not a night ruined by snobs, or guilt over ordering a hundred dollar steak.

Carrie smiled wide, proud to be on the arm of her handsome husband. It made her want to scream, "Look at me!"

Every time she walked through the doors of the Blue Bayou Café, the ambiance of the place took her breath away—she loved it. She and Eddie had never been to New Orleans, though this is what she imagined walking into an old jazz or blues bar must be like, minus the cloud of smoke. The Blue Bayou prided itself on being a Jazz club, as such, and a few musicians played in a small area off to their left as they entered. Immediately past the small niche where the band played, a long bar stretched along the entire left side of the restaurant.

Carrie squeezed Eddie's arm, unable to express her happiness.

Carrie and Eddie stood at the elevated entrance with an eagle's eye view of the entire restaurant below them, another unique element adding to the ambiance. They checked in with the hostess, who then led them down the stairs into the restaurant itself. They made their way past the bar on the left, with the main dining room behind, a half wall to the right. Carrie always enjoyed the low soft light, making it feel like receiving an intimate hug from an old friend. Carrie thought it was the most romantic place in the world.

Once seated, Eddie stared into his wife's beautiful hazel eyes, watching the flame from the candle between them dance. "I love you, Carrie Washington. Thank you for this." He couldn't have been more sincere.

Carrie felt a tear well up in the corner of her eye, threatening to ruin her make-up. "I love you too, Detective Edward Thaddeus Washington. Now and always." She was so overwhelmed she nearly choked on the words.

"Not detective yet. Don't jinx it, honey." Eddie swelled with pride, despite the rebuke. "No tears, dear. This is a happy night, we're here to celebrate."

"It's a good tear, my love." Carrie patted at the wetness that had escaped, trying not to smudge her make-up. "I know it's not official yet, a technicality. You and I both know it'll be true soon enough. When it is we'll just have to celebrate again!" She smiled at him with her cheeks beginning to ache from the effort, an ache she would gladly bear.

Their waitress arrived before Eddie could respond. "Good evening and welcome to the Blue Bayou Café. I'm Melissa, I'll be your server tonight." She beamed at them. "How are you folks this evening? Celebrating an anniversary tonight?"

"We're excellent, Melissa. We're celebrating—just not our anniversary. This extraordinarily handsome gentleman—who I get to call my husband— received a promotion to detective in the Buffalo Police Department today!" Carrie beamed like a child with a report card sporting straight A's.

"Fantastic! Congratulations!" The waitress smiled, knowing a big tip was likely coming her way.

"Thank you. Though my lovely wife is a bit over zealous." Eddie blushed, uncomfortable being the center of attention.

"Now, detective, would you want a wife who didn't beam at your accomplishments? Every man should be so lucky." They all laughed. "I'll give you a little time to look over the menu. Our specials this evening are a grilled mahi-mahi with avocado chile salsa, a bacon wrapped filet mignon with a side of lobster and truffle, cheesy pasta or we have a swordfish steak topped with baby shrimp smothered in butter and basil. I can tell you all of those are exquisite, as our chef is simply outstanding. How about something from the bar while you think about it?"

They placed their drink orders, a cosmopolitan for Carrie and scotch on the rocks for Eddie, waiting for Melissa to walk away before resuming their conversation.

Carrie debated to herself over whether to tell Eddie about their meal being on Jamie or not. She wanted him to be free to choose what he really wanted and not contemplate prices but she also didn't want to hurt his pride either. She struggled a moment and then finally decided to tell him.

"I need to tell you something, Eddie. I'm going to warn you up front not to get upset about it or no dessert for you when we get home, understand?" Carrie gave him a serious look then blew him a kiss to lighten the mood.

"Honey, you can't ask me to temper my reaction to an unknown, though knowing you as I do, I'm positive whatever you have to say is not as contentious as you've made it in your mind." He leaned forward raising his eyebrows at her. "So spit it out."

"You do know me too well. Here goes…Jamie says congratulations and shut up, she's picking up the tab tonight." She held up her hand, seeing Eddie begin to protest. "Shush! First, our new client has deep pockets and second, this is your night to celebrate, so I don't want you holding back because you're worried about the bill. So loosen up and order something expensive just because you can. You got it mister?"

Eddie saw protesting was pointless. "Fine, whatever. If that's how it's gonna be, then let me see. Do they have a forty ounce filet with a side of gold and a bowl of diamonds for dessert?" He chuckled. "That'd teach Jamie a lesson."

"I wish! Also if I knew she was going to do this I'd have booked us a table at The Chop House. You might be able to get all that there!" They laughed again since The Chop House was the most expensive restaurant in the city.

Melissa returned with their drinks, interrupting their fun. "I see we're in a great mood this evening!" She set their drinks down. "In honor of your promotion, Detective, these are on the house. We're proud you picked the Bayou Café to celebrate. Are we ready to order?"

"Thank you, you're too kind." Eddie conjured his officer persona to quell his laughter. "Before we order, I have a question. Is there anything I can order that would be so ridiculously expensive a person would have to be insane or a billionaire to order it? I'm thinking like a five pound filet mignon with gold flakes or perhaps diamond encrusted?" Eddie smiled seeing the shocked look on the waitress' face.

"Ignore him, Melissa." Carrie shot her husband the evil eye. "He's being a sarcastic jerk because I just told him my boss, is picking up our tab as her way of congratulating him. Apparently, his macho pea-brain can't handle it."

Melissa smiled, positive a big tip was coming her way now. "I'm glad I'm not the only one with a wise-cracker at home. Sorry, you came to the wrong place if you really wanna stick it to your friend, everything here is pretty reasonable unless you double up!"

"He's done goofing around. Right, Edward?" Carrie shot him her best disapproving look.

"Yes, dear."

"Good. Now, I know what I'd like."

"My apologies, Melissa. Yes, since my stunningly beautiful wife is ready to order, I better be or I'll have to stay here tonight." He gave Carrie a wink and a smile.

"I can see this is going to be my favorite table tonight. So, what can I get for you two love birds?"

Melissa took their meal order—the filet mignon special for Carrie and the swordfish for Eddie—promising to return with a basket of fresh warm bread momentarily.

"Now, Detective Washington, we have business to take care of before I forget. When would you like to come in and talk to Jamie? She told me to set a time and she'll make sure she's in the office for you. There's an open slot mid-morning tomorrow if you're free. She has a client appointment in the morning so you could come right after. Is that okay?"

"That's fine. What time, hun?"

"Ten thirty, to be safe. I think her morning client will be quick so if you're early it should be alright."

"Seems Jamie has become the center of my world. First, she's connected to the body I found, albeit indirect, then remember the call I rushed out for today?"

Carrie nodded.

"It was for a missing couple in Jamie's neighborhood, only a couple blocks away from her house." He leaned in, lowering his voice. "It looks like foul play, unfortunately." Eddie straightened back up. "Now here I am with her buying me dinner. Everything does come in threes, I guess."

Eddie had peaked his wife's curiosity, though didn't want anyone overhearing them. She leaned in speaking softly. "Is it connected to the body you found, to the serial killer?"

"We don't think so but it's way too early to say yet." Eddie wanted to share everything with his wife, but if anyone found out, he'd end up a bike cop in the park handing out tickets to idiots for not picking up dog poop for the next twenty years.

Melissa returned with a smile, bread and two fresh drinks, interrupting Eddie's news to Carrie's irritation.

Eddie saw the interruption as an opportunity to change the subject before he said something he shouldn't. "Anyway, you know I can't say much about it. I gotta tell you though, Detective Barker—the one who brought me in on all this?"

Carrie nodded her head, still a bit disappointed.

"Well, this guy, he looks just like Columbo. I mean, he's the spitting image of Peter Faulk. I almost laugh every time I look at him."

"Excuse me, ma'am, just one more thing." Carrie did her best, yet horrible, Columbo impersonation then laughed. "Please, please, please tell me he says things like that!"

Eddie laughed. "Oh God, no! I'd never hold it together if he did. Honestly, Carrie, he's one grumpy, miserable SOB. However, he's also one damn good detective. I do want to buy him a frumpy old raincoat, though he'd likely kill me!"

"I'll keep my eye out!" They both laughed. "You know I'll do it too!"

"Yes, I certainly do."

"Eventually I'd like to meet this man who's going to be stealing my husband away from me for long hours and late nights." Carrie smiled though she was deadly serious.

"I'm sure there will certainly be some long days and nights ahead. Honestly, you're lucky I made it here tonight. We expected to simply turn the case over to missing persons, but unfortunately, it didn't work out that way. Tomorrow I'll be interviewing the neighbors, coworkers and what not. It won't be a problem sneaking off to meet Jamie though, Barker made it a priority." Eddie inadvertently slipped into his "just the facts" cop tone.

"Yes, sir, Detective Washington." She saluted him with a wink, the way she always did, to remind him he wasn't at work. "Well, I'm glad he saw how awesome you are and trusts you with all of this."

"He made me prove myself, several times, then admitted he spoke to Captain Hitchcock about having me transferred before he even called me. Obviously, if I laid an egg at Dr. Ketchum's office, another call would've been made. Oh, that reminds me—"

Carrie cut him off, knowing exactly what he was about to say. "You're gonna need to buy a couple new suits!"

"Stop it! You freak me out when you read my mind." Eddie smiled.

Carrie shrugged her shoulders. "Maybe you're just too predictable." She stuck her tongue out at him. "Saturday? I thought we'd go to that warehouse shop on

Elmwood—I forget the name of it—you know the one I mean."

Eddie nodded.

"They're reasonable for really nice suits, without breaking the bank. You have what? Three?"

"Maybe four."

"A couple more should do, then a few new dress shirts and…" She looked at him with disdain. "Some decent ties! I'll pick 'em out so your new partner doesn't think he's working with a mentally challenged ten year old."

"What?" Eddie recoiled in mock shock.

"You know dang well what, Edward Thaddeus Washington. How many Batman ties are hanging in the closet?" Eddie smiled at her scolding eyes. "None should be the answer, so you have too damn many. If this Barker is the curmudgeon you say, then he'll bust you down to the guy walking behind the police horse shoveling up shit for wearing some crap like that!" Carrie broke into laughter though Eddie knew she was serious.

"You're probably right."

"Probably? Looks like you're talking your way right out of dessert tonight."

"I'm sorry, my dear." Eddie stuck out his lower lip. "You are beautiful and you're always right."

"Now you're getting it! Don't think for a second I won't be writing that down to remind you of later either."

Eddie tried giving her a hate filled stare, which failed almost immediately when both busted out in laughter again.

Melissa, the waitress, arrived with their meals, once again interrupting their fun.

Carrie remained amazed just how much they still enjoyed each other's company after so many years together. They started out as high school sweethearts, yet every day she felt even closer to her husband. She never worried about him—dangerous as a police officer's job can be—she trusted him to come home. Eddie had always made her feel safe and secure by his mere presence, so her thoughts rarely conjured tragedy. If she ever got the fateful knock on the door some day, she knew it would absolutely crush her. She pushed thoughts like that far away. Memories of nights like the one they were sharing now would be her nightmares if they day ever came when her Eddie didn't come home. Carrie smiled sweetly at the love of her life, choosing to live in the moment rather than dwell on tragedy that may never come.

Eddie returned her smile, warmed to the marrow by their love for each other.

6

Jamie fidgeted as she waited impatiently for Thomas to flip through the files she'd brought. He claimed not to recognize most of the names, though some of the faces in the faded pictures that accompanied over half the information sheets seemed familiar. She saved the "James" file until last rather than crush her hope for answers from the start. She couldn't even imagine the memories the ghosts of Thomas' past must be dredging up. She'd be amazed if any of the children in these files escaped Mormont without suffering some form of post-traumatic stress disorder. She didn't wish to bring him nightmares, though she saw no choice. These files were her only lead so far.

Jamie watched and waited, trying not to scream out in frustration. Patience was not a virtue she had ever possessed. Her mind wandered off on tangents. Just how many times had that awful red door opened, leading children to midnight beatings or worse? She felt anger welling up inside her just thinking of the atrocities committed at Mormont. Then her mind drifted to the three predators Carrie tracked down for her. The names Rollins, Keane and DeLong swirled around in a sea of red, along with visions of the suffering she'd inflict if they chose to be tight lipped. She knew, whether they spoke freely or not, she was going to make them suffer before the end.

"What's with the smile?" Thomas' voice caught Jamie by surprise.

She had been so lost in thought she hadn't realized a smile creeping across her lips. "I'll tell you later, when this is all over." She frowned at him. "No, I wasn't thinking about you and I'm not spending the night either."

"A heartbreaker too! You are a woman of many masks, aren't you, Ms. Windstein?" Thomas clutched at his chest, making them both laugh.

"Oh, shut it! Believe me, Mr. Combs, you couldn't handle me with two hearts and four arms." Jamie enjoyed flirting with Thomas, but they had business to conduct. "So any luck? Anything at all?"

Thomas frowned and let out a little sigh. "I'm sorry. I only vaguely recognized a few of the faces in there—possibly a few names. Why these files were hidden away, I have no clue. I can tell you, most likely all of those kids were taken there at one time or another." He gave a wry smile. "Which is about as helpful as telling you water is wet. I'm sure you already knew that."

"Unfortunately, I did suspect as much. However, I put together one last file I'd like you to look at carefully. I pulled out every boy named James and put them together." Jamie handed the last file to Thomas. "None have the last name Reimse, which is why I asked you about a possible false name earlier. There's no reason for him to do so, but people tend to do unexpected weird shit for no reason. If they didn't, I wouldn't have a job." She chuckled. "Maybe we'll get lucky and strike gold. I do apologize for this. I can't even begin to imagine the horrible memories these files must drag up for you."

"I'm okay. No need for apologies. Too many suffered there when they should have been building a library of happy memories filled with puppies and days playing in the sun. I hope this won't be another dead-end."

"I hope so too. You know, no matter how many terrible things I see, it always takes me aback at how cruel people are to each other. Some people read a Stephen King book and think that's horror, but if you want a real horror story just read a history book. Read the memoirs of Holocaust survivors or just read a book about Mengele. They didn't call that sick fucker the Angel of Death for nothing! Those are real horror stories—no book or movie can even compete with the real world." Jamie surprised herself with her rage filled mini-rant fueled by frustration and vodka. "Sorry, I get upset thinking about it."

"It's quite alright. I can't say I disagree with anything you said. No matter how vivid the imagination of even the most talented writers or artists, horror fiction pales in comparison to real life." Thomas smiled despite the grim subject. "It'll drive you mad if you dwell on it. Best to tune it out and buy a puppy or something."

"I won't be buying any damn puppy!" Jamie forced a smile. "Unfortunately, you know horror better than most. Now, find something in that damn file before I lose it completely. I need another damn drink!"

"If you'd be so kind." He wiggled his glass at her while opening the James file.

Jamie slammed a few ice cubes in each glass loudly, trying to let out some of her frustration. She downed two fingers of vodka and then poured another along with filling Thomas' glass. She couldn't help feeling the night was going to be a total bust.

"Sorry, Jamie. If any of those kids are my Jimmy, there's no picture and none of the last names are familiar." Thomas shrugged his shoulders in defeat.

"Well, fuck me!" Jamie threw her arms up in defeat. "Great! All fucking questions and no fucking answers! Were you sent to me by Satan, Mr. Combs? Only the other day, I was a happy go lucky PI just taking photos of cheating perverts! Now, look at me, I'm obsessed with finding a man I can't even seem to prove existed and a major cover up involving an orphanage of torture. What's next? You gonna ask me to find the meaning of life for you? Curse you, Thomas Combs!"

"You love this and you know it!" He winked at her. "You've been on the case for less than two days and you already learned more than I did in two years. Just how in the hell did you find that room anyway? Are you a witch?"

"Ancient Chinese secret, Tommy ol' boy! I could tell you but then…"

"You'd have to kill me? Try it." He laughed.

"No, Tommy, then I'd have to cut your balls off. Still want me to try it?" She winked at him, took a drink, and brandished her best drunken smile. "Honestly though, it was really just dumb luck, plain and simple. I noticed a finger smudge by chance, it looked out of place then—wah-la!—the door opened. Easy peasy Japanesy." She laughed.

"You are amazing! Again, and I can't say it enough, I see I hired the right person for the job. If anyone can find Jimmy it's you. I know it. Thank you so much, Jamie."

"But wait…there's more!" Jamie did her best infomercial impression.

"Oh?"

"I didn't tell you why I was smiling earlier—and it just might finally yield some bleeding answers! I happen to have the addresses for three little scumbags in need of some—shall we say—thorough interrogation. I doubt I can squeeze them all in tomorrow, however, I will be paying a visit to Anthony Rollins, Robert Keane and the devil herself, Eva 'The Evil Fucking Cunt' DeLong! It may please you to know Ms. DeLong is currently a resident of a local nursing home, a terrible one with any luck." Jamie finished with a self-satisfied smile.

"Damn! You really are amazing!" Without thinking, he grabbed Jamie, and before she had time to react, planted a kiss on her lips.

The kiss lingered beyond the friendly range, giving them both a rush. Jamie felt her cheeks flush, though the heat created wasn't contained to her face. She instinctively put a hand to Thomas' chest, pushing him gently back, even though she didn't actually want him to stop. Thomas held his lips to hers a moment longer before relenting.

"Sorry." He blushed. "I…I don't know what came over me."

"Relax, it's alright. Maybe, once I solve this damn case, we can revisit this moment. For now, though, you're my boss, so let's keep it professional, 'kay?" Despite her words, she felt a rush of lust.

"Yes, you're right. I am sorry. I promise I'm not some sexual predator. I still can't thank you enough, and I really hope we can revisit this later." He looked her straight in her beautiful green eyes, smiling from ear to ear. "You really can't help it, can you?"

"Help what?"

"Being perfectly irresistible." He watched her reaction closely. "Now, since I've been absolutely zero help—and you've shot me down on a night you'd never forget—can I call you a cab, or would you trust me to be a gentleman and take the very comfortable couch over there?"

Jamie blushed a deep red and considered her options. "I know you're a gentleman. Unfortunately, I don't trust anyone, including myself. Maybe if you had supplied me with some answers tonight I would have rewarded you with a night I guarantee *you'd* never forget." She shot him a sly smile. "But…you supplied all of jack and shit—so you lose! So, I shall require a cab, good sir!"

Thomas looked at her like she had just murdered his family in front of him. "Damn, Jamie! You make me wish I wasn't such a gentleman! Maybe tomorrow will be my lucky day!" They both had a good laugh. "A yellow chariot for the lady it shall be!"

7

He slid the key into her lock, knowing he needed to be in and out quick. He didn't like having to rush— that's how mistakes happened. He knew he had more than enough time, though knowing didn't ease his mind. He couldn't understand why his anxiety was so high, usually nothing ever got to him. His one and only friend often quipped about the ice flowing through his veins, yet his heart raced like it was his first time up to mischief. He felt like a rookie and he didn't like it. Deep down he knew the reason why, but knowing did nothing to slow his heart. The issue was the combination of Jamie's reaction to his first "gift" coupled with her secret hiding place. He wasn't sure whether to be excited by her or afraid of her. He hadn't felt anything close to fear since childhood.

He snuck through her garage, sticking to the shadows, until he reached the side door. Even though he knew that if she had security cameras, his little game would be over already. He paused a moment before entering to gaze down at the shelving unit that hid her secrets. He couldn't place the foreign feeling welling up in him. Was it fear or guilt? He couldn't decide, but he knew neither were good. He tried to shake it off, whatever emotion it was, yet it continued to linger. He paused with his hand on the door knob, attempting to get himself under control before making an error he'd regret later. It felt like it took forever, but finally his heart slowed. He slid the key into the lock with a sudden urge to finish his business quickly.

Once inside, he moved quickly to the counter and set the black plastic bag he carried down at his feet. He clicked on the small LED light strapped around his head—he still had an uneasy feeling he couldn't seem to shake. He undid the twist-tie that held the bag closed, eager to finish his business. He pulled Abigail's torso out of the bag, setting it on the counter in the same spot he had set the heads. Positioning the torso in the same fashion as before, he hoped it would be the first thing Jamie saw. The first time didn't go exactly as he planned, though now she'd expect something.

He picked up the bag, double checking for anything left behind. Seeing nothing, he stuffed the empty bag into the small pack that was strapped across his back. He could relax with the task complete, though he was still unnerved that he let his emotions get the better of him— even if only momentarily. Jamie turned out to be more surprising than he ever imagined, though he knew he shouldn't have let it rattle him. Due to her secret, his plan may need some minor adjusting. He prided himself on his planning and being methodical, and he desperately hated monkey wrenches. He survived by paying meticulous attention to every little detail, sticking to a routine. He thought, he planned and then he executed. His plan for Jamie never included her being the proverbial fly in the ointment. She was still a mystery to him. One he hoped this deadly business would help him solve.

He paused before exiting, with the nagging feeling he was forgetting something. Looking around, he saw nothing out of the ordinary, yet the same feeling lingered. It unsettled him, even though he tried shaking it off, telling himself to stop the second guessing. Losers second guessed everything—not him. Guys rotting in prison for life, or on death row did that. He was not of their ilk. He was better.

His cell phone began to vibrate, interrupting the thought as he exited the house.

He knew the caller without looking. "Yeah…'K…All set." He let out a sigh of relief. He had time to get to his monitors before Jamie arrived home and he missed her reaction.

8

Once she stepped out of the cab, Jamie realized she drank more than she'd thought as she stumbled her way to the front door, nearly tripping over her own feet several times. She zig zagged her way up the walk, desperately trying not to fall over—she knew she'd lay there all night if she did. She hoped none of her neighbors were peeping out their windows at her obvious inebriation. She kept her distance from her neighbors. It was likely none of them even knew her name although she knew every single one of them. She'd selected her home carefully, based on its lack of some nosy old lady nearby with nothing better to do than stare out the window all day. She fumbled with her keys, dropping them three times and loudly cursing when she banged her head against the door retrieving them. Finally she managed to unlock the door.

"Fuck, I'm drunk," she admitted as she pushed the door open hard.

She nearly fell on her face as she tripped over the threshold, sending her into a whirling dervish of wildly flailing arms as she tried to catch her balance. Luckily, her hand found the edge of a chair, ending her out of control ballerina act.

She stood there a moment, door wide open, until she felt stable enough to move again. She stepped forward, slamming the door shut behind her so hard it shook the walls. She nearly fell over again when something went crashing loudly to the floor.

"Honey, I'm home!" Her voice boomed in the darkness, before breaking into drunken laughter.

Jamie staggered forward and considered dropping down on all fours to safely crawl like a baby, instead of wobbling on her unsteady legs. She managed to navigate the few feet across her living room, collapsing onto her comfortable old couch once her knees bumped against the edge of it.

She stared up into the dark, hoping the room didn't start spinning. "Big day tomorrow, motherfuckers! Some motherfuckers gonna wish they never met Jamie, motherfuckin' Windstein!"

She howled another round of drunken laughter, then laid back, laughing at nothing and everything until her face and belly ached from the effort. The ache made her laugh even more, subconsciously relieved for her mind's reprieve from the unanswered questions filling it. *Wasn't escape why people became alcoholics in the first place?* she thought. Her riotous laughter continued for several minutes until she couldn't remember what had been so funny. The thought only lit another spark of hilarity in her alcohol addled mind for another belly busting round.

It took several minutes for her to calm down and stop laughing at nothing. Jamie lay, staring up into the darkness on what she usually referred to as "the world's most uncomfortable hunk of shit" and tried to clear her mind through the din of buzzing brought on by too much alcohol. It worked momentarily, until the multitude of questions without answers smashed through her mind's Zen wall and shattered it into a million pieces. Her compromised brain was unable to slow the flow as the flood gates opened wide.

Where was Jimmy? Who was Jimmy? Why had Mormont closed? What happened to the money? What happened to the trust fund? Why did Thomas Combs never have any answers? Hadn't he been looking for Jimmy for two damn years? Why, with all his money, had he turned up jack shit? Why did he hire her when he could afford an army of better PIs? Fuck! Who in the fuck broke into her house? Why leave two severed fucking heads? Just what in the holy fuck did "Blood Remembers" mean? Blood remembers what?

She had been abandoned as a baby—orphaned. Jamie assumed "blood" meant family. *How the hell is an orphaned baby supposed to remember family? Did somebody else's blood need to remember? If so, why the fuck leave the message for her? Fuck, fuck, fuckity fuck!* Then what about Eddie Washington, Officer Eddie Washington, soon to be Detective Eddie Washington? What if he found a trail leading to her? If it were anyone else she'd add them to her collection in a heartbeat, but Eddie? Really! Fucking Eddie! Could she do it? Would she? It would kill Carrie. Her questions and doubts spun out of control in the infinite loops of a downward spiral spreading out in only two directions, one leading to insanity, the other to the porcelain god.

Jamie stared up into the darkness, a prisoner of her own mind, until the concept of time returned. Sobriety slowly crept its way back into her veins as her blood alcohol level peaked and then began its descent. She knew the feeling well. She had been on the verge of sickness, maybe even blackout, and managed to ride the wave back to shore.

Then came the alcoholic's pronouncement, shattering any potential catharsis. "More vodka! The answer is vodka! I don't fucking care what the question is, damn it!"

She hoped the uproar might, at least, scare the shit out of any little critters making a home in her attic. The thought had her giggling like a school girl again. She pictured a squirrel—or tree rat as she called them—scampering to get away from the crazy lady yelling below. "Fuck you, Rocket J. Squirrel!" The thought of Bullwinkle Moose's cartoon pal made her laugh even harder. It only got worse when she nearly fell on the floor in her struggle to sit up. Her difficulty in "un-couching" herself brought the idea that maybe, just maybe, she didn't need any more vodka. She quickly pushed away such an evil thought.

Jamie managed—after a half dozen attempts—to sit up, putting her feet flat on the floor and leaning forward with her elbows on her knees. She paused there, breathing deep until the lightheadedness brought on by the change in position, faded away. She placed her hands on her knees and pushed out a big breath in the effort to stand, though her muscles failed to move. She tried again, this time rising part way, fully expecting to fall back on her ass. She braced for a fall that didn't come and then staggered toward the kitchen, maintaining her balance by a very thin thread. For the stability her legs lacked, she made for the wall, though it felt miles away in her present state. She covered the distance without falling over, a small miracle, then felt her way to the edge where the refrigerator stood.

Celebration of the small victory was cut short when she nearly tripped over her garbage bin. She held onto the refrigerator's handle for dear life and used it to swing herself into the kitchen. Her free hand found the knob for the kitchen's dimmer switch, turning it slowly so she didn't blind herself. She squeezed her eyes to narrow slits, knowing the light would likely bring a headache she'd still be fighting in the morning. The struggle to keep herself upright made her forget why she had come to the kitchen in the first place.

"Vodka!" The light went on in Jamie's drunken head.

Jamie froze in place with her hand on the freezer door, catching something out of the corner of her eye. She tried not to look but it was too late. She turned her head slowly. On the edge of the kitchen counter—where she'd found the heads the previous night—sat the naked torso of a woman. Staring at the perfect, perky breasts, she waited for her brain to make sense of the image. Her eyes scanned the torso slowly from top to bottom, first taking in the red, raw oval where the poor woman's head once sat. Her eyes continued down. She took note of the smooth, even cuts below the shoulder, where the arms had been removed. The still perky breasts told her the kill wasn't very old, nor was the woman. Her alcohol blurred brain saw the woman's nipples as eyes which nearly brought on another fit of laughter. She did her best to stay focused. She scanned down to the even stumps of what she imagined, had been very shapely legs that the torso rested on. Only then did she let her eyes return to the new message carved into the torso's abdomen, starting immediately beneath the breasts. The words were carved, rather than written in bold black ink, yet she could see the same hand had performed the task. Her eyes fixed on the words, unable to look away. The phrase "Madness Comes" burned themselves into her retinas, though she felt neither shock nor alarm. The carved words bore the same child-like style as her previous message and were legible from any distance. Jamie felt a twinge of empathy for the unknown woman, whose fate ended up being a grisly riddle to a stranger.

"Great!" Jamie threw up her arms in disgust. "Another fucking riddle!"

In frustration, she turned her back on the new message and grabbed her bottle from the freezer. She unscrewed the cap, letting it drop to the floor out of apathy, where it rolled noisily away and into the corner. Foregoing a glass, she lifted the bottle to her lips for one long pull. She only stopped to catch her breath, absently wiping the back of her hand across her lips before turning back to the dead girl's torso with a grimace.

"I don't know who you are, what your message means, or who left you here. But I promise you, I will find out and when I do, they'll get a message from me. Loud and clear. Nobody fucks with Jamie Windstein, not ever."

Chapter Eight: Blood-Soaked Memories

1: Sometime in the '80s

The two boys lay face down, crying into their pillows to muffle the sound from themselves, and from Head Mistress DeLong and her Goon Squad. It took every ounce of their will to suppress their screams behind the red door, however, the instant their bedroom door had closed, the pain flooded to the surface. Fat red welts, crisscrossed by gaping slashes covered their backs and oozed blood as though their skin wept along with their eyes. Some of the welts continued to swell and split apart their tender skin, while they could do nothing except lie still and weep. The pain burned like the fires of hell and fed the boys' hate of everything Mormont.

Lost in a world of his own pain, Tommy prayed for the burning agony to subside. He began to wonder if he was going to survive. Tears streamed from his eyes while he bit his pillow as every throbbing wave rippled relentlessly across his back. The worst pain he'd ever felt came from breaking his thumb a few years prior, and it paled in comparison to this. To Tommy, it felt like someone constantly pouring gasoline on a fire burning from his neck to his butt. One word reverberated in his mind and helped him through it all—escape. The intention of the beating was to drive that word from his brain. Head Mistress DeLong would be disappointed to discover it achieved the exact opposite effect. He wanted to escape from this hell now more than ever.

Tommy hadn't noticed Jimmy get up until he felt a hand on his shoulder. Instantly, the mantra playing in his head stopped. Out of fear, he recoiled from the touch, sending a tidal wave of agony up his spine before he noticed it was only Jimmy's hand.

Jimmy's calm face quelled the mighty inferno threatening to fully consume him momentarily. The world had faded away into oblivion, forgotten, until Jimmy roused him from the isolation of his own suffering. He could see the torment in Jimmy's eyes, reminding him he was not alone. The kinship he saw there, finally dampened the fire that threatened to turn him to ash.

"Grit your teeth and bear it, Tommy. They love hearing us suffer, so don't give them the satisfaction. They feed off our misery, so starve 'em, Tommy. Give those fuckers nothing."

The resolve in Jimmy's face gave Tommy strength. "I...I...I'm trying, Jimmy." He nearly choked on the words.

"Do it! I promise you, Tommy, one day we'll escape. Then...they pay. We'll make them pay for every kid they ever took to that place, for every beating. Revenge, Tommy, revenge for all of us. I promise. Replace the pain with what we'll do to them. Don't let it destroy you. Push it down and save it for the day we destroy them. Together, Tommy." Jimmy's conviction convinced Tommy it would happen one day.

The whispered words of vengeance made all the difference and the burning receded. Tommy knew he'd survive after all. Dreams of escape and revenge left no room for pain, and made him smile. The thought of one day turning the tables on DeLong and her cronies filled him with hope for a future that he didn't believe existed a few seconds before. It also lit a dark spark of desire deep inside him. His black ball of hate began to pulsate in his mind and it burned a path across the world, leaving only scorched Earth in its wake.

The image in Tommy's head showed him the truth of Jimmy's whispered words. They'd get revenge no matter how long it took them. Tommy had a vision of Head Mistress DeLong engulfed in flames and screaming while he watched her drop all the way to hell. The image brought immense joy that he hadn't believed possible only a moment ago. He felt reborn by his confidence that one day the hell he'd unleash on DeLong and her cronies would pale in comparison to what he just experienced. A wave of satisfaction washed over him at the thought of unleashing such misery on DeLong that the Devil himself would cringe and look away. Unconsciously, his smile widened over his tear streaked face.

Tommy pulled Jimmy close, staring at him with stone cold seriousness. "Together. You and me, Jimmy. Together, we'll burn every one of them to ash. I don't care how long it takes as long as DeLong suffers the most."

Jimmy stared back with a smile. "Together. We're brothers now, Tommy. Bonded in blood. We'll make them sorry they ever fucking met us!"

"Blood brothers." Tommy savored the words. "Yes! We'll make it out together. Then we'll make them sorry they didn't kills us."

"Guaranteed, brother!" Jimmy gripped Tommy's hand and sealed their pact.

Jimmy slipped back to his bed so they wouldn't get caught talking. Tommy wiped away his tears—the sting of the whip feeling a million miles away. He laid his head back down, feeling renewed and unbreakable. He no longer had a single friend, he had a brother. His mantra changed again, this time the words "Escape to Revenge" echoed their way through his skull and allowed him to drift off to sleep. He whispered the words aloud before slipping away to a dreamland filled with fire and screaming. His lips curved upward in a menacing smile.

2: Present Day

Blood covered everything—the walls, floor—not even the ceiling escaped a fresh coat of bright red crimson. Every visible surface showed a thick coating, as if a blood bank had exploded and pooled on the floor in a shimmering red lake. Natural light showcased an empty room, absent of any furniture. The walls held no paintings or pictures of some smiling family—the kind a little boy made a silly face in to ruin the moment for his mother. Nothing decorated the room aside from the bright crimson everywhere.

Suddenly, a baby appeared out of nowhere. It sat naked and silent, smack dab in the middle of the impromptu pond of blood. The baby began splashing its hands in the blood, no different than it would in crystal clear bathwater. The baby smiled away, while splashing and sending viscous fluid flying in every direction. The baby appeared clean, unlike everything else, until it continued to splash in the pool of red. Streaks of crimson rolled down the little cherub face and within seconds coated its soft skin from tiny head to cute little toes. While the scent of death slowly replaced the smell of baby shampoo and sunshine, the smile of the tiny angel turned demonic. The newborn sat there, flashing from cherub to demon, as if bathed in a horrifying strobe light that had been extracted straight out of hell. One strobe flash showed smiling newborn perfection—happiness personified—followed the next instant by a tiny demon covered in drying crimson, the smile twisting to an evil grin that masked a lust to destroy.

Jamie stood as a simple observer, unable to move or speak to whatever atrocity had taken place in the room. Watching the baby with curiosity, she stared in wide-eyed horror at the blood soaked room. She stood frozen in place, unable to do anything as the lake of blood began to rise. She struggled to make her feet move—helpless to do more than watch—as the little cherub faced child disappeared beneath the rising crimson. It continued to fill the room—reaching Jamie's knees, moving up to her waist, covering her breasts and then quickly rising over her head. The blood choked her, drowning her, until she felt nothing.

Jamie's eyes shot wide open in a flash. Now filled with light glinting off pristine walls, floor, and ceiling, she stood in the doorway. Her limbs were no longer frozen, and all traces of blood had disappeared. She tentatively stepped forward, her foot sinking into the surface and nearly tripped head first into the room. The blood was back, covering her foot to the ankle. She looked out at a sea of it where the floor was only a moment before—though it was no longer just blood. She stared, while partially submerged body parts floated along the crimson surface—an arm passed to her left, a leg to the right. She waded further out into the viscera unafraid, toward what appeared to be a pair of heads bobbing up and down in the corner of the room, one male and one female. The heads laid on their sides, half coated in red, yet she sensed something familiar about them. She tried searching her memory for an identity when something popped up to the surface with a splash in the opposite corner. It was a woman's torso with vivacious breasts, though lacking a head, arms, and legs. Jamie began to panic when the torso rolled onto its side and instead of nipples a pair of eyes stared directly at her. She waded further through the blood as it deepened every inch she went forward. Her steps began to feel like she was treading through quickly drying cement, slowing her movement to a crawl. She stopped and attempted to catch her breath when an eviscerated male torso, split almost completely in two, popped up in front of the female torso. She was happy to have the creepy breast eyes blocked from her view. Jamie remained eerily calm despite wading through waist deep blood and viscera.

Lightning struck in the middle of the room and Jamie stood in the doorway once more. The baby was back at the room's center, sitting in a shallow pool of blood with the mangled body parts gone. The child no longer smiled and its tiny hands no longer happily splashed in the dark claret. The angelic face turned, staring her straight in the eyes. She found herself overcome with a sudden motherly instinct, a foreign feeling to her. A sudden urge to rush to the child overwhelmed her. She needed to hold it tight, tell it everything would be okay. She felt a tear spill from the corner of her eye.

Jamie and the child stared at each other, locked onto each other like lovers, neither seemingly able to move. Jamie nearly stepped forward when the child raised its tiny index finger to point at her. She froze stiff. The child's eyes turned pitch black and its jaw dropped as it unleashed an ear-piercing, scream. Jamie immediately covered her ears, though it made little difference. The child's wail threatened to tear her skull in two if she stopped holding it together. She began to scream herself, as she felt a fissure rising from the base of her skull across the crown, then splitting her face in half. The baby's screech grew louder until the pain became so excruciating Jamie could do nothing but scream and scream.

Jamie's eyes exploded open to the sound of wailing. It took her a few seconds to realize it was coming from her own gaping mouth, along with the realization that the child, the blood and the room were all her nightmare. Sweat soaked her shirt, while her hands still white-knuckled the arms of her recliner, aching from the effort. She sat stiff on the verge of hyperventilating while her heart threatened to burst through her ribcage, pounding away like a jackhammer in her chest. Her mind filled with confusion until the fog slowly cleared from her brain. She was awake, no longer trapped in the nightmare world of blood and a baby's screams. She closed her eyes, trying to get herself under control while the nightmare faded out of memory.

The nightmare felt so real Jamie couldn't believe it had really just been a dream. It felt like a demented reality. She struggled to make any sense of it. Alcohol fueled dark fantasies visited her mind often but this nightmare seemed to be something else entirely. The words "twisted memory" entered her head, though her brain rejected any notion of her nightmare being some remnant of something real. That thought was simply too horrible. She shook it off. She imbibed a little too much after thinking of the horrors of Mormont all day. She told herself her brain had simply taken the ball and ran with it while she was too inebriated to stop it. Severed heads and limbless bodies were on her mind when she blacked out, nothing more. Jamie's mind wouldn't stop asking, "but what about the baby?"

"The last thing you need is another fucking mystery, Jamie Windstein. Let it go." Talking to herself in the dark, among her collection, did nothing to quell her curiosity, even though her subconscious began singing the lyrics to "Hush, Little Baby".

Jamie caught herself and slapped her cheek in the hopes it would shake off the cobwebs. *Keep your shit together*, she scolded herself. It worked until her brain finally, registered her surroundings.

She didn't remember coming down to her special room, yet here she was, nonetheless. The night was a total blur after leaving Thomas' hotel room. *Cab! I took a cab.* The thought popped in her head like a light bulb springing to life. She looked down, nearly jumping out of her chair. The woman's torso sat in front of her in all its headless, limbless glory. The latest message from her mysterious and unwanted secret admirer scrawled below the breasts. Her nightmare flashed back into her mind, reminding her why she had come down here. The words stared at her, burning themselves onto her retinas.

"*Blood Remembers*, now *Madness Comes*?" She looked around at the deaf ears assembled in her secret place. "What in the fuck does it mean?" She flung her arms down dismissively. "Fuck it! It's too early for this shit!"

Frustrated and annoyed, Jamie slid her newest gift onto the bottom shelf, below the heads she'd received the day before. She stared at the two messages, trying to find some sense in the words. She needed to come back with her camera then bag up and dispose of the messages before they left a stink in her special room that would never come out. She grabbed the empty bottle of vodka at her feet and exited her special place with a hangover headache beginning as she ascended the stairs.

The nightmare remained fresh in Jamie's mind momentarily blocking out thoughts on what the messages might mean. The nightmare clung to her mind like Velcro and refused to simply fade away, the way any other dream should have already. The fog of too many unanswered questions pounded away at her temples, fueling the start of a major hangover. She rubbed at her head, attempting feebly to will the pain away to no avail. She resolved to get some answers today even if she had to kill to get them. She smiled, knowing the damage she planned to inflict whether or not she received any answers.

She pushed the shelves back across the hidden door and pulled her phone from her pocket, expecting to find nothing except maybe a message from Carrie about meeting with Eddie. She squinted at the phone's far too bright screen to see the time. Only six in the morning—far too early. The pleasant thought of letting her head hit the pillow for another hour immediately jettisoned from her mind. She had one message and it wasn't from Carrie. Who the hell messaged me in the middle of the damn night? Anger crept in seeing *Unknown Number* attached to the message. *This better be a wrong number,* she thought. Her heart sank once she opened it.

"You've been a naughty girl, Jamie Windstein. See you soon." A photo of the room she had just exited accompanied the message.

3

Kirk Scheidt clocked in fifteen minutes early for work, too bored to wait in his car any longer, and too excited to get the day started. Aside from his normal daily torments, today he had the task of making sure his favorite patient behaved with her special visitor. He was more anxious than a ten-year-old expecting a new bike on his birthday. His shiny new bicycle with a big red bow on it would be coming in the form of a very attractive woman—or so he had been informed—full of questions. He was also told she had no love for his favorite patient and may do some tormenting of her own.

Kirk's assignment was to watch, listen, and then report—especially if the nasty old bitch decided to spill anything she had been warned not to. He had an extra bounce in his step and a big, dumb smile plastered all across his face. His joy nearly disappeared when he whacked his head on the door casing of the employee breakroom for the millionth time. He was used to it, being six foot seven inches tall, so his smile had returned to full force by the time he tossed his lunch box into the employee refrigerator.

"Someone get lucky last night, big guy?" Nancy mocked his goofy smile.

He knew none of his co-workers liked him, yet they also feared him, which generally held their tongues in check. "Actually yes, by the way. Your mom says hello, Nancy." Kirk responded, a bit sarcastic and annoyed.

"Hope you had fun digging her up, dumbass."

"Funny, she was still warmer than you." He didn't wait for her shocked reaction as he exited the breakroom, careful not to bang his head and ruin his zinger.

Kirk wasn't about to let a bitch like Nancy ruin his good mood. Not this morning. He marched down the hall, his smile widening as he heard her complain loudly to some of their other coworkers. He never sought their acceptance, even though it never seemed to stop them from asking for his help every five minutes. If they didn't like his attitude, he mused, they could break their backs moving the heavier residents around today. He endured their nastiness in order to have access to his favorite patient, whose time was nearly up.

The imminent demise of Eva DeLong only served to brighten Kirk's smile further. He made it his mission in life to make her every waking second pure misery, even though he hadn't actually expected to enjoy it so much. He wanted her to have nightmares about him, knowing they likely paled in comparison to the ones he suffered in the aftermath of the broom closet. His biggest fear once he'd taken this job, was that his nightmares would return with a vengeance and so he'd been pleasantly surprised to find it had the opposite effect. He had never slept better in his entire life than since taking on the care of his nemesis, the source of his worst nightmares. He did feel a twinge of remorse for today possibly being her last at Lake View Manor Nursing Home—he had come to enjoy tormenting her more than he ever expected. Any remorse he felt was tempered with the happiness he'd feel telling his coworkers to go fuck themselves when he quit. He saw no downside for him so he wanted to enjoy every last minute.

Kirk couldn't help humming happily to himself as he rounded the final corner on his way to DeLong's room. He was determined to stay upbeat, regardless of the hate DeLong would no doubt spew at him or anything his coworkers said or did. He barely slept in anticipation of what this day could bring and then arrived over an hour early, anxious to get the day started. He wanted to give his favorite patient an absolutely horrible day, a day he hoped would be his last. He also found himself excited and curious to see this Jamie Windstein he'd been told about. He had been told she was a demoness wrapped in an angel suit—a description he yearned to see for himself. Seeing an attractive woman was certainly a welcomed change from the wrinkled up elderly that surrounded him every day. The anticipation of meeting Jamie contributed to his good mood as much as the thought of his mortal enemy's demise.

"Top o' the morning, Ms. DeLong! And how is my most favoritest resident in the whole wide world today?" He loved seeing her grimace at his loud, overly cheerful morning greetings.

Former Head Mistress Eva DeLong didn't turn to curse him or give him a nasty look today like she normally did. Panic shot through him like a bolt of lightning at the thought of the old bitch dying in her sleep. His grin disappeared, along with the happy tune he'd been humming. He rushed to her bedside while the color drained from his face and turned him pale as a ghost. He shook her foot, trying to rouse her but she didn't stir. Grabbing her wrist, he checked for a pulse. The sudden burst of adrenaline sent panic coursing through his veins, making it difficult to feel anything but his own skittering pulse. Fear forced beads of sweat from his forehead while time seemed to stand still. He was desperate to feel the familiar thump against his fingers, telling him she still was still among living. Eva DeLong passing peacefully in her sleep would be a miscarriage of justice of the highest order. Dread immediately filled Kirk. How would he break the news to his friends? She wasn't supposed to die at peace. Every second that passed without feeling a pulse, his panic rose even though it was possible he was gripping her wrist too tight in his frenzied state.

Suddenly, DeLong rolled over laughing. "Hahaha! Think I was dead, dumbass?"

Kirk nearly fell over at the shock. "Why you sly old cunt. You got me!" He shook his head in disbelief. "Soon, we'll see who has the last laugh. I'm only here to make sure you suffer all the way to hell and you best remember that. It can get worse." He kept his voice low so only she could hear him.

"Fuck you, nigger! Now get me in my chair! Or does the big baby need a diaper change?" She knew she'd end up regretting the prank, though the smile of satisfaction on her lips didn't show it.

Kirk leaned in closer. "Best get your fun in now, you shriveled up old cunt. Once your visit is over, you have no use left. So behave, or you can sit in that fucking chair all day with a broken hip. Your call, Head Mistress, I'd be happy to do it." He didn't wait for her response. He picked her up like a sack of potatoes and slammed her down into her wheelchair hard.

"I still remember you crying like a little girl and soiling yourself. You may be bigger now but we both know you're still a fucking pussy." She hissed the words through clenched teeth while her eyes welled up from the pain.

The sound of footsteps in the hall prevented Kirk from continuing their nasty banter. "Yes, ma'am! My favoritest patient needs to keep her strength up with a good healthy breakfast. Nothing but sunshine and roses for my beautiful lady!" Kirk leaned down to whisper. "I'll shit on your grave every damn day. You can count on it. I hope you die slowly." Kirk pushed DeLong down to the dining hall with a big, dumb smile back on this face.

4

Edward Washington laid awake and enjoyed the warmth of his lovely wife asleep on his chest, still feeling euphoric from their after-dinner celebration. A satisfied smile covered his face while he waited for the alarm to go off. He couldn't sleep, too eager to start his first full day as Detective Edward Washington. Soon to be detective—as long as he didn't screw up. It still felt like a dream to him. Most waited decades for a chance at working homicide and here Barker had leap frogged him straight to the front of the line. It was his dream job, though it hadn't fully sunk in yet.

Eddie felt it deep in his marrow that he was going to have a wonderful day. The aroma of coffee wafted into the bedroom while the first few rays of morning filtered through the curtain and created a halo around his lovely wife's head. His very own angel.

The sun made Carrie's blonde locks shimmer like pure gold, transforming her into a sleeping goddess. He cherished these little moments, given the dangers inherit to his chosen profession, though he never told her. It would only make her worry to know he took mental photos of her in case one day he didn't make it home. These moments were his alone, stored away in a tiny lockbox in his brain, where the ugliness he dealt with on a daily basis couldn't touch them. Few took the time to appreciate the little things, the precious moments you only get once, the ones that make life worth living. Eddie knew without these beautiful moments, no matter how small, the world was just a cold ugly place. Police only see the ugly bits of humanity most of the time, which can make the most positive soul jaded. He held onto moments like this to remind himself that, at the end of the day, he was still a human being.

All good things come to an end, this time harshly when the alarm erupted into its annoying buzz. Eddie's angel roused from her peaceful slumber, removing her warmth in the process. His precious moments never seemed to last long enough. Alas time marches in but one direction, he thought, ever forward. His moment vanished completely when Carrie, still half asleep, reached to end the annoying buzz. She couldn't quite reach it so she slapped away like a drunkard until finally smacking the right spot after several attempts and bringing silence back to the room. However, Eddie's special moment was gone forever.

"Why does morning come so early?"

"Because God hates us and if it came any later it'd be afternoon and we'd hate that time of day instead." He laughed, brushing the hair out of her face.

"It's too early for jokes." She half-heartedly smacked at him. "Coffee first, then jokes…maybe."

"As you wish." He mimicked a line from her favorite movie, *The Princess Bride*, leaning down to kiss her forehead. "I could do better than coffee for a wake up."

"Mmm, I thought I wore you out last night, but keep talking, mister. We can both be late for work." She looked up at her husband with a sly, sexy smile.

"Isn't that your boss' job?"

"What? Being late? Or have my husband's thoughts strayed from his beautiful Princess Bride?" Carrie shot him a sarcastic disapproving look.

"Weeellllll."

Carrie smacked him.

"Ow! I meant late, jeez!" He winked at her rubbing his arm.

"Watch it, Officer Washington, or I'll give your new partner a different homicide to investigate!"

"Threatening an officer is a crime, Mrs. Washington. I'm afraid I'm gonna have to frisk you for any concealed weapons."

"Aren't you all full of piss and vinegar this morning? Get your butt in the shower and maybe I'll come frisk you if you're lucky."

"As you wish." Eddie winked, jumping up to run into the bathroom.

Carrie laid her head back on her pillow with a smile, believing no one in the world could possibly be as happy or lucky as she was. She felt blessed for the years they'd shared together. They seemed to grow closer with every passing year, while everyone else they knew seemed to grow apart. She knew a relationship like theirs was rare and wonderful. The thought made her think of her boss and best friend, Jamie Windstein. Carrie couldn't imagine her life without Eddie, whereas a two-week relationship would set a record for Jamie. She wished everyone could know happiness like she did, especially her best friend. The thought lingered until her phone vibrated unexpectedly.

Carrie jumped in surprise. No one ever called her this early, yet the bigger shock was the name showing on her phone's screen. "What in the hell are you doing up this early, Ms. Windstein? Don't tell me you were up all night again." Carrie realized how much she sounded like her mother and frowned.

"Well, good morning to you too! I slept, I promise. Don't get all bitchy with me—it's too early in the morning for that, girlfriend!"

"Fine. Good morning then. Actually you must have ESP because I was just thinking about you. So what's the special occasion?"

"Oh, well I hope I didn't interrupt you inappropriately touching yourself!" Jamie laughed then got down to business. "Two questions for you. One, do I have any appointments today? And two, when is Eddie coming into talk to me?"

"Pervert! And it's yes to the first question. Al…something—I forget the last name—is scheduled for nine thirty. As for the second, I told Eddie to stop in about ten thirty, right after the first appointment, but he'll be in closer to ten. Why?"

"Shit! Okay, I'll be there. I…um…I'm just anxious to talk to those three you tracked down for me yesterday, that's all."

"Want me to pick you up anything on my way in?"

"Thanks, sweets. No. I'll probably beat you in, so same question back at ya."

"Ooh, dinner and breakfast on the boss! I am a lucky girl! I'll take a large double and a blueberry muffin."

"Double cream, double sugar, got it. You and your damn sugar," Jamie laughed. "You sure you don't want a triple?"

"Damn if you didn't just read my mind!"

"K, see you soon."

"Thanks, sug…" Carrie stopped, the line went dead as Jamie hung up the way she always did.

Eddie exited the bathroom a few minutes later, freshly showered, shaved and wearing one of the few suits he owned, proudly sporting one of his Batman ties. He wanted to see how long it would take Carrie to notice and explode.

"I don't think so, mister!" She caught it instantly. "My husband will not look like an overgrown five-year-old his first official day on the job!"

Eddie doubled over laughing. "It's your fault. You didn't come supervise so I had to do it all by myself." He winked. "Who called so early?"

"You don't miss a thing…except taste in neckwear," she threw in sarcastically. "It was just Jamie checking the morning schedule. She wanted to know if you were stopping in. She sounded off, but then she's never up this early. It's probably nothing. She's anxious about this new case. I guess the client has super deep pockets so I think she's nervous. Either that or she slept with him last night. Who knows? She's picking me up Timmy Ho's, so I don't care."

"Dinner and breakfast? You sure she isn't sick?" Eddie laughed.

"Ha! I said the same thing! I dunno, she sounded odd. Like something got under her skin, y'know? She can be a grouch but never just off. I don't know how to explain it. Probably nothing."

"Well, you'll drag whatever it is out of her soon enough. Now, would my lovely wife like to pick out a more appropriate tie—something more professional, or should I stick with the mentally challenged child look?"

"I should make you keep the mentally challenged look just to be a jerk!"

"Okay, I'll see you in a couple hours then." Eddie made a move toward the door.

"You freeze right there, jackass." She ran to the closet and returned with a normal tie. "Here." She handed him the tie. "Now throw that damn thing away!"

"Sacrilege!" Eddie feigned offense.

"Fine. You can use it to hang yourself when your incredibly beautiful wife leaves you! About all it's good for."

Eddie changed his tie. "Happy now?"

"I'm always happy with you, baby." She kissed her husband goodbye.

"Well, now we're both happy. I'll see you in a couple hours, sugar."

"Not if I see you first!"

Carrie always felt a twinge of sadness when she watched him leave. She did her best not to think about it, but he was a police officer. Every goodbye had the potential to be last goodbye. She made it a point, since he joined the force, to always send him out the door happy, knowing she loved him. You just never knew.

Carrie did her best to shake the feeling away. It may have been reality, but she didn't have to dwell on it. She headed to the bathroom to get ready for her own day, still baffled by Jamie calling. It wasn't like her friend to be awake this early, nor to check her schedule, regardless of the reason she gave for doing so. Jamie never cared if a client waited forever, or even walked out. "So be it!" she would say. Carrie made a mental note—as if she'd forget—to grill her boss when she got in. Jamie Windstein was never "off" and it nagged at her mind like an itch she couldn't reach.

5

Jamie dried her hair quickly with a towel and checked to see if she had any clothes that were actually clean. She sent up a silent prayer hoping to at least find a single pair of clean jeans hanging in her closet. To her surprise she found some, along with three clean shirts. It must be her lucky day! She smiled slyly, thinking whether today was her lucky day or not. Not everyone would feel very lucky once she crossed their path.

Jamie hoped her new client, Al—whatever his name was—didn't drone on forever with his sob story. She never relished pretending to give a shit about her clients. She had become a master of faux sympathy over the years, though it never ceased to get on her last nerve. The best case scenario to her was for him to get to the point quickly, tell her who he needed pictures of and then get the fuck out. She wanted—no—needed him to be quick and easy. If today turned out to truly be her lucky day, then Eddie would be quick too. She desperately wanted to get on with the business of finding Jimmy Reimse. The fact that it might result in a few intense interrogations made her all the more eager.

Jamie dressed quickly, impatient to get on with her day. Before rushing out the door, she decided to check her dirty pants' pockets in case she forgot anything in her drunken stupor. She reached in and pulled out a book of matches with the Adam's Mark logo on them and a folded up twenty-dollar bill. She smacked herself in the forehead. "Leon!" She realized she nearly forgot about him again.

Nearly everyone in the neighborhood treated Leon like shit because he was a simpleton. The bastards rarely paid him, even though he kept their lawns manicured better than most professional landscaping outfits. Leon worked hard every day, did a great job and asked for nothing in return. It pissed Jamie off to no end that her piece of shit neighbors took advantage of the man simply because he wasn't very smart and too nice to bill for the services he provided. The poor man covered a ten or fifteen block radius, never asking for a glass of water—let alone payment—yet they all turned their noses up at him. It made her so angry she wished she could douse the entire area in gasoline and then drop a fucking match just to watch it burn.

City of Good Neighbors, my fucking ass, Jamie thought. She hated how the city's nickname got hauled out on the one or two occasions a year it actually applied. She saw the dirty underbelly of Buffalo. She saw the people walking by the homeless turning up their noses unable to be bothered to give them some change or buy them a sandwich—the same way it happened in any other city on the planet. Meanwhile those same people patted themselves on the back as "good neighbors" because once a year during a big snow storm some strangers share some fucking hot cocoa or something. She found it pathetic. Buffalonians were no better than people in any other damn city. All people held the same basic principle no matter where you happened to be born. It was a simple principle, "I'll help, but what's in it for me?" Jamie didn't think anyone needed to look very hard to see that people equaled shit—period. She didn't care if people called her a cynical bitch for thinking that way. She considered it a truth everyone knows, yet refuses to say out loud.

Jamie let her internal rant drop as she rushed down the stairs not bothering to grab her customary morning vodka coffee. She needed a clear head today, especially after her weird nightmare and latest message, though thankfully, her hangover headache had mostly subsided. She admitted the one good thing about being a heavy drinker was that the after effects faded quickly. She paused, her hand on the doorknob to the garage entrance, staring at the counter where her "gifts" kept appearing. The messages had her at a loss, who was messing with her and why? Obviously, they didn't want the police involved so what in the hell did they want? She tried to push the thought out of mind. The answer would reveal itself eventually, so she saw no point worrying about it. However, she hoped her secret admirer would take the night off. It was going to be a long enough day without having another mystery to deal with once she returned home.

When Jamie finally exited, she decided not to bother locking up. It didn't really seem to make much difference. She should be mad, yet she found herself impressed. Whoever her secret admirer turned out to be—and she would find out—they were quite intelligent. Not only had they found her secret room, they'd also bypassed her security. She wished for a second that she had installed cameras, though her reason for not doing so remained. Photographic or video evidence was never a good thing, especially when performing criminal acts. She desperately tried to shrug it all off as she grabbed the garbage bag containing her gifts to dispose of elsewhere. She tossed the bag in the trunk then pulled out, hoping it didn't take her too long to find Leon.

Jamie hadn't driven far before spotting the man trimming the hedges in front of an older home a few blocks away. He had only begun, yet it already looked better than the surrounding yards. She parked at the curb getting out behind him, since he was too involved in his work to notice her. Leon loved his job whether anyone else noticed. Although they'd damn sure notice if he stopped one day. *They'd be sorry when they had to tend to their own damn yards or hire a service*, she thought. Then they'd piss and moan about Leon not doing it for free. She walked around the hedge Leon was trimming and waved her arms to get his attention while, trying not to frighten him. Luckily, he noticed her almost instantly and shut off the trimmer.

"Hey, Leon!" She greeted him with a friendly smile. "I'm so sorry I forgot to pay you like I promised. I was a little preoccupied, please forgive me."

"Oh, Miss Jamie, you far too kind to ol' Leon. You know you doesn't have to pay me nuthin." Leon gave her a big toothy grin with his trucker cap crooked on his head.

"You deserve ten times that for all you do, Leon." She handed him the folded up twenty. "Thank you. You deserve to hear that more often, too! Can I get you anything? Do you need some new overalls or maybe a new hat?" Regardless of his answer she'd find something for him when she had the time.

"You done enough, Miss Jamie. Leon has his PB & J and sunshine. Leon don't need nuthin' else, Miss Jamie. If yous could make it rain to keep these lawns a'growin' I sure would 'preciate that!"

"I'll do my best, big guy." She looked up at him, squinting her eyes at the sun that was creating a halo around him. "You enjoy the sun today, but don't you work too hard, Leon. These people don't deserve you."

"P'haps not, Miss Jamie, but the grass sho' like ol' Leon. That good enough for Leon!" He beamed with pride.

"I'll leave you to it then. You need anything at all you know where I live. Have great day, Leon." She waved goodbye starting toward her car.

"Leon know where e'eryone lives, Miss Jamie." Leon turned back to his work as she walked away.

She froze with his words immediately hitting home. Leon was always in the neighborhood, dawn to dusk every day. She turned back to him waving to get his attention again.

"Yessum, Miss Jamie?" He looked at her with curiosity.

"Leon, have you noticed anyone strange in the neighborhood? Anyone who doesn't belong? Maybe creeping around or peeking in windows, anything like that?" She wasn't sure Leon was observant enough to notice but it was worth a shot.

"I sees a mangy old black cat creeping 'roun' sometimes. No peoples though. I keep my eyes peeled for Miss Jamie. Leon be like Shirley Homes for you, Miss Jamie!" Leon threw up his hand in a salute so hard Jamie thought he might knock himself out.

"Thank you, Leon." She tried not to laugh at his awkward salute, coughing quickly so she wouldn't. "Now you're a real private investigator like me! Just keep your eyes open for any strangers, okay?"

"Invinctigator, Leon is on the case, Miss Jamie!"

Jamie couldn't help thinking of the old Benny Hill shows she watched as a child with her grandfather. Leon looked just like one of characters Hill had played on the British sketch comedy show, with his awkward salute. The only thing missing was the goofy smile Hill always had on his face when he did it. She couldn't stop a giggle escaping her lips.

She smiled and returned his salute. "If you see anything, just leave a note in my mailbox, okay, Invinctigator Leon?"

"You gots it, Miss Jamie!"

Jamie smiled all the way to her car, feeling better than the day Thomas Combs walked into her office. *What a couple of days it's been,* she mused. Two big mysteries—the missing Jimmy Reimse, and who the hell was breaking into her house to leave riddles on dead body parts? Her smile turned devious as she thought about extracting answers with pliers and a blow torch.

Jamie waved again at Leon and pulled away, while in the rearview mirror she watched him return to his hedge trimming.

Suddenly, with Leon shrinking out of sight behind her, pieces of the nightmare returned. The image of the baby sitting in a pool of blood, pointing at her and staring with those black eyes flashed in her mind. She had never really believed that dreams meant anything—Freud had been a drug addicted hack, as far as she could tell—but she did have to admit that this nightmare felt different. She knew it was impossible, but it felt more like a memory than a terrible dream. It baffled her. If it recurred perhaps she'd consider trying to decipher it, but for now she needed to focus her mind on other things.

Chapter Nine: Something's Off

1

Emily Bresson sat sipping her morning tea in her favorite chair with her fat orange tabby purring in her lap. She divided her attention between the hustle and bustle outside the window, and her early morning programs—which she used to tell the time more than the clock on the wall. When a familiar car pulled up in front of her house, she knew it wasn't quite eight in the morning yet, because *Good Morning America* hadn't started. This was the second one to arrive at her neighbor's house since yesterday. She wasn't surprised when the younger of the two men—the more handsome one—got out, looking first to her neighbor's empty house, then back at hers. Emily stayed seated until the bell sounded so she could make a big production out of answering the door.

"Hang on a minute!" She did her best impression of shock and annoyance—as if she hadn't seen her young caller from the moment he'd pulled up in front of her house.

Emily set her plump old cat down on the floor, much to his irritation though. In general, cats are easily irritated by nothing. She stood up from her reclining chair with a stretch, making her joints sound off like gunfire in protest. She loudly moaned and groaned her way to the door, attempting to garner maximum sympathy from her early morning caller. When she wanted to see what was going on outside, she was as spry as her old cat, yet when it came to her own door, she shuffled slower than someone twenty years her elder. She decide to play it up further, throwing a few loud sighs in to accompany her groans. This was her show and she planned to give it her all.

Finally, Emily turned the deadbolt and opened the door as far as the security chain would allow. "Can I help you?"

"Emily Bresson?"

"Yes, that's me." She did her best to sound aggravated and ignorant. "Who are you and what do you want?"

Eddie continued, unfettered. "Ma'am, I'm Officer Washington, Buffalo Police. I need to ask you a few questions about your neighbors, if I may." Cop mode engaged, Eddie did his best to be polite yet direct.

Emily feigned surprise. "Oh my, yes, certainly. Would you like to come in? I was just about to make another cup of tea." She quickly pushed the door closed enough to slide the chain off and then opened it wide, not waiting for Eddie to respond. "Come in, come in."

Eddie thanked her and stepped across the threshold. He knew ladies like Emily Bresson well—pegging her for a drama queen even before he'd pressed the doorbell. He suspected everyone had that one busybody who kept tabs on all their neighbors. The kind who only missed something when they were too busy exchanging gossip with other busybodies. Emily Bresson was not unique, merely one of millions of professional people watchers and gossipers peeking out windows all over the world. He followed her to the kitchen, knowing full well that she wouldn't take no for an answer on the offer of tea. He also knew she'd make a big production of it—ladies like her made a big production of everything. Men weren't any better, he thought, especially older men who enjoyed gossiping more than the old ladies though they'd never *call* it gossip.

A moment later she handed him a steaming cup of tea. "Cream or sugar? Please, sit."

"Touch of cream, if it's no bother, please."

"No bother at all, dear. My pleasure to assist Buffalo's finest any way I can." She smiled at him looking like the world's friendliest grandmother.

"I appreciate it, ma'am."

"Please. I'm not that old! Call me, Emily."

"Okay, Emily. Could you tell me the last time you remember seeing your next door neighbors, Karen and David Osbourne?" Eddie sat with his pen and notebook at the ready.

"Just the other night—I guess that would have been Saturday night—I noticed they left together about the time the evening news started, so about six. I'm no nosy neighbor, mind you. The window across from my chair faces their driveway, that's all. So I really can't help seeing them come and go, you see. I'm usually sitting there with Tigger, my baby, in my lap." She reached down to scratch her orange tabby's head while he rubbed against her leg.

"It's alright, Emily. Tigger is a lovely cat." He smiled politely. "Right now, we're simply trying to establish a timeline so we can figure out exactly when they might have gone missing."

"Of course. Well, given the time of day, I assumed they were heading for one of their usual Saturday nights out. Date night, the kids call it these days."

"Most do! In fact, my wife and I went on one last night."

"Ooh! Lucky lady! My husband, Dexter—God rest his soul—was never what you would call romantic, so our date night usually involved me driving him home from Clancy's after he was three sheets to the wind, if you get my meaning." She smiled, reminiscing. "Oh, my Dexter did love to tip 'em back. Lord bless him."

"I'm sorry, Ms. Bresson. I didn't realize you were a widow." He looked down, before gently nudging her back on topic. "Now, if we could get back to the Osbornes."

"Yes, thank you. Anywho…most Saturday's Karen and David had their date night. She told me they usually went out for dinner then to a movie, unless they were invited somewhere, y'know? They were such a lovely couple. It isn't like them to just up and disappear. That's why I reported it so quick. It's just so odd."

"We thank you for that. So…they left about six," he prompted. "Did you see when they arrived back home, or was it after you retired for the evening?"

"No, it was still early or early-ish. They weren't ones to stay out late very often, not that I ever noticed anyway. I'd say they pulled in between ten and ten thirty. The X Files was still on, so it had to be before the eleven o'clock news. I saw David's car pull into the garage and that was it. That's the last time I saw them. I don't understand what could have happened." She gripped a tissue in her fist.

"So they arrived home between ten and eleven. You never saw or heard anything in the middle of the night?"

"No. Nothing. When I noticed neither of them left for work Monday morning I got worried. I tried calling

Karen, but there was no answer," she said, dabbing at her eyes with the tissue, genuinely upset. "I called the police because I was worried. I just know something bad happened."

"It's alright, Emily. We aren't sure what happened yet. It's still just a missing persons case." He knew better than to give her much information—half the city would already hear of his visit the second he walked out the door.

"But I saw you and that little man, the short one who looks like Columbo. I saw you block off the house with the yellow tape. I'm sorry. I assumed you found something bad." She looked at him with puppy dog eyes, hoping he'd divulge some information.

"Unfortunately, what we didn't find was Karen or David Osbourne. We know they haven't been to work and that it seems you may have been the last one to see them. Did you happen to see any suspicious movement inside or outside their house? Even if you thought it was nothing at the time. Maybe something out of the corner of your eye? A strange vehicle in the neighborhood— anything at all?"

Emily thought about it for a moment. "I would have noticed a strange car for sure, so that's a no. I didn't even notice them turning on a light that night. I just thought—you know—young couple home after a date…they were doing what young couples do." Emily blushed at the tawdry admission.

"I understand. So you didn't notice anything out of the ordinary at all until they didn't leave for work Monday morning?"

"No, nothing at all."

"What time did they normally leave for work?"

"Well, Karen worked at the bank, so she usually left between eight and eight thirty—and David worked in some office in the north towns, so he left a little before her. You know how bad traffic can be in the morning."

"Don't we all?" He smiled at her. "Well I think that's about all the questions I have, Emily. Thank you so much for all your help and acting so quickly in calling us. And for the tea, of course."

"I think we all have a duty to keep an eye on each other these days, don't you? It seems every time I turn on the TV there's been some murder or some whacko shooting up a school or church or something. If we don't look out for each other, who will? No offense to the police, of course, but you can't put a patrol car in everyone's driveway."

"You certainly are correct there. People need to look out for one another. I can tell you as a police officer, that it doesn't happen nearly often enough. Now, here's my partner, Detective Barker's card. If you think of anything else, give him a call, okay?"

"Why can't I call you? You're such a nice young man. No offense but your partner looked a little, well…not very sociable?"

"I'll admit Detective Barker is a bit rough around the edges but trust me, he's one of the absolute best. You can certainly ask for me—Officer Washington—but I just transferred, so I don't have my own number or cards yet," He smiled apologetically. "I'm sorry."

"Well if I think of anything or see anything I'll definitely call you. I do hope you find them, they were such a pleasant young couple. Has anyone contacted their families yet?" She couldn't resist trying to get every last drop of information she could.

"Another officer will be speaking to them today, along with any friends and coworkers we can. You have a great day, Emily. Call if you think of anything, no matter how minor you think it may seem, okay?"

"Will do, Officer Washington. Good luck and you stay safe out there!"

"My wife insists on it, ma'am."

Eddie walked back to his vehicle, knowing little old Emily Bresson probably never sprinted to her phone so quickly in her entire life. He had to admit she was friendly enough, and the thought of her running to her phone made him chuckle. Once back in his car he pulled his cell out to inform Barker of what he had learned. He was anxious about making the call, since he really had nothing new to report. Barker wasn't exactly friendly on his best day, but he didn't have much of a choice. He punched in the number.

"Yeah." Barker sounded annoyed, per usual.

"It's Eddie. I just interviewed the neighbor, Emily Bresson. She didn't see anything strange—no strangers, no out of place vehicle. She saw the Osbournes leave for their usual Saturday date night about six, and then she says they returned home between ten and eleven. She never saw them again. When she noticed neither went to work on Monday morning she attempted to call the wife, Karen. When she got no answer she called us. That's it."

"About what we figured. Did you set up a meet with that Windstein, PI?" Barker never wasted time on pleasantries.

"Meeting with her this morning. I was about to start heading that way. Doubtful I'll get more out of any of the other neighbors."

"Probably right, but check anyway. I'm heading over to meet with Ketchum, see if he has anything on the mattress yet. Call me after you're done with Windstein, and we'll see what's next."

Eddie started to respond, then stopped when he heard the click of Barker hanging up. He shook his head, checking his watch to see if he had enough time to interview a few neighbors before heading to Jamie's office. He did, and so he moved his car up to the Osbourne's driveway to be out of the way and block it off. It wasn't likely he'd learn anything more, but sometimes you got lucky and some teenager sneaking in late saw something without realizing it. He knew most cases broke on some small, seemingly insignificant, fragment of information that was initially thought unimportant. Catching a murderer, especially a serial killer, was like winning the lottery—sometimes you needed to simply get lucky.

2

A morning when Jamie Windstein entered her office first was beyond rare. She couldn't think of a single occurrence since the day she hired Carrie to be her secretary. It took her a few minutes to even remember where the light switches were. She set the large cup of coffee and the blueberry muffin on the counter for Carrie, and then took her own extra-large coffee into her office. Before her new client came in, she planned on killing a couple hours, plotting out her day and possibly some research on the kids' names in the files she found. If it was truly her lucky day, maybe one or more of them lived near the three scumbags she expected to visit.

Looking at the list Carrie had given her, the closest to the office was DeLong's former goon, Anthony Rollins, at about a fifteen minute drive away. She planned to make him her first stop after Eddie left. DeLong's nursing home sat only slightly further away, but sneaking in a visit could depend on visiting restrictions. Lastly, DeLong's head goon—Robert Keane—lived a solid hour away, making him unlikely to have the pleasure of her company today.

Jamie wanted answers badly, and yet she also wanted DeLong and her Goon Squad to be difficult. She didn't need any excuse to inflict a little grievous bodily harm on these child-abusing scumbags, though she'd use it if necessary. To vent her frustration, doling out some pain might be just what the doctor ordered.

DeLong immediately sprang to her mind. If that wrinkled up old cunt was now an invalid and lying in a damn nursing home she might snap. She wanted blood from that bitch badly after seeing the secret room and hearing Thomas' story. She hadn't added anything of her own to her special collection in over a week, giving her a deadly itch she needed to scratch in the worst way.

Jamie pushed her dark thoughts to the back of her mind by plugging the three addresses into her GPS. It worked for a temporary distraction. She pulled the files from her satchel, ready to get to work when she heard Carrie enter the office.

A shit eating grin smeared itself across her face, overwhelmed by the urge to rib her best friend on such a rare occasion. "Missus Washington! I think we need to talk about your blatant tardiness. I trust you have a good reason for being sooo late? Dog steal your keys? Car break down so you had to walk the last ten blocks?" She barked like a drill sergeant on the first day of boot camp, though she found it difficult not to burst out laughing. "Well, out with it or out with you!"

"I'll have you know I'm—" Carrie glanced at the clock. "—twenty damn minutes early, and the bitch I work for is lucky I come in at all with the way she treats me! Slave! I'm just a slave, I tells ya! Massa Jamie, cans I pleeeaaaasssseee use the bathroom? I's promise I's be good, Massa Jamie. Cans I please take off these chains?" Carrie batted her eyelashes at Jamie and they both lost it bursting into hysterical laughter.

Once she regained a modicum of her composure, Jamie tried to start in again. "Looks like the raise I was going to give you just went bye-bye! Where's my whip at, so I can get you to actually do some work around here? And you can wait 'til your break to use the lady's or I'm docking your pay!" A fresh round of laughter ensued.

"Guess I'll just pittle at my desk then, and when we can't get any clients because of the smell in here, maybe—just maybe—you'll think about being a little nicer to me!"

"Don't bet on it, bitch!"

The two went back and forth longer than they should, but they still had plenty of time to kill, and it made them laugh. Nothing makes time fly by faster than some good gut busting laughter.

Once they calmed down, Carrie went about getting herself set for the day, and Jamie dove into the files stacked in front of her, still hoping they weren't completely useless.

Carrie sat at the front desk for several minutes, thinking about her best friend a few feet away. She still had the feeling something was off about Jamie, but she debated whether or not to pry. She knew Jamie drank far too much, and was prone to depression, yet it seemed like something else. She knew Jamie was more protective of her privacy than even her clients were, but something still nagged at her mind. It took Carrie a few more minutes to work up the courage to broach the subject, knowing Jamie would likely clam up or get irritated. Finally, she was ready to approach her best friend.

"What's up, girlfriend?" Jamie smiled, still in a good mood for the moment.

"Well first, thank you for dinner last night. Eddie didn't even bitch about it, if you can imagine that. But..." Carrie began tentatively.

"You're very welcome. But what?"

"Well, Jams, can I be serious with you for a minute?"

"Oh, this can't be good." Jamie shot her friend a curious look. "But, go ahead."

"Well you seem…um, what I mean to say is…you've seemed troubled lately, and I know it has to be more than just this Combs case. It feels like there's something else eating away at you." Carrie felt like she was in the principal's office in elementary school after misbehaving. "I'd like to help, if I can. You know I love your bitchy ass."

Jamie sat silent a moment, unsure of what to say. She couldn't tell Carrie about her gruesome gifts with their odd riddles. She couldn't tell her about the text message she received with the attached picture of her secret trophy room. She couldn't tell her that the decapitated body Eddie found, leading to his promotion, was one of her many victims. She couldn't tell Carrie the possible consequences if Eddie somehow figured it all out and came knocking on her door one day. On top of all that— the Combs case was no closer to being solved. *So what's troubling me, Carrie, my only friend? My world is imploding, leaving me nowhere to fucking hide!*

"You shouldn't worry about me." Jamie saw only one way out of this interrogation. "You're right, it's not the Combs case and yet it is. Yesterday I paid a visit to the abandoned building which used to be The Mormont Home For Children—the orphanage where Thomas met the person he hired me to find. You saw those files I brought in?"

Carrie nodded.

"You know how much I despise anyone who abuses children, right?"

Again Carrie nodded.

"While I was looking around, I found a secret room I wish I hadn't seen. I can only imagine what actually went on in there. I asked Mr. Combs about it, but I know he held back. A place like that exists for only one purpose, and all completely unseen and unheard. The files I brought back were in there. I'm still trying to figure out why. I haven't found anything useful in them yet." Jamie hoped this story would satisfy her best friend, because, technically she wasn't lying.

Carrie stood in awe, her imagination running wild with the horror she imagined was committed in a place like that. "Oh my God, Jamie! That's…that's just awful. I'll never understand how people can be so cruel, especially to children. You don't think they…" Carrie put her hand over her mouth, unable to say her dark thought out loud.

"I didn't see any evidence of sexual abuse and I didn't have the heart to ask Thomas directly. He didn't even hint at it, so perhaps it was simply their little torture chamber. Unfortunately, I can't see why it wouldn't occur there when it seems to happen everywhere else. Horrible physical abuse definitely took place and where there's one—there's usually the other. Knowing about the abuse, while important, doesn't really get me any closer to finding Thomas' friend, Jimmy." Jamie could see revealing the abuse and the secret room would likely quell any further inquiry from her friend.

"I just don't understand how people can do things like to children. No punishment is too severe for scum who hurt kids. I hope they all died of ass cancer or worse!"

Jamie smiled in agreement, thinking of all the things she'd do to make their punishment worse than any cancer. "Unfortunately—er, fortunately?—some of the culprits are alive and well. Those three I gave you to search for me?"

Carrie nodded.

"Those three are the scum we're talking about. The Head Mistress, Eva DeLong, who ran the place, and then her two main thugs. Thomas told me the kids called them The Goon Squad. They'll be getting a visit from yours truly once I'm done with this new client and then, Eddie, of course."

"Good. I wish you could pull out their fingernails, or something, to make 'em talk." Carrie added with disgust.

"Pulling out fingernails is a little too good for them, but it's a start." She winked at Carrie.

Carrie turned to leave satisfied with Jamie's terrible answer, and then stopped short. "Wait…Thomas? You never call a client by their first name." She raised a curious eyebrow at Jamie. "I'd ask if you got lucky last night, but if you did you'd be in a better mood." A sly smile crossed her lips. "So are you getting 'friendly' with a client?"

"Don't go gettin' that little matchmaker brain of yours fired up. Last night was all business, okay? He isn't exactly hard on the eyes, and I wouldn't mind having my own sugar daddy—and but no—nothing happened. Nor will it."

"Fine, fine. Though, why not?" Carrie questioned. "Maybe my boss would be a little less bitchy if she got laid once in a while." She winked.

"Oh? Well then, maybe I'll see if Eddie is free tonight." Jamie licked her lips wickedly.

"Exactly what I mean! You're such a bitch! You keep your little hands off my Eddie, or else!" Carrie picked up a letter opener and waved it around like a sword.

"Oh, threatening the boss, eh? That's it! No raise for you!" Jamie did her best impression of Seinfeld's Soup Nazi.

Carrie dropped her head with a pout before looking back up and smirking. "I may as well do it then! Don't forget, my Eddie's a cop. We'll make you disappear, lady." Carrie held out her hand with her fingers extended together and then spread them wide. "Poof! You're gone!"

"Funny, Eddie whispered the same thing in my ear about you last night...after..." Jamie wiggled her eyebrows up and down.

"Sorry, bitch, that man was occupied. All. Night. Long. So you, my dear, are a big fat liar." A satisfied smile played over Carrie's lips.

"He was just practicing for tonight, honey!" Jamie added all the snark she could muster, making them both bust out laughing.

Their banter finally ended when the office phone rang.

"Saved by the bell!" Carrie dashed out to her desk. "Windstein Investigations, how may I help you?" She answered the phone with practiced professionalism—not even a hint of the smile that was still on her face. "Yes, sir, one moment please." Carrie hit the "hold" button before yelling. "Jamie! It's *Thomas*." She accentuated his name with purpose. "Line 2." She winked at her friend, wishing Jamie would actually let someone into her life for once.

"Smart ass!" Jamie couldn't resist a reply as she shut the door behind her.

3

He started up the dirt driveway on foot, after parking his vehicle safely behind some trees about a quarter mile down the road. He tossed a few branches in front of it for extra precaution.

It was early with the sun shining bright in a cloudless sky. The day had all the makings of another beautiful day. The weatherman had stated the mercury would cross the eighty-degree mark before noon. The comfort of a light breeze accompanied him as he made his way up the long dirt driveway to his destination. It wasn't his first visit—he'd made several throughout the years—though he felt fairly confidant this would be the last.

The old man's mangy black cat took notice of him from its hiding spot beneath the steps that led up to the front door of the small house at the end of the driveway. The ill-tempered cat eyed him with the casual curiosity and general apathy only felines are capable of displaying. In other words, it saw him—though it didn't really give a shit so long as he left it alone. Cats—though apathetic, he'd observed—were also the world's original narcissists. They had a need to be the center of attention, unless they didn't want it, like when they were on the prowl. As if on que, the old black cat stood and casually stretched to ensure its presence was known.

Once he placed a foot on the first step the feline darted off. He smiled at the thought of cats being—quite possibly—the world's worst guard animals. However, he was glad that the old man had chosen a cat for a pet, rather than some beast of a guard dog. He wasn't afraid of dogs, but they do tend to announce the arrival of strangers with ferocity.

The rickety, rotting door creaked loud enough to wake the dead as he pulled it open, decimating his attempt at a stealth approach. Not that it really mattered much. Between the dust, the ornery cat, the door screeching like nails on a chalkboard and being surrounded by the threat of contracting a serious tetanus infection at every turn, he absolutely despised coming out here to the middle of nowhere to see a man he disliked even more. He stepped inside the hovel this man called home, and shrunk back from the stink of rotten garbage and body odor. He'd been in worse places, though to call the place unkempt would be a drastic understatement. Dirty dishes had been stacked in and around the sink for so long they appeared as towers of dust. Empty containers laid strewn about everywhere and the ashtrays overflowed with avalanches of discarded cigarette butts. Disgusting, but to him the real trash here was the piece of filth who lived in it. He had little choice though, so he powered his way through the ocean of filth to the back door where the old man could generally be found. He carefully maneuvered his way through the house as a dust storm twinkled in the few sun rays that penetrated the dirt-caked windows. He held a deep-seated, pure hatred for filth. Not only the kind laying everywhere, but the kind which came in human form as well. It made him absolutely loathe his trips here every single time. He wanted to deliver his message, then be gone before becoming infected with some rare disease.

The sound of a trigger being cocked back froze him where he stood.

"What the fuck you doing in my house, mister?" The old man's scratchy voice followed.

He could smack himself for his carelessness, even though he had no fear of the old man. He pivoted on his right, turning to find himself staring down the twin barrels of a shotgun. He couldn't believe his own stupidity, but he had been concentrating so much on his footing through the heaps of garbage, that he'd forgotten to check the bedroom. The old man stood a step back from the bedroom doorway in a stained white undershirt and matching stained underpants, shakily holding a double barrel shotgun in his weak alcoholic hands.

He raised his hands, coldly staring, and waiting for the old man to recognize his target. He knew the man's mind had been slowly fading away for some time, though he hoped it wasn't gone completely yet. "Is that any way to greet an old friend, Counselor Bob?"

Robert Keane paused, studying the intruder in a desperate attempt to force his mind to work. *Do I know this man? Why did he call me Counselor? I'm no counselor, am I? Blast my damn memory!* Thinking made him feel like he was trying to swim in quicksand these days. He felt lucky he remembered to get up to use the pisser most of the time—admittedly not always.

"Do I know you? Why you callin' me counselor? Who the fuck are you? Speak up, or I'll blast ya, young man!" His hands shook worse the more he spoke.

"Set the gun down before you hurt yourself, Bob." He took a step toward the old man.

"Don't you fuckin' move! I still know how to use this thing." His confusion caused his hands to shake worse and he nearly dropped the shotgun.

He took another step. "You're gonna blow your fool head off with that thing, Bob. Put it down! You know me, so stop fucking around." He took another step, putting the barrel only a few inches from his face.

"I said don't move! I don't know who the fuck you are so state your business or fuck off! I'd prefer you just fuck off!" Bob was more agitated by his confusion than his visitor, making him angry.

Had Robert Keane been any other man, sympathy is what he'd feel—maybe even pity the poor soul—but that wasn't the case. This was Robert Keane—Counselor Bob—a former goon who had done terrible things. Counselor Bob didn't deserve an ounce of sympathy, nor would he be receiving any. Counselor Bob deserved to suffer, slowly, to his final, bitter end. Counselor Bob deserved pain while someone reminded him of each and every one of his many, many sins. Slipping slowly into dementia, wiping clean the memory of those sins, behind vacant cataract eyes was far too good an end for the likes of Counselor Bob. He wanted Robert Keane to be haunted by his sins until his light finally went out, only after suffering as much misery as he had dished out in his lifetime. Anything less was far too good for a man like him.

"Shit! I… I remember you. You, son of a bitch!" The old man's eyes went wide with recognition flooding back in.

Swifter than Mr. Whiskers pouncing on an unsuspecting squirrel, he sidestepped to the right and in one fluid motion, pushed the barrel of the shotgun up to the ceiling with his left hand. Before Robert Keane's shaky finger could pull the trigger, the shotgun was wrenched from his grasp. Robert Keane could only stand in his disgustingly pit stained shirt and tighty-whities, with a dumbfounded, shocked look on his face. He was the pathetic and feeble old man he had become. Keane had been unarmed in the blink of an eye by a man he should have disposed of as a child decades ago. Regret came too late. Now he was left standing in bewilderment and trying not to soil himself.

"Now sit the fuck down, Counselor Bob! Jesus! I came here to deliver a message, not have you wave your useless pecker replacement in my face. You do remember our little talks, don't you, Bob? I know I've always enjoyed them." He jammed the butt end of the gun into Bob's gut hard enough to make him double over, pushing the old man back onto his bed and moaning in agony.

Tears welled up in Robert Keane's eyes, though he hung his head to hide it. He crossed his arms across his stomach from the pain and to protect himself from another blow. He looked like the very definition of haggard. His body and mind soured by his many years. Robert Keane never married, never let much happiness into his personal life at all. The only joy he had ever known came from inflicting pain on the young and weak. The irony of now being the weak one at someone's mercy, was not completely lost on him, despite the dementia setting in.

Finally, Bob looked up at his visitor, twisting his pain into hate. "I remember you. I should've buried you all those years ago. You always were a nasty little cuss."

"Ah, but you didn't, Bob. You can cry about it after I'm gone." He looked around disgusted by everything he saw. "I'm nasty? Just where do you think I learned it from, Bob? You think maybe, just maybe, I had some good teachers, Bob? You wanna whine about the rotten fruit you cultivated all those years ago? We're here, right now, in this place because of what you did—what you all did, Bob. Your home is a fucking pig sty, Bob. I suppose that's fitting, since a big, fucking pig lives here." He took a moment to look with contempt around him. "Now, on your feet. Let's go out to your favorite spot on the back porch so I can breathe some clean air instead of your rotten stench." He loomed over Bob scowling. "You disgust me, Bob."

He held the shotgun on the old man, not because he needed to, because he knew the old bastard hated it. Following Bob out the back, he wondered if the old fool had even loaded the thing. He kept a steady eye on Bob, while popping the double barrels open. Surprisingly, a shell sat in both barrels. He had no intention of using the gun, but he knew he might need it to accentuate his message if Bob failed to get the point.

The old man pushed the screen door open, sending an eruption of dust into the air, then plopped himself into the rocking chair where he spent most of his time. Bob looked dejected with, perhaps, a twinge of fear in his eyes. He delighted seeing his one-time tormentor in such a frail state, nearly trembling in fear the way he had years ago when their roles were reversed. Robert Keane was but a ghost of the man who had once virtually beaten him to death. He enjoyed watching the man wither away through the years but was also glad to have the end so near.

"So what the fuck do you want, asshole?" The old man's voice lacked any power it had once possessed.

"For you to die slowly and painfully, then burn in hell. That's not why I'm here today though, you old bastard. A young woman is going to come visit you later today, maybe tomorrow."

The old man perked up at the word woman.

"She's coming to you with questions. Many questions, Bob. Questions you'll have forgotten all the answers to, understand? Shouldn't be too much of a stretch for you. All you need to do is sit here like the feeble old fuck you are, Bob, and say nothing. She's going to ask you about a young boy. You're not going to remember who that young boy is, Bob. If you do, I'll come back. You don't want me to come back, Bob, do you? I won't be happy if I have to come back here. I don't like you and I don't like it here, *Bob*, so if I have to come back it'll be so you can watch your mangy cur of a feline companion make a meal of your nuts. Get my meaning, Bob?" He held the shotgun squarely between Bob's eyes to emphasize the seriousness of the situation.

"Yeah, yeah. I got it, asshole. Now get that thing out of my face before I shove it straight up your ass! Something I shoulda done years ago!" The old man sneered.

"You did plenty—which probably isn't very wise to remind me of when I have a shotgun pointed at your face, Bob. I understand you probably wanna die now that your noggin is all fucked up—but trust me, it'll happen soon. I should mention to you, this woman won't be very happy when you don't answer her. She may get very angry, in fact. Maybe, if you ask her real nice, she'll finally put you out of your misery, Bob." He returned the sneer.

"You came to us a bad seed. Eva saw it. I told her we shoulda just put you down. Some seeds are flowers. Some are weeds. Weeds get plucked." Disdain was clear on the old man's face.

"You were the stinking fertilizer, Bob, and look at what a beautiful flower you cultivated." He smiled broadly. "About time I scraped you off the bottom of my shoe though, I have no use for shit anymore, Bob." His voice was calm and cold while the knuckle of his trigger finger turned white with the burning need to be done with Robert Keane for good.

"Well then, stop being such a fuckin' pussy and pull the damn trigger! Pull it! Pull it, you fucking coward!"

His finger strained against the trigger no more than a hair from setting off both barrels straight into the old man's face. He couldn't think of much he'd love more than seeing Robert Keane's head explode in a burst of red like a firework display on the Fourth of July. He let out a sigh, relieving the tension—blowing Keane's face off wasn't part of his plan. He straightened his finger, lowering the shotgun, and smiled at the helpless old man in a filthy shirt and underwear. Then he laughed.

He shook his finger at the old man. "You almost had me, Bob. Almost. But then you'd miss all the fun!" He reared his head back in laughter as the old man scowled from his rocking chair. "Now, keep your mouth shut and I promise you'll never see me again. Jamie Windstein is the woman coming to see you, Bob. I don't think it'll be a pleasant visit, whether you give her any answers or not. You think I'm wicked, Bob? You ain't seen nothing yet."

He popped the shotgun open and lifted out both shells, tossing them into the field before giving the old man his gun back. He turned, walking back inside without a further word—he had nothing left to say. He left Robert Keane to sit rocking back and forth, waiting for him to finally leave for good. Inside, he rummaged around for any extra shells the old man might have hidden away. He wouldn't put it past the old bastard to fire both barrels into Jamie before she could try to get her answers, given his message. He wouldn't have it, that wouldn't do at all.

4

"I will meditate my way through all this shit," Jamie whispered to herself, contemplating the past few days.

She desperately wanted Thomas' call to end up helpful, though she found herself filled with doubt. Either way, it would most likely take her several days of research to find out, and she didn't have the time or the patience. While she pondered Thomas' call, Carrie buzzed her phone and interrupted further thought on the matter.

"Mister Jourgensen is here, Miss Windstein."

"Thank you, Carrie. I'll be right out."

Jamie took a deep breath, trying to clear her mind before pushing her chair back and heading out to greet her potential new client. She swung her office door open with confidence and stepped out into the small waiting area in front of Carrie's desk.

A middle-aged man sat, his head down as he fidgeted with his fingers, visibly nervous—a pose Jamie had become accustomed to from her clients. Al Jourgensen had the beginnings of what would become a major comb-over on his prematurely balding head. It made him appear like a man in his early fifties, though his face told a different story. The lack of wrinkles or any crow's feet around his eyes put him more accurately in his mid-thirties—maybe forty at most. While the name Jourgensen suggested a Scandinavian descent, his dark hair and slightly olive complexion suggested an Italian heritage. He seemed fairly short, though likely taller than herself, as almost everyone was. He was also overweight and she guessed him to be headed for a heart attack by the time his chronological age caught up with his appearance. She had little doubt he had come about a cheating spouse—his body language screamed it. She completed her initial assessment in the five steps it took her to cross the room to greet the man.

She smiled politely and held out her hand. "Good morning, Mister Jourgensen. I'll be with you in just one moment, if that's alright?"

"Please, take your time, Miss Windstein. I appreciate you seeing me so quickly."

Jamie smiled as she stepped over to Carrie's desk and leaned down. "Carrie, can you make some calls for me while I meet with Mister Jourgensen?"

Carrie nodded.

"I need to find out where all the records on The Mormont Home are kept. The place was cleared out, so they have to be stored somewhere. See if you can track them down for me. I know adoption records are sealed, but if I can get permission to look through any from the home, it would be exceptionally helpful."

"I'll get right on it. Hopefully they're in the archives at City Hall. The adoption records might be a different story. I'll see what I can do."

"I know you'll do your best. Thanks, sweets." Jamie winked at Carrie and then turned back to her client. "Alright, Mister Jourgensen, follow me."

Jourgensen shuffled his feet behind her like a school child on his way to the principal's office. Once in her office, Jamie offered him a seat before sitting down across from him. She had cleared some of the major clutter before he arrived, though her desk remained a maze of stacked files and assorted brick a brac. She had managed to reduce the total chaos to merely a tidy mess.

"So, what can I do for you, Mister Jourgensen?" Jamie was pleasant, though prayed he'd be quick.

"Well…I'm hoping you can help me, Miss Windstein," she began tentatively.

"Please, just Jamie. I'll help if I can. Take your time and just start from the beginning." Jamie resisted screaming—her agitation wasn't his fault.

"Oh okay, Jamie," he said politely. "I need your help to find my sister. We were separated as children, you see, and she's the only family I have." He hung his head in shame, unable to look Jamie in the eye.

Jamie was more than a little shocked, having expected the usual sob story about a wife suspected of infidelity. "I'm sorry, Mister Jourgensen, that's terrible." She feigned sympathy even though the unexpected request roused her curiosity.

Al reached into his suit jacket, pulling a photo from the pocket. He gazed at it longingly a moment before handing it to Jamie. It was an old, badly faded Polaroid photo. She could make out what looked like a boy of maybe nine or ten years old holding a baby wrapped in a pink crocheted blanket. She glanced at Mr. Jourgensen over the photo. The years hadn't been very kind—she couldn't really see in him the boy he had been. But clients lied to her all the time, and she was suspicious even though the photo was old. It wasn't unusual that an adult would be unrecognizable from the child they once were.

Tears welled up as he tried to continue. "That…that picture is all I know of her. My parents—my adoptive parents—passed away unexpectedly earlier this year and…that's when I found…it." He dropped his head into his hands, weeping uncontrollably.

Beneath the photo, in barely visible blue ink, someone had written, "Albert & Melissa '83." Jamie flipped the photo over to find nothing further on the back side. She stared intently at the children, getting a strange feeling of déjà vu with no idea why. She shrugged it off gently, handing the photo back to Jourgensen.

"Take your time, Mister Jourgensen. It's alright," Jamie said sincerely, consoling him.

He regained his composure finally. "I'm sorry, Jamie, it's just…I'm so ashamed. I…" he paused, trying to regain his composure. "I forgot about her. I forgot my own sister! Then I found this photo in an old box in my parents' basement. What kind of person forgets they have a sister? How do you forget a thing like that?" Unable to hold himself together any longer, he broke down completely.

She handed him a box of tissues. "It's alright, Albert, you were very young. You can't beat yourself up over it. Maybe you were only with her briefly and you were just a boy. Can you remember your birth parents at all?" Jamie thought maybe a slight change of subject would help.

Several deep breaths later, he responded. "Barely. They died in a car accident. It couldn't have been long after that photo was taken." Tears streamed down his cheeks. "I don't know why they separated us. I ended up at The Mormont Home for Children and I don't know where she would've been taken. I know she wasn't at Mormont with me."

Jamie's ears perked up considerably at the mention of Mormont as Al continued. "Her name is Muh…Muh…Melissa—it's written there on the photo. Please, please help me find her, Jamie," he pleaded. "I need to tell her I'm sorry." He dropped his head into his hands to muffle his weeping.

Jamie sat back stunned for a moment as she waited for him to regain his composure. The Mormont Home coming up once again was either worrisome or fortunate. She didn't like irony and she didn't believe in coincidence. This Jourgensen seemed sincere, though she couldn't help but wonder if this was a new game set up by her demented secret admirer. She refused to let her curiosity get the better of her, deciding instead, to proceed with caution. She sat, quietly thinking, while Al calmed himself enough to proceed.

Jamie chose to test the waters a little and changed the subject. "Perhaps, we may be able to help each other, Mr. Jourgensen. You said you were sent to The Mormont Home?"

Jourgensen nodded in the affirmative, looking quizzically at her.

"Then, honestly, it's ironic you coming to me right now," she began. "A few days ago another former resident of Mormont hired me. Do you possibly remember a boy named James or Jimmy Reimse?" Holding her breath, she watched his reaction.

Jourgensen gave her nothing. He sat with a blank expression, tears shimmering on his reddened cheeks before responding. "I can remember more than one boy named Jimmy. I'm sorry though, Reimse doesn't ring any bells. Do you know anything else about him? Maybe something to jog my memory?"

"It appears he was last seen after an escape attempt in the playground area with another boy—his roommate, Tommy Basnett. Do you remember Tommy?" Again Jamie held her breath as she waited for his answer.

"Oh, I remember the incident! I remember Tommy but his roommate wasn't—what did you say his name was?—Jimmy Reimse? His roommate was Makowski, Jimmy Makowski. A real troublemaker, that one! He got all of us in trouble many times. No one liked him very much, except Tommy, of course."

Jamie's jaw was nearly on her desk. "You're positive? The boy's name was Makowski?"

"Who could forget him? That kid was evil incarnate. We were all afraid of him, almost as much as DeLong and her crew of goons. I remember one time this kid tried to start a fight with Jimmy—big mistake! Jimmy pushed him down and bit his ear off! His fucking ear! Absolutely disgusting! I can still see the look on his face when he spit it out as far as he could, spraying blood and spit everywhere. He looked like the damn devil himself!" He shuddered. "If Jimmy's still alive, my guess is he's rotting in prison somewhere. I wouldn't wanna run into him—not then, not ever—I can tell you that, Ms. Windstein."

Jamie studied Mr. Jourgensen's face, looking for any sign he'd fabricated or made up the story he'd told, but found none. "Thank you! You've been a huge help, believe me." Jamie smiled. "Now getting back to Melissa. Is Jourgensen your birth name or your adopted name?"

"Jourgensen is my adopted name. My birth name…well, I guess *our* birth name is Dowd. Her name was Melissa Dowd. I can only assume it no longer is, obviously. I did a simple name search that got me nowhere. It isn't much to go on, but I didn't know what else to do—I'm no detective." His cleared his throat, clearly still on the verge of tears.

Jamie couldn't let go of her suspicions quite yet. "Can I ask, why me? Did someone refer you? I'm listed almost last in the phone book, so most people get referred to me, unless they just close their eyes and pick at random."

"No random pick, Ms. Windstein, I was referred to you. I believe you know Sandy Largulis, the divorce lawyer? I work for her. She told me you're the best, so here I am."

She could check his story before he left the office if she chose, so she really had no choice but to believe him.

"Ah, good ol' Sandy, the Shark." They both chuckled. "I'm sorry—I'm not trying to give you the fifth degree or anything—I just don't get many missing person cases. Please thank her for me, I appreciate the referral and the accolades." She smiled at him. "I'll make a deal with you, Mr. Jourgensen. If what you told me about Jimmy aids my other case, I'll do everything I can to find your sister, Pro Bono." Jamie *never* worked Pro Bono, but Thomas Combs had paid her enough for *ten* cases, and his bill just increased drastically.

Jourgensen's face nearly cracked in two with joy. "Wow! I'll kiss Sandy for you, if that's the case! I'm not a rich man but I can pay for your services, Ms. Windstein—sorry—Jamie. If you find my sister, I'll forever be in your debt." His eyes welled.

"The information you shared is worth far more than you know, Mr. Jourgensen. Trust me. Plus, I'm an orphan myself, and if I had a brother out there I'd want to know about it. It'd be my pleasure to reunite the two of you if I can. It may take me some time, so if you don't hear from me for a few days, please don't worry— I'm on the case." Jamie smiled thinking it may be her lucky day after all. "If you think of anything else just call; otherwise, I'll let you go so I can get started."

"I believe I've told you all I know. I'm still going through my adopted parents' things, so if I find anything of use I'll let you know ASAP." He stood, extending his hand to shake hers vigorously before making his exit.

Jamie sat stunned, unable to believe what had just happened. She seriously had never been a believer in coincidence. If he was telling the truth though, she'd live up to her word and try to find his sister, free of charge. However, if he'd lied—then no God could help him.

Thomas Combs popped into her mind. Why had he deliberately lied to her from the start? Was he the secret admirer? A blinding hot rage flowed through her limbs—she wanted to wrap her hands around his neck and pull the answer right out of his lying throat.

5

Detective Stephen Barker made his way through the County Medical Examiner's building and down to the dungeon—his nickname for Dr. Clive Ketchum's corner in this living hell. He also liked to joke with his friend that he was a prisoner to his work, making the reference an apt one. He hadn't told Officer Washington, nor would he ever admit, how much he hated coming to this place. He detested the sting of ammonia in his nostrils and the stench of death it failed to mask. The irony of a homicide detective despising the smell of death wasn't lost on him.

Barker pushed open the doors to the morgue with force, sending a thundering echo through the entire basement. He was annoyed by simply being here. On top of that, there was also the lack of a single lead on either the Snyder or Osbourne homicides. It irked him to have no answers—even more so this time because there was no doubt that the Snyder murder was absolutely the work of The Executioner. Then he had the Osbourne crime scene that lacked the bodies to even prove it a homicide, though he had no doubt. He needed to know if these two cases were connected before it drove him insane. Everyone wondered why he had such an ill temper all the time. Cases like these. Not that he cared what people thought—his perpetual bad mood kept everyone around him on their toes; his new young partner being a perfect case in point.

"Stephen! Welcome!" Dr. Ketchum beamed from behind his desk in the back corner.

Barker waved with a grimace. He detested raising his voice, whether friendly or not. He liked Ketchum far more than he let on, yet he found the doctor's boisterous nature abhorrent. He made his way with purpose to the doctor's desk. Ketchum's official office lay three floors overhead, though he rarely used it unless forced by circumstance. Ketchum felt more at home in the morgue—among the dead—than in his actual home. Barker knew the doctor would sleep here if his wife allowed it.

Barker waited until he was at Ketchum's side before speaking. "Anything at all for me, doc?"

"Probably a nasty strain of bird flu, though I suspect you don't want it." Ketchum shot Barker a big, dumb smile.

"How about I nail your nuts to that chair and see if you're still able to make wise cracks?" Barker couldn't hide his irritation.

"Well, good morning to you too, Sunshine!"

Barker glared. "Tell me you have something, or there's nothing good about it."

"Y'know I've known you—what? Ten years now?"

Barker nodded.

"And in all that time I think I've seen you smile—well…smirk is probably more accurate—exactly three times!"

Barker sighed loudly in aggravation.

"You're a cop. I don't believe 'must be humorless cunt at all times' is in the handbook anywhere." He chuckled. "So tell me, copper, where in the hell do I find a hooker in this city—because you, sir, need a blow job more than any man in history! Or would carnal relations still not lighten your mood?" Ketchum gave a full blown laugh while Barker remained unamused.

"Stealing jokes from a dead man now? Oh, how far the mighty have fallen." Barker frowned.

"Steal? Why, I never!"

"Robin Williams, *Good Morning Vietnam*, 1987. Committed suicide 2014, so you stole a joke from a dead man." Barker acted annoyed even though this was a game they'd played dozens of times.

"Fine. I'll point out that the dead *are* my business, Detective Barker, so shoot me." Ketchum shrugged. "You know it's true."

"Shut it and don't tempt me. I haven't shot anyone in far too long so careful what you wish for, Doc. Now, do you have anything for me or am I wasting time in a place I despise in the first place?" Barker sneered. "I can't say I care for the company much either."

"You didn't waste your time. And the company is fantastic, I'll have you know!" he muttered under his breath. "However, I can't say your mood is going to improve much, not that it ever does anyway."

He snagged one of the numerous manila file folders off his desk and handed it to the detective, then sat back waiting for the inevitable grouchy retort. He knew the report contained almost nothing unexpected—almost.

"So, all the blood is from our suspected victims. None from our perp. No hair, no fibers or anything else that wasn't there already." Barker dropped the file back on the pile it came from. "Would you say it was a fatal amount of blood found?"

"The stain in the center of the mattress, no. The splatter at the head of the mattress, absolutely. Karen and David Osbourne—wherever their bodies may be— are almost certainly deceased, unless our Un Sub had an ample supply of blood on hand to transfuse them."

"Great! So I'm looking at a double homicide with no suspects, no leads and not even the damn bodies!" Barker threw up his hands in frustration. "Anything at all to go on from the mattress? Aside from the blood, obviously. Any gears turning in that big brain of yours, Doc?"

"Possibly. I would like to hear Eddie's thoughts on it though. Nice big brain on that one too." He feigned looking around for Eddie. "Where is your apprentice this morning? You didn't fire him already, did you? Did he decide partnering with you isn't worth the pay increase?"

"Would you shut your big fat fucking mouth? Jesus! I sent him to interview the Osbourne's nosy old neighbor this morning—the one who reported them missing. He turned up bupkis other than a time frame for the murders of about thirty-six hours. It had to happen sometime between approximately ten Saturday night and Monday morning when the old woman called it in. She didn't see any stranger or strange vehicle, or anything else important. He's checking with the other neighbors, but I doubt anyone else saw anything if the nosy neighbor didn't." He glanced at his watch. "Right about now, he should be interviewing that PI—Windstein—about the Snyder victim. Long and short, he'll be tied up for another hour or two, so why don't you just get on with whatever you have to say and you can ask Eddie his thoughts later. If you don't mind, Doc?" He finished sarcastically.

Ketchum returned the condescending glare. "Fine. Guess I'll have to make do with the likes of you."

Barker's lip twitched at the backhanded insult. "Well, you noticed the blood obviously, but anything else?"

"Visual observation only, I didn't want to disturb any possible evidence. You know that, so get on with it."

"You are no fun at all! Humorless—that's what my wife says, you know, Barker is simply humorless." Ketchum smirked.

"I'll show you just how humorless if you don't get to the damn point!" Barker shook his fist in frustration.

"Yes. Yes. It's the blood stain near the center of the mattress I found most interesting. When I examined it closely I found a puncture mark. It's not very large but it goes completely through the mattress from top to bottom. Inside the hole I found our victims' blood, along with a trace amount of soil. There's nothing special about the soil unfortunately, other than its presence though. Based on the size of the puncture hole, my guess is our first weapon is a long round bar or tube somewhere between a quarter to a half an inch in diameter. I assume it was metal in order to be strong enough to pierce through two bodies and the mattress. I suspect a killer that was smart enough to remove the bodies and clean up—albeit lightly—was smart enough not to chance a wooden stake breaking off and leaving evidence for us. Once his victims were pinned to the mattress, I have to assume the Un Sub used a blade of some sort, beheading the couple and causing the massive amount of blood at the head of the bed. After that, he moved them to the bathtub to cut them up for disposal. Now, this is assuming we're looking at one perpetrator." Ketchum relayed his opinion like delivering a post-op report. "So put yourself in the killer's shoes a moment, what do you think happened?"

Barker stood rubbing his chin trying to absorb all the information Ketchum relayed. He closed his eyes a moment, visualizing the bedroom at the Osbourne house during the incident. The house had been dark that night. Dim light filtered in through the curtains from the streetlights outside. He pictured Karen and David Osbourne coming home after their date night, laughing and smiling the way any young couple would after a night out enjoying each other's company. He saw them ending their evening in the throes of lust. They kissed their way to the bedroom, leaving a trail of clothes all the way until they hit the bed. Barker watched in his mind as the killer slipped in, silent and unseen, with his intended victims oblivious to the world around them, lost in each other's eyes.

"Well?" Ketchum impatiently interrupted.

"Don't rush me!" He grumbled. "So, it's Saturday night. Our victims come home after their normal date night, dinner and a movie. They arrive home probably feeling a little frisky. They make their way to the bedroom to put the exclamation point on their evening. So they're on the bed, oblivious to the world around them. Our killer silently enters the room. Maybe he broke in earlier and waited—it doesn't matter. He comes up behind the couple and by that point, unless he let out a big ol' war whoop, they didn't hear or see him coming. He raises his long spear, or whatever it was, and stabs the couple so hard he drives the thing right through the couple into the mattress. This tells me our perp is almost certainly male, and no ninety pound weakling either— that took some strength. At this point, the couple are pinned down at his mercy, or lack thereof. Our guy doesn't waste any time moving around the couple, either slicing their throats or beheading them. It had to be quick or the nosy neighbor might hear a scream. He's cased the house—he knows they have a busy body next door. Then our killer takes them into the bathroom, tosses the bodies in the tub where he cuts them up for easier removal from the house. Then our killer thoroughly cleans the tub, telling us this is premeditated, not a spur of the moment crime of passion. He knows to leave no trace of himself behind. Then he gives the bedroom a cursory wipe down, just enough so if someone peeps through the window they don't notice anything blatant. Finally he takes the bodies out—God knows where—then locks up like he was never even there. Monday morning, the neighbor calls and we show up that afternoon to find the obvious crime scene and nothing else. Sound about right to you, doc?"

Ketchum clapped. "Excellent! You hit all the essentials, I think. I do have a little to add, though." Ketchum smirked like the Cheshire cat.

"What, pray tell, do you wish to add, good doctor? I ain't got all damn day."

"The initial puncture wound." He began. "I think you're correct about our killer approaching from behind, while the victims were consumed by passion, but from the angle, I don't believe he stood behind or to the side. I think the only way our killer could have delivered his blow—almost perfectly straight through and with enough force to penetrate two bodies, a mattress and into the bed springs—is if he was straddling them and driving the spear straight down with both hands. Our killer isn't just strong but also fairly tall. I'd say six-three, six-four at a minimum. I also believe he was already in the house waiting. I think he watched them and I think he waited until precisely the moment he wanted. I'm no profiler, detective, so I can't give you a psychological analysis but now I've come to the bad news portion of this sad story." Ketchum frowned.

"Bad news?"

"I don't believe the Osbournes' killer is *The Executioner.*"

"You sure?"

"Not one hundred percent, but pretty close. Nothing about any of The Executioner's victims point to anything even remotely sexual. Plus the fact of this being a double homicide. I know it isn't proof positive, but to my knowledge none of our Executioner cases have been double murders. Every Executioner victim seems to be a single homicide—he isolates his victim before going in for the kill. If we ever locate the Osbournes' bodies, perhaps it'll tell us a different story, however for now, I think we're looking at a different killer here. This one seems patient and sadistic, but that's the only similarity I see to The Executioner. This murder took patience and skill, making it highly doubtful they were his first victims." He paused. "Which brings me to the next bit of bad news: this is the work of an experienced killer—not some first time novice. Our Un Sub was methodical, leading me to believe this was planned well in advance. This wasn't someone who was going to be surprised. I'll bet he knew the nosy neighbor wouldn't take long to call it in, too. I suspect he selected this couple well ahead of time—watched them and waited for the right time. I'm sure he selected the Osbournes for a reason. I hate to say it, Stephen, but this killer may not be The Executioner. I'd bet anything we're looking at a serial killer, though—it just isn't the one we thought it was," Ketchum finished, wishing he had better news for his old friend.

Barker looked dejected. "Have you checked with the FBI yet?"

"No, not yet. I wanted to talk to you first. I don't see any way around it on this one. We need to see if this matches the MO of any other murders around the country. If it crosses state lines, you know they'll take it over."

"Yeah, I know. We've been able to keep The Executioner off their radar because it's been all local, but you know they'll take that too, once they dig in." Disgusted, Barker spit the words out.

"Well, our work is off the books—and will stay that way—but the bodies aren't, nor the case files. All we can do is cross our fingers, unless our double homicide matches nothing—which I'd find hard to believe. I think it's a coin flip at best, my friend." Ketchum shrugged.

"We don't have a choice. Maybe if you keep them focused on this crime scene they won't go poking around. I don't need them coming in and causing a damn panic in the city. Fuckers leak to the press like there's no tomorrow."

"I know. I do have a contact who I might be able to convince to be discreet, but if he finds anything he won't be able to keep it quiet. I'll see what he says," Ketchum said.

"Well fuck! It ain't your fault, Doc. I'll meet up with Washington after he's done with the PI, you call me if you find out anything else. Hopefully, the kid has better news than your sorry old ass did." He patted the doctor on the shoulder and tried not to look too disappointed.

"You ain't no spring chicken yourself, you grumpy bastard. Sorry I couldn't improve your mood. Wait…your mood never improves!" Ketchum laughed. "Say hello to Edward for me. I hope this doesn't end his ascension—I was looking forward to working with that one. And he's a damn site more pleasant to be around than you!"

"Fuck yourself, Doc. Don't worry, I plan on keeping him around for a while. It's rare finding one who isn't a complete moron with delusions of becoming Commissioner someday. He seems to be a rare breed these days, a cop who wants to be a cop. Later, Doc! Let me know what you find out."

"Will do!"

Barker went over all the new information in his head while making his way out of the building. He knew Ketchum was right about it being a different killer, though he hated to admit it. He had known it from the moment he and Eddie lifted the mattress. The Executioner killed one at a time, took one head at a time.

Something about this couple bothered him though. He couldn't shake it. Some called it gut instinct, though he didn't buy into any of that mumbo jumbo. He had years of experience, and sometimes your subconscious recognizes something that the rest of your brain has to figure out later. It was instinct alright, from the deep recesses of the brain and not the gut. The brain is simply one amazing machine, he thought, even though Doctor Ketchum tried teaching him all the details and nuance of it. Knowing how it worked didn't help him in figuring out what his brain was trying to tell him about these cases. The connection lay hidden in his subconscious somewhere, the rest of him needed to catch up, and quick.

6

Jamie picked up her phone the second she heard Al Jourgensen exit through the outer office door. It took only a moment to punch in Sandy Largulis' number from her rolodex. She chuckled to herself, thinking she just may be the last person on Earth still using one, as Sandy's secretary put her on hold.

"Hey, Jamie! How's the prettiest PI in all of Western New York?" Sandy's gravelly, yet pleasant, voice boomed in Jamie's ear.

"Hey, Sandy. Got a quick question for you."

"Shoot."

"Did you refer an Al Jourgensen from your office to me, by chance?"

"Such a nice little man and one hell of a legal aide, I'll have you know! Wish he'd shave his head—blasted comb over! Ugh!" Sandy had earned her nickname, the Shark, with her brutal honesty. "But yeah, when he told me his story I told him he should contact you. Any problems?"

"No, I just don't believe in coincidence, so I thought I better check. You know me, hun, trust but verify." Jamie lightheartedly giggled.

"Ya can never be too careful, sugar. What coincidence though, if I may ask?" Sly Sandy always had her ear to the ground for dirt on anyone.

Jamie knew Sandy to be the biggest gossip on the East Coast, easily making her regret mentioning the coincidence. "Not a big deal. He unexpectedly had some information about one of my other cases. I ain't never been lucky and, like I said, I don't believe in coincidence, so I thought I better double check his story with you. Truthfully, I would've checked with you regardless, since I don't know the man." She hoped that would satisfy Sandy the Shark's curiosity, even though she had her doubts.

"Ah, I see. Well, good thing I pointed him in your direction then. Keep me in mind if you get any cheaters who need the best damn divorce lawyer in Buffalo." Sandy the Shark never missed an opportunity to plug her services either.

"You know I will! Gotta run, Sandy, I'll talk to you later." Jamie didn't wait for the other woman's goodbye, plunking the receiver back in its cradle with a smile. She knew Sandy hated being hung up on.

Jourgensen was legit, she thought, or at least he hadn't lied about where he worked, nor his identity. The name he had given her—Jimmy Makowski—now nagged at her. Was that name in the file? It didn't sound familiar to her, but what really drove her nuts was why Thomas knowingly gave her a false name. It didn't make any sense at all. She didn't believe for a second he didn't know his friend's actual name. So who was playing games with her? Thomas? Albert? Both? Jamie's impulse was to pick up the phone and drag some answers out of Thomas, but then she thought, why tip her hand? If one or both of them were playing her for a fool, wasn't the smart play to let them keep on thinking her a fool? The need for answers burned in her gut like napalm, yet she needed solid facts before confronting the best paying client she'd ever had. If she found out Thomas had been playing some game this whole time, she'd make him regret it more than anything he had ever done in his life. Now her only hope for the truth was if she could drag the answers out of DeLong or one of her former goons. She cracked her knuckles with a smile, hoping they'd make her pull every last word from their treacherous throats.

"Eddie's here, Jams!" Carrie buzzed in, interrupting before Jamie slipped too deeply into dark thought.

"Thank goodness! I was so lonely in here all by myself." Jamie laughed, but internally cursed the delay.

"Oh, you bit—"

Jamie hung up, cutting her cursing short. She paused a moment before getting up. It took some effort to push her anger to the back of her mind so she could be pleasant. A little levity with her only friends would help, yet visions of her hands wrapped around some deserving throats danced in her head. She sighed loudly then stood to get her mini interrogation with Eddie over with so she could go find her answers.

"Eddie! I told you meeting here at the office will only make Carrie suspicious. Why not question me later in our usual room at the Shady Lady Motel?"

"Sorry, Jams, someone booked Room 69." Eddie feigned sorrow and wiped fake tears from his eyes. "Tomorrow?"

"You two are damn devils!" Carrie threw up her hands in defeat. "Fine! Take him, Jams. I give up! Word to the wise, you two, I know thirty seven different fatal poisons." She batted her eyes with a wicked smile. "Now, can I get you two some coffee?"

"I think we'll skip the coffee, sugar. You better put in earplugs though, 'cause it's gonna get loud in there!" Jamie returned a wicked smile of her own.

Jamie and Carrie locked eyes in a stare down while Eddie looked back and forth between the two. They looked too serious for his comfort.

"Alright, ladies. I know I'm a prime hunk o'meat and all but, honestly, you can share." He joked to break some of the tension.

The girls held their stare down for a moment longer, knowing exactly what they were doing. Finally, with Eddie nearly in a sweat, they burst out in laughter.

"Guys are so damn gullible! See why I stay single now, Care Bear?"

"Just keep your damned hands off my man or you'll find yourself in an early grave." Carrie warned.

Eddie burst out laughing. "What a couple of bitches! Is this what you two do all day?"

Jamie and Carrie looked at each other, shrugged their shoulders and then looked at Eddie. "Yeah. Duh!" they replied in unison.

Eddie could only shake his head as the girls laughed. Jamie—at least for a moment—managed to put her anger on hold. Eddie then made a point to thank her for dinner the previous night which she blew off, of course. Carrie handed Jamie the Snyder case file, now that all the pleasantries were out of the way. Jamie took the file leading Eddie back to her office. She left the door open knowing they weren't going to discuss anything sensitive.

"So, what can I answer for you, Eddie? Carrie tells me you found Michael Snyder's body?" Jamie put on her game face for business.

"Yeah, I was almost home the other night when I got the call. I assume one of the homeless down there called in reporting that they saw a body by the old railroad underpass. I figured it'd be some homeless guy passed out or—at worst—hit by a train, but nope, it ended up being Snyder." Eddie did his best to be nonchalant, giving up none of the details.

"Carrie tells me there may be more to it?" Jamie tried pumping him for information.

"Possible," he shrugged. "All we know, for now, is that it was no accident. Snyder was definitely murdered, and it didn't happen where I found his body either. No blood, no nothing. Please keep all this confidential, Jamie. I know you know that but I've already said too much."

"Any suspects?" Jamie pushed him a bit further.

He shifted uncomfortably in his chair. "Sadly, no. It's why I wanted to talk to you. I know you're limited in what you can tell me because of confidentiality and so am I. Mainly, we just want to know if maybe you can think of any enemies he might have had, aside from his ex who I assume wasn't his biggest fan. Anything at all you can provide would be a huge help."

"I'm not sure how helpful I can be but I'll try." Jamie was careful to hide the smile that threatened to sneak out, hearing there was no evidence found. "I remember this guy, even though I didn't have to tail him for very long, maybe a week or so." She looked down at the file to act like she was double-checking. "Yeah, here it is. I followed him around for a full week, though two days would have been sufficient. Snyder was a real piece of shit, Eddie, both as a husband and a human being, in general. In the first two days—two damn days!—I observed him on 'dates' with three different women. He met one for a nooner and the other two were in the evening." She scanned through the file. "Oh and on the third day he had a nooner with a fourth woman and then picked up a prostitute later that night." She rolled her eyes. "Like I said, a real piece of shit."

"Damn! No wonder his wife wanted a divorce. I hope she took him for everything." Eddie shook his head. "Do you have names on any of his 'dates' by chance?"

"It's my understanding that he beat the wife, too. I suppose if she had ever called you guys, you'd have a record of that to confirm, but like a lot of women, she never reported it. I didn't doubt her story." Jamie flipped further into the file. "I don't have them all, but if you don't say where you came by the information, I can get you their names and any information I found on them. Carrie can make copies. Technically, it's not a breach of confidentiality, but I have a reputation for maintaining privacy, so I'd prefer to keep this on the *way* down low. Okay? I know I can trust you, Eddie."

"Absolutely. You know I don't blab, Jams. It's a very small team working on this case specially—just me, my new partner, and the County Medical Examiner. They already know I'm meeting with you. They're even more discreet than me, believe me." Eddie lowered his voice despite being alone with Jamie.

"I do trust you, Eddie. Honestly, I hope it helps. I can't say I'm sorry to hear a scumbag like Snyder ended up dead." Jamie thought of Michael Snyder's head in a jar on her shelf, content to know he'd never hurt another woman again. "Anything else I can do for you?"

"Yes and no, actually."

"Oh, now I'm intrigued." Jamie's eyes lit up. "Need a suggestion on something sexy to get for Carrie or something?"

"Oh no, nothing like that. Though I guess I couldn't complain if you have one." He smiled thinking of his wife in sexy lingerie, and then visibly shook his head. "No, what I wanted to say…well…I don't really know how to put it, I guess."

"Just spill. We're friends here unless you ever cheat on my girl."

"Never!" He smiled. "It's just that you sort of keep coming up in my cases lately. Obviously, you know about Snyder but um…there seems to have been a double murder in your neighborhood just a couple days ago."

"My neighborhood? Seriously?" Jamie was genuinely surprised.

"Unfortunately, yeah. Just a couple blocks away from you. You see…I shouldn't really tell you anything, but I know I can trust you. We think Snyder may be the victim of a serial killer. One who has, apparently, been in the city for years." He took a breath. "That's the small task force I told you about. We got a call that this couple near you might be missing. My partner thought there may be a slim chance it might be connected to our killer so we checked it out. No bodies, Jams, but there was so much blood on their mattress." Eddie paused. "I don't believe we'll find them alive and well. My partner is with Ketchum right now trying to figure out if there's any link. It was just weird finding out you investigated this Snyder victim and then I get a call right in your backyard. Freaky, huh?"

"Damn! That *is* freaky! Who was the couple? If you don't mind me asking, maybe I know them or saw them around."

"Karen and David Osbourne over on Alaska."

A light went off in Jamie's head. It was their heads on her counter. She knew they looked familiar. She hoped Eddie mistook her reaction for surprise. "Were they fairly young? Maybe late twenties or early thirties?"

"Yeah. The woman was twenty-eight and her husband was twenty-nine. Ever talk to them?"

"No, not that I can remember. I don't actually know them but I used to see them out on walks occasionally or working in front of their house, I think. Have you talked to Leon?"

"Leon?"

"Leon works all around the neighborhood mowing everyone's lawn, trimming hedges and stuff like that. He's kind of a simpleton, so most everyone treats him like shit or ignores him entirely. He's always around the neighborhood working, even in the rain most of the time. He's a big dude, but he wouldn't hurt a fly. In fact, he'd probably try to nurse someone back to health if he found them hurt. He's white, no beard or mustache, and damn huge—probably at least six five if not taller. You can't miss him. He always wears blue jean overalls and a big trucker hat that's always on crooked. He looks like a white version of that big black guy from *The Green Mile*, only not quite as muscular, but close. You know the guy I mean?"

"Yeah. Carrie loves that movie. I forget his name. You know how much Carrie loves anything Stephen King, books or movies. So yeah, I've seen it…many times." He grimaced jokingly. "Why do you think Leon would know anything? If we're right, and this couple met with foul play, it likely happened late at night."

"He might not, but if whoever killed that young couple didn't pick them at random—y'know, picked them—then maybe Leon saw someone hanging around, or saw a strange car on the street. Besides, Leon is super friendly and would love the attention. I just joked with him this morning about keeping his eyes peeled for anything suspicious." She laughed. "He started calling himself, Invinctigator Leon. He's too damn cute!"

"Thank you. I need to go back to interview a few other neighbors who weren't home this morning anyway, so I'll look for him. Thanks for the tip and the list."

"Glad to help, Eddie. I don't know how much good that list will do you. It's from about six months ago. At the rate he was going through them, you might end up questioning half the women in Buffalo and still not get to them all!" Jamie chuckled.

"It's more of a lead than I had when I walked in here. Plus, you told me about Leon, so if not one then maybe the other. Now—please Jamie—stop coming up in murder investigations or I'll just have to arrest you in the interest of public safety." Eddie joked.

"Oh, you'd never catch me, detective. I'm a cannibal, no evidence ever!" She laughed as much from the thought, as from happiness that Eddie wasn't going to suspect her of anything nefarious anytime soon.

Jamie stood to walk Eddie out, inciting another round of bawdy jokes with Carrie, who made a copy of the Snyder list while they discussed grabbing lunch or dinner sometime soon.

Eddie's partner called forcing him to leave and Jamie informed Carrie she'd be leaving soon, as well, and may not make it back before the end of the day.

Jamie made to head out when Carrie stopped her. "Just checking to be sure you're okay, boss." She smiled kindly.

"No, sugar, I'm not."

"Anything I can do? All you gotta do is ask, y'know?"

"Wish you could, but I'm going to do something about it right now. I'm alright, don't worry yourself." Jamie stood and held the office door open. "Something's off, girlfriend, but I'm off to find the answers—or, at least, I hope so!"

Jamie made her way down the stairs, her anger growing with every step. Everything was off kilter right now. She resolved to get the answers she needed to right the ship. If she had to kill her way through the entire city, then that's just what she had to do. There was no room for mercy left in her heart. God help anyone who got in her way today.

Chapter Ten: Enlightened To Extinction

1: Sometime in the '80s

Tommy and Jimmy bided their time for weeks. They stayed on their best behavior and avoided any confrontations with Head Mistress DeLong and her Goon Squad no matter how much they were provoked. They were on their toes at all times. Delong and her goons watched them like hawks even while they slept. The door would click as it was unlocked, randomly, in the middle of the night and then one of the goons—or DeLong herself—would poke their head in to make sure the boys weren't up conspiring their next escape. They had nearly been caught talking after lights out several times, always narrowly managing to make it to their beds just in time to save themselves another trip to the broom closet. They made a vow to each other to escape Mormont, or die trying, pledging to stick together no matter what happened.

Each night they played the same game. They'd pretend to go right to sleep, while they waited for the spying eyes to go away. They knew DeLong and her goons didn't trust them, but they couldn't watch them every second either. Once they were safely locked in their room, they'd wait until they saw the shadow feet below the door move off and then they'd meet between their beds. It was their time to whisper their plans, what they would do when they made it out or reaffirm their pledge to each other.

"Do you think we're playing it too safe, Jimmy?" Tommy worried no one bought their good act. "I think they know something's up. I don't wanna get beat again. Maybe we're being too good." Tommy wore his concern on his face.

"We turned a new leaf." Jimmy shrugged. "All they care about is we're not being a problem for them. Give 'em enough time and they'll move on to some other kids, trust me. We've tried to escape three times just since you got here, so it's gonna take a while. Be patient and they'll let their guard down. We just have to wait them out, then we're gone for good, Tommy." Jimmy's confidence never seemed to wane no matter what happened.

Tommy wanted to believe that, but he felt their eyes on him all the time, even when he was alone. He desperately wanted Jimmy to be right—he needed him to be right. He ached to be away from Mormont so bad he could almost taste it. "Escape to Revenge," he reminded himself.

The phrase had become his daily affirmation. Jimmy did everything he could to calm his friend. One day while they were in the library, Jimmy set a copy of The Count of Monte Cristo down in front of Tommy and told him to read it. "Learn from Edmond Dantes." Jimmy told him.

Tommy devoured the book, learning that it had taken Dantes years of plotting and planning to escape and then earn his revenge.

Patience is the key, Jimmy preached to him during their nightly talks. He was reaffirming himself every bit as much as Tommy.

Tommy studied Dantes like it was his job. "Patience puts them to sleep."

Jimmy smiled in the dark. "Exactly. Be like Dante. We wait for our moment. Then we wait again until we take our revenge."

Anxiousness grew in Tommy. Regardless of Jimmy being right, staying patient was damn hard in this place. He hated everything about Mormont; the way it looked, the way it smelled, and most of all, Head Mistress DeLong and her goons. Counselors Bob and Tony got off on the beatings, but DeLong was even worse. Demented was the only word that came to Tommy's mind for the way she just watched, cackling out encouragement while cracking her whip. The Goon Squad also had their little torments, like walking through the cafeteria bopping kids on the head with the blackjacks they carried or randomly coming up behind a kid, pinching and twisting their ears or noses. They'd pull kids up to their feet by the hair, or any of a million other little painful torments they could think of and, all the while, DeLong would simply look on smiling her approval. Tommy saw the immense pleasure she took watching the sudden fear wash over the face of an unsuspecting kid. She seemed to enjoy that more than her goons enjoyed supplying the pain.

"Be patient, like Dantes." Tommy constantly reminded himself against the endless provocation. He pushed the pain, the indignation and his hate deep down into his gut. He began to believe if he spent much longer here, there'd be no room left. He felt it consuming him. He pushed it all down the best he could, swallowing every miserable drop. He squeezed his ball of hate so tight, he imagined if he let go the explosion would make the Big Bang look like a balloon popping. "Just breathe and remember Dantes." Jimmy told him during the times his rage began to consume him. He had made a pact, and he'd fulfill his commitment to Jimmy; to revenge, no matter what he must endure to achieve it. Tommy knew only one thing for certain; if they escaped The Mormont Home for Children alive, their suffering would be paid back tenfold.

Tommy and Jimmy spent weeks waiting for the eyes watching them to turn away. In the beginning, they spent several days simply practicing getting back in their beds quickly from where they met in the middle. They spent a solid week practicing, while noting how often someone looked in on them in the night. The frequency of the check-ins slowly decreased from about twice an hour to—now after weeks—just a few predictable times each night. The first click of their lock would come within the first hour after lights out, then about an hour later. The last check-in would come sometime in the middle of the night, usually after they had returned to their beds anyway.

They timed the check-ins perfectly, three seconds from hearing the key sliding into the lock, to someone's head poking in. It didn't seem like much time at first, but now it felt like an eternity. They practiced until they were able to get into their beds in about one second, and continued to practice even though the frequency of check-ins slowed. Jimmy insisted they didn't get lazy or complacent, turning their practice into a competition. Randomly, Jimmy would whisper "Door", starting their race to see who could get in bed first. Jimmy almost always won, and the competition kept them on their toes. They knew the punishment they faced if caught out of bed, let alone trying to escape again. They were determined not to get caught.

Tommy couldn't shake the feeling that DeLong knew exactly what they were doing, despite how careful they were or how well they behaved. Counselors Bob and Tony may be growing bored with them, but he feared Delong never would. Jimmy kept telling him he was overthinking, though it didn't stop him from worrying they were being too clever. Jimmy's assurances that Bob and Tony were morons did nothing to assuage his fear of DeLong. Jimmy insisted DeLong suspected nothing, as long as they maintained their good behavior, though Tommy remained unconvinced.

Kenny Von Nagel, a name which seemed to incite bullying, was one of only a few kids who could be considered lucky at Mormont. Tommy had only talked to the boy a few times in the three months he been there. Jimmy avoided talking to pretty much everyone except Tommy, unless he had no choice.

Kenny was incredibly shy, horribly weak—even for an eleven year old—and rather ugly. Somehow he had managed to catch the eye of one of the couples who visited the home occasionally, despite all that. Tommy thought, perhaps he inspired pity, like the runt of a litter might at an animal shelter.

Tommy always felt like a puppy in a pet store window when he'd see the young couples visit. The couples visited, flipped through files containing each child's photo along with whatever was known of their family history and behavioral record. Once the couple picked a handful of children that interested them, the potential adoptees were rounded up and brought into what looked like an interrogation room at a police station. The children led in, one by one, for what was essentially a job interview. Child wanted, only one position available, are you the son or daughter we always wanted? Very few kids ever got adopted out of Mormont, despite the fairly frequent visits from desiring couples. The main reason was the sad fact that the majority of Mormont's orphans were too old being over the ripe age of ten. Most couples wanted to adopt babies, or the very young—those under three or four, who had yet to become corrupted by the system they had no choice in being a part of in the first place. They wanted children they could still teach and mold, not those already fully formed. Tommy found their thinking counterintuitive. At least with a kid like him, they could see what they were getting. A baby or toddler might grow up to be ugly or have learning disabilities no one could predetermine. Kenny von Nagel had been one of the lucky ones, despite the obstacles. He escaped, to the envy of every other kid at Mormont. Tommy wished Kenny's new parents knew the hell they were saving him from. Perhaps then they would have saved more.

Kenny Von Nagel was forever burned onto Tommy's memory, not because they were close friends but because of what happened the day he escaped to a happy life away from the hell of the Mormont Home. After dinner on the day Kenny escaped, Tommy and Jimmy were heading to their room, only to find Head Mistress DeLong waiting there for them. She stood in front of the door with the same evil look she had the night she sat cackling while they were mercilessly whipped after their last escape attempt. Tommy half expected horns to sprout from her head and a forked tail to rise up behind her, proving she was a demon straight from hell. They both froze seeing her there, waiting for them. They knew they had done nothing wrong, yet they also knew she wasn't there for a social call.

Tommy feared she had finally grown bored of their game—or worse, had she overheard them conspiring in the night? He knew it made no difference why DeLong was there, the woman didn't need a reason. They both assumed she came to punish them for something, or even nothing at all other than her pure sadistic desires.

"Good evening, boys!" DeLong acted happy to see them, sinking what little hope they had of this ending well. "I want you to know that you two nasty, little boys aren't fooling anyone. You do know that, don't you?" Both boys stood before her—stoic like marble statues—while their hearts lurched inside their shirts. "I know you're up to something. There's no way in heaven or hell that you two, especially you..." she nodded at Jimmy, "have turned over a new leaf. So, I'm here with an opportunity for the two of you. Option one is to confess now and you can have another peaceful night dreaming of gumdrops and rainbows. Trust me, boys, you don't want option two." She smiled her wicked demoness smile, slapping a blackjack into the palm of her hand.

"We're not up to anything," Jimmy began defiantly. "We don't want to be hurt anymore. That's all, honest." He hung his head, near desperate tears to stop whatever DeLong had planned for them.

"Please, Head Mistress. We're telling the truth, we're not up to anything." Tommy chimed in, following Jimmy's lead.

Head Mistress DeLong acted shocked, her wicked smile momentarily fading before it returned, more wicked than ever. "Bob. Tony." The large hands of DeLong's Goons slammed down on each boys' shoulders, catching them by surprise because they hadn't noticed them sneak in from behind. "What do you think? Have these two naughty little bastards reformed their ways? Do they look repentant to you?"

"We've been nothing but good. We ain't up to nothing, honest, Head Mistress." Tommy knew the futility of his words before they left his mouth.

DeLong leaned down to the boys' eye level. "So, no confession then?" She looked from Tommy to Jimmy as she waited for a reply. "Last chance." She glared at the boys. "Okay. Hard way it is then! You've chosen wisely, boys." She motioned to her goons. "I told you they wouldn't talk. Lock 'em in 'til after lights out," she instructed. "See you soon, sweethearts. Best get some rest—it's gonna be a very long night."

The beating they took that night was the most brutal either boy had ever received. The blackjacks flailed and the whip cracked, yet neither Tommy nor Jimmy broke. The tears streamed from their eyes, but their mouths never opened, either to scream or spill their secrets. Head Mistress DeLong and her goons doled out all the punishment they could muster and still, the boys remained silent. The beating continued for hours until, finally, Head Mistress DeLong's patience seemed to wear out. She ordered her goons to unshackle them, and they all laughed as the boys collapsed to the floor like sacks of potatoes. The goons dragged Tommy and Jimmy back to their room, with DeLong leading the way. She was visibly frustrated by the boys' silence. When they reached the boys' door, DeLong stopped and turned to face her limp wards.

"I'll give you one final chance to talk, boys." The words oozed like venom from DeLong's lips.

She bent down, and with two fingers under his chin, lifted up Tommy's head. Tommy could barely open his blackened eyes and he remained silent. Jimmy did the same. DeLong let out a growl of frustration before standing and instructing her goons.

"Well you leave me no choice boys. It seems your night of fun isn't over yet. Counselor Tony," DeLong snapped, lifting Tommy's head with the tip of her boot. "Take this one to Room 126 since Von Nagel is gone." She moved to Jimmy and lifted his head in the same manner, addressing Robert Keane. "This one is yours for the night, Counselor Bob. Counselors, enlighten these young gentlemen on the subject of carnal desire."

Head Mistress DeLong walked away, cackling all the way down the hall.

2

Bethlehem Steel ceased major production in 1983, leaving Buffalo to slowly die. It was nothing uncommon at the time, turning many cities, big and small, into ghosts of their former selves. Manufacturing began its steep decline during the '80s, a decline continuing to the present day. The decline turned a wide swath of the country into what we now call the Rust Belt. Most say, correctly, the middle class also began to die during the same period. Time seemed to stop in Buffalo in that moment, as though the city became trapped in suspended animation. People talked reverently about the city up to that point, like a forty year old talking about his glory days in high school when he quarterbacked his team to a state championship. Jamie never understood those people who acted like their lives ended at high school graduation, with nothing worthwhile or important ever happening again. She thought it rather pathetic to have that mentality. Life has good times and bad times and neither last forever. Time only travels in one direction—there's no stopping, no going back, you move forward or you get left behind. In Jamie's mind, it was that simple.

She made her way to the south side of the city, closing in on the skeleton of the old steel plant. It reminded her of how she hated coming here as a child. For decades, anyone traveling toward the south side of Buffalo had to deal with the foul stench of rotten eggs due to the sulfur rising out of the smoke stacks of the steel mill. Jamie was happy when the mill closed. Now downtown Buffalo smelled like Cheerios from the General Mills plant, instead of a cesspool of filth. Sadly, when the steel plant died, so did a large portion of Buffalo as thousands of high paying jobs were snuffed out, along with the furnaces. Jamie couldn't get over how perpetually stuck in the mid '80s Buffalo was sometimes. She suspected the band, Journey, was more popular in the city today than they had been at the time. She chuckled to herself every time she saw people go crazy for them. Jamie saw Buffalo as the jock who was reliving his glory days in perpetuity. Only over the past few years did it seem the city had begun to finally move on. Driving toward the south side of the city, Jamie laughed at the insanity of it all though she was also saddened that the area she was entering hadn't even begun to recover in the last thirty years.

She couldn't help thinking about how the city had changed so much and so little in her lifetime. Certain areas were finally beginning to recover, to rebuild—like downtown—yet progress comes slowly. Driving around the city you couldn't help noticing block after block of old, empty abandoned manufacturing buildings with broken out or boarded up windows and crumbling abandoned homes everywhere. It made her sad to see a once proud city, a true hub of industry, reduced to death and decay clinging desperately to the last vestiges of its life. Anger overwhelmed her sadness when she thought about all the development plans that stalled out or died entirely. She saw plans for everything from a new Peace Bridge—the bridge connecting Buffalo to Canada—to waterfront development along Lake Erie and so much more all die a slow death of bureaucratic red tape until in the end nothing ever actually happened. Jamie had no patience for politics. She knew if she were the mayor or a councilman there was no way in hell she'd be able to stop herself from showing up to a meeting one day with a machete, and hack every single one of them into tiny bits. She knew Buffalo was not unique; many cities had similar issues, but how it didn't incite a new revolution or rioting in the streets, she would never understand.

Driving into some of the worst neighborhoods in the city to reach the former Mormont Home counselor, Tony Rollins, brought all the city's failures in the last three or four decades to the forefront of her mind. The frustration of it all only served to fuel the hatred she planned to release upon Mister Rollins, whether he supplied answers or not. The only solace she found lay in the satisfaction of seeing a scumbag like Rollins ending up in a shithole like this. He didn't even deserve it this good—a home on the verge of being condemned in a decrepit rat infested, drug addled neighborhood. In her opinion a hovel carved into a garbage heap would be too good for a child abusing waste of a human being like him. She grinned, hoping more than ever, he'd refuse to cooperate so he could learn just how difficult she could be too.

Jamie had to circle around the neighborhood twice, since half the street signs were either stolen or missing. She finally managed to find and turn down Ronkwe Drive, only to find that figuring out the correct house would be an equally difficult task. People in this kind of neighborhood either removed their house number so the police couldn't find them, or they simply let the numbers fall off as their homes dilapidated. Rolling down the street slowly made her thankful she didn't own something new and shiny that stood out, even though being an unfamiliar vehicle in this neighborhood automatically singled her out. Drug dealers would wonder if she was an undercover cop, and paranoid old ladies peeking through dirty windows would fear she was scoping out homes to rob. Luckily it was daylight—

driving along this slow after dark would have likely had her dodging gunfire, hoping to escape with her life.

Finally, she believed she found Rollins' rundown abode; 1915 Ronkwe Drive. She parked in front, putting the odds at fifty/fifty at best that her car was still there when she returned. She knew locking the doors made no difference, but she figured if someone was going to steal her car, she wasn't going to make it any easier for them.

Jamie walked up the steps slowly, in part to be cautious, but also out of fear of falling through with a single wrong step. The boards cried out in screams of creaks and groans under her tiny hundred pound frame as she carefully ascended toward the front door. Aside from the threat of a case of tetanus if her foot plunged through the worn boards, she could also see that she'd be falling into a petri dish of filth that was piled up beneath them. Jamie scrunched her face in disgust at the thought of that mess.

A sigh of relief escaped her lips when she reached the top step, even though she could see she wasn't out of the woods just yet. The boards of the small porch were in no better shape than those of the steps, forcing her to tiptoe carefully forward. Once at the door, she pulled the encrusted screen open with an ear piercing screech and a cloud of dust. She cringed, hoping this visit wouldn't end up in a trip to the emergency room for a tetanus shot or worse. The screen—what was left of it—hung limply like a dirt blanket, while the rusted hinges hung so precariously. Soon it wouldn't be a door at all.

She shook her head whispering to herself, "What a complete shithole!"

Jamie knocked and kept her eyes peeled for any "unwelcoming" committee while she waited for a response. No one seemed to be paying her any attention—unwanted or otherwise. Perhaps they didn't like Rollins enough to care who paid him a visit. The silence was deafening as she stood waiting.

Jamie knocked a second time, louder, unable to hear any movement or voice from inside. By the looks of the place, either Rollins was a shut in, or had abandoned the place. She prayed for it to simply be the former. The seconds ticked by slowly with no sound from inside, making her hope she hadn't come to such a decrepit area in vain. She knocked a third time and was still greeted with nothing but silence. Calling out wasn't an option, as it would only attract more unwanted attention. She tested the doorknob—which reluctantly creaked, but turned—and pushed against the old wooden door. It didn't want to budge. *Shit, a freakin' deadbolt on a shit box,* she thought. Perhaps she had been wrong about the deadbolt, because when she pushed a little harder, she felt it give slightly. She looked around again for any faces peeking through curtains and saw none.

Jamie took a deep breath as she rammed her shoulder hard into the solid oak door, sending a shock wave of sharp pain rippling through her bones. The door popped open, the rusted hinges screaming their protests as she pushed it open far enough to slide her tiny frame through the threshold.

"Anthony Rollins? Mr. Rollins, are you home?" She called out softly at first then a bit louder receiving no response.

Jamie closed the door behind her, taking in the decrepit surroundings. It was not an easy feat, but the house was far worse on the inside than the outside. Stacks of garbage, newspapers and magazines sat everywhere in piles rising from floor to ceiling. It was the stench that hit her first and nearly took her breath away. Anthony Rollins was certainly a hoarder, as well as a child abusing asshole, but what he seemed to hoard had no value of any kind. It was trash, all trash. She found the stench indescribable. It was like a dead sewer rat had been rolled in raw sewage and then vomited on by a sick dog with halitosis and finally dipped in hot garbage. Even that would smell better than the home of Anthony Rollins, she mused. She coughed from the extreme reek that hung in the air, desperately trying to keep the contents of her stomach down. Covering her mouth and nose with her shirt did little but it was better than nothing. How anyone could live in such deplorable conditions was beyond her, yet sadly, this may not even be the worst house in this neighborhood. Part of her found it fitting that a piece of human filth like former Counselor Tony lived this way. *Shit deserves shit,* thought Jamie Windstein.

3

Thomas Combs stepped out of the shower with steam hanging in the air and began to towel off. He moved with no hurry, knowing he had hours before actually needing to be anywhere. He paused a moment, admiring his six pack abs in the mirror—vanity he never showed in public—proud of the shape he kept himself in. He thought it a shame that no one ever got to see that he was chiseled steel beneath the three piece suits he generally wore. Thomas knew he was no GQ cover model, but he was modestly handsome and a fairly average six foot tall, which gave him the benefit of easily blending into a crowd. His common, short black hair and brown eyes didn't make him stand out either.

He was handsome enough to catch the ladies' eyes on occasion, although sadly, most took notice of his wallet first and his pleasant appearance second. He learned quickly that with a fat enough bank account, it really didn't matter if you were fat or ugly when it came to garnering companionship with the opposite sex. Perhaps money couldn't buy happiness, though it could buy shallow companionship, and sometimes that was all he desired. In general—the cost of a dinner was less than the cost of a prostitute. He found the companionship of gold diggers came cheap—they did it for just the mere promise of money. They were trying to use him, and so he had no guilt in using them.

His vain moment of smug arrogance ended abruptly when he turned his back to the mirror. The sight never failed to humble him, a reminder of his true self. The reflection always brought Dantes front and center in his mind. He looked over his shoulder at the pattern of scars carved into his skin, renewing the black ball of hate that forever burned in his gut. The scars were a constant reminder of the pact he'd made with his blood brother all those years ago in the dark, while they shook with fear. The road from escape to revenge had been a long and winding one—his scars reminding him of that every day. Now the end was so close he could taste it. Their plan was working out perfectly.

Thomas felt a smirk crawl over his lips as he dressed, thinking how right about now private investigator extraordinaire, Jamie Windstein, should be winding her way through the putrescent mountains of 1915 Ronkwe Drive to the resident sage of filth himself, Anthony Rollins. How unfortunate for her to crawl through that vomitory just for Rollins to provide her no answers at all, he thought. He honestly felt bad for a second. He wished he'd installed a camera right on Rollins' forehead so he could see that look on her face when she finally found him. *Now that would be priceless!*

Jimmy wanted Jamie to interrogate all of them ,but Thomas insisted on taking revenge on Rollins personally and refused to let Jamie be his surrogate. Thomas knew Rollins was a degenerate alcoholic with a loose tongue, willing to spill his guts for a fifth of cheap whiskey and potentially ruining their whole plan. More importantly, Thomas needed to take personal revenge on Rollins, and it wasn't something he was willing to sacrifice for anything. Jimmy knew the reasons why, so it wasn't a hard sell. Jimmy only insisted Thomas leave Rollins alive for Jamie to finish off. After Thomas explained what he had in mind for Rollins, they both laughed at the horrible nature of it and the discussion ended. The only real worry they had was whether Jamie would be able to make it through the stinking putrescence to find him or not. Their worries faded after the discovery of her little secret, and they saw she was certainly strong enough to make it.

Thomas had called Jamie right before his old pal Jourgensen arrived to throw her another preplanned little monkey wrench. He informed Jamie he thought the children's names from the file were all adopted, though he couldn't be certain. It was a lie, of course. Every child in that folder—the folder he placed for her to find—had suffered one of two fates. Either they were dead after too severe of a beating behind the red door— in which case they had been hauled away by either Rollins or Keane in the trunk of their car—or their fate was even worse. Even Thomas had a hard time coping with the fact that being beaten to death was actually the lesser evil, yet it was true. The children not carted away to be buried like a dog in an unmarked grave had been sold into a child sex ring that'd been run by Head Mistress, Eva DeLong. The prestigious pedophiles DeLong supplied made her, quite simply, untouchable. Her client list was full of the elite, the rich—politicians and anyone else with power. Delong's clientele were her insurance policy against Mormont and the potential investigation of her activities. All DeLong had to do was thoroughly misplace the children's paperwork— something she usually did quite efficiently—in the coal furnace. He and Jimmy never discovered where Rollins and Keane had dumped the bodies of the dead. They were generally too drunk to remember doing it at all. And though most of them were dead by now, they'd never discover all of DeLong's perverted clientele.

Thomas didn't see any need in involving Jamie in this elaborate plan. In the beginning, he pleaded with Jimmy that they could simply tell her the truth, or at least most of it. He didn't see any reason to play this extravagant game, with the potential to blow up in their faces and ruin their revenge. Jimmy insisted it was the perfect way to exact their revenge, while having some fun. Jimmy was adamant that Jamie needed to discover—to learn and remember on her own—or she would never believe it.

"She loves a good mystery," Jimmy spoke his case. "So let's give her the best one she'll ever get to solve."

After discovering her secret, Thomas got excited, while Jimmy seemed both proud and disappointed at the same time. Jamie Windstein certainly epitomized the saying, "an enigma wrapped in a mystery wrapped in a riddle." Jimmy was the only person Thomas could say the same thing about. And they were going to meet soon.

Starting at the Mormont Home, he and Jimmy shared everything through their years of friendship. And although they knew each other's secrets, there was always one thing that Jimmy held back.

"When the time is right, I will tell you. Until then it is my burden to bear alone. But on the day I tell you, it will be your burden as well," Jimmy had whispered one night very long ago.

Thomas knew whatever Jimmy's final secret was, that it must be extremely important because they had shared every other deep, dark secret with each other. He couldn't fathom a guess at what it could be, but he knew somehow that Jamie was at the very heart of it. He had no idea how that could be, yet she was nonetheless. He would be finding out very soon now that their plan was drawing toward its conclusion. He was ready for it to be over.

The sound of his ringing phone snapped him back to reality and he smiled as he recognized the number. "Yeah…Good…Perfect…Tomorrow. Noon." Thomas hung up with a wide grin covering his face. It was going to be a good day.

4

"Mr. Rollins?" Jamie called as she ventured past the heaps of garbage. She received no response back. She passed through the small entryway and what she believed was a family room to her right—a possible dining room to her left, though it was impossible to tell what was what with the mountains of garbage everywhere. She made her way along a narrow footpath that wound through the maze of detritus piled high over her head. She had never felt claustrophobic before, but she thought the teetering piles could bring it out in just about anyone. The further she traveled inside, the more she felt trapped. An anxiety attack loomed, leaving her even more on edge. She wanted to bolt to the nearest exit, but her gut told her Rollins was in here somewhere. Whether he was still among the living was a different question. She was determined to find out.

Jamie inched her way along. She was careful not to bump anything that could cause an avalanche and bury her alive under a ton of filth. The house was quite large—similar to others in this neighborhood—and likely had once been a beautiful home. It was hard to imagine in its current state, but at one time a lovely family likely lived here. Now it was just another decaying reminder that beauty doesn't last forever. Everything rots eventually.

Jamie reached what had once been a very nice, perhaps quaint, kitchen. It had fallen to despair and all the appliances had been removed, stolen or sold for scrap. The garbage, like in every other room, was piled to the ceiling. She never understood how anyone could live like this. The stench of decay would make just about anyone nauseous and yet, incredibly, that wasn't the worst of it. The pungent stench of ammonia from the rodent droppings everywhere stung her eyes and burned her lungs. They made a thick carpet along the footpath and crunched under her feet with every step. She tried to tell herself it was something else, but her mind wasn't fooled so easily. She wasn't sure how long her lungs would let her take it and the last thing she wanted was to pass out in this filth.

Jamie searched the entire downstairs, finding nothing—no sign of Anthony Rollins nor anyone else living among the filth. She dreaded the thought of climbing the stairs, which she assumed were precarious at best. Luckily, they were surprisingly sturdy when she cautiously began her ascent along an even narrower footpath through the refuse. She made it about half way up before a new, even more pungent stench began to assault her nostrils. She didn't think the stench could be worse, and yet it was. The thought of perhaps being through the worst of it was only stripped further away with every step. Whatever nastiness awaited her on the second floor seemed more foul than anything she ever thought possible. She hated the cold of winter, but right now, she wished for a sub-zero day in January rather than a warm day in June. Jamie knew the smell of death better than a mortician, and what assaulted her nostrils now was worse than anything she'd ever encountered before. She knew whatever was dead up there was definitely large and she didn't know whether to hope it was Rollins or something else.

Near the top of the stairs the stench was so overpowering, Jamie felt as if she had hit a brick wall.

"Fuck!" Jamie choked and tried desperately to hold back spewing her morning coffee everywhere. She couldn't see how it could be anything other than the bloated, decaying corpse of Anthony Rollins. She fought the urge to turn around and run for the exit but she had to know if it was him or something else. She ascended the last few steps, extra mindful of her footing as the putrid aroma threatened to push her back with every step.

Jamie didn't want her story to end buried in an avalanche of shit after she'd fractured her skull from tumbling down the staircase. The thought of a rescue team needing a bulldozer and gas masks to recover her body flashed in her mind. Under any other circumstance, this may have brought on a good belly laugh, but laughter was no option while she was gagging against a stench that only seemed to be getting thicker. She had adjusted to the foulness on the first floor, even if only slightly, but here at the top it was overpowering. Her grandfather used to say that terrible smells were enough to make a billy goat puke, however, she was inclined to believe a dung beetle would puke in this place. She still held her shirt over her mouth and nose, not that it really did any good against the foulness of the air.

Jamie stood at the top of the landing holding on to the rail for a moment to steady herself before moving forward. Whatever was creating the smell seemed to be emanating from the room at the far end of the hall. She waited until she felt as sturdy on her feet as she was going to get. She kept her right hand on the rail as much to steady herself as to pull herself down the hallway. She released the railing to duck her head into the first room she came upon, finding it filled to overflowing with more trash—not the source of the stench. The smell grew in ferocity with every step she took, making her question why she was putting herself through this. She knew the answer. It was a mystery and she had to find the solution no matter what.

The next room down turned out to be a bathroom, or at least, it *had* been when the plumbing worked. She managed to peek inside for a few seconds too many. Even holding her breath didn't stop the reek from hitting her like a wall. The bathroom was full of trash, which was the least of the problem. Someone had continued to use the toilet long after it had no longer functioned and there was now a mountain of feces atop it. It made for an indescribably disgusting sight, and then there were the maggots wriggling beneath a halo of flies. Jamie always thought of herself as having an iron gut, but that bathroom was more than she could take. She felt the bile rising up her throat at the sight, no longer able to choke it back. The bathroom did show her something more horrible than the image of the feces that now burned in her mind. It wasn't the main source of the stench that had been choking her all the way up the stairs. In the room at the end of the hall was something even more monstrously foul. Jamie's head swam at the thought, and she wished she could unsee the room, but it was an image that would stick with her forever.

Without thinking, Jamie drew in a deep breath and tried to stave off the compulsion to vomit. She instantly realized her mistake in breathing just then, but it was too late and she doubled over, blasting out the contents of her stomach. All she had taken in—a couple cups of coffee—came out in one mighty heave. The mixture of coffee and stomach acid splashed against the heaps of trash and splattered onto her legs and shoes. It was all coming up and her head spun so wildly she didn't have time to care where she puked. She retched until she had nothing left to spew out, holding her shirt tight to her mouth, desperate to calm herself before her gagging brought up bitter, burning bile.

"Fuck, fuck, fuckity fuck!"

Jamie's outburst didn't vent all of her anger and frustration but it helped. She wiped her mouth on her sleeve and braced herself for another wave of nausea. She no longer wished to continue this adventure, but having come this far, there was little point in walking away with no answers. *How much worse could it possibly get now?* she thought, but wasn't sure she wanted the answer. All Jamie wanted now was confirmation that Anthony Rollins was one dead cocksucker and then she'd haul ass out of this hell as fast as humanly possible, hopefully without burying herself in a tidal wave of filth. One last door and then she could sprint to the nearest shower, even though she feared she'd smell this place in her skin for weeks.

A foot away from the final door, the stench was so strong it made Jamie's eyes water and her stomach churn. She paused, frozen in place, bracing herself for whatever abomination she was about to stumble into. In that moment, the nightmare that had started her day came rushing back like an out of control locomotive, hell-bent to run her down.

The baby's screams echoed in her ears, yet this time a voice came with it. It sounded like a little boy to her, though she didn't trust her mind at the moment. *What was he saying?* She couldn't make out the words against the baby's high pitched wails. *Was he saying a name?* She stood frozen, her eyes closed with her hand on the doorknob. She strained to hear, as though the little boy was here with her now. Was her subconscious warning her not to open the door? She tried to concentrate, but the baby was drowning out everything. Then there was the blood—blood everywhere she looked. Every surface was coated in crimson; it even appeared to be raining down from the ceiling. She felt it hitting her skin in thick red globules until it fell like a waterfall. Suddenly the vision was gone as quickly as it had come. There was no baby, no little boy, and no blood. Reality came rushing back on Jamie Windstein. She stood outside the last door in Anthony Rollins' rancid home with her eyes watering (or was she crying? She couldn't be sure.) while holding back the bile rising up her esophagus.

Jamie turned the doorknob and braced for the wave of vomit inducing odor she knew would overpower her olfactory nerves the instant she pulled it open. She took as deep a breath as she dared to—through her shirt—mentally preparing herself for whatever lay inside. She shut her eyes tight, holding her breath until she was about to burst. She told herself it couldn't possibly be worse than the bathroom, though she knew it was likely far worse.

Jamie counted to three and then pulled the door slowly open, not wanting to look inside. Slowly, she peeked, her curiosity twisting to complete shock. She knew immediately that nothing, not even the disgusting bathroom, could have prepared her for the sight spilling out behind the door. She fought her stomach which rebelled against the vile stench, hitting her like a flood while her eyes struggled to make sense of what they were seeing. She gagged and again pressed her shirt hard against her mouth.

Jamie stood in the doorway for over a minute trying to wrap her head around the horrid scene set before her. Bright rays of sun shot through the window and highlighted every little nuance in vivid detail. The room appeared to be the lone area of the house that had not been packed to the gills with refuse—but more trash would have been better than this. She could see it had once been a very beautiful room, with dark oak floors, ornate woodwork and intricately patterned wallpaper now hanging in limp curls as it peeled away from the walls. It had once been the master bedroom and deserving of the name. Its glory years were long gone, never to return now, just like the rest of the house. Jamie stared blankly, seeing there was no amount of remodeling that could ever restore this house to anything remotely near glory—let alone even livable again.

Jamie stared unblinking into the heart of the horror, unable to fathom how anyone was capable of doing such a thing. Her brain refused to make any sense of it at first, then slowly she started to regain focus. She had never seen anything so revolting.

Stacked in the center of the once beautiful master bedroom was a literal mountain of dead, rotting animals. A multitude of uncountable critters from rats to deer, all in various stages of decay. The carcasses at the bottom were little more than a few gelatinous flaps of pelt oozing away, exposing the bones beneath. The middle of the pile was a gooey ocean of discharge, gently writhing in waves as though the whole stinking mass were alive. Which it was, in a way—alive with what had to be millions of masticating maggots. Eventually all those maggots would mature and join the plague of flies buzzing over the fetid pile like a living shadow.

There were fresh remains at the top, which looked like they had been added this very morning, and for all she knew, they had been. Some of the animals were so decayed they were no longer recognizable, though Jamie could make out far more than she wished she could. From dogs and cats to raccoons, rabbits, skunks, squirrels and even a decaying deer carcass. The massive pile of putrescence put every other disgusting thing in the house to shame—she had never seen anything like it, nor did she want to ever again. The flies accumulated in the largest numbers, feasting at their fetid trough, but they weren't alone. All manner of multilegged monstrosities crawled through the decomposing clutter taking part in the barbarous banquet. Cockroaches skittered in and out of rotting corpses, while creeping centipedes slinked silently about and winged parasites hovered overhead—all too numerous to fathom. The pile, disgusting and reeking as it was, wasn't the worst spectacle in the room, though Jamie would admit it was a matter of perspective. Somehow, despite the foul sight, Jamie found herself more curious than frightened.

Jamie stepped further into the room, pushing past the thick stench which seemed to resist her every step. What she saw sticking up from behind the mountain of rot drove her to press on, despite the nausea churning her empty stomach. At first she thought her eyes must be playing a trick on her, but then the further she moved forward it became clearer and it was not the light nor trick of her mind.

On the opposite side of the death pile, someone was hanging upside down on the wall. She moved closer, fighting back the bile rising in her throat with every step. Halfway there she could see definitively that it was a man, hanging inverted on the wall. She had no doubt it was the man she had come here to question.

Jamie carefully made her way around the rotting pile, doing her best not to step in the green-black discharge oozing from it. When she reached the far side, any remaining uncertainty left her—the man clearly was Anthony Rollins. His old, withered, naked body hung in an inverted crucifixion. And that wasn't even the worst part of his punishment. Whoever did this had not only hung him this way, but had also flayed him open from his sternum to his testicles, although the cut was not deep. They had peeled back only the very top layer of skin with surgical precision. The wound wasn't intended to kill him—not directly anyway. There was no mistaking that the man was Anthony Rollins and she decided she definitely wasn't getting any answers out of him, and so she turned to leave.

He froze her in her tracks before she took a step away.

"Heelllppp mmmmeeee." His voice was extremely weak, and so faint that the sound of buzzing flies nearly drowned him out.

Jamie stood in shock, amazed the man was somehow still alive. Without saying a word, she turned to take a good long look at his predicament. Her nose and twisting gut screamed at her to bolt for the exit, yet she had to brave it for a few more moments. She looked closer at Rollins, taking in the full scope of what had been done to him. She couldn't help but admire the handiwork of his torturer. It made her want to shake their hand—a feeling that would be shared by every child ever to have the misfortune of being under his care at The Mormont Home for Children.

The first thing she noted was his inverted crucifixion pose, minus the cross. The slow death set up for him made that the least of his worries. Whoever the perpetrator was, they obviously didn't think Rollins deserved a quick death, but then, neither did she. His ankles were crossed one over the other with a rather large rusty nail—closer to a railroad spike—piercing through them and into the wall. Similar, though smaller, rusty spikes had been driven into each wrist and then the center of each palm as well, ensuring that if one spike failed the other would hold him in place. The top layer of skin was flayed from his sternum straight down to his testicles then tacked to the wall on each side. His penis had been removed then perfectly split in half and tacked to the wall beside his head so he could watch it rot while the bugs consumed it. The cut to his torso wasn't meant to kill him, it was meant to make him suffer until someone came along to put him out of his misery. She nearly laughed seeing that it wasn't just her lucky day, it was Rollins' too.

The shallow wound that slit Rollins open had formed a small pool of blood beneath his head, though he was in no danger of bleeding to death. It was superficial—the perpetrator had been careful to slice only through the skin. Rollins' internal organs and intestines were in no jeopardy of spilling out, even though they were beginning to bulge.

Jamie stood in awe of the ingeniousness. The reason for the shallow wound, coupled with the stinking mound of rotting animal carcasses, wasn't simply shock value to whoever stumbled in—or even the heart of Rollins' torture. She found the whole scenario devious and completely fucking evil.

Jamie thought whoever did this must hate Rollins more than anyone had ever been hated in the history of man. Rollins, in essence, had been turned into a living roach motel, though any crawling critter who wished to call his carcass home was doing so. Maggots were the main residents, and no squirming creepy-crawly was refused entry into The Rollins Roach Motel. She saw a thin white wriggling line crossing the floor from the death pile through the pool of Rollins' blood, up the wall then entering the motel through multiple ports of entry. The giant carcass pile ensured an endless mass of maggots to gnaw away while Rollins hung there slowly rotting away. Maggots only feast on dead flesh, however, soon that would be all that was left of Rollins—dead flesh. The death pile ensured a near infinite supply of maggots, plus all their little bug buddies, to munch away on Anthony Rollins until they devoured him down to the bones. Jamie knew of easier ways to make a child abusing pedophile suffer, but she had to stand in awe of the time, creativity and effort put into making Rollins suffer so slowly all the way to the bitter end. Sadly, she would be getting no answers from him now, though it did upset her seeing him this way. Anthony Rollins certainly hadn't gotten off easy. He may still be alive—biologically speaking—though his mind must have abandoned him days or even weeks ago, judging by his state of decay and the size of the pile.

Jamie knelt down as close to him as she dared so he would hear her clearly, "You earned this asshole."

"Kiiilllll mmmeeeee."

"Where's Jimmy Makowski?" She figured it was worth a shot.

"Kiiiilllll mmmeeeee."

She wanted to laugh, but managed to hold it back. "Sorry, I don't do charity work. You still have hell to look forward to, you old cocksucker." She turned to exit, disappointed yet content about finding no answers.

Jamie wanted to sprint from the house straight for a bleach shower, even though she knew running spelled disaster in this place. She didn't think the stench from this place could be washed away with a thousand showers and a steel wool scrub. She figured she could at least burn her clothes. She made her way out quickly, while trying not to stumble down the stairs or bury herself under an avalanche of garbage. She feared being here too long already. The last thing she needed, no matter how unlikely, was some nosy neighbor calling the cops or worse—and more likely—alerting a neighborhood gang. She made it back to the front door quicker than she thought possible, but according to her nose, not quick enough. Relief swept over her and she pulled in a giant gulp of fresh air, opening the door. She felt her nausea wane and her stomach stop churning in protest against the fetid air inside the house with that one single breath. Another wave of relief hit her when she saw her car still parked out front, with all four tires still attached. She smiled. This truly was her lucky day.

Jamie closed the door behind her and stepped further out onto the porch. She pulled in deep breaths of fresh air, trying to purge the foulness from her lungs. Her joy died when she turned back to the door and froze in place like a statue. It wasn't another vision of blood and screaming babies this time—it was a message she instantly knew was intended for her, along with the deeper meaning it carried with it. She knew Rollins must have been left here for days as a maggot motel—probably weeks—and this new message told her, beyond a shadow of a doubt, that the Combs case and her new secret admirer were connected, too. If not, it was a major coincidence—a coincidence about as likely as the sun shining at night. Plus, she thought, two coincidences involving the same case on the same day was near impossible.

Carved into the door frame over Anthony Rollins' front door was a message intended for her eyes alone. She stared blankly at the words, *Madness Goes*, written in the same childish scrawl as her previous messages. Jamie was instantly angry. Someone was playing games with her. Thomas Combs was certainly involved, she thought, and now she knew he must have at least one partner. She knew Jourgensen may be in on the scheme, but he was definitely not the partner. He was no killer. Her mind began to spin out of control with the possibilities.

Jamie took her cell phone from her pocket and snapped a picture of the words, then slid it back in her pocket. She stood on the porch in deep thought for a moment. She pulled the book of matches from her pocket—the matches Chris the bartender had given her the previous evening. She wished for a cigarette, needed one. A thought, like a light bulb went off in her head as she remembered she kept an old pack in her glove compartment for the rare occasions when she couldn't resist. She rushed down the rickety steps, not caring if her foot went through this time. She unlocked the passenger door, retrieving a cancer stick and immediately struck a match. Taking a long pull, she felt the smoke burn deep into her lungs. Damn, it felt good. Maybe it would burn out some of the house's stench. She shook the box of matches in her hand, knowing what she had to do now. Slowly, she walked to the back of her car and opened the trunk, rummaging through its few random contents.

Jamie slammed the trunk down once she found what she needed. Raising her free hand, she shielded her eyes from the bright afternoon sun as she scanned for any prying eyes. She found none. It appeared no one cared she was there or why. Suddenly, it dawned on her while standing there that she was probably taking way too long. The sun still sat high in the sky, even though she had wandered around in Rollins' stinking home for what felt like hours. She pulled out her cell to check the time and found it was already past four in the afternoon. She technically had time to visit one of the other two on her list, but she had the need to stand under a steaming hot shower for a solid hour to even begin to feel somewhat clean.

She decided to check in with Carrie, hit up the liquor store, and call it a day. She needed to think before she made any more moves.

"Hey, girlfriend! Just checking to see if there's anything new." Jamie crossed her fingers, hoping for a typically slow day at the office.

"Hey, Jams! Nothing new here. How'd the interview go?"

"Hardly worth the effort. I think the old bastard has dementia or something. His place was a complete shithole. I think I need to bathe in acid if I want to get the stink off me." She grimaced. "Any appointments in the morning?"

"Ewww!" Carrie laughed, "Sorry it was for nothing." The sound of papers rustling could be heard. "Nope, nothing scheduled for tomorrow. You thinking of playing hooky?"

"I wish, but no," she said ruefully. "I was going to head south in the morning to try the scumbag down there. You can take off whenever you want and sleep in tomorrow. Give that hunk o'man a real good morning!" Jamie laughed.

"You're terrible! Speaking of Eddie—I think he's going to be working late. Want a little company? Girls night?"

"Maybe another night, hun. I'm exhausted and I seriously need to soak in bleach to even begin getting the stench of that place out of my skin. Soon though, I promise."

"Well, if you're that stinky, maybe it's best you have some alone time." Carrie giggled.

"You have no idea, Care Bear."

"You be safe and get some rest. I'll talk to you tomorrow."

Jamie smiled as she walked back up the steps with a metal can in one hand and the box of matches in the other. She opened the front door again, taking one small step inside. Spraying what remained of the only flammable liquid she found in her trunk—half a can of WD-40—until it blew only air. She didn't want to take any chances even though she knew an accelerant probably wasn't necessary. Stepping back into the doorway, she plucked one match from the box. She struck it against the side, lit the entire box and tossed it down. The floor instantly burst into blue flames and she closed the door, walking away.

"Anthony Rollins, you've been enlightened. Enjoy hell, fucker." She got into her vehicle. Looking back to see the house already engulfed in flames, Jamie let out a giggle before turning the key and driving away.

5

Eddie Washington swiped the key card Barker had given him earlier in the afternoon. The indicator light changed from red to green with an audible click as the door's lock disengaged, granting him access inside. The cool air hitting his face felt great, even though he had only been standing out in the heat for a few minutes. Sentinel Storage was one of only a few public storage businesses that offered climate-controlled units and had been the reason Barker and Ketchum selected the place. Plus, it was only a stone's throw away from the station.

Eddie still couldn't believe this was all happening. He considered it dumb luck that he was in the area of the railyard when taking the call, with only a few minutes left of his shift. If he hadn't found Michael Snyder's headless body, he may never have encountered Detective Barker, and he'd probably be writing jaywalking tickets right about now.

Eddie stepped onto the elevator, his thoughts stuck on why he had become a cop. He loved being a cop. However, handing out citations for minor crimes that he felt should be overlooked ninety percent of the time wasn't what he dreamed being a cop would be like. Almost all children play cops & robbers, dreaming that one day they'll grow up to stop real bad guys like bank robbers and murderers. But they sure didn't daydream of running a speed trap to ensure their city earns enough money from the fines to pay their salary. For the first time since donning the uniform, Eddie actually felt like a cop. He felt like he may actually be able to make a difference in his city.

Barker was giving him the opportunity to do some real police work, maybe even earn his detective badge. He didn't plan to squander it. He had a real chance to take down an honest to God serial killer—he'd be lying if he said he wasn't excited about it. He knew how very dangerous it could be, but he was confident in his ability to handle himself. It certainly didn't hurt that his lovely wife shared his confidence. If she were the type of woman who constantly worried about her husband being a cop he probably wouldn't be able to do it. He couldn't put her through that, no matter how bad he wanted it. He'd gladly ride a bicycle in the park and cite people for littering if he must. Thank God, Carrie was tougher than that. Thinking of wife's lovely golden locks and smiling face filled him with joy as he reached his destination, Unit #731.

Eddie knocked twice, paused and then knocked three more times, the way Barker had instructed him. The metal door rippled loudly as it was pulled up from the inside. Barker ushered him inside as Ketchum smiled at him from the back of the small ten by ten foot space. Eddie could see the pair had been operating here for a considerable amount of time. As he entered, he noticed the file boxes stacked up to the ceiling along the side wall to his left. There were two small desks set up in an L-shape to his right but it was the back wall of the unit which caught his attention. It was covered from one end to the other with a couple dozen 8x10 photos, each with a sheet of information hanging beneath it. On the right side of the wall, there was a large map of the city with red pushpins dotted across it, each holding a number, along with white pins also numbered. There were also several grey pushpins holding a question mark and, finally, a large amount of blue ones holding nothing.

"Welcome, Edward!" Dr. Ketchum bellowed as Barker dropped the door back down with a clang.

"Hey, Doc!" Eddie looked around in wide-eyed amazement. "This is some set up."

Dr. Ketchum stepped forward with his hand extended. "Welcome to The Executioner's Exhumation." He smiled, vigorously shaking Eddie's hand. "I'm so glad you're on board with us now."

"Exhumation?" Eddie twisted his face in confusion.

"Too much? My idea of a little coroner humor."

"Nothin' funny 'bout it." Barker looked at Ketchum with disapproval. "You should bury it."

"Look who's not funny now." Ketchum stared back at Barker with a frown.

"Okay, okay. How about the bickering Hendersons stop and explain what I'm looking at here." Eddie tried not to laugh.

"Nice one, Eddie! Glad I finally have someone to work with on this who isn't a completely humorless cunt." Ketchum folded his arms across his chest with satisfaction as Barker grunted his irritation. "You're only proving my point, Stephen. Now, Edward, I'm guessing you can surmise a good deal of what we have here." He swept his arm across the swath of photos. "These are obviously victims whose bodies were dumped, minus their heads. The locations where the bodies turned up are the numbered red tacks, and the corresponding white tacks are where they lived. Which, in each case, is also the last place they were seen alive. The grey tacks with a question mark represent missing persons we highly suspect are Executioner victims—but whose bodies haven't been found. And the blue tacks, sadly, represent all missing persons in the city over the age of twenty-five. The youngest confirmed victim was thirty-one, but we didn't want to rule out anyone except teenagers. The Executioner has never attacked anyone so young as far as we can tell, and if we included them, all you'd see would be a virtual sea of blue. The files over there," he pointed to the boxes, "are all information we have on the known victims. Any questions, Edward?" Ketchum finished with a smile.

"Several." Eddie looked around him. "First, why set all this up here? I feel like a spy, slinking around to make shady drop-offs or something."

"It's not to hide what we're doing—not really." Ketchum shrugged his shoulders, not really being able to answer the question.

"Look, kid, what we're doing here isn't illegal but it is off the books," Barker said. "This little team is sanctioned by the big wigs, but if one word gets to the press or we screw up in some way…there's no team and our names are mud. Got it?"

"Yeah, I got it. Everyone wants to play CYA while a serial killer is loose in my city." Eddie couldn't help the anger that crept into his voice.

"Nail on the head, Edward. If there's one thing you can count on in this world, it's that those in power will cover their asses at the expense of you, me or anyone else. We've managed to keep our work on the down low for a long time but…" Ketchum trailed off and glanced at Barker.

"But nothing, Clive." Barker gave his longtime friend a grave look. "What the Doc is trying to say, is that our time alone on this case may get cut short very soon. I told you earlier that our other murder, The Osbournes, isn't the work of our killer."

Eddie nodded his head.

"Well, what I didn't tell you, is Doc and I think it's probably another serial. We had to contact the FBI to check on similarities to any other cases. It's entirely possible it could put the feds on the scent of our Executioner. If that happens, they'll come in like a tornado and we'll be left to clean up the mess—supposing we still have our jobs." He looked at Eddie imploringly. "Doc and I understand if you wanna walk away."

Eddie stood and looked around at all the work his new partners had already done on the case, thinking about Barker's offer to walk away. He knew if the FBI stepped in, they'd smile, thank them for their files and then never even consult them on the case. He could count his time on this team on one hand, but it's exactly what he wanted. He didn't want to do this case for the glory of capturing *The Executioner*. He needed to go home at the end, look his wife in the eye and tell her the city was safe because of him. The look of pride in her eyes would be unparalled, making it the true reward, far beyond any accolades anyone else might bestow upon him.

"Walk away? You couldn't drag me off this case with a team of horses! You brought me in because you thought I could help and I intend to do just that. Let's get this son of a bitch!"

"Did I tell you or did I tell you he was the right man, Stephen?" Ketchum slapped Eddie on the back with gusto.

"I brought him to you, Doc." Barker scowled. "I hope we don't end up regretting it."

"Always the optimist, Stephen, aren't you?" Ketchum joked while Barker continued to look sour. "So now that we have all that nonsense out of way, what other questions do you have, Edward?"

With his arms crossed, Eddie turned to the wall of photos and the map. "You told me before that you hadn't found anything connecting all the victims to each other, but what connections have you found? Any work at the same place? Frequent the same restaurants, stores, parks? Anything at all?"

"Not much of anything really, other than a few cases of happenstance, at best. This is why we wanted to bring you in, Edward. Stephen and I have been working on this case for about two years now. Stephen started, informally, even longer. We needed fresh eyes. I know it's a lot to ask, but what we want you to do is go back through all these files. See if you can find a connection we missed, some common link, anything to point us in another direction. Right now we really only know one thing." He paused to look Eddie in the eyes. "That *The Executioner* will kill again…and again—until we stop him."

"Yes and eventually he'll make a mistake." Barker chimed in.

"There is one thing they all have in common." Eddie remarked, with a straight face.

Skeptical, Barker and Ketchum stared at him. There was no way he had found the connection after five minutes on the case.

Eddie broke into a huge smile. "All their heads are still missing."

Barker feigned annoyance. "You ain't here to tell jokes. I've already got one damn comedian, and that's one too many!" He scowled in Ketchum's direction.

"No, no. I'm not making a joke." Eddie scrambled. "Well…sort of. What I mean is, most serial killers collect souvenirs—a piece of clothing, a lock of hair, even teeth. What if the reason the heads are never found is because they are his trophies? What if he keeps them somewhere? Going by the known victims—that's what? Two dozen heads? That has to take up a lot of space, assuming there are even more victims than we know about."

"Still doesn't really help us. We already assumed he keeps the heads." Barker sighed, though the annoyance had mostly left his voice.

"Maybe, but it's something." Eddie helplessly shrugged his shoulders.

"Okay," Ketchum began. "Let's assume Edward is correct, *The Executioner* keeps the heads as trophies. If he left them out somewhere to rot, it'd stink to high heaven, and someone might notice. He's shown a meticulous attention to detail, not leaving so much as a single carpet fiber on any victim, so far. Someone with that kind of attention to detail wouldn't take the risk of getting caught due to a neighbor reporting a bad odor. Let alone live with it himself." Ketchum closed his eyes to think. "I see only a couple of options. One—he keeps them in specimen jars. Jars of that size can't be very common, or easy to purchase." He looked to the other men. "That's something you two can look into. The only other option I can think of would be to strip them down to the skull by chemical means or even fire. Though I don't like either of those options if the heads are his trophies. They'd get ruined in the process." Ketchum concentrated. "Now, I believe taxidermists use a particular species of beetle to do that. They devour all the flesh and leave the bones completely clean." Ketchum's eye widened. "Edward, I could kiss you! Did I tell you or did I fucking tell you!" Ketchum jabbed Barker in the arm.

"Nice work, kid," Barker said under his breath, just loud enough for Eddie to hear.

Eddie couldn't stop smiling. He felt like a detective for the first time in his life. It was too bad he wouldn't be able to share this with Carrie.

"I heard that!" Ketchum poked Barker again.

"Shut it, Doc." Barker meant to sound like his normal grumpy self but he couldn't hide the smile that played at the corners of his mouth for a brief second. "Eddie, you start going through those files. Doc, looks like you and I get to search for unusual jar, acid and bug purchases."

Eddie grabbed the folding chair, brought in especially for him, and took a seat next to the file boxes. He thumbed through some files, thinking he wouldn't find anything Ketchum or Barker didn't catch the first time. However, he was happy—he had already contributed something. It might end up a dead end, but if it didn't it would be because of him. He truly hoped the FBI didn't come in and take over now that he actually felt like a real member of the team. Carrie's voice went off in his head, *Don't worry about what you have no control over.* He silently agreed with his wife and put his head down, diving into the small mountain of boxes.

Chapter Eleven: The Death We Owe

1: Sometime in the 80s

No one knows for certain where the term *omertà* first derived. Linguistic scholars are torn over the origins of the word, arguing over whether it derived from a Spanish word for manliness or a Latin word for humility. The word had not yet entered the lexicon of either Tommy or Jimmy, but they epitomized its meaning. *Omertà*—for lack of a better term—simply means code of silence. It is the refusal to speak—or "rat"—born out of extreme loyalty. No matter the threat, no matter the personal harm one must endure, up to and including death, a man never rats out his brother; this is *omertà*. The term has an obvious negative association with the mafia, however for Jimmy and Tommy, their code of silence meant the difference between life and death.

If DeLong's intention had been to break them, then her efforts could be summed up simply as a failure. Their brutal beating, followed by the unspeakable bestial violations of her goons, left both boys on the brink of their final breath and yet their loyalty to each other stayed intact. Though nearly convinced the pair had truly turned a new leaf, DeLong remained skeptical. She couldn't fathom how they could remain silent if it wasn't real, however their silence bothered her. She knew a beating, no matter how severe, was something they could likely endure, because they had so many times already. Her sadistic side couldn't resist coming out to play, though. What had her convinced of her wards' innocence, was their silence after her goons' heinous violations after the beating. Neither young man spoke a word, nor screamed out during the savagery. She found it more troubling that she hadn't heard them utter a word since. She had the fleeting thought that she had gone too far.

Tommy and Jimmy lay in their beds for three full days after the vicious assault, silently praying for death—a death which seemed as likely as not. Rollins had carried Tommy's limp, bloody body back to his own bed that night and dropped him like a sack of potatoes. Guilt seemed to get the better of Rollins momentarily, and he checked Tommy's wrist for a pulse. Rollins was normally callous and indifferent to any of the children's well-being—even after a brutal session behind the red door—so perhaps he felt a twinge of fear over graduating to murder. It was a fleeting moment. He dropped Tommy's limp arm the second he felt a weak pulse and exited nonchalantly, like it was just another night.

Fortunately, Jimmy's heart had refused to stop beating also, despite Goon Keane showing him no mercy whatsoever. The beating and rape had been brutal, but they had both survived somehow. Time seemed to stop for the three days following the inhumanity they suffered. They upheld their *omertà* despite everything—neither let their plan slip out.

DeLong marched down the hallway, making no effort to dampen the click of her heels on the tiled floor. She knew the chills of fear it sent up the spines of every single child under her care in the Mormont Home. She allowed her two most troublesome wards to recover for a week. They were now well enough to speak. She intended to extract their plan, unless somehow she really was wrong. She unlocked their door, shoving it open hard for a grand entrance. The wicked smile on her lips quivered momentarily when the boys barely even looked up, though she tried to act unfazed.

"Hello, my little darlings!" She spit her words with venom.

The boys remained stoic.

"Good evening. I trust you're well on your way back to your normal, nasty old selves. Perhaps a little worse for wear, but you're still breathing, so count your blessings."

Tommy and Jimmy remained silent, showing no emotion or the pain that still racked their bodies. They were finally able to roll over onto their backs that afternoon. They hadn't spoken a word to anyone, including each other so far. They didn't need to speak. The horrendous night had done nothing except harden their resolve. They endured the worst DeLong and her Goon Squad could throw at them, and had survived. Each knew the other gave up nothing, and so there was nothing they needed to say now. Tommy and Jimmy looked at each other—empty eyes meeting empty eyes—then returned their cold stare to DeLong. Visions of murdering everyone danced in their minds.

"Nothing? Really?" DeLong could see that escape wasn't in their minds at the moment. "I can't blame you, you know? If I were you, I'd be thinking of terrible things too." She gave them a knowing look, though neither boy acknowledged her. "I know the two of you are plotting something—or you were. I think it should be obvious to you both by now that neither of you are ever going to leave this place, well…at least, not to anywhere you'd want to be. You think this place is terrible? That Counselor Bob and Counselor Tony are terrible? And I know you think I'm terrible, but I'll let you two in on a little secret—and you'll want to remember it. There are worse places than this. There are people worse than you can even imagine. Did you think the other night was horrible? Maybe you think that's the worst it can get? Maybe?" Delong let out a long, sarcastic sigh. "I came here to tell you that you're not half as smart as you think you are, and let me tell you, I could send you places that would make you beg to come back to your Head Mistress DeLong's loving bosom." DeLong knew how evil she sounded, and yet the two boys barely blinked.

Tommy and Jimmy stared apathetically at Delong and maintained their silence, refusing to show any emotion though their hatred for her and her goons occupied every fiber of their being. The brutality visited upon them only served to harden their hate and their resolve. None of DeLong's threats mattered to them now. Any fear remaining in them a week ago died as their bloody, beaten bodies were held face down in a pillow and grown men drove out their last remnants of innocence. They drew strength from the only thing they had left; their pact to each other. *Escape to revenge* moved beyond a mantra and into the sole purpose for their existence. When death refused to come, their bond became unbreakable.

"Still nothing to say?" DeLong paused for effect. "The escape you were planning is best put out of your minds now. You hate us. I can't blame you, but I will be watching. No matter where you go, no matter how slick you think you are, I'll be there waiting. One false move, one time caught out of your beds after lights out, either of you gets even an inch out of line and the other night will feel like a Candyland dream of gumdrops and rainbows compared to what I can really do to you. You think you're in hell now? Step out of line again and you'll find out what hell is. Are we clear?" DeLong looked from Tommy to Jimmy, staring into each of their cold, empty eyes only to be disappointed that she could glean nothing from either one.

Neither Tommy nor Jimmy got any satisfaction from sending Head Mistress DeLong away merely disappointed. While she spoke, Tommy had visions dancing behind his cold stare of stabbing her over and over and then cutting her into little bits to feed to the stray cats that occasionally wandered around the playground. Meanwhile Jimmy's visions went even darker. He wanted them all to suffer long and slow. During DeLong's little speech, his imagination he was turning the tables on their abusers. He saw them chained to the wall in the secret dungeon behind the bright red broom closet door. He'd keep them there for years, doing the most horrible things he could imagine, until their skin rotted off their bones and he watched and laughed. Eventually they told each other their visions of revenge, while DeLong attempted to scare them. Once she left the room though, they simply laid back, closed their eyes and willed the pain to stop.

The two boys laid in their beds for another week in total silence before they finally healed enough to get up and walk. Amazingly neither had any broken bones, but that was of little consolation. Every movement brought a new torture. Their muscles ached, bone deep bruises cried out with every breath, and the scabs of still healing wounds tugged against their tender skin. Tommy breathed his way through that pain, and yet the pain burning his insides below the waist wasn't so easily dismissed. Every step he took felt like a gut punch from a heavyweight boxer while a rhinoceros rammed its horn up his ass. Saddle sore was the term used in cowboy times to describe the feeling of riding a horse for days or weeks at a time. Tommy felt like he had ridden a bucking bronco across the country then back again.

Tommy and Jimmy made a silent pact to never speak of what happened—even to each other. They had no reason to do so. No words could describe it even if they'd wanted to. They had both been there, so speaking of it served no purpose. It took another three days before they healed enough to walk outside their room and join the other children. Their appearance came as a shock since most of them believed the pair were dead.

Tommy and Jimmy's late night talks remained on hold for several more weeks while their bodies continued to heal. They had little to say to each other anyway, they both knew the other hadn't changed his mind nor intended to renege on their pact. In time, despite the threat, Delong's eyes did drift away. DeLong and her Goon Squad assumed they had broken the pair, despite their cold, empty eyes and continued silence. They no longer seemed to find Tommy and Jimmy a threat, a sentiment the boys reaffirmed whenever possible by shrinking from them any time they came near or passed by in the hallway. The boys even flinched at the sound of their voices, to sell their compliance to the fullest extent. The first time they had whispered between their beds in the middle of the night again, Jimmy insisted that they do this.

The days crawled slowly into weeks, while Tommy and Jimmy bided their time. They didn't simply need to put the watchful eyes to sleep, they also had to wait for Mother Nature to cooperate. Their plan required nice weather—weather to allow the Mormont children to go outside to play. They also decided they needed to wait for the nights to be warmer as well, since they'd be leaving with nothing. They fought against impatience and desperation, waiting for the right time. They knew they'd only have one shot, since they weren't likely to survive another punishment for a failed attempt. They knew their conspiring, alone, would prove fatal if they got caught.

During this time, Tommy suggested they appear to make friends with some of the other kids, to make them seem more normal. They kept on their best behavior for months, even though it had brought about their last punishment. During one of their late night talks, Tommy advised that they only looked more suspicious by keeping to themselves. He suggested to Jimmy they prove they had reformed by being more sociable. He told Jimmy they were more visible to DeLong and her goons because they were so anti-social—they were outcasts making them easy to watch. Jimmy saw the truth in it and yet he protested, saying none of the other kids would have anything to do with them even if they tried. They wouldn't want to chance being found guilty by association. Tommy couldn't argue with that logic, but suggested they try befriending a couple of newer kids who weren't jaded against them. Jimmy wanted new friends like he wanted another beating, though he knew Tommy had a point.

Kirk Phillips was a natural outcast at the Mormont Home. First, he had dark skin, being the son of a black father and Dominican mother. Second, even though he was barely ten years old, he was already nearly six foot tall, making him tower over everyone his own age as well as a good number of adults. Many of the kids at Mormont had mixed ethnic backgrounds, however Head Mistress DeLong did her best to keep dark skinned children out by using the excuse that they were harder to adopt out. This was true to an extent, since racism permeates all of American society, though DeLong used the excuse to cover for her own supremacist attitude.

Kirk became an instant outcast upon his arrival at Mormont, from his peers and staff alike. However, this made the boy perfect for Tommy's plan.

Tommy saw two perks to having Kirk as a friend. First, he was huge, which could be a useful asset, and second, it would piss off DeLong and her Goon Squad. It would be like giving the whole crew a big middle finger.

Laughing with his friend, Jimmy agreed, making the decision a total win all the way around.

Lunch seemed like the perfect time for Tommy and Jimmy to make their move. Breakfast was generally too quiet, with everyone filtering into the cafeteria still rubbing the sleep from their eyes. Only a few kids seemed chipper at that time and Kirk wasn't one of them. Tommy or Jimmy weren't either. During lunch, everyone was more talkative and in the best mood they were likely to be in for the day—making it the best time for Tommy and Jimmy to move in. Kirk made it even easier because he always sat alone so the other kids wouldn't stare at him like a freak. It made it the perfect time to sit down and try to make a new friend.

The day they tried, their plan turned out to go better than they had anticipated. Tommy and Jimmy hung back, making sure they were the last—or nearly last—to enter the cafeteria. They made their way through the lunch line, getting their daily dose of mystery meat and vegetables—the cuisine at Mormont was no better than any other aspect of the place. One of the only things they could count on was the milk being cold and pretty fresh since western New York is dairy country. The food might be inedible, but they considered it a small miracle they received anything at all as far as the Mormont children were concerned.

Tommy and Jimmy weaved their way through the tables to where their unsuspecting new friend sat at the back corner. They smiled at each other when they got closer, seeing it was possibly going to be a twofer. Little Albert James sat across from big Kirk, a sight almost so comical the boys nearly burst out laughing before they said hello. Albert was the shortest kid at Mormont and quite possibly the palest, making the contradiction between the two almost too much to take.

"Talk about David and Goliath," Tommy whispered to Jimmy.

Jimmy reached the table first and set down his lunch tray with a clack. "Good afternoon. Can we sit with you?" Jimmy smiled, a real rarity for him.

He received a blank stare of disbelief from Albert while Kirk showed immediate suspicion. "Why?"

"It's quite simple really, we need a place to sit and eat our lunch and the two of you look…well, lonely." Jimmy ignored the giant's suspicion.

"We're outcasts here, you're outcasts here. Seems like a natural fit. Don't you think?" Tommy attempted to alleviate the tension.

Albert looked to Kirk with sad puppy dog eyes for his two cents.

"We don't want any trouble. If you intend on bringing trouble, then find somewhere else to sit." Kirk remained cold and unfriendly.

"No trouble, we promise." Jimmy looked to Tommy, who nodded in agreement. "We've had more than our fair share. We ain't lookin' for more."

"Alright then." Kirk granted his approval while Albert beamed like a kid in a candy store.

Jimmy sat next to Kirk, facing the rest of the cafeteria while Tommy took the seat across from him, next to Albert. Tommy and Jimmy discussed taking it slow, not wanting to be too overzealous which would not only push away their potential friends but also raise the suspicion of DeLong and her crew. Kirk wasn't much of a talker, while Albert, on the other hand, only stopped talking to momentarily chew.

Albert was short for his age and the kind of kid whose grandmother would call him *chunky* instead of fat. He talked a blue streak, which drove most people away after only a few seconds. The boy just never seemed to shut up. For the sake of being friendly, Tommy and Jimmy smiled and nodded along with his non-stop banter. Tommy was amazed by the short boy who seemed to go on without ever taking a breath.

"Albert, hush." Kirk broke in. "Let these boys eat in peace. I'm sorry guys, I think he only shuts up when he's sleeping."

"It's alright, we didn't sit with you for quiet time." Tommy smiled.

"Apparently we came to the wrong table if quiet is what we wanted." Jimmy laughed sarcastically, bringing a smile to the giant's face.

"He'll be quiet when he's dead…maybe." Kirk laughed and wagged his fork at Albert.

"Haha. You guys are soooo funny. The midget talks a lot, hardy-har-har." Albert shrugged off the sarcasm he'd heard about a million times in his short life.

"Y'know I just realized something." Tommy added. "Any of you ever see that cartoon with the little dog trying to be friends with the big dog? He runs circles around the big dog and constantly tells the big dog how awesome he is and stuff? That's totally you two!" Tommy laughed.

Kirk burst out in a big belly laugh, slapping the table so hard all of their trays jumped up in the air. "Oops, sorry. I should kick your butt for calling me a dog, but that's too damn funny."

Unfortunately, their fun was short lived. Kirk's loud guffaw caught the attention of DeLong and everyone else in the cafeteria. She sauntered across the room toward them, catching Jimmy's attention, while all the kids held their collective breath for whatever terrible thing they were sure was about to happen.

"Guys, cool it." Jimmy whispered. "DeLong's headed this way."

DeLong's name brought immediate silence to the table as all of their smiles fell away. Tommy and Jimmy wanted DeLong to see them being social. They didn't intend to attract unwanted attention even though they expected it. The woman was predictable.

DeLong stopped at the end of their table, putting her hands down deliberately on the edge and leaned down. "Well, well, well. What do we have here?" Her presence froze the boys stiff. "You two—Giant and Pee Wee— why you associating with these two? They your new girlfriends? Is that what we have going on here? Making a little love nest in my cafeteria? Somebody better speak up!" Now the whole cafeteria went silent.

"We just thought…" Jimmy began, but DeLong cut him off.

"Thought? You just thought? Boy, you ain't never had a thought worth a shit your whole damn life." DeLong leaned in close and whispered so only Jimmy could hear. "Best shut your fucking mouth before I give Counselor Bob the keys to your room tonight." She shot him an evil smile. "You two, why you let these two troublemakers sit with you? Answer me!"

Albert spoke first in his high pitched nasally voice. "They asked to sit with us, Head Mistress DeLong. That's all."

DeLong bolted around the table to stand behind little Albert. She grabbed hold of his ear with her thumb and forefinger twisting until he yelped out like a puppy getting kicked. Tears sprang to his eyes as she twisted until his ear turned several different shades of red and purple.

"You think you fool me, you little elf? Maybe you need a visit to the broom closet tonight." DeLong sneered, her voice lowered even though everyone heard her in the silent room.

"He spoke the truth, Head Mistress. Tommy and Jimmy asked if they could sit with us. I told them it was okay, not Albert. I gave them permission." Kirk shook with fear but he never lied, and he protected his friends with a ferocity.

Head Mistress DeLong scowled at him with the fire of hell in her eyes. It didn't take much to bring her sadistic side to the surface and she knew she needed to get herself under control, at least, for the moment. She stared daggers at the dark giant across the table until she no longer saw a boy, just a raw piece of meat to sculpt as she saw fit. He was big, making it a challenge, and that made her smile. She loved a challenge.

Tommy's heart sunk in his chest, seeing DeLong's mouth curve upward. He knew the look too well. He saw no way these two could possibly be their friends now, not when they would pay the price for it. His tight black ball of hate grew a little more in that moment. He was glad to see these boys defend themselves, but when they found out the price of insolence at Mormont Home, there was little chance they'd care to pay it a second time.

DeLong stared daggers at the dark giant across the table, but made no move other than twisting Albert's ear until it turned a deep purple. Kirk defiantly met her eyes, not daring to back down before she did. He wasn't familiar with its meaning, and Tommy thought that was why he didn't flinch at her wicked smile. He frowned, knowing DeLong would see to it that he didn't make the mistake twice.

"Okay, newbie." DeLong finally ended the silence, still locked in her stare down with Kirk. "If you wish to dine with swine then by all means…enjoy your lunch. Now you owe me and—rest assured—I collect my debts in full." She looked around the table still holding Albert's ear so tight it appeared she might take it with her. "Please, enjoy the rest of your lunch, boys." Then she locked onto Kirk once again. "And you, dark meat, you have a pleasant afternoon. Save your energy—I'll be back later to collect."

Delong let go of Albert's ear and walked nonchalantly away as though nothing had happened. The boys sat in uneasy silence and waited for the other children to stop staring and go back to eating their lunch. Albert's sobs were the only sound in the entire cafeteria for several minutes. He sat holding his ear with a river of tears, and eventually snot, running down his face. No one dared breathe, let alone speak to break the dead silence filling the room. Eventually the other children returned to their lunches, bringing a din of forks scraping plastic trays and hushed conversation about the four boys that were still sitting silent in the back corner.

Jimmy, feeling it was safe, broke the silence. "Kirk, Albert." He addressed their table mates somberly, looking to one then the other. "We apologize. We didn't intend to bring trouble when we asked to sit with you. We truly just wanted to make friends." He looked at Tommy. "I know I speak for both of us and we understand if you want nothing to do with us." Jimmy spoke soft, slow and deliberate with sincerity.

Albert started to speak up but Kirk raised a hand for him to stop. "If you really want to be friends, please stay. If all you wanted was to take the heat off your backs and place it on ours, then you just gained two more enemies in this place, and you can fuck off." Kirk ended with a deadly serious stare.

Jimmy and Tommy exchanged a look of delighted surprise. They weren't expecting to find a kindred spirit in this place. They liked Kirk instantly and he had earned their trust just as quickly. They suspected Albert might fold like a sheet, but they could see Kirk would never break under any amount of pressure.

"You do realize what's going to happen to you tonight after lights out?" Jimmy kept his voice low.

"I can guess." Kirk seemed to already be preparing himself mentally.

"What about you, Albert? She'll likely come for you too."

They all waited patiently for Albert's response. None of them expected the severely undersized boy to have any spine whatsoever. They couldn't blame him if he wanted to slink away, keep his head down and pray he survived this place. They all expected him to make a hasty exit.

Albert looked up, still holding his ear. He knew they expected him to run away screaming like a scared little girl. He wiped away his tears as best he could, and accepted a napkin from Tommy to blow his nose. He wasn't proud that he'd been reduced to a blubbering mass from a simple ear twist even though he was helpless against the pain. He cried easily. He was short and fat. However, he wasn't weak nor stupid despite what everyone believed.

Albert gathered himself the best he could and looked at each of them one by one, through his own burning bloodshot pupils. "After lights out, that evil bitch is going to enter our rooms with one or more of her fucking goons. They're going to march both us down to the blood red door. They're going to take us through to the secret room, hidden behind the false wall. They're going to strip us naked or, at least, down to our skivvies. They're going to shackle us to the wall. Then they're going to beat us without mercy, and march us back to our rooms to cry and bleed until morning. Did I leave anything out?"

The other three boys sat staring at little Albert in shock, stunned by his accuracy and the cold, calculated way he related the information, like a lawyer speaking in court. They knew then they had drastically underestimated their tiny new friend. Albert, for his part, wasn't finished yet.

"Yes, I know exactly what goes on in this hell once the lights go out. As my gigantic friend said, if you two truly want to be our friends I think we can all use a few in this place. Also, if you want to be my friend, then call me Al, not Albert. Don't make fun of me for being short and don't ask my large associate how the weather is up there—he doesn't like it." Al enjoyed the stunned looks he received. Everyone underestimated him. He continued, "Now, since you've literally put our asses on the line, why don't you tell us why you really sat with us today? It wasn't for our charming good looks."

"Wow! I think I can speak for both of us, you're a pretty cool dude."

Jimmy nodded his agreement.

"I'll speak because it was my idea to sit with the two of you. Jimmy and I get watched more than anyone in here because we've tried to escape a few times. We've suffered greatly for our failed attempts. If we're going to survive this place and possibly succeed, it's my belief that we need some friends to trust. We didn't expect DeLong to threaten you so quickly, but I'd be lying if I said we didn't expect it sooner or later. For that, we are truly sorry. If you're still willing to be our friends after tonight, then we will be the most loyal friends you've ever had. If you choose to walk away, there will be no hard feelings and we will leave you alone." Tommy finished, holding his breath for a reaction.

"I don't need to wait until tomorrow—" Kirk started, but was cut off by Al.

"My father raised me. I never knew my mother—I was told she died giving birth to me. Unlike a lot of men in that position, my father didn't take it out on me. My dad was an attorney, though unfortunately, he failed to learn from my mother's death. One day while I was at school, my father crossed the street on his way to get his favorite lunch. 'Best cheap lunch in the country,' he used to tell me. He used to get the same thing every day, he even took me with him in the summer. Every day he got a foot-long hot dog, a soda and a bag of chips for one dollar from the same pushcart vendor. Then one day he crossed the street, heading back to his office, and some car going the wrong way down the one-way street ran him over. Fucker never even looked back and left him to die in the street like a dog. Two days later I found myself here." The other boys tried giving their condolences but Al waved them off. "My father was a good man, a smart man. Ironically, a couple of days before he died he sat me down for a serious talk. He never did that, so I found it odd. He said to me, 'Al, life is a funny, fickle thing. It seems so strong at one moment then in a flash it shows you how fragile it can be—like your mother dying. I thought that was it for me. I thought I was square with the house again. I thought I was in the black in the big ledger Saint Peter keeps on us all. I hope that's the truth. Al,' he said, 'we all have a death we owe. The price of original sin, the religious nuts will tell you. We all die one day, there's no getting around it, but that's not the death we owe, that's the death we are given. Understand son?' I shook my head, utterly clueless but wanting him to continue. 'We owe a death to the house, sometimes for things we've done ourselves and sometimes we owe the death of others who've run too far into the red.' I still don't completely understand what he was talking about that day but now that I'm here I do get his meaning. DeLong and her goons are deep in the red and, one day, I hope it's one of us who helps them get even with the house again. The deaths we owe are theirs."

The four boys stared at each other in silence. Instantly a pact between two became the pact between four.

2

Jamie stepped out of the shower with steam still hanging in the air and flowing out under the door. She felt she could shower for the next week straight and still not shed the stench embedded in her skin. Since arriving back home, she had stood under the hot water of her shower until the water went cold five times, yet still it didn't feel like enough. The pungent stench seemed to writhe under her skin like maggots in dead flesh with no end in sight. She seriously considered dousing herself in gasoline and striking another match, though she doubted even that would do the trick. She knew it was mostly just in her head now, yet knowing didn't do much to help the situation. She never thought, after all she had seen and done in her life, anything could get to her, make her skin crawl this badly. She had never been more wrong. She needed a serious distraction to get her mind off the toxic green cloud that seemed to hang over her. She desperately hoped interrogating Keane may do the trick.

Jamie dressed, mired in the disappointment of being unable to interrogate Rollins or adding his head to her collection. She admired the time, effort, and patience it took of whoever may be responsible. Obviously, they wanted him to suffer immensely. She stood in awe of how completely disgusting his suffering appeared, yet confounded by the extreme overkill of it. She couldn't say the man didn't deserve it, because he did. She had to admit, seeing him suffer such a horrible fate—aside from wishing she had worn a HazMat suit complete with oxygen tank—was tremendously satisfying. It wasn't a total loss though. Despite her disappointment, Rollins had given her an important detail. He'd told her the search for Jimmy and her secret admirer were definitely connected.

Jamie rushed down the stairs, knowing the long day she faced. She planned to interrogate both Keane and DeLong as well as confront Thomas about lying to her from the very beginning. Anger brewed inside her knowing she may find Robert Keane in a similar state as Anthony Rollins, making the trip a waste of time. However, she had no way of knowing without seeing for herself. She needed solid, honest answers, though getting to the facts about Jimmy and Mormont appeared to be nearly as elusive as finding Bigfoot. If she found Keane unable to supply answers, then Thomas Combs would discover there is something worse than The Mormont Home For Children and its Head Mistress, Eva DeLong—a pissed off Jamie Windstein.

Jamie turned the key in her car's ignition, excited to get on her way. The possibility of answers coupled with the possibility of another head for her collection put her in a great mood, a rarity for her before her first drink of the day. She also loved a road trip, even one this short. The open road and music blasting from the speakers always put her in a good mood. Road trips bring out a sense of adventure no matter how mundane the destination might be, which never failed to bring her joy. She found it exhilarating, though inevitably on the return home, the excitement wanes.

Pretty much all highway driving requires is holding the wheel straight, so Jamie cranked the music once her wheels hit the highway and let her mind wander back to the revolting scene at Rollins' house. To the pure artistry of Rollins' torment, while trying to leave out the stench and filth. She saw the majesty of creation in the scene once she got past the vileness. She thought of how Anthony Rollins, despite all else, was a child abusing piece of shit for over a decade at the Mormont Home. If she remembered correctly, his employment record listed him as an employee for about a dozen years. In that time he had abused dozens of children, at a minimum, not including what atrocities he committed before and after his time there. Rollins was human garbage who also happened, appropriately, to live in garbage. She envisioned the way he was crucified upside down, castrated, and then split from stim to stern so the creepy crawlies could eat him. Then, of course, she burned him alive to finish the deed. She thought it may be terrible, but the cruelty of his death was justified by his lifetime of evil deeds. No mercy for child abusing scum, she thought. She only wished she had taken a picture to hang on the door of every church, school, and display in every newspaper in the world with the headline:

"Justice For The Broken."

She laughed out loud at the thought.

It was another beautiful sunny day, prompting Jamie to roll the windows down in hopes the fresh air may finally blow away what remained of the reek hanging on her skin. A good day to crank up some tunes and let her hair down, while she sang along. She hoped Carrie took her advice and had taken the day off. Nothing needed done at the office that couldn't wait until tomorrow. If they missed a client, it wouldn't be the end of the world. She thought about calling Carrie to remind her to stay home even though she knew well enough Carrie may arrive late but she'd be in the office no matter what she was told. She wished she could make this trip with her best friend along for the ride, however, Carrie would not approve of her interrogation methods, nor the justice she planned to extract before she left. She was also aware that she may find Keane in a similar situation as his old buddy, Rollins. That was a scene she didn't want Carrie exposed to, now or ever.

The trip down Interstate 90 was certainly a boring one with little to see, yet there wasn't a quicker route. The back way, though slightly more scenic, took nearly twice the time and the scenery consisted of mainly dairy farms with the fine smell of cow manure wafting out— not exactly what she needed after yesterday. She actually grew up not far from where Keane called home, so she knew the area well, making him less difficult for her to find. She once had a friend who lived just down the road from Keane's address, though she wasn't familiar with his exact location.

The tunes blasted from the radio while she sang along to the ones she knew and faked it through the ones she didn't. Jamie tooled along, happy to be alone with no one to correct her lyric violations, nor hear how terrible she sang them. It helped pass the time, while keeping her mind from buzzing at a million miles an hour with unanswered questions.

As Jamie passed by, a young boy looked at her strangely. She didn't care. Other than that no one seemed to pay her much attention. She liked feeling invisible, anonymous.

Jamie reached her exit off the dull Interstate. She still had nearly a twenty-minute ride ahead of her, but it was familiar territory. Once off the thruway she pulled into a service station to fuel up and get herself something cool to drink. It felt strange being back here. She had grown up here, though she hadn't been back since moving to

Buffalo over a decade ago. She remembered meeting her weed guy behind this very gas station numerous times to pick up a nickel or dime bag, something she also hadn't done in several years. While she pumped her gas, her mind drifted through old memories from a lifetime ago. She'd attended elementary school, high school and even college all within a twenty mile radius of where she now stood. Her first drink and losing her virginity lay within the same radius. The memories of her younger days seemed to belong to someone else now.

She was so lost in thought, that when the fuel pump handle clicked, she just about jumped out of her skin. She nearly laughed at herself until the image of the screaming baby sitting in a pool of blood resurfaced. She froze stiff, fully immersed in the scene. She heard the boy's voice calling out faintly, nearly inaudible over the baby's wailing. She still found herself unable to make out his words, no matter how hard she tried. She strained her ears, as if it could help hearing an imaginary voice inside her own head. The boy's words eluded her, seeming so close yet so far away. She thought she might be able to hear the boy's voice if only the damn baby would stop crying and splashing in the blood for a second. In her mind, Jamie stepped toward the child, hoping to quiet it for a second. The baby was within her reach when reality flooded back in.

"Excuse me, ma'am. Are you alright?" An older man in a dirty green and yellow trucker's cap stood in front of Jamie, genuine concern on his face.

The voice snapped Jamie out of her vision. "Ah…yeah." She responded slowly, while reality crashed back in. "Yeah, yeah, sorry. I'm alright. I was just, um, lost in thought for a moment. I used to live around here. Old memories y'know?"

"Oh, I have way too many of those. When you get to my age old memories are all your memories." He chuckled, a big country smile brightening his face. "Beautiful day to daydream, that's for sure! Back for a visit, are ya?"

She wasn't in the mood for small talk, though she saw no need to be rude to the nice old man either. "Visiting my grandpa for the afternoon. He gets lonely now that gram passed." Jamie had always been a world class liar, thinking quick on her feet. For her, it was a necessity.

"Well bless your heart, young lady! Seems my grandchildren are always too busy with their video games or dang computers to be bothered paying a visit to their old granddad."

"These days their heads are buried in their dang phones no matter where they are. Ironic that they're too busy on social media to actually socialize with real people when they're in a room full of 'em." They laughed together.

"Ain't that the dang truth! Well, I won't keep ya from your business, ma'am. You have a wonderful day now!"

"You too, sir!" She smiled as the old man turned back to his vehicle. She let out a long sigh, steadying herself before bopping into the convenience store for something cold to drink.

About fifteen minutes later she pulled slowly up Robert Keane's dirt driveway, trying to keep quiet and not kick up too much dust. The house sat over a quarter mile off the main road in a carved out patch of land surrounded by trees, making it impossible to see until she rounded the final curve. She said a silent prayer for Keane to be in better shape than his old pedophile buddy, Anthony Rollins.

She realized quickly if she intended to sneak up on Robert Keane she would've needed some sort of stealth mode installed in her car. Her tires threw dust high in the air no matter how slowly she crept along. Also

Keane's homestead was so calm and serene that even an electric car would sound like a chainsaw pulling up. Keane's house was really a large shack, looking every bit abandoned as Rollins' place had been, which made her heart sink in her chest a little. She hoped like hell Keane was in better shape than his old friend.

She parked and exited, slamming the door loudly. If her presence hadn't been noticed by now, then Keane was already dead. She approached the front steps cautiously, spying a big black cat darting off the edge of the porch in a hurry to get out of her way.

"Well, at least someone's home." She sighed.

Jamie put her foot on the first step and flinched as it creaked loud enough to wake the dead. She almost laughed and remembered why no one needed an alarm in the country. Keane would have to be deaf and blind to be unaware he had a visitor. She raised her fist to knock, when a voice called out from the backside of the house.

"Back here, young lady." Keane's voice was gravelly and unpleasant.

Jamie breathed a sigh of relief. It was definitely an old man's voice and relatively healthy. Keane may not be the picture of health, but he wasn't hanging upside down a few feet from a rotting pile of dead animals.

Keane's screen door was so caked in dirt she could barely see anything at all inside. What she could see reminded her of Rollins' home. Garbage was strewn everywhere. The difference being, while Rollins seemed to be a hoarder, Keane looked to be just a lazy slob. Neither were ever going to make the cover of *Good Housekeeping* or *Better Homes and Gardens*.

She stepped back down the creaky wooden steps and walked cautiously around to the backside of the house, doing her best to avoid twisting an ankle across the uneven lawn. Rounding the corner of the house she saw a wrinkled, grumpy looking old man in a rocking chair.

Keane may have aged poorly, but she recognized his ugly mug from his old photos. He was definitely Robert Keane, no doubt about it. The old man stared at her with either suspicion or contempt, she wasn't necessarily sure which, but she had business with him whether he liked it or not.

Jamie shot him a friendly smile, like she had the gentleman at the gas station only a moment ago. She'd play nice until it was time not to. "Good morning! Robert Keane?"

"You can drop the 'happy to see you act', missy. I know who you are." Keane growled.

Her face mistakenly showed the surprise his words created.

"That's right. I knew you was a comin' today. Bet your skinny little ass didn't expect that, did ya? Bet you're wonderin' how I knew." He looked downright giddy.

"Well, I've had a strange week so go ahead, shoot. How did you know who I am—if that's even true—and how did you know I was coming?" She was genuinely curious if he'd talk voluntarily.

"*He* told me. And if you think for even a second, Imma tellin' you who *he* is, you best think again, Jamie Wine-stine." Keane rocked in his chair, extremely satisfied with himself.

Jamie was a little disappointed even though she wasn't exactly surprised by the turn of events. Any doubt remaining about her being a pawn in someone's little game were removed by Keane's vague confession. The message at Rollins' house had confirmed the search for Jimmy and her secret admirer were connected, however, Keane's admission had just narrowed it down to either Thomas or Jimmy. The why is what she needed to know now.

Her friendly smile returned as she thought about how much fun she was going to have interrogating this withered pedophile in a rocking chair. Robert Keane owed his life for his many thefts of innocence. Jamie grew excited thinking of how slowly and painfully she was going to get her answers, along with justice for every child this human filth left broken along the way.

2

Thomas Combs sat outside of Spot Coffee, in what had become his usual seat, sipping his double espresso. The sun shone on his face while he flipped through the financial pages of the *Wall Street Journal*. He knew his company ran just fine without him there, but he liked to check his stock prices anyway. The technological age the world enjoyed, in part due to his own company, made it easy to communicate no matter where he happened to be physically, yet he liked to be a hands on type of manager. He found the old adage of the mice coming out to play when the cat's away true most of the time. It wasn't his employees goofing off that made him uneasy. His office was his home, his safe place. He was the All Seeing Eye in that place—nothing came or went without him knowing. He missed the sense of security he found only there, though he would never admit it.

A rusting dark blue Olds Delta 88 pulled up to the curb in front of his table and he swept his longing for home aside. Downing the last of his espresso, he set the cup and saucer on top of his paper and made his way to the vehicle. No one paid any attention to him, but he glanced around for prying eyes before opening the door of the beat up jalopy. The car pulled away down Elmwood Avenue.

"Did she see your final message?"

"I thought we were going to need to switch to Plan B for a minute, but then she saw it on her way out." The driver's deep voice boomed in the small space.

"So why are we meeting? If she saw us right now everything would be ruined."

"She's on her way to Keane right now. You need to see what she did. I think you'll be pleased."

"Did she make it to him? Did she see what I did?" Thomas smiled anxiously. "I don't think I could make it through there without the mask. It was bad enough with it."

"Oh, she made it alright. It was touch and go for a minute, but she pulled through like a champ." The driver grinned with pride. "She tossed her cookies at the bathroom but then pushed on through it. She got up close and personal with good ol' Tony."

"I assume he didn't talk."

"Just a plea for death. I doubt he had any more than that in him. She didn't bother questioning him, though she did inspect your handiwork for a good long time. I think you impressed her."

"Still better than the bastard deserved. I should've funneled leeches down his ass." Thomas sneered. "Did she take his head?"

"No. And she didn't grant him a quick death either. You'll see when we get there."

The pair drove into a rundown area of Buffalo. Many cities had fallen further into disrepair than Buffalo, yet the reasons remained the same. High paying manufacturing jobs moved overseas for cheap labor and little to no safety regulations, or became automated, leaving rusting skeletons of machinery and brick, while the homes of former workers crumbled into decay. For those with dark purpose, it made for endless playgrounds away from the spying eyes of morality.

"Smell it yet?" The driver smiled as he wove his way toward their destination.

"Other than decay?"

"Yes, Tommy. Besides the normal shit smell of this neighborhood."

"Alright, alright, don't bite my damn head off," Thomas shot back.

Thomas didn't know what he was supposed to be smelling. Normally he held his breath when rolling through this neighborhood. The fetid stench of decay was usually so overwhelming it overpowered anything else. It emanated from every crumbling abandoned factory and the houses rotting away, inside and out. It may not have the foul odor of rotting flesh, but it was no less pungent. Finally he started to smell it. Something burned here recently, though the scent of cooked meat also hung in the air.

"She set the place on fire?" Thomas smiled with pleasant surprise.

"I like to think of it as Jamie roasting our old friend like a pig on a spit." The driver smiled back.

"And she left him alive for it? I can't think of a more fitting end for the bastard, outside of dropping the match myself."

They turned onto Rollins' street, only a block up from where his house stood only twenty-four hours earlier. They came to a stop across from 1915 Ronkwe Drive, now a pile of ash with a few charred remains of the frame and a charred toilet. It didn't look like the fire department made any real attempt at saving it, instead only hosing down the adjoining properties to prevent the fire from spreading into a disaster. The home of Anthony Rollins, once filled to the brim with trash, was reduced to still smoldering ash and little else. The scene brought great joy to the car's two occupants.

"One down, two to go, Tommy."

"The death I owed. I'm glad he suffered to his last smoke filled breath. I hope he choked on it." No mercy nor regret was to be found from Thomas.

"I pretty much guarantee he did."

"You sure you aren't letting Keane off too easy?"

"Have you learned nothing from watching Jamie? I give you credit for your creativity with ol' Tony, but I have faith in the girl. She'll make him suffer, and take her trophy. And then I'll be in the black, right along with you."

"Almost. DeLong is the death we both owe."

"Indeed, but not just ours. She is for all four of us. Her death wipes the slate clean for every kid who ever had the misfortune of seeing the inside of the room. I promised you we'd get our revenge. We're close now."

"Now will you tell me the reason for bringing Jamie Windstein into this?" Thomas annoyed his friend with the question for the millionth time.

"Patience, Thomas. Soon you'll both get that answer."

3

Once again Eddie Washington found himself in Jamie Windstein's neighborhood, which was becoming a weird coincidence. He wasn't the slightest bit suspicious of his wife's boss, even though this was twice he ended up here for a possible murder victim. Then she also had a connection, tangentially though it may be, to a confirmed Executioner victim, Michael Snyder. His Spidey Sense tingled from the string of coincidences, even though they seemed to be just that—coincidences.

Eddie thought about stopping to have a cup of coffee with Carrie before remembering she had the day off because Jamie was travelling down to the south towns. He knew his wife wasn't taking the whole day off, just going in late. He tried convincing her to take the day to relax but she would hear none of it. Carrie told him she wasn't going to sit around watching the boob tube all damn day. When he went to kiss her goodbye, he tried convincing her again, but she brushed him off. He'd headed out the door, knowing belaboring the point would only anger her.

Eddie pulled to a stop in front of 4514 Jasta Street and was pleasantly surprised to see he somehow managed to beat Detective Barker to the scene. On another day they would have considered this a waste of time, however, after the Osbourne discovery only a few blocks away they weren't taking chances. Barker hadn't told him much other than a young woman, Abigail Peterson, appeared to be missing and—given the proximity to the Osbourne house—another potential murder victim. Nothing seemed impossible at this point.

While he waited for Barker to show, he couldn't help thinking about what a whirlwind the last several days had been. The fact that Barker and Ketchum invited him to their private work space was amazing alone, but then having them ask him onto their team astonished him. Only a few days ago he knew nothing of *The Executioner* or even that a serial killer existed in Buffalo, and now his job was to hunt down and capture him. It blew his mind. His adrenaline was pumping just thinking about it.

They had no luck tracking down large sales of medical containers yet, though they were only just beginning. They hoped *The Executioner* was dumb enough to buy in bulk rather than spreading purchases all over to buy one or two at a time. The Executioner showed no sign of being stupid, aside from it being nothing more than a wild goose chase in the first place. Eddie saw hours of tedious research in his future, making it completely pointless in the end.

The thought of days spent in front of a computer screen until the entire world blurred filled Eddie's mind, until Barker pulled in behind him. It took all the restraint Eddie could muster to hold back busting on his chronically grumpy new partner for beating him to the scene. For his part, Barker barely acknowledged Eddie's presence heading up the driveway to the house with nothing more than a cursory wave of his hand. Eddie hadn't really expected more from the man so he fell in step behind his new mentor.

Barker knocked on the front door loudly several times, receiving no answer, the same as they had done at the Osbourne's house. He tried the knob to find it locked as expected. They checked the perimeter, with Barker going to the left and Eddie going around the right, starting at the garage. Eddie peeked inside, seeing the potential victim's car there, finding it locked tight. They met around the backside of the small house at a door which seemed to be their only possible entry point. Nothing seemed out of the ordinary, giving them justification for breaking the door in and they didn't need it.

At the backdoor, Eddie turned the handle and found it unlocked to his and Barker's surprise. He looked to Barker in shock before pushing it open a crack.

Barker drew his service revolver from its holster, doubting he needed it but he'd rather be safe than sorry. Eddie followed suit then silently counted to three pushing the door fully open. Barker entered cautiously, taking a few steps into the kitchen. Eddie followed. They listened for any sound of movement but found only silence. They proceeded further in with caution, though the house appeared to be vacant. They re-holstered their weapons to search more thoroughly once they saw each room was clear.

There were no signs of struggle anywhere. The home's sole occupant, Abigail Peterson, seemed to have vanished with her car safely nestled in the garage and all of her possessions left behind. Eddie wisely checked under the mattress, finding nothing there this time. Both detectives' hearts sank, noticing the strong smell of bleach in the master bathroom—the same as the Osbourne house.

"Well, what do you think, Washington?" Barker seemed to genuinely want a response.

"I think it's too eerily similar to the Osbourne scene to call it coincidence. No sign of forced entry. No sign of a struggle. Nothing out of the ordinary except the occupant is missing and her vehicle is safely locked in the garage. Also there's a strong smell of cleaner in the master bathroom, same as the Osbourne's place. The only notable difference is the clean mattress here—no blood. I can't say I have any doubt that Abigail Peterson was likely murdered by the same perp." Eddie felt like a police robot relaying the obvious, the Officer Eddie T-1000.

"I agree. So walk me through how you see what happened here. It's not a test, Eddie. I just want to see how you think."

Eddie was taken aback that Barker actually sounded friendly for the first time since Eddie met him. Eddie looked around the master bedroom, gathering his thoughts. Abigail Peterson didn't have any pictures of friends or family hung up or setting on her dresser or nightstand. A small jewelry box sat closed atop the dresser with nothing sitting out. The entire house was tidy, though only the bathroom smelled of fresh cleaning products. Eddie didn't remember any art hanging about, though there were several inspirational posters about running with a large sticker on the mirror over her dresser stating, *Run Like You're Being Chased by a Cheetah.*

Eddie closed his eyes, took a deep breath then opened them before beginning. "Since we assume our perp was already inside, waiting for the Osbournes when they returned from their date night, I think it's safe to assume the same scenario happened here. So our perp was inside the house waiting for Miss Peterson to return home. She was obviously a runner, so she comes home—young single woman—she probably felt safe once inside with the doors locked. She walks in, likely after a run or coming from the gym. She's hot, tired and sweating. She tosses her keys on the counter and walks straight through to her bedroom. She strips off her workout clothes to hop in the shower. Maybe our perp knew her habits, or simply just waited for the right opportunity to take her by surprise. Since now she's already in the shower where he planned to cut up the body afterward anyway, he takes his chance to perform a little *Psycho* reenactment, making the cleanup super easy. Our perp is highly intelligent, so I assume he left the backdoor unlocked on purpose. How he disposes of the bodies is anyone's guess, but I doubt we'll ever find them unless he wants us to."

"You're creepy, Officer Washington."

Eddie wasn't sure if Barker was giving him a compliment or not but, he felt proud of himself. Finally, he was doing some real police work instead of writing stupid tickets in order to justify his job.

"Now, what conclusion do you draw from all that?"

"Well, if this isn't the same perp who murdered the Osbournes, I'll turn in my badge." Eddie didn't hesitate.

"You and me both." Barker tossed Eddie his keys. "Do me a favor and grab the kit in my trunk. Let's see if there's anything for forensics."

Barker stood with his hands on his hips looking exactly like Peter Faulk as TV's *Columbo*. He was well aware of the resemblance, which is the exact reason he would never own a rain coat. He was truly pleased by Eddie's observational skills and deductive reasoning. He knew it usually took years to build those skills and they seemed to be innate in his new partner. He saw in Eddie, a downright scary good detective with a little more experience under his belt. He hid the smile playing over the corners of his mouth.

Eddie returned a minute later with Barker's small black bag that reminded him of a doctor's satchel in old movies. He handed it off and followed Barker into the bathroom.

Barker pulled back the shower curtain slowly and then set his bag on the floor, kneeling down alongside the edge of the tub. Barker pulled out the bottle of Luminal and sprayed some around the drain. Eddie watched, trying to take in every little detail as Barker pulled a battery powered ultra-violet light from the bag.

"Hit the lights," Barker instructed.

Eddie moved to flip off the switch, rushing back to see if anything appeared. Nothing glowed—not a drop of blood left behind. Barker sprayed around the faucet to find nothing still. Everything seemed wiped completely clean, leaving no blood, fingerprints or any other bodily fluid behind. Determined to find something, Barker sprayed the tile above the faucet—nothing. He sprayed the inside of the tub in random spots, waving the ultra-violet light over top and yet still they found nothing. Frustrated, Barker stood up about to call it quits. He pointed the bottle of Luminal at the tiles and wildly sprayed a few areas, wishing to vent his frustration with the firearm instead. Then Barker and Eddie froze stiff when Barker held up the UV light and illuminated light green fingerprints. A whole slew of them.

"I know I'm new, but please tell me you've never seen anything like this." Eddie stared wide eyed at their discovery.

"Trust me, no one has. Better get Ketchum and his team down here. He needs to see this."

<h2 style="text-align:center">4</h2>

Jamie scowled as Robert Keane rocked slowly back and forth, with a smug look on his face. The last few days' worth of information ran through her mind and she fought the urge to run up the steps and rip Keane's head straight off his shoulders with her bare hands. The old bastard held answers, and she planned to pull them out of him if it took her all damn day.

"So, you know who I am, huh? Well did *he* tell you that your old friend, Tony Rollins, is dead?" Jamie was already enjoying this. "He died horribly, y'know? I'd be happy to tell you all about it."

"Tony, eh? I thought that sumbitch died years ago. It makes no never mind to me, young lady, so you may as well hop back in your little rice burning piece of Jap crap and fuck off right back down the road." Keane smiled, full of self-confidence even though he must have known that today was likely his last.

"Quite the foul mouth you got there. Not that I expected any less from an old cocksucker like you," Jamie sneered. "I think you need to know how your old child abusing buddy passed from this world. He suffered to his last breath. And who knows? Maybe you will too. The world is definitely better off with one less child abusing asshole in it, don't you think?" Jamie shot Keane a sly smile. "Oh wait…do you feel that? I think the world is a little better already."

"You think I care how you feel about anything, bitch? So good ol' Tony is dead. You ain't gonna see me shed no tear about it. Now, if you ain't gonna fuck off, why don't you make yourself useful and fetch me a fresh drink—or are you one of them modern type cunts who thinks the whole world owes 'em something? A bitch can catch more bees with honey than vinegar, or didn't your daddy ever teach you that?" He wiggled his glass at her, letting the last few slivers of ice clank loudly.

"How about I piss in that glass and force it down some old fucker's throat instead? I've got a better idea. How about we play a little game called *how many fingers is Robert Keane willing to lose before he tells me what I want to know*?" She winked at him, knowing it would piss him off. "Or you can pretend you're not a miserable old prick and answer my questions with a fresh cold drink in your hand. Makes no difference to me, Bob, but it might to you."

Keane stared hatefully down at her, aware that he had no real play here. "I ain't tellin' no bitch a fucking thing. The hedge clippers are in the barn if you got the balls, cunt!"

Jamie smiled. Keane had just made her day. "Sweet! I hoped you'd choose the hard way! We could've done this over a couple cold drinks like real civilized folk, but I'm glad you're not the pinky-up-while-sippin'-tea type, Bob. By the way, I can do so much better than your hedge clippers." Satan would have envied the smile Jamie shot him.

She approached Keane slow and deliberate—without fear—and silently sauntered up to his rocking chair, until she stood directly in front of him. Leaning down equally slow, she savored the smell of fear that oozed from his pores. She enjoyed seeing him squirm in his seat.

"I want you to know…" She was close enough that her lips could tickle his ear. "I'm going to enjoy this."

"Enjoy what, bitch?" His hands trembled despite his brave words.

The sentence barely escaped Keane's lips when Jamie struck, faster than old Mr. Whiskers pouncing on an unsuspecting squirrel. She forcibly slammed her left hand down on Keane's knee, while simultaneously grabbing him by the ankle with her right. Keane's knee popped like an old dead stick. It echoed across the field, to Jamie's delight, followed immediately by a blood curdling scream from Keane. She repeated the process on his left knee before the echo died out.

Jamie stood with a satisfied grin. "Now don't you run off on me, sweetie. I'll be right back." She flashed him a hundred watt smile before leaving him to writhe in pain as she retrieved her tools from the trunk of her car.

Robert Keane was still yowling like a stuck pig when Jamie returned. He uselessly gripped his thighs, hoping somehow that the pain would ease. She slid a wooden chair across the back porch and set her small black duffle bag down at her feet. She unzipped it slowly and deliberately, enjoying the sound of Keane's suffering, as his eyes bulged in fear of what she might do next. Jamie sized up his head—the few wisps of white hair, the sagging jowls—it was going to make a nice addition to her collection. A spot had been cleared for it right next to the other child abusers and pedophiles that she had already emancipated from the world.

"You, fucking bitch!"

"Oh, I'm sorry. Did that hurt? It sounded like pure agony." Jamie smiled. "Was it worse than it sounded? I hope so, 'cause it sounded awful." She batted her eyelashes at him.

"You, go fuck yourself!" Keane spit between strained teeth.

Jamie only laughed. "Now, Mr. Keane, where are your manners? You may wanna start thinking about being nice to this fucking bitch, trust me. What I just did to those useless, old knees of yours…" She reached over and pat his right knee with a smile. "That's as good as it's gonna get, darlin'. Best get those annoying screams out now."

"I hope *he* kills you nice and fucking slow." Keane pushed the words through his clenched teeth.

Jamie ignored him. "Now, I have a few questions for you and I'm just dying for the answers. I'm gonna need your undivided attention, Bob." She reached into her bag.

Keane shifted in the rocking chair, clearly afraid. "I told you, you ain't getting shit outta me. I hope he makes you scream before he kills you, cunt!" Keane knew the threat was weak, but it was all he had.

"I'm pretty sure I told you nicely to mind your manners, Bob. Apparently, there's a certain old cocksucker here who desperately needs to work on his listening skills. Don't you agree, Mr. Keane?" Jamie smiled up at him, her hand hiding inside the bag at her feet. "I suggest you shut your cum-guzzler until I tell you otherwise or I'm just gonna have to knock every last tooth out of that fucking ugly head of yours, Bob. You don't need teeth to give me the answers I want." She batted her eyes again before pulling her hand from her bag and coming out with a ball-peen hammer.

Keane shifted uncomfortably at the sight of the instrument, holding his tongue. In plain view, Jamie held it in her lap. She enjoyed watching Keane squirm while she sat, tapping it slowly against her leg. She wanted his mind to race with horrible possibilities of what was to come. She had only just begun to play her little game with him. Keane flinched as she stood up, slowly moving around her chair before setting her hammer down on the table next to his nearly empty glass. His eyes widened in fear when she reached back into her bag and pulled out a box of eight penny nails. She set the box down next to her hammer, letting Keane take a good look at his fate.

He stiffened, still rubbing his legs. Jamie relished the smell of fear oozing off of the old man. With a smile, she sniffed the air loudly, while Keane broke out in a fearful sweat. Her dark emerald eyes seemed to glow with excitement. Keane's pupils went wide, dreading her next move. She loved seeing his mind race, the wheels slowly turning, trying to see any way out. There was none. She picked up her hammer, making Keane cringe.

Jamie put her free hand on his shoulder. "Don't you go running off, sugar. I'll be right back."

She slammed the hammer down on his knee, then immediately turned away, letting him howl as she entered the house through the backdoor. She intended to grab his bottle of whiskey since she wanted a shot or two herself. She noted Keane's little hovel wasn't filled with the heaps of garbage like Rollins' home, but it wasn't much better. Everything was covered in a thick carpet of dust, with random garbage strewn all over. Robert Keane was no Little Susie Homemaker. Luckily, his bottle of whiskey sat out in the open on the center of his filthy table. She grabbed it, making a quick exit before the dust brought on a sneezing fit. She exited, and set the bottle on the little table, next to his glass.

Jamie sat down in front of Keane to begin anew. "Now, Bob, I'm afraid we might have gotten off on the wrong foot—or knee—am I right?" She winked and slapped his knee with an open hand, making him yowl. "Oh sorry. I'll tell you what we're gonna do, Bob. We're gonna play a little game. Let's call it tit for tat, just for shits and giggles. Here's how it works: each time you answer one of my questions, you get yourself a shot of whiskey. We'll call that the tit. Sounds pretty good, right? Now the tat…each time you refuse to answer, or lie, or otherwise fail to give me an honest answer—well, then I take one of these nails," she held one up for him to get a good look, "and drive it into your body at various points. Oh, and I also get to take a shot of your cheap rot gut if I want. What do you say, Bob? Sounds fun, doesn't it? I hope you like the game. It's one of my favorites." Jamie did her best game show host impression while making no attempt to hide her contempt for her lone contestant. "I could just play all day."

"Burn in hell, cunt!" Keane growled.

"Aw. Wrong answer, Bob! You don't seem to be very good at this game…but you'll learn." Jamie smiled and grabbed a nail from the box. Before Keane's mind registered what was happening, she moved the nail over his right hand, dropping the hammer fast and hard. The nail slid through his old flesh and into the rocking chair's arm with a satisfying crunch. To Jamie's delight, Keane's howls echoed once more across the open field.

5

Detective Barker, Officer Eddie Washington and Dr. Ketchum stood abreast in front of Abigail Peterson's bathtub in awe of the sight revealed there. In the glow of the ultra-violet light rig set up along the back wall, the three men were stunned at the brazenness of whoever had certainly murdered young Ms. Peterson. The words illuminated in light green swirls of fingerprints would stick with them for the rest of their lives.

What horrors of human sacrifice have you seen, Executioner? – JXK

"Anyone have a damn clue what this means?" Barker grumbled with his arms folded across his chest.

Silence was the only reply Barker received. The three men stared, amazed at the confidence on bold display, trying to comprehend why their killer left a message at all. They only knew that someone with a giant ego would take the time to do something like this. It also made no sense to them why someone would attempt to communicate with another serial killer in this manner. *The Executioner* had no way of seeing these words, making their presence even more of a mystery.

"What are the chances the fingerprints are the killer's, doc?" Barker broke the long silence.

"I'll need to find a sample from the victim, but my guess is our killer used her prints for his message. He's far too intelligent to use his own, even if he knows they aren't in the system." Ketchum's opinion elicited a groan from the detective. "I'm bothered by something else, though. Is it just me or does this message seem as though it isn't intended for us?"

"If this is an attempt to communicate with our Executioner, it seems an odd way to do it. Unless we leak this to the press, we're basically the only ones who will know about it, am I wrong?" Eddie voiced what they were all thinking.

"Quite an astute observation, don't you think, Stephen?" Ketchum jabbed at Barker.

"Hey, I already praised the kid for his thoughts on what happened here. Don't go swelling his head any further, or he won't make it out the door."

Ketchum smiled, knowing how much Barker hated doling out praise to anyone while Eddie tried to hide his pleasure.

Eddie had an idea, and pulled his phone from his pocket. He tapped the search icon and began frantically typing.

"What the hell are you doing, Eddie?" Barker squinted his eyes.

"Just a second. Yes, here it is. This line is part of a poem called *The Executioner's Dream* by a Kwesi Brew, an African poet from, uh, Ghana." Eddie relayed. "I don't know if that means anything, though."

"I don't see how it would, but none of this makes any sense yet." Ketchum rubbed his chin in thought.

"Anything else significant in the poem?" Barker asked Eddie.

"Nothing as far as I can tell. I was never much of a poetry aficionado. It's all pretty much gibberish to me." Eddie shrugged his shoulders.

"I'm with ya there, kid," Barker said. "What about that big brain of yours, doc?"

"I'll print out the poem back at the office, but I'm not sure the poem itself is the killer's point. It seems to almost be a taunt like, 'I've lived through hell, what have you done?' But it's like Edward stated before. Why leave a message to *The Executioner* where *we* would find it and not him? Perhaps it's this new killer's way of telling us he's not *The Executioner*?" Ketchum pondered.

"It gives us a whole new question then. How does he even know about *The Executioner*? That name has never been leaked to the press. The victims were—of course—but only as suspected homicides." Barker was clearly frustrated.

"Well whoever this JXK is, I suspect he knows exactly who *The Executioner* is. If we catch one, then maybe we get both." Ketchum added, hoping to calm Barker down.

"You hear anything back from your FBI contact yet?" Barker asked.

"Not yet. He's doing me a favor, trying not to set off any alarm bells. It'll probably take him a day or two if he finds anything. It wasn't much to go on."

"Not sure if this," Barker pointed to the message, "will help keep it low key. You need to update him, but is there anyway you can leave the message out? Maybe just pass along the initials?"

"He's discreet. I'm not worried about him. It's anyone who sees what he's up to. They track everyone's usage, but he'll do what he can."

"So what you're telling us, is that we can expect the FBI to start nosing around unless we catch this guy in about the next forty-eight hours, give or take?" Barker sounded hopeless and dejected.

"I'm afraid that's a pretty accurate assessment, Stephen. Though don't lose faith yet—we do have those forty-eight hours to work with." Ketchum's attempt at being cheerful didn't work.

"Well, fuck." Barker sighed. "I don't think there's anything left for us to do here, Eddie. I'll head downtown and get started on the paperwork. Why don't you see if you can track down that lawnmower guy. What's his name?"

"Leon. Jamie said he isn't very hard to find. Should be around this neighborhood somewhere. Want me to meet you back at the station to help with the pencil pushing when I'm done?" Eddie tried sounding positive.

"Call first and we'll go from there."

"Shouldn't take long." Eddie turned to Ketchum. "Doc, I'll see you later?" Eddie implied meeting up at the storage unit.

"I certainly hope so, Edward. We'll talk soon." Ketchum smiled.

Eddie followed Barker out, unable to get the killer's message out of his mind. This killer was intelligent, so why leave a cryptic message to another serial killer who would never see it? Was it, like Dr. Ketchum suggested, simply to let them know he wasn't *The Executioner*? A pointless endeavor because they already knew that. It made no sense. The initials were worthless too—*if* they were even the killer's own initials and not some even more cryptic message.

It gave him a headache. Eddie plopped into the driver's seat of his car, feeling completely crestfallen. Two serial killers were running around his city now and he didn't have a single good lead on either one. He hoped Leon, the lawnmower man, knew something. He hoped, even though he expected another big, fat dead end.

6

Jamie Windstein had a sick sense of humor, and yet sometimes she surprised even herself with how much enjoyment she got out of inflicting pain on some scumbag. She couldn't think of anything that made her happier—not even sex made her feel *this* good. She laughed while Keane howled in pain, knowing he was helpless to stop her from doing whatever she desired. She gave him a moment to recover before starting her game again.

"Now, let's see how fast you learn, Bob. Now my first question—oops I mean second—is an easy one. Why did The Mormont Home close its doors?" She paused and waited for his answer, letting the hammer rock back and forth like a pendulum. "Tick tock, Bob."

Robert Keane sat silent, contemplating whether to answer or not. "They found out."

"A little too vague, Bob. I'll give you another try since you're new at this." She smiled with the hammer in front of her face. "Tick tock, Bob."

"Alright, alright. Some rich asshole came around looking for a kid who wasn't...wasn't around anymore. That rich asshole knew some politician who wasn't in our pocket. Bam! Closed. Good enough for you, Cunt?"

"Hmm, I'm gonna let that one slide, Bob. I'd suggest you mind your fucking manners from here on out." She shot him another big smile. "I'll warn you, the questions do get tougher as we go. But first, another easy one for you—what happened to the trust fund that was used to run the place?"

"DeLong raided it for years. I assume she completely wiped it out when the shit hit the fan. The trustee was one of her special clients. He let her do anything she wanted."

"Clients? Elaborate, Bob." She waved the hammer back and forth.

"She ran a sex ring for rich sickos. Occasionally, they bought a kid from her, okay?"

Jamie was taken aback by this admission, though she wasn't really surprised. She knew it wasn't uncommon for children, especially orphans, to be sold as sex slaves, even though, usually when you heard about it, it happened in some third world country. She handed Keane the bottle of whiskey, he'd earned himself a shot or two. He guzzled down a good portion before she pulled it back.

"That it?" He grunted, whiskey dripping down his chin.

"Not even close, Bob. Now, for the million dollar question. Where's Jimmy Reimse—or Makowski?" Jamie leaned in, wanting the answer so badly she could taste it.

Keane started laughing. It was the wrong thing to do. She grabbed another nail and drove it down through his already shattered right knee cap. His laughter instantly transformed into a howl of pain.

"That's not an answer, Bob." Jamie glared, fire lighting her eyes.

He stared at her, his pain obvious as he spit through gritted teeth. "You don't have a fucking clue who you're dealing with, do you? Jimmy is gonna pluck your cold, black heart from your chest and choke you with it, bitch!"

Without hesitation, Jamie drove another nail through his left hand, securing him firmly to his rocking chair. His defiance made her want more. She grabbed another nail, stopping herself with it poised over his left knee. *Keep it together, Jamie, we're not done yet,* she told herself. Taking a deep breath, she regained her composure even through Keane's choked laughter.

She looked up at him with the nail still poised over his left knee cap. "What is Jimmy's real name, Bob? Answer me now—nails are the least I can do." Jamie hated sounding desperate but couldn't help it.

"That's your million dollar question?" Keane strained, gnashing his teeth through the pain. "You are one daft cunt, aren't you? You think knowing his name is going to tell you anything? It won't. You best get on with it! Kill me!"

Keane's defiance astounded her, even though she didn't show it. She didn't plan to let him off the hook so easily. She whacked his knee with the nail three times, until it could go no further. It took all the will power she could muster not to drive the entire box into the old bastard.

"You haven't seen the worst I can do yet, Bob. Talk," she spit out.

"It doesn't matter. He changes his name every few years—maybe more. You don't get it. His name isn't who *he* is, bitch! That's what you really want to know and you don't even know it! You can fill me with nails. You can kill me. I don't fucking care! Look at me! This body was broken and useless before you showed up today! And guess what? My mind is half gone too. Didn't know that, didya? Maybe everything I told you is bullshit. Did you even think of that, you stinking cunt?

No!" Keane lifted his head high in defiance, accepting his death with open arms. "So fuck me or fucking kill me, I don't give a damn! Do it if you have the balls, or fuck off and let the crows finish the job! I'm done talking!"

Jamie Windstein was rarely stunned by anyone, but Keane's resilience had her more shocked than she had ever been. She felt the rage building inside her. She needed to get herself under control or she'd end up fulfilling Keane's request for death too soon. He had filled in a couple blanks about Mormont for her, but it was inconsequential. She couldn't fathom why he was resisting the one answer she needed above all others. It was maddening. She sat back to think for a moment to regain her composure. Would DeLong supply the rest of her answers? It seemed doubtful, since Keane had been warned she was coming—surely DeLong had or would be too. Why? Why did Thomas hire her to find someone who obviously wasn't missing, and then do everything he could to keep her in the dark? It didn't make any sense. She knew there had to be some logical reason, but damned if she could see it. It made her mind spin.

Jamie thought perhaps changing the question might help. "What about Thomas Combs? You knew him as Tommy Basnett. Has he been here recently?"

Keane laughed loudly. "You don't have a fuckin' clue about anything, do ya? Those two have been visiting me—visiting all of us—for fucking years! They pop up every now and again to threaten, torture and torment us. They made sure we all had to look over our shoulders and live in fear. Fucking psychopaths! If you haven't figured that out yet, you're pretty but you're fuckin' stupid. Now, I'm done!" His lip had started to quiver. "You can all go fuck yourselves! I ain't sayin' no more! Kill me, send me to prison or whatever the hell you're gonna do—just do it! Look at me! I'm old. I'm weak. My mind is on the fritz. What the hell do I care anymore? Do it, or leave me a knife or a gun so I can do it myself!" Tears had started to stream from Keane's eyes.

Jamie sighed knowing he gave her all he was going to give. "Just one last thing, Bob. Why did you abuse and beat those kids? Were you just doing DeLong's bidding or did you enjoy it?" Jamie suspected she already knew the truth, she just wanted to hear him say it. "Did you ever do more than just beat them? I need to know, Bob."

"Beat, fuck, beat again. I did it all and I'd do it again. I'd do it right now if this crippled old body allowed it. What do you think of that, you pathetic cunt?" He spat his venom at her, knowing it would provoke the end he wanted.

Jamie made no reply. She reached into her black duffle bag and pulled out a razor sharp machete, moving silently behind Keane. The sun glinted off the blade. It felt majestic in her hand. Like God himself was blessing this particular kill. She raised the blade, feeling more apathetic than normal. Few deserved to die by her hand more than Robert Keane.

"Cunt," Robert Keane spat his final word.

Jamie Windstein took his head.

Chapter Twelve: Hear This Prayer For Her

1: June 27, 1983

Marie Keenan ran out from the bedroom to see what all the commotion was. She heard the doorbell ring and James yelling out that he'd answer it. After that, it sounded like stampeding elephants had entered the house. She rounded the corner to find one man sitting on her husband's chest while two other men kicked him—one from behind and the other from the side.

Marie screamed and dove for the man sitting on her husband, but the other man caught her and threw her back as if she were a rag doll. He was on top of her before she regained her senses. Her attacker wasn't tall, though he was thick with muscle. She looked up at him just in time to see his fist—big as a cinder block—coming straight down at her face. She had time to scream for her husband before everything went black.

"What did you tell them, you fucking little rat?" Piotr's deep voice bellowed.

Marie opened her eyes, feeling like she was waking up from a bad hangover. Her vision hadn't even cleared before the pain hit her. She had a pounding headache, though it took her a minute to remember why, before recalling she'd been punched in the face. She instinctively put her hands to her face and felt warm sticky blood still running from her smashed nose. She screamed bloody murder. She had no idea what was happening to them and where her children were.

"Shut her the fuck up!" Piotr commanded.

Aleksander clamped his hand over Marie's mouth from behind, pulling her head back hard. Her eyes widened in panic. She began to thrash, trying desperately to break free so she could breathe, but the man's grip was like a vice.

Aleksander leaned down to her ear. "Calm the fuck down or I'll knock you the fuck back out. Understand?"

Marie nodded her head.

"Good. Now I'm going to remove my hand, but if you scream again, you'll be sorry. Understand?"

Again, she nodded, and Aleksander let go.

Marie gasped in the air like a fish out of water, nearly hyperventilating before she calmed herself enough to suck in a deep breath. Confusion filled her, even though all she could do—for now—was wait and watch. Three strange men were in her house with obvious bad intentions. She had been moved to one end of their floral print couch, and the man who had possibly broken her nose sat on the matching ottoman, while her husband was at the opposite end with the other man behind him.

Now that the wife had calmed down Piotr turned his attention back to the husband seated in front of him. "What did you tell them, rat?"

"I swear I haven't said nothin' to nobody," James said emphatically.

Piotr kept his calm and placed a hand on James' knee. "There's an easy way and a hard way here, James. Care to revise your answer?"

"Guys, I swear I haven't talked to anyone. Please!" James looked from one man to the next, hoping for sympathy.

Piotr nodded to Jakub, who stood behind James.

Holding his breath, James waited on a punch or some other punishment that didn't come.

Jakub turned away instead, entering the kitchen, while sweat dripped down James' forehead and Piotr sat, doing nothing more than staring at him. He heard the man rummaging around in the kitchen, opening and closing drawers for a minute before returning in complete silence.

Piotr nodded to Jakub again. This time he grabbed James by his left wrist, and sliced the palm with a knife he'd brought back with him.

James sucked in a sharp breath, then began to howl when Jakub poured the contents of a salt shaker in the open wound. When James stopped yelling to catch his breath, Jakub tossed a dish towel on his lap for him to wrap around his bleeding hand.

"You were seen coming out of the DA's office, James. What did you tell them?" Piotr continued as though nothing happened.

James looked to his wife, her eyes pleading with him to tell these men what they wanted to know. He knew she thought this would end if he spilled his guts. If he talked, he was sure it would be the end for them. His mind scrambled for an excuse, anything they might believe. He wished he had taken the offer of protection now, but it was too late. He killed his family by talking—unfortunately, saving them wasn't going to be that easy.

"There are no answers over there, rat." Piotr grabbed James by his lacerated hand and squeezed until the bones nearly snapped. "See the fear on your wife's face, James? She wants you to tell us what we want to know before things get out of hand. You know who we work for, so talk and we'll leave." Piotr never raised his voice making his words even more malicious. "Your wife really wants us to leave, James. Your kids want us to leave too."

"Leave my children alone!" James leaned forward, although there really wasn't much he could do and he knew it.

Piotr sent James flying into the back of the couch with one punch square in the chest. Marie began to whimper before Aleksander clamped a hand over her mouth again. She made a futile struggle for a moment and Aleksander moved his hand to her throat, letting her know silently not to protest again.

Piotr looked menacingly from James to Marie. "Either of you move again, and I'll walk in that room—" He pointed to the children's bedroom, "—and I'll cut both their fucking throats right in front of you." He turned his steely gaze back to the man. "Now, James. You're seriously trying my patience and making your lovely wife nervous. Talk or this gets so much worse. You can't even imagine."

"I swear on my children, I was never at the DA's office. I don't even know where it is." James tried pleading his innocence once more.

Piotr looked up at Jakub then over to Aleksander, giving a slight nod. Marie's legs suddenly stiffened as Aleksander gripped her throat, not hard enough to kill her, just enough to cause panic. Jakub turned to the counter separating the kitchen from the living room, sucking up one of the lines of coke he had just laid out.

"Last chance, James. I'm out of patience. Talk now, before it's too late."

"I swear, there's nothing to tell." Tears streamed from his eyes.

"Bring out the kids." Piotr instructed Jakub. "They get to watch."

Jakub snorted up another line and then went into the bedroom. When he returned, he gripped the shoulders of a young boy carrying a baby in his arms.

Marie struggled hopelessly against Aleksander's hold on her throat, unable to protect her children.

Marching the children to a chair in the far corner, Jakub sat the pair down, and then leaned forward until his forehead touched the boy's. "If you move from this chair, I'll have to hurt you. You don't want me to hurt you, do you?"

The little boy shook his head no.

"Good boy. Now stay put and stay quiet." Jakub returned to stand behind James with the devious thoughts in his head making him smile. He especially loved when things got rough.

Piotr was the cold, calculating leader of the group and Aleksander was the loyal, trustworthy muscle. But when they needed unadulterated depravity, Jakub is who they relied upon. It was his time to shine. He couldn't wait for it to begin. Piotr gave him the nod and Jakub reached over the back of the couch to pull James' arms behind his back. He pinned them with one arm, then put James in a headlock, leaving the man the ability to kick with his legs, and nothing more.

Piotr stood up once Jakub had secured James. He placed his hands on James' thighs and leaned in, up close and personal.

His smile instantly struck fear in James. It was like staring into the eyes of the devil incarnated in his own living room.

"We don't care if you talk anymore. The boss already knows. This could have gone real easy for you, if you talked. I would've given you a quick death." Piotr eyed up Marie before turning back to James. "You brought this on yourself, rat. We thank you." He glanced to Marie. "She won't. If you believe in God, I suggest you hope he hears your prayer for her." Piotr nodded in Jakub's. "Don't let him look away. Cut off his fucking eyelids if he tries."

"With pleasure, boss."

Jakub squeezed James' head and arms like a boa constrictor, ensuring he couldn't look away from the savagery about to be visited upon his wife.

Walking behind Jakub, Piotr snorted a few lines of coke, then focused his attention on Marie Keenan. He let the drug fuel his adrenaline before moving around Aleksander to James' lovely wife. He made no attempt to hide his intentions as he grabbed Marie's breasts and squeezed uncomfortably hard, snatching the collar of her shirt with both hands. He ripped it off her in the blink of an eye as if it were made of paper.

Marie squirmed against the hand at her throat, struggling to cover herself while kicking at Piotr at the same time. She knew it was futile, but she'd be damned if she'd make it easy for them.

Piotr punched her in the gut, knocking the wind out of her for the effort. "The more you fight the worse it will be." He sneered, hovering over her. "Please fight though. I love a battle for my prize."

A few seconds later he tore away her bra and panties, tossing them away without a care. Piotr was first to brutally rape Marie Keenan while her husband watched helplessly. Her young son had the good sense to shield the baby's eyes while squeezing his own tight to block out the horrific image, although the sounds he heard that day would be forever burned into his memory—if he even survived.

Piotr and Aleksander traded spots, though eventually all three men took a turn. Jakub went last with the most brutal violation of them all. The vicious assault seemed it would never end. Marie laid there in tears, helpless against the assault on a body that failed to feel like her own anymore. The men endlessly taunted James with lude and cruel comments until finally, it was over.

Marie felt like her insides had been filled with hot coals when the horrific ordeal was finished. The violation left her covered in blood from her waist to her knees. She looked to her young son with her eyes nearly swollen shut, and sent up a silent prayer to a God she no longer believed in that he still sat with eyes squeezed tight, shielding the baby's. The nightmare wasn't over, yet Marie already prayed for death.

Piotr walked back to James and punched him square in the nose. "Don't think we've forgotten about you, ya fuckin rat!" He looked to Aleksander. "Grab me the lil slugger, and the hammer out of the bag."

James' eyes went wild. He expected a brutal beating, but his fear only grew, not knowing what the large man had in mind. He'd share his wife's sentiments of wishing for death soon. He wanted to be strong for her but sheer terror was getting the better of him. He squirmed, causing the arm around his neck to squeeze him harder. He feared his head may actually burst.

"Turn him around," Piotr barked the order out.

James stiffened, instinct making the job more difficult. Jakub twisted James' neck so hard it nearly snapped before James complied and turned his back to the leader.

Pulling James forward, Jakub flipped him over the back of the couch. Jakub leaned with all his weight on the back of James' neck, choking him against the couch.

James turned purple from the pressure, although he was able to suck in just enough air, the sweet release of unconsciousness was staved off.

With no emotion, Aleksander made a point to let him see what he'd retrieved for Piotr before handing the tools to his leader. He dangled a miniature wooden baseball bat and a mini sledge hammer in front of James, removing the mystery of what came next. James struggled, only bringing him closer to being choked into blackness.

Piotr taunted James by banging the little bat and hammer together loudly. Marie flinched each time they clinked together, but had no more energy to even lift her head to see what it was. Piotr stopped a moment to pull James' pants down to his ankles, while James began to weep uncontrollably, helpless to prevent his defilement.

"We didn't want you to feel left out, rat. We let your pretty little wife off easy." His deep belly laugh sent a chill down James' spine. "You aren't going to be so lucky. I'm afraid this is going to hurt you a helluva lot more than it's going to hurt me."

"Still think blabbing was worth it now, you stinking fuckin rat?" Jakub bellowed in James' face, spit flying.

James didn't have enough air in his lungs to scream when Piotr smacked the end of the bat with the hammer. It felt like a rhinoceros had rammed into him. Piotr smacked the bat again and James was sure he would split in two. He'd never stepped foot in a church for anything other than a wedding in his life, but he prayed now. There simply was nothing else he could do, but he'd run out of prayers by the fourth smack when—mercifully—he fell into the black void of unconsciousness.

Minutes—hours?—later James regained consciousness. He was slumped over the back of the couch, free of the arm around his neck and was able to breathe again. It was little solace, though—his gut felt like it had taken a blast from a cannon. It took a few seconds for him to recover enough to notice the moans coming from the other side of the couch. With great effort, he managed to turn his head enough to see the three men had begun to sodomize his wife. If God existed, he thought, he most certainly was on vacation.

Jakub saw James conscious again. He laughed as he pulled Marie's arms down and bent her over the back of the couch like her husband. "Well look whose back with us! I gotta tell ya, rat fuck, your wife is one hell of an entertainer!"

James had no response, not that it mattered if he had. He watched Marie's head wobble on her shoulders with every thrust of the thug behind her, faint moans giving the only clue that she was still alive. He let his head drop, unable to watch, wishing to silence the awful sounds of his wife's brutalization just as easy. Tears rolled down his cheeks, knowing he'd brought this fate down on his family. He thought he had been so careful. He tried to do the right thing. He couldn't help thinking maybe he deserved this. But she didn't.

When they finally finished, Jakub spun Marie's nearly lifeless body around, letting her slump over like a sack of potatoes. James tried to maneuver, only to find even the slightest movement made him feel like he was being disemboweled. Breathing shallow didn't stem the feeling of evisceration, even for a second. Jakub made it a moot point when he twisted James around to face forward. James felt like he was being torn in half at the waist. When he dared open his eyes, he expected his legs to be sitting beside him. He couldn't hold himself upright and began slumping over toward his wife until Jakub caught him. The python wound back around his neck, this time only holding him upright instead of choking him. The leader sat on the ottoman in front of him, the way he had at the beginning.

"Does it hurt, rat? It looked like it hurt real bad." Piotr slapped him lightly on the cheek. "I mean, I didn't think it would fit, but you took it like a champ!" He laughed at his own sick humor. "I'm afraid we tired your poor wife out. I—I mean we—do have to say that she's been a delightful hostess. Look at her, rat." Jakub turned James' head, but the man closed his eyes, eliciting a punch from Piotr. "I said, fucking look at her! Look at what *you* did! *You* did this, rat. You just had to run your mouth instead of just doing your pathetically simple fucking job. Now look at her, rat. I'm afraid we broke her, not that it matters now." Piotr motioned to Jakub to turn James back to him. "Don't worry, it's almost over now, you little rat bastard. It has been a real blast though, eh boys?" Jakub and Aleksander answered with laughter.

Piotr stood, stretching to his full five foot four inch height so thick with muscle he looked like a human bulldozer. He nodded to Aleksander, who had resumed his place behind Marie Keenan, prompting him to move.

Piotr then turned his attention to the children sitting quietly in the chair Jakub had placed them in. The boy shook in fear, eyes not once opening, while the baby had whimpered itself to sleep on his lap. Piotr picked up the baby, turning back to its father.

"So precious at this age, ain't they?"

James only sobbed. Marie instinctively reached out her arms, as though she could save her baby on the other side of the room. But she could only look on, helpless to stop whatever the thug planned to do. Piotr rocked the baby in his arms lightly, then set it down in the center of the room, returning to the boy. He reached down and lifted the boy to his feet, leading him to stand facing his parents on the couch, his back to the baby on the floor. Piotr knelt down and turned the boy to look at him.

"Do you know what a rat is, boy?"

The trembling child shook his head no, opening his eyes for the first time. "A rat is someone who tattles on his friends. That's what your daddy did. He tried to get his own friend in trouble after that friend gave him everything. That's not very nice, is it?"

The only response the boy gave was the uncontrollable shaking.

"No, it's not very nice at all. Look at your mommy and daddy. See? That's what happens when you're not nice. Now, I'm going to show you what we do with rats. You sit down here and watch. When you grow up don't you ever rat on someone—not ever. If you do, I'll be back to do this to you. So be a good boy, never ever be a rat."

The Keenan's young son sat and watched while Piotr Paprota, Jakub Kislyi and Aleksander Kaczmarek showed him what happens to rats. Wide eyed this time, afraid to even blink, he sat while Aleksander handed a large, long machete to each of his friends. The trio then took turns hacking his mom and dad to pieces. They kept the couple alive as long as possible, slowly going about their ghastly business. Blood flew in all directions, while the Keenan's son watched as his parents were meticulously butchered.

The trio started with hands and feet followed by elbows and knees, saving the heads for last.

Like watching a horror movie in slow motion, the boy was helpless to look away. Blood flew everywhere coating himself and even his baby sister. When it was finally over, he sat drenched in a pool of his parents' blood. He watched, numb, as Piotr carved the word "RAT" into his father's forehead.

The other two men stacked the rest of the pieces in the back corner of the room opposite the chair he'd sat in while holding his little sister. Like the wooden blocks he'd played with earlier, his parents' body pieces were piled—with the heads on top—leaning one against the other. They made a perfect menagerie of gore, one that would stay locked in his mind forever.

After the trio cleaned themselves up, the leader came back to the young boy. He expected him to be crying uncontrollably, yet to his amazement, he sat silent, his eyes glazed over. The baby had whimpered here and there, but that had been about it. Piotr nearly laughed, thinking kids really were amazing creatures.

"You be good, Junior." Piotr patted the boy on the head. "Don't make us have to come back for you someday. Understand?"

The boy didn't respond at all.

Piotr shrugged his shoulders, not really caring what happened to either of the children after they left. Killing the children was out of the question for him, he did have *some* standards. He'd been paid to do a job—depraved as that job may be—but he wasn't a baby killer.

"Sorry about your parents, kid. They had it comin'," he said, unemotionally. "Speak of this and I'll come back for you. Understand?"

The boy remained motionless, and Piotr shrugged before turning to his companions. "Let's go boys, we're done here."

The three men entered with the ferocity of a rabid bear and now left with the care of a kitten strolling through wild flowers. They immediately put the brutality and carnage of the past few hours in their rearview—for them it was all over. Rumors of what happened here would make them legends in their world, which was the most important part for them. They walked out into the night air as proud men. They never spoke of the two tiny crushed souls they left behind. The second the door closed behind them, the children were gone from their thoughts, as if they'd never existed.

2

The drive north up Interstate 90 passed in slow motion. Much to Jamie's dismay, removing Robert Keane's head gave her little, if any, satisfaction at all. She'd received some answers but not the big one she'd been looking for. The one rolling around in her head until everything spun out of focus. Who the hell was Jimmy Reimse—or Jimmy Makowski, or whatever the fuck his real name was? What did Keane mean when he'd said the name wouldn't tell her who Jimmy was? These questions did nothing but bring her back to the other giant elephant in the room. Why did Thomas, who was obviously working with Jimmy, hire her in the first damn place? She couldn't make it make any sense no matter how many times she asked the question. The way she saw it, she had one advantage over the pair. They didn't know how much she knew. Keane had been told to say nothing, but he was only a slightly better listener than he had been a caregiver to the children of Mormont.

Jamie had returned to Buffalo before she knew it and— lucky for her—it was still early. She couldn't justify wasting time paying a visit to DeLong, who likely had also been told to keep quiet. Also it was going to be difficult to extract information from the old bitch, since she assumed the nursing home frowned on patient torture. The old Head Mistress deserved to suffer more than any of them, but she was going to have to wait. The upside was that DeLong wasn't going anywhere unless she had the misfortune of croaking without Jamie's hands wrapped around her throat—a truly disappointing thought. Thinking of the old bitch's head in her collection made her very happy though. For now, she wanted peace and quiet to think things through. She needed a plan.

Jamie pulled into her garage feeling dejected and desperate, two feelings she hated. The few answers Keane gave her, coupled with his head for her collection should've made this an extremely happy morning for her if she wasn't plagued by the answers she didn't have. She wanted to feel good about ridding the world of a low life, child abusing, pedophile, piece of filth like Robert Keane, yet there was nothing to celebrate just yet.

Exhaustion and frustration hit her hard. Her recent late nights and early mornings were catching up to her like being slammed head first into a brick wall. On top of it all, she needed a damn drink. *First things first*, she thought as she removed Keane's head from the trunk, carrying it in a bag rather than by the hair this time out of fear the old bastard's few wisps of white hair wouldn't survive the journey otherwise. She headed down to her not-so-secret room.

Jamie descended the steps and set Keane's head down on her small table, temporarily rolling the edges of the bag down to get a good look at his ugly mug. She smiled, happy the bastard was dead, although she wouldn't be fully satisfied until she had all her answers.

Her thoughts ran rampant. Thomas had picked *her*. He had singled her out over every other, far more talented, PIs. Why? His hidden reason threatened to drive her mad. She was just some piece in a well thought out larger puzzle, but she didn't have the slightest clue what the puzzle was or how big a piece she may be in it. All she knew was Tommy and Jimmy had been building their plan for a long time, regardless of how big her part was. She didn't know how she fit in and she needed to figure that out to get ahead of the pair. *What's the big fucking picture? Damn it! Drink,* she thought, *I need a fucking drink now!*

She needed to calm down and think. They had kept the upper hand on her, but she intended to turn the tables—or die trying. Jamie entered her kitchen and let out a huge sigh, trying to get her spinning thoughts to stop a moment. At least no new gift sat waiting on the counter for her this time, though that only sent her mind racing off on another tangent. *Just what in holy hell did those damn messages mean?* Blood Remembers, Madness Comes and finally Madness Goes. *What exactly did that shit mean?*

"Because I sure as fuck don't," she blurted, not actually meaning to answer out loud.

Jamie grabbed a glass from the cupboard, filled it with ice and topped it off with vodka. She took the glass and the bottle back down to her special room, plopping down in her chair with a thud. She took a long swallow, the last few days events playing in her head. She looked over to Keane's head sitting on her work table with a grimace.

"Okay, you child molesting fuckstick, so I know Thomas met Jimmy at Mormont where they became friends. They bonded stronger than most kids—in large part due to you, your buddy, Tony and that bitch, DeLong. In fact, they are friends to this day and have spent the last couple decades tormenting you and your asshole partners. I can't blame them for that. In fact, I fucking applaud them. So why hire me to find Jimmy, who was never missing in the first place? Answer me, asshole!" She stared at Keane's head like it might actually speak if she waited long enough. "Nothing? No answer for sweet, Jamie Windstein? Well fuck you, Bob! And now you tell me DeLong was selling kids as sex slaves until the wrong person found out, which got the school closed down even though one of DeLong's elite clientele hushed it all up! That makes no sense, Bob! Plus, DeLong swiped all the money from the trust fund, which did her so much good she's rotting in a nursing home? All that did was keep her bitch ass out of prison!" Jamie slammed down another glass of vodka, continuing her rant at Keane's head. "Then, you piece of shit, you tell me it doesn't matter what Jimmy's name is? Doesn't matter! You say the important thing is *who* he is! Well who the fuck is he, Bob? Answer me, damn it! He wasn't some rich fuck's kid or he wouldn't have been at Mormont. So how can *who he is* be of any fucking importance at all? Fuck! Fuck! Fuck!" Jamie downed another glass of vodka. "So riddle me this, Batman. Why me? Why. Fucking. Me. Why pick me for this wild goose chase? It doesn't make any God damned sense, Bob! So why? Why?" The vodka did nothing to stem her growing anger. "And what about their little fucking messages? What the fuck does *Blood Remembers* or *Madness Comes* or fucking *Madness Goes* even mean? Is it some weird code? And why break into my fucking sanctuary? What game are they playing? God fucking damn it! Think, Jamie—you stupid fucking twit!" She hoped saying it all out loud would make her feel better, but it didn't.

She drained her glass, filled it then drained it again still trying to calm herself. She forced herself to take a few deep breaths, and that helped a little. She needed to think rationally and form her own plan, instead of letting her anger lead her to a mistake. She drew another deep breath to focus. She could forget DeLong and her Goon Squad, they were inconsequential—a diversion. For some reason, either Thomas or Jimmy wanted her to know about them and the Mormont Home, to know their past. Why, was anyone's guess. It didn't tell her anything about them other than what they went through. They chose her, over anyone else, for a reason—a reason she couldn't decipher. Somehow, she fit in the story, but she could do nothing but wait. Did they know about her dark deeds before they had broken in? Anger grew in her again, because only two people knew the answers she needed, but they didn't seem to want to part with them.

Jimmy could be anyone or anywhere, but Thomas wasn't hiding. Keane told her they were both psychopaths—probably more like sociopaths—though she couldn't expect a doofus like Keane to know the difference. The point being, they were dangerous. Thomas knew she had part of the story and so she needed to get close to him without tipping her hand. She had lethal skills, but taking on two men with bad intentions at the same time would be a cataclysmic failure. Her anger only grew until, finally, a light bulb finally went off inside her head. She saw it all. She knew how to get the answers she needed.

3

Eddie circled the neighborhood for what felt like hours with no sign of Leon. He started to think the lawnmower man had taken the day off. As he drove around, he couldn't help his mind buzzing from the note their new killer left for them. *What horrors of human sacrifice have you seen, Executioner? – JXK* The words kept playing in his head on an endless loop. The message perplexed him because it was obviously intended for *The Executioner*, so why leave a message for someone who would never see it? Unless either Barker or Ketchum happened to be *The Executioner*—and they weren't, it made no sense to him. His mind reeled. Perhaps, it was as Ketchum suggested, simply the killer's way of telling them he wasn't *The Executioner*, which made it even more frustrating, since they knew that already. Sure, this new killer wasn't aware that they knew. To make things more frustrating, he knew the name—The *Executioner*—which only a few police knew. None of it made any sense.

Eddie tried to stop obsessing over it. Unfortunately, doing so was like trying to make water less wet. He drove along slowly with his front windows down, hoping to see or hear some sign of Leon, though he was about to give up. He rolled past Jamie's street for the second time, wishing she was home so he could stop in for a coffee or something to break up the monotony. The thought made him think again of the coincidence of Jamie's tangential connection to his entire week so far, though everyone in this neighborhood faced the same coincidence—aside from the headless corpse that had put him here to begin with. He still wanted to ask her about Abigail Peterson the next time he saw her though.

Jamie Windstein was still on his mind when he rolled up to the next block. A young female jogger was coming up the street toward him, and he stopped, hoping she knew where he could find Leon.

Eddie hopped out of his vehicle, realizing he wasn't in his cruiser or his uniform. He still wasn't used to it and, being so lost in thought, it had slipped his mind. He pulled his badge and police ID from his back pocket and held it up for the young jogger to see, so she didn't think he was some pervert or mugger looking to harass her. The woman stopped and pulled the earbuds from her ears.

"Good morning, ma'am!" Eddie smiled politely. "I'm Officer Edward Washington. I was wondering if you could help me?"

"Sure." She was reluctantly cautious, the same as anyone speaking to a cop for an unknown reason. "How can I help?"

"I'm looking for Leon. Friendly fellow I'm told mows lawns around the neighborhood. Have you seen him this morning, by chance, Miss…?"

"Chris. Er, Christina Barnes. I'm pretty sure ol' Leon was a couple blocks back up that way. I think, on Arizona." Chris pointed back the way she had come. "He's not in any trouble is he?"

"No, no he's not in any trouble. I'm hoping maybe he can help me. Couple questions about something he may have seen is all. Nothing to worry about."

"Oh, about the Osbournes?" She had the decency to blush. "Sorry, you probably can't tell me. The whole neighborhood is buzzing about it. You know how rumors are."

"Unfortunately, I do. I can't really say much, but to put your mind at ease, I just need to ask Leon if he saw anything suspicious. He's not a suspect or anything. I don't need the neighborhood getting suspicious. A friend of mine tells me a lot of folks don't treat Leon very well."

"Sad but true, I'm afraid. Poor guy. I haven't seen anything suspicious either, by the way. Officer Washington, was it?" Chris eyed him up with a flirty smile.

"Thank you for your help, Miss Barnes." Eddie returned the smile, holding up his wedding band for her to see. "I'll let you get back to your jog."

"My pleasure, Officer."

Eddie turned back to his vehicle, noticing Christina Barnes lingering a moment to watch him. He would never cheat on Carrie in a million years, but he had to admit, it felt good to know he still had it. Of course, some ladies are a sucker for a man in uniform. He put the woman out of mind and got back into his car.

He rolled up to the next cross street—Arizona—and turned down it. He wanted to confirm Leon didn't know anything, so he could get back to doing real work on the case with Barker. He knew the odds of Leon being able to help were slim to none and he hated wasting any more time on a likely dead end. He glanced at the clock, frowning that he had lost nearly an hour already in this search for nothing.

Finally about three blocks away, Eddie heard the buzzing of a lawnmower. Halfway down the block, he came to a stop in front of an ordinary ranch style house like so many others in the area. He heard the lawnmower coming from the back and hoped it was Leon. Since he could hear the lawnmower on the opposite side, he walked around on the left of the house, wanting Leon to see him coming so as not to spook him.

Eddie smiled and waved to get Leon's attention, walking slowly toward him, though Leon seemed oblivious to his presence. Eddie moved further to the back of the property, still working on getting his attention. He was halfway across the yard when Leon finally noticed him. Leon waved back, shooting Eddie a big toothy grin, and pushed the lawnmower behind a trio of tall lilac bushes. Eddie came around the other side and Leon killed the motor, dropping the pair into abrupt silence.

"Leon?"

"Yessir! I'ms Leon. Who is you?" Leon wiped the sweat from his brow.

Eddie looked Leon over quickly, noting how large of a man he was—something he hadn't realized. Leon stood at about six and a half feet tall and was far more muscular than Eddie imagined. Leon smiled at Eddie, wearing his usual blue jean overalls, a plain dark green t-shirt and his always crooked trucker's cap. Eddie noted that while Leon seemed harmless, his bulging forearms and biceps screamed caution. His physical appearance took Eddie aback.

"Hi, Leon! I'm Officer Washington." Eddie showed Leon his badge and ID. "I'm a friend of Jamie's."

"Miz Jamie sure is nice to Leon. She asked Leon to be an Invinctigator just like her!" Leon beamed.

"Yes, she told me." Eddie smiled up at the big man. "That's why I want to talk to you, Leon. May I ask you a few questions?"

"Sure, sure."

"Do you know Karen and David Osbourne, a couple streets over on Alaska? Do you remember which house is theirs?" Eddie prayed he wouldn't need to drive Leon to the house in order for him to know which he meant.

Leon thought for a second. "Leon thinks so. Miz Karen always real nice. She brought Leon cookies once for no reason at all. They was good too!"

"So you remember where they live?"

"Sho' do. They has the prettiest rose bush on the block!"

Another big toothy grin.

"Okay, Leon. Now I need you to think real hard for me. Around the end of last week, did you notice any strange person lurking around or maybe a car you didn't recognize? Anything out of the ordinary, even if it was a block or two away?"

Leon thought about it, removing his cap to rub his head. "Leon can't 'member anything strange. This a real nice neighborhood, Oskifer Washinton."

"It's okay, Leon. I didn't think you did, but it's my job to check."

"I haven't seen Miz Karen 'roun. Is they okay?"

"We're not sure yet, Leon. I'm sure they'll turn up. You can get back to cutting the grass, now."

"Invinctigator Leon keep his eyes open. Miz Jamie— she told Leon to do that." He proclaimed, proud as a peacock.

Eddie smiled back, unsure if he should to say anything else or just head back to his vehicle. He settled on the latter, thinking it best to let Leon finish mowing the lawn. When Leon turned away, Eddie noticed the mesh tool bag strapped to Leon's back. Eddie could see a pair of hedge trimmers, a pair of pliers and a couple of screwdrivers. What caught Eddie's attention was a long thin pole with a handle poking out the top of the bag and the sharp point sticking through the bottom. Nothing unusual for Leon to have—it was made for picking up paper litter. Alarm bells went off in Eddie's head though. Could it be what made the odd piercing through the Osbournes' mattress, and likely through the Osbournes themselves?

"Excuse me, Leon?" Eddie's voice cracked slightly.

"Yessir." Leon spun back around to face Eddie again.

Leon saw the panicked look on Eddie's face, though he refused to acknowledge it. He looked down for a second and waited to see if Eddie would pull out his service revolver. Neither the sound of Eddie popping the snap of his holster nor the swoosh of a draw greeted his ears. He smiled, even though he knew the game was going to be up in a few seconds. He looked up at Eddie, dropping the façade of the simple lawnmower man, Leon. He stepped forward, showing his true face to Officer Edward Washington.

Eddie reached for his still holstered gun, but it was too late, Leon was on him. Leon put Eddie in a bear hug so tight it felt like a pair of anacondas were crushing him. The simpleton that Eddie had come to question had vanished before his eyes to be replaced by a monster intent on crushing the life from him. Eddie struggled like a two year old in its father's arms, with the same amount of success. He kicked his legs, squirming back and forth to no effect. Eddie saw Carrie's face before him bathed in sunlight. He was content thinking she would be the last image his mind recalled. Darkness was coming.

"What horrors of human sacrifice have you seen, Officer Washington?" Leon's voice was gone, replaced by something dark and sinister.

Eddie's eyes went wide as he recognized the words but it was too late.

4

Thomas hated waiting, the boredom of it being the source of his ire. He and Jimmy kicked the balls into motion, and now came the waiting to see where they all came to rest. He knew the famous quote from Robert Burns well, "The best-laid plans of mice and men often go awry." They plotted. They planned. The details they included certainly seemed perfect at the outset. However, Thomas knew too well there always seemed to be one damn ball you couldn't see. Chaos is the villain to well laid plans. Thomas liked predictability, and yet so far, despite facing many unpredicted obstacles, the plan still seemed to be falling neatly into place. The balls were ending up where they were supposed to be.

Jimmy, on the other hand, was a fan of chaos. He often recounted to Thomas about how it was the natural order of the universe. Jimmy was the yin to Thomas' yang, opposites—though necessary and complementary. Jamie Windstein seemed to be pure chaos from Thomas' perspective. He feared she might whack everything out of place. She was anything but predictable. Thomas wished they had simply taken their revenge on DeLong and her Goon Squad like they planned all those years ago. It was Jimmy who insisted on this plan. Jimmy still hadn't told him why Jamie was so important to him, or why he needed to leave his messages for her. Thomas didn't like being kept in the dark by his only friend in the entire world.

Thomas conceded it wasn't complete chaos, even though their plan wasn't neat and tidy the way he liked. He smiled, thinking of Jamie roasting Rollins alive rather than putting the man out of his misery quickly. It was an unexpected but pleasant touch. Jamie had cleansed the place by fire, though the thought of the BPD doing forensic work in Rollins' shithole was laughable. However, Jimmy preached that it was always better to be overly cautious than careless. He wondered for a moment if Jamie cared that she could have burned down half the neighborhood if the fire department arrived a little late. He suspected that was part of her reason for doing it, though he did look forward to asking her at the appropriate time.

Finally when his boredom reached its peak, his cell phone buzzed with Jamie's number. "Good afternoon, Jamie!" He grinned with anticipation. "Sure, I'm just sitting around here bored out of my mind…The bar? Sounds good to me…Oh, Jaime? Wait, have you eaten yet?…Sure, I know the place…An hour? Perfect. I'll see you then."

Thomas hung up with a self-satisfied grin on his face. He didn't know what Keane had told her, though whatever he said, it seemed to peak her curiosity. Maybe this little chaotic ball was going to land exactly where he intended after all. It bothered him that Jamie hadn't visited DeLong yet. He expected her to do so after finding Rollins or, at least, after her visit with Keane. He didn't like being wrong. Now he'd have to tell Jimmy to go visit the old bitch again to make sure she remembered her instructions. He hated going to see her, partially due to the nursing home smell, but mostly because he wanted her dead. He wanted to stab her until his arm went numb from the effort. The thought made him smile.

Thomas picked up his phone, once again bringing up Jimmy's number. "She's back. Looks like she didn't visit DeLong yet…You did what?...Fuck, Jimmy!...Alright, alright…Well she's meeting me in an hour for dinner…I'll do my best…It better not be a problem…I'll call you when she leaves…Why?...Are we completely fucked?...Yeah…I got it, Jimmy. Take care of the problem. I'll call when I'm all set."

Well avoiding complete chaos was out of the question now, he mused. Why did it have to be Jamie's cop friend instead of some anonymous uniform they could dump in the lake or something? But, no! It had to be the husband of Jamie's best friend, who came asking questions. Damn it! It didn't blow their plan, though it would drastically speed things up. He warned Jimmy that "Leon" played too large a roll, and now it just blew up in their faces. As he got up to get ready for dinner with the lovely, little mystery woman, Jamie Windstein, he told himself there was no point in crying over spilled milk.

An hour later Thomas was waiting when Jamie finally entered the Pearl Street Grill & Brewery. He smiled, waving to her like an old friend. She waved back and sauntered up to the bar next to him. He handed her the vodka on the rocks he'd ordered for her.

"Sorry I'm a little late. I couldn't find a damn parking spot. Is there a city anywhere in the world with ample parking?" Jamie laughed.

"None I've been in. There has to be one somewhere, I guess—law of averages and all that." Thomas raised his eyebrows with a smile.

They sat at the bar, making small talk until their table was ready. Jamie casually flirted with Thomas, trying her best to keep him away from the topic that had her mind buzzing. He continued playing his game, and so she needed to play hers. She intended to keep things friendly and cordial until the time was right. She wasn't about to reveal what she knew yet and had never met a man she couldn't manipulate to her own ends. All she had to do was giggle at the proper times, bat a seductive eye, show a little leg—maybe some cleavage—and men put themselves right where you wanted them. They were predictable creatures, even a sociopath like Thomas. He may be playing a game with her but, in the end, he was no different than the others.

"So why did you need to meet with me, or did you just miss my charming good looks?" Thomas pried for any hint of what Jamie knew.

Jamie giggled appropriately. "I missed your charming good looks, of course!" She shifted in her seat and watched his eyes fall straight to her breasts, barely contained by her low-cut black dress. "Seriously, though I had a few questions and I hate asking the important ones over the phone. Plus, I wanted to see you, charming good looks and all that." She looked at him with a flirtatious smile.

Jamie reminded herself to be careful and not to lay it on too thick, making him suspicious. After the other night in his hotel room when she shunned his advance, if she came on too strong, he'd definitely catch on to her game. She held his interest, which was enough for now.

"Why so serious? No, Jamie Windstein. I won't marry you." Thomas winked at her. "Though it would really piss off the relatives to see competition for my will. I guess, you'll have to convince me."

She could tell it wasn't his first time using that line. It probably got him laid often, and so she played along. "Thomas Combs, how ever did you know? Maybe you should be the investigator." She playfully slapped at his arm. "Seriously though, what I want—no, need—to know is why me? I know you said Killian recommended me but, seriously, in the world of private investigation I'm not big enough to be called small fry. I mean, I'm damn good and all but I'm as small time as they come." She knew she wouldn't get a straight answer. She was watching for his reaction.

"Well—like I told you—Killian told me you were the absolute best and he's someone I trust in business matters. Honestly, that's all I needed to hear. Then I saw you and I said damn, she's sexy too!" He finished with a hundred-watt smile.

"Sorry to harp on it. It just keeps catching in my brain like a scratch I can't itch. With your money, you could've hired the second coming of Sherlock Holmes or something, and yet you picked little ol' me. But I'll take you at your word and drop it." She humbly lowered her eyes, pushing her chest out slightly to keep his mind on her body. "Now, the next one is a little tougher. A potential client came in yesterday. Excuse me for not divulging his name—confidentiality, y'know? Anyway, it turns out he has a missing person case. You don't know this about me but I really hate coincidences and this man provided two of them. First, it's a missing person case, giving me two back-to-back, when I'm usually lucky to get two in a whole year. Second, he also happened to spend time at The Mormont Home. Crazy, right?" She watched him for any hint he was in on it. "Of course, I checked him out and he seems legit. The coincidence just gets under my skin, y'know? I take confidentiality seriously so I didn't mention you or your case to him. I want to assure you of that, Thomas. However, I did ask him if he remembered Jimmy." She watched him intently for any subtle sign of surprise. "Wanna take a stab at what he told me?"

Thomas sat stoic, fully aware of who she meant and what he told her. "I understand suspicion over the coincidence. I would be too. Perhaps this man is playing some game with you for his own weird reasons. I don't really know. I truly don't have a clue what he may have said about Jimmy, though."

Jamie wanted to hand Thomas an Oscar for the performance. "He told me he did remember both of you. Then he surprised me." She raised an eyebrow at him. "He told me Jimmy's last name wasn't Reimse. He said it was Makowski." She paused to gauge his reaction, but he still showed her nothing. "Any reason Jimmy would lie to either you or another boy at the home? It makes no fucking sense, Thomas. Pardon my French." She studied his face for the slightest reaction, any hint of a tick or anything at all.

Thomas gave nothing away. "That certainly is strange. This man claims he remembers me too, hmm? I'm guessing you invited me here to figure out which one of us is the liar, correct?" He smirked.

"Yes and yes." Jamie eyed him.

"I suppose it's possible this man was mistaken. There is another possibility you wouldn't be aware of though. You see, Jimmy hated the staff. We all did for obvious reasons, but he didn't really like anyone there, except me. He got in a lot of fights. He was damn good too, so it's possible this man that came to see you got his ass kicked—possibly several times—by Jimmy. I don't know why he would think giving you false information would help him get back at Jimmy, or me, but maybe it's that simple." Thomas shrugged.

Jamie lowered her accusing eyes though not at all done being skeptical. "I suppose anything's possible. Whether it was true or not was of no consequence, since it didn't help me at all." She felt disappointed by his lack of reaction even though the absence was telling in and of itself.

Jamie dropped her questioning seeing as Thomas wasn't going to give her any truth voluntarily. Their dinner arrived, so she returned to small talk and flirting, hoping she hadn't pushed it too far. Once they finished their meal, She offered Thomas a ride back to his hotel, assuming he would ask her up for a drink. As she swung into the parking garage next to the hotel where he was staying, he did just as expected, asking her up for a nightcap. She took his arm like a proper lady, letting him escort her to his suite exactly according to her plan.

"Make yourself at home. Mi casa, su casa. I trust you remember your way around?"

She took a seat on one of the leather sofas at the back of the room, hoping he'd sit next to her without any prompting. "Make mine a double on the double, Mr. Combs." She added a flirty giggle.

"Well you're certainly full of spunk tonight. Good day?" Thomas raised a curious eyebrow at her from the bar.

"Just another day down in the trenches with the lowlifes, as always. Now hurry up with my drink and come sit with me." She hoped she wasn't coming on too strong.

"Yes, m'lady." He flirted back, topping off their drinks before joining her on the sofa.

"Cheers! A toast! To answers and finding Jimmy!" She clinked her glass against his.

"Answers? Do tell, are you close?" He raised the same eyebrow at her again.

"All shall be revealed in good time. Now drink up. Pleasure before business," she whispered seductively in his ear while rubbing the back of his neck.

Thomas smiled broadly. "I'll drink to that!" He tipped his head back and drained his glass in one giant gulp.

Jamie followed suit, draining her own glass. "Another, barkeep. And keep 'em coming!"

"Aye aye!" Thomas stood and took her glass. He walked to the bar to refill both glasses and quickly returned to the sofa. Handing Jamie her vodka on the rocks, he then sat back down next to her.

Jamie gulped it again in one swallow and set it down on the side table. She had Thomas right where she wanted him. Men were so easy. She returned to rubbing his neck, while her other hand slid down to his thigh. She rubbed the inseam of his pant gently, knowing the affect it should have on him. For a moment, she wished she'd come for this purpose alone. He was handsome and she hadn't satisfied her own carnal urges in such a long time. Thomas leaned his head back, enjoying the tingles traveling up and down his spine. He moved into her, hoping to feel her full lips on his, but was met instead, with the room swimming out of focus. He wobbled and nearly collapsed on his beautiful companion.

"Oh, poor Tommy. Can't handle his liquor. Nighty night, asshole."

Jamie slapped him hard across the cheek with an open palm. He didn't stir so she slapped again, harder, forcing a groan from his lips. "Time to wake up, Thomas!"

The black void began to fade as Thomas blinked his eyes groggily. Slowly consciousness crept back into his head like a snail on a long journey. His head felt like a semi-truck crashed into it at warp speed. Jamie waved a tube of smelling salts under his nose and roused him to her satisfaction.

"Okay, okay! I'm awake!" He recoiled from the smell.

Jamie paced back and forth in front of him, waiting for him to fully regain his senses. Thomas was tied to a chair in the center of the room, between the bar and the leather couch they had been sitting on. Jamie had him on the chair backwards with his hands tied around the front, a rope midway up his back prevented him from leaning back. His ankles were bound to the back legs, leaving him in an awkward position and unable to get any leverage in case he got the wise idea to tip the chair over. She also cleared the area around him, leaving nothing to chance. The last thing she wanted was a visit from some peon from the front desk checking on a noise complaint. She had hung the "Do Not Disturb" sign on the hotel door, ensuring she'd have all the undisturbed time with Thomas she wanted.

"What the…? What the hell do you think you're doing, Jamie?" Thomas was angry and annoyed.

She continued to pace. "It's past time for you to start shooting straight with me, Thomas. I have questions. I know you have the answers—or most of them anyway." Jamie stopped for a moment, leaning down until they were eye to eye. "You're going to start being honest with me or this is going to get very uncomfortable, very fast. I know you are no stranger to pain, Thomas. However, you've left me no choice. I do hope you're more—shall we say— forthcoming than your old pal, Robert Keane. I really had to squeeze that one to get anything. Thankfully, I have all the time in the world here in this lovely suite with you." Jamie smiled like a dominatrix, looking forward to a long night of punishment.

"I don't understand. What is it you think I know?" Thomas played the innocent victim to a tee, pleading his case in an Oscar worthy performance.

Jamie pulled another chair in front of him and took a seat. She had changed out of the low-cut, sexy black dress she wore to dinner and into tight black cargo pants and a long sleeve, tight black shirt. She smiled, setting her duffle bag at her feet.

"I commend you on the fine performance, Thomas, but you can stop playing games now." She pulled a small glass box from her bag. "I know you know that I'm not some little girl to be trifled with. You saw my room. So last chance. You sure there isn't anything you need to tell me?"

"Jamie, please! Whatever answers you think I have, I don't. Jamie, I swear! I don't have the answers you need." He alleged ignorance once more.

Jamie hadn't expected him to spill his guts easily. She had to try though. Sometimes, when a rival sees the jig is up they cave in quick. Thomas wasn't about to give her anything without a fight, so Jamie didn't need to say another word. She held up the little glass box, opening the top slowly to see if she could elicit any fear in this man who had seen so much, so early in his life. Thomas showed no fear at all, though he wasn't sure what he faced just yet. Jamie plucked a small sliver from inside the box and held it up for Thomas to get a good look. He sat indifferently, staring at the little brown sliver she held between her thumb and forefinger, as if it were nothing to fear. She expected it—no one ever saw something so small as dangerous. She reached out and grabbed his right pinkie finger in her left hand, forcing it out straight. She looked into his eyes with a smile and shoved the tiny sliver slowly under the nail until it could go no further. A tear dripped from the man's eye, yet he didn't yell out.

Jamie leaned in, trailing her tongue over the tear from his cheek. "Mmm, delicious." She licked the wicked smile on her lips. "I have so many more for you." She shook the little box, emphasizing the fact. "Are you going to make me use all of them, or will you give poor little Jamie some answers?" She mocked him and stuck her bottom lip out in a pout. "Now, who is Jimmy? Why did you hire me? Simple questions, Thomas. So how about some simple fucking answers before I really get angry?" She batted her eyes at him.

"I...I, Jesus Fuck! Jamie, I...I can't. Honestly, I don't have the answers you need," Thomas pleaded through teeth clenched from the intense pain.

"I'm really sorry to hear that." She feigned disappointment. Jamie didn't wait for any further stonewalling from Thomas. She plucked another sliver from the box, jabbing it slowly under his ring finger. She worked her way across his right hand without a pause to ask him questions he didn't seem ready or willing to answer. The slivers in the little glass box were fragments of a beer bottle she'd smashed up with a hammer. She had only used them once before to make a pedophile divulge the names of each and every one of his victims. The pathetically weak bastard spilled his guts after the second sliver. Jamie wasn't sure how long Thomas could hold out. She reached for his left hand, to continue the treatment. She knew her slivers caused more pain than just about anything else in her bag. He would break soon—he had to.

After she slid a sliver of glass under the nail of his middle finger, Thomas began pleading with her to stop. "Fuck!" He screamed sending tears and sweat flying in all directions. "I...I don't have the answers you need. Honestly, Jamie." He spit out the words through gritted teeth. "Jimmy...you need Jimmy."

"You wouldn't lie to me now? I mean, you have...since the day you walked in my office. You're a liar, Thomas. A fucking liar. Now, you want me to believe you? Only Jimmy can provide the answers?"

"Yes."

Jamie picked up Thomas' cell phone, swinging it back and forth in front of his face. "Code."

"71094."

She pressed in the numbers and unlocked his phone, surprised to find Thomas had made no attempt to disguise Jimmy's number. "Tell him to come now or I use your balls for a pin cushion. Warn him and I'll make you swallow them. Understand?" Thomas nodded his head and Jamie hit the number, holding it out on speaker so she could hear everything.

Jimmy answered on the first ring like usual.

"I need you to come to the suite."

"Why?"

"Keane spilled more than he should have. We need to talk."

"What's wrong?"

Jamie shook her box of glass slivers.

"I stubbed my toe. Just get over here."

"'Kay." Jimmy hung up.

"How long?" Jamie squeezed Thomas' pinky for emphasis.

"Ahhhh! Damn it, Jamie! Less than twenty minutes, depends on where he is exactly," Thomas spit out through the pain.

"Does he have his own key card?"

"Yes."

Jamie picked up the box and shook it again. "Looks like we have a few more minutes to get acquainted. Now, did you send Jourgensen?"

"Yes."

"Why?"

"To throw you a curve ball. Al was one of our only friends at Mormont—the lookout on our final escape attempt."

"What happened?"

"We escaped. We got away."

"Did the Combs' really adopt you?"

"Yes. They adopted both of us."

"Then why didn't I see Jimmy's name in any of the articles about you?"

"He ran away a couple years later. I kept him hidden. I convinced them not to talk about him. Told them it was for Jimmy's safety and they bought it."

"Did you tell them about what happened at Mormont?"

"Not everything, but enough. We couldn't hide the scars. Mr. Combs had some political connections so he made some calls and the home got shut down. They kept it all nice and quiet but no more kids had to suffer in that place." Fresh tears came to Thomas' eyes from the painful memory.

"Which of you came up with the idea for Rollins? Fucking brilliant, by the way—though I should slit your throat for making me suffer through the stench. Disgusting—absolutely genius—but disgusting. You know, I had to shower like ten times and burn my clothes after being in that fucking place."

"My idea. I wish it was DeLong, but with her in the damn nursing home we couldn't risk it. For me, Rollins was the next best thing. I couldn't exactly warn you. Thank you for not killing him quick. Jimmy drove me by the smoldering remains this morning."

"You're welcome. I was impressed. That bathroom though—I lost my breakfast over it. Not nice." As punishment, she squeezed his right hand.

"Fuck! Jamie, stop!" Thomas roared. "I'm sorry! The bathroom wasn't my doing!"

"Hush. I saw your back—you can take it. You wouldn't have survived Mormont if you couldn't." She rolled her eyes. "You could've at least left me a gas mask."

"You got me there." His shoulders sagged in defeat.

"How many have you killed?"

"For Jimmy, it's more than I know. He doesn't always tell me about them, but it's a lot. Me? I have to be more careful, being in the public eye and all. Maybe fifty," he admitted.

Jamie squeezed his damaged fingers again. "Number."

"Fifty-three! Fuck!"

She smiled sarcastically. "Thank you for your honesty." "Stay right here okay, sweets? I need to get ready for your partner. Oh, and before you go getting any ideas, it would take you days to loosen those knots. But feel free to waste your energy if it pleases you." Jamie reached into her bag and pulled out a ball gag. "I know you're trustworthy and all, however I think if I were in your position I'd yell out a warning to Jimmy the second he opened the door. I'm not really a risk taker. It's better to be overly cautious, I always say." She winked at him then shoved the ball gag in his mouth strapping it on tight.

Jamie double checked the knots for her own peace of mind. Better safe than sorry. There was nothing left to do but wait for Jimmy, so she hurried to the hiding spot she'd picked out.

Not much later, Jimmy slid his keycard through the slot and unlocked the door with an audible click. He entered and immediately froze at the sight of his friend tied up.

Thomas screamed a warning through the ball gag even though it was futile. Taking a cautious step forward, Jimmy resisted the urge to rush to his friend's aid, knowing it'd be a mistake.

It was already too late, though. Jamie stepped out from behind the door, jabbing a hypodermic needle in Jimmy's right butt cheek. Before he'd even had a chance to turn around, he was dropping to the floor with a thud.

Like nothing had happened, Jamie closed the door quietly behind him. She put the protective sheath back over the needle so she didn't poke herself by accident and slipped it into one of her pockets. She flipped the unconscious body at her feet over onto its back—and received the shock of her life. Jamie Windstein loved a good mystery, but she hated surprises. The last person she expected to see was the sweet, lawnmowing simpleton, Leon.

5

Jamie sat stunned, trying to absorb the shock of the Jimmy revelation. She came to Thomas' room unable to make sense of the game being played, and now it made even less sense. Good, sweet Leon was nothing but a character in the game—a fiction, a total fraud. She racked her brain trying to remember how long she had known Leon as the lawnmowing simpleton—when had he first appeared? He'd been a well-known fixture of the neighborhood for several years. She felt like an incompetent fool. How in holy hell had she missed something this big? Some investigator she turned out to be! She'd have to worry about it later, her sedative was powerful but not long lasting.

With difficulty, Jamie dragged Jimmy's limp body across the room. The man had to have been at least a full foot taller than her and a good hundred and fifty pounds heavier. She moved as quickly as she could, though. It was a good thing that she was much stronger than she looked. She set a chair next to Thomas, separating them by about two feet, and then hauled Jimmy's dead weight onto it. She tied him in the same fashion as she had Thomas, deciding to add an extra length of rope around the midsection—just in case. Jimmy looked like a giant in comparison to Thomas.

After securing Jimmy to the chair, she fixed herself a vodka. Draining the glass in one gulp she refilled and drained it again. She checked her watch and calculated that Jimmy should come around within five minutes. She topped off her glass again and returned to her seat in front of her captive, watching for the sedative to wear off. Before long, she saw Jimmy's breathing change. It was nearly time. She moved her chair over, placing herself directly in front of Leon, the imposter.

Just like she had done to Thomas, she smacked him across the cheek, only this time it felt so good she added a half dozen more, until her palm was warm and had begun to sting. She felt betrayed. She was furious over being deceived by Leon. She was the only one in the entire neighborhood who'd went out of their way to be nice to him. And it had been a lie the entire time! She was hurt more than she'd ever admit and to make herself feel a bit better, she struck him again, even though he'd already begun to stir.

Jamie stood up and walked over to the bar, desperately needing another drink, if only to get her emotions under control. She had never been an extremely emotional woman, but on occasion, her rage took over. The revelation that Leon was actually Jimmy had her feeling everything from hurt to bloodlust. She downed her vodka and then walked back over to the big man, punching him square in the nose before she plopped down in a chair. It was time for the Q & A session. She would get the answers she needed no matter what she had to do.

Trying to get the world to come back into focus, Jimmy blinked several times, drawing in giant gulps of air. It took him a moment to remember where he was. Bound to a chair next to his best friend who was tied in a similar fashion, but also gagged. Last but definitely not least, the petite dark haired, green eyed beauty,

Jamie Windstein came into focus. Jimmy looked up at her with the most sincere smile he'd ever bestowed upon anyone. He was right where he wanted to be.

"I fucking hate you, just so you know." Jamie leaned forward, the anger evident in her voice. "Now, this is how it works. I ask, you answer. If you lie, or I just don't like your answers, then you get hurt. Like I told Thomas, I'm sincerely sorry for what you were forced to endure at Mormont. I know that experience gave you an extraordinarily high pain tolerance but I need honest answers and you, obviously, are not an honest man. On the positive side, we have all the time in the world. I implore you to please, please, be difficult. I'm looking forward to extracting what I want to know in the most excruciating ways possible. Am I making myself clear?" Jamie tried to keep her tone even, matter of factly, though she found it impossible to keep her anger at bay.

"Yes. Now, pardon me if I'm speaking out of turn, but what did you inject me with? And how on Earth did you get it?" Jimmy ignored her threats, curiously fascinated.

"Like it?" She smiled, giving him credit for how calm he seemed. "I know some unique people. In my profession, sometimes you need to crawl through a little slime. You never know what you're going to find. Many years ago I found a chemist swimming in the primordial ooze of mankind. Now, he makes it for me. And it never fails—even on a big fucker like you. The only negative is a short knockout duration. That and if you use slightly too much…well…the knockout is permanent." She shrugged nonchalantly.

To keep her captives off guard, Jamie stood. She needed to keep her head in the game. When she looked at Jimmy, all she saw was Leon. And she'd had such simple affection for him. She fought the urge to cry at the overwhelming feeling of loss. It was as if he'd suddenly died. She tried to push her feelings down.

"Keep your mouth shut unless I ask you a fucking question. Understand?" Thomas nodded his head and she removed the ball gag. "You'll be verifying his answers when necessary. If I think one or both of you are lying, you know I'll make you pay." She pulled his hands over to within Jimmy's vision, letting the big man see what she had done to Thomas already. "Tell him honesty is the best policy when dealing with me."

Thomas' bloody hands trembled in her grip. "No point in secrets now, brother." He dropped his head, pain clear in his eyes.

Jamie dropped Thomas' hands and sat back down in front of Jimmy. "We start easy, but the questions will get harder as we go." She reached into her duffle bag, pulling out a thin piece of shiny metal. "Now, what is your real name? Reimse? Makowski? Leon? None of the above?" She narrowed her eyes, a scowl playing on her shapely lips.

Jimmy took a deep breath, "James Xavier Keenan. Junior."

Jamie looked to the other man. "Is that correct, Thomas?"

"The truth is I don't know, Jamie. He told me his name was James Ward my first day at Mormont, but I believe he's telling you the truth." Thomas seemed to answer honestly.

"Thank you, Thomas."

Jamie held up the small, thin piece of metal she had pulled from her bag, holding it up for both of them to get a good look. It was approximately four or five inches long and about a quarter of an inch in diameter. Sticking up from the top of her fist were several long thin strips of jagged black metal. They looked like small strips of bandsaw blades, though neither man had seen a bandsaw that was small enough to fit them. Jamie carefully reached under the blades and extended the small piece of metal slowly to its full length of eighteen inches. Without warning she smacked Jimmy across the left cheek, slicing him open before whipping it around and smacking Thomas' right cheek. The retractable thin metal looked similar to a radio antenna and acted like a whip when swung. The tiny blades made little paper cuts and were extremely painful.

Jamie smiled, clearly enjoying herself. "Sorry. I can't be sure that was the truth, and there's no way to verify it. And that's really just as good as a lie. I'll let it slide for now. I call this little thing the stinger." She held it up. "It only stings a little at first, but you'll find it gets worse as we go. Test me on this, I beg you." She eyed them both, eyes steely, letting them see just how serious she was. "Now, James. Why did you have Thomas hire me?"

After flinching from the strike, Jimmy relaxed. "I wanted you to remember."

She kept her cool, although his answer angered her. "Remember what?"

Jimmy looked her straight in the eye. "All you've forgotten."

In frustration, Jamie brought the stinger down onto Jimmy's shoulders several times. Deep cuts bled through the holes in his now shredded t-shirt sleeves, though he never flinched.

Jamie sat back, taking a deep breath to get herself under control. This was not the time to let her rage get the better of her. "Jamie Windstein doesn't forget a fucking thing. Ever." She decided to switch tactics. "Why masquerade as Leon?"

Jimmy saw the bloodlust in her eyes and maintained his calm demeanor. "To keep an eye on you. And to gain your trust. My intention was never to hurt you, and it still isn't. The cloak of Leon was invincible, it gained me access to every home in a ten-block radius. I hid in plain sight. No one pays any attention to the neighborhood simpleton."

"Is that true, Thomas?"

Thomas didn't hesitate. "Yes."

She returned her hateful gaze to Jimmy. "Why keep an eye on me? Why am I so fucking special to you? You better start making sense real quick."

Jimmy sighed. "Because, I care about you."

"I don't even fucking know you. Are you some sort of pervert? Should I consider myself lucky you didn't rape me or something?" Jamie raised the stinger to strike again, catching herself mid-swing. "It'd be the last mistake you ever made."

"I've known you your entire life. I was afraid you wouldn't remember me." A great sadness resonated in Jimmy's voice. An honesty she didn't expect. "And I see that you don't."

"Fucking impossible! My whole life? Bullshit!" Jamie nearly took out Jimmy's eye when she swung the stinger as hard as she could. "I was a baby when I was found on the doorstep of the Windsteins! They took me in. They raised me as their own. You're a fucking liar!"

With reckless abandon, not caring where it struck, Jamie wielded the stinger. She didn't want to hear any more of his lies. Jimmy sat perfectly still, taking every sting without the slightest reaction as he waited for her to finish.

"Jamie..." A single tear spilled from his right eye. "Who do you think put you on that doorstep?"

Instantly, she saw red and leapt up, lashing out again with her homemade whip. "Liar!" She swung hysterically, hitting both men with a deluge of blows. The onslaught continued until, exhausted, her arm fell to her side.

Jamie collapsed hard on her chair, her head swimming from exertion and Jimmy's implication. Behind his bloodied face, Thomas appeared just as shocked. The room spun out of focus before disappearing completely.

Jamie found herself sitting in a pool of blood with a baby cradled in her arms in the center of the room. Blood poured down in endless sheets of red, covering everything. The little boy's voice came faintly once again—distant, yet this time, she could make out what he said. He called her name—though it wasn't her name. In a blur of crimson, the room spun around. Again, the boy called the name that wasn't her name and then began to sing words more familiar than any she'd ever heard. Her entire world spiraled out of focus. The baby in her arms was screaming in a blur of red, while the boy called her the wrong name and sung a song she knew, but couldn't remember. Jamie felt herself melting away.

The vision suddenly vanished and she was back in Thomas' suite, glaring at the two bloody men tied to chairs in front of her. Reality returned and yet nothing felt real anymore.

She stared daggers at Jimmy. "Lies. You're a fucking liar! Why couldn't you just leave me the fuck alone? My world was fine until you two showed up!" To get some control, she took a deep breath. Anger had her on the edge of eviscerating both of them and just being done with it.

Despite the deep cuts the stinger had made all over his face and arms, Jimmy maintained his calm. "I'm truly sorry for shattering all you thought you knew, but it's time you knew the truth. Your real name is Melissa

Angela Keenan. You were born on March 15, 1983 to James and Marie Keenan—our parents. You are my little sister. I left you on the doorstep of The Windsteins." He finished with a sigh.

Jamie's rage began to melt, but she tried hard to keep her focus. "I…I can't…I don't believe you. Lies! All lies!" The denial lacked much conviction.

"No, little sister," Jimmy said softly. "I swear, it's the truth. I can see you know it too." Another tear slid from his eye, to roll down a bloodied cheek. He looked to his friend. "Now it's time, Thomas. It's time you both knew the truth. Jamie, I've never told this story—our story—to anyone. I had to wait until you were ready. Thomas, I couldn't tell you before, because it isn't just my story. It's our story, Melissa. At least, what I know of it. May I?"

Jamie had never heard anyone sound more sincere. She sat, completely dumbfounded and stared at this man who claimed to be her long lost brother. She had never felt fear before—not ever—though she believed it was what she was feeling now. She'd only ever known Kurt and Sheila Windstein as her parents. When she was fifteen, they had sat her down and told her how, one night, they had found her on their doorstep. She naturally assumed her birth mother was either extremely young, or possibly an addict. Whether they provided her DNA or not, she considered them her parents. She never felt any need to search for her true identity. The thought of just killing them both and walking away crossed her mind, but now she needed to know. What was this man who claimed to be her brother going to tell her?

Tears glassed Jamie's eyes, though she refused to let them fall. "If this is another game you're playing, I'll make you think Rollins got off easy."

Jimmy took a deep breath, meeting her gaze. "I swear to you, sister. The game is finished. You deserve to know the truth, or what I know of it. I've never been able to find out who did it, or why. Despite my best attempt. If I did know, I swear this story would include our vengeance on them.

"Jamie, I was ten and you were just a baby. One afternoon I was playing quietly with my Matchbox cars in my room, when I heard a knock at the door. Our father—James—yelled to mom that he'd get it since she was busy changing your diaper or something. I remember dad opening the door with the chain still in place. I saw him look out and then immediately try to slam it closed. But it was too late." He took a deep breath. "Three men—they looked like giants to me—burst in and knocked dad to the floor. I remember they started just punching and kicking him. Mom handed you to me and told me to go in my room and lock the door. Next I heard mom screaming. I set you down on my racecar bed and went back to the door to peek out. The shortest guy of the three seemed to be the leader and was telling the others what to do. I remember him punching mom in the face so hard she went flying across the room, then he grabbed dad by the hair and dragged him into the living room. He lifted dad up by the hair then pushed him on the couch. Mom got up and jumped on the back of one of the men, but it was useless." The words were coming out fast. "He tossed her like a rag doll down on the couch, on the opposite side from dad, then punched her in the face again. I was afraid, so I closed the door after that, but I could hear them yelling at dad, calling him a rat and asking him what he had said. The best I can figure is dad was working with or for some criminals, but I never found out who they were. I have to assume dad talked to the cops or something like that. Maybe he witnessed something he wasn't supposed to see, I don't know." He paused. "I want you to know I tried, Jamie. I really did, but I think someone must've destroyed any evidence of dad's connection. I've never been able to find out anything. I couldn't even find a record of any homicide investigation of them."

"Wait—" She cut him off, confused. "Why come to me with this game of finding you? If you were going to play a game, why not have me look into our parent's murder?"

"No offense, but they're dead. I'm alive. I wanted to see if you were able to remember anything. You were only about three months old. I hoped the memory was in there somewhere, buried down deep."

"After I kill you, I'll find out what happened to our parents. You can count on it! I don't know why you didn't bring this to me years ago. I don't know what the fuck you waited for." She was starting to feel exasperated.

Jimmy frowned before continuing. "I'm sorry. I didn't think you were ready. I wanted you to learn my story, about what happened to me after. Call me selfish, if you wish."

"Narcissistic is probably more accurate." Jamie sneered.

"Fair enough. Now, where was I?"

"The men threw the Keenans on the couch, knocked our so-called mother out, and called James a rat."

"Yes, thank you. They worked dad over for some time, keeping him on one end of the couch and mom on the other. One guy stood behind mom and held her by the throat, while the other stood behind dad. The leader sat on a footstool asking questions. Then he sent the tall guy—I think he called him Alex—to get me and you. I had been peeking out the bedroom door up to that point. I carried you while he marched me to a chair in the corner, facing the couch so I saw everything they did. This Alex set us on the chair and told me to keep my mouth shut or they'd hurt you and me too. So that's what I did. Sometimes I wish I had just started screaming, or fought back so they would have had to kill me. I couldn't, though. I was the big brother. My job was to protect you. They could kill me, but I couldn't let them kill you." Jimmy paused for a moment, overwhelmed by the tears spilling from his eyes.

"You were what? Nine? Ten? There was nothing you could have done." Jamie's doubt had waned, listening to Jimmy recant the story. His eyes showed the truth.

"You…you were just so peaceful. Somehow you managed to sleep through some of the worst parts. They held dad in a headlock while they brutally gang raped our mother. When they finally finished, the leader told dad he didn't want him feeling left out. Jamie, he…he used a hammer." Jimmy paused at the painful memory. "He used a hammer to force one of those miniature bats…" Jimmy trailed off unable to finish.

"You don't have to say it." Jamie cringed at the mental images flying through her mind.

"No, you need to know what happened. Dad passed out after the first few whacks. The leader didn't stop though. He hit that bat until it refused to go any further. I had my eyes squeezed shut for as much of it as I could, but they said if I looked away…" Jimmy hung his head in shame. "He looked right at me. The bastard was smiling when he pumped the bat in and out. Dad was gushing blood. I thought he was dead. Then they went back to mom. She was already bleeding everywhere but those animals didn't care. I thought they were both dead. I thought they had raped our parents to death. They were laughing and high fiving each other like it was a game. A damn game! Then it got even worse."

"Worse? How?" Jamie was horrified.

"They weren't dead yet. The tall guy that put me in the chair came back over. He had mom's blood all over him and the fucker was smiling like it was fucking Christmas or something. He took you out of my arms and laid you down in the middle of the room. Then he came back for me. He marched me over to give me a front row seat for what came next. I sat in front of you so you couldn't see what they did. They all had machetes. They didn't make it quick. They hacked our parents apart, one little piece at a time. Fingers, toes, arms and legs. They chopped them up into little pieces, slowly. They hacked mom apart first, forcing dad to watch, and then they went to work on him. Blood flew everywhere. I was coated in it, you were coated in it. I didn't dare look away by that point. I barely dared to breathe. Then they took all the pieces and stacked them up in the corner of the room, topping the pile with their heads. The leader carved the word 'RAT' into dad's forehead. That was it, they were done. They washed up like it was all nothing, like they had been working in the garden all day or something, then they just left. The room looked like a tornado of blood blew through. I don't know how long I sat there after they left. I couldn't move until you started screaming and screaming. I didn't know what to do. You wouldn't stop." Jimmy paused again, choking on emotion.

"There was nothing you could do." Her visions now made sense. Finally she let the tears fall.

Jimmy swallowed hard. "You witnessed it too, sister. I honestly hoped you didn't remember but then I saw your secret room. I knew you remembered, whether you realized it or not. It still feels like a nightmare that happened to someone else. That's why Mormont didn't break me. What happened there only filled me with hate. The thugs who killed our parents are likely long dead but I'd love to get my hands on them."

"No argument here. Did you know The Windsteins? Did you just hope it'd be a good home?"

"I don't know how long we sat there in a pool of our parents' blood. Five minutes, five days? I finally got up and took you in the bathroom to clean us both up. I was completely detached from the world. I just felt cold, numb. Somehow, I got us both into clean clothes, put you in a baby carrier and stepped outside. I remember it was dark and I just started walking. I kept looking behind us expecting those thugs to come after us and kill us too. But they must have been long gone. I carried you for several blocks—I don't know how far—I just knew I had to get as far away as possible. Finally, when I couldn't carry you any more, I looked for the nicest house I could find and set you down in front of the door. I kissed you goodbye, rang the doorbell and then I just ran and ran and ran until I didn't think my legs could carry me anymore. I'm not sure where I was when the cops found me. When they asked my name all I could remember was James. Then Ward popped in my head for some reason, but I couldn't remember what our address was. One of the cops—an Officer Barker—he was real nice. He bought me a hamburger and a chocolate shake. Then social services showed up. Of course, no one reported me missing, so after a couple days they delivered me to the Mormont Home. The rest of the story you know." He paused. "It took me years to find you again. When I did, I assumed the identity of Leon, and I've been watching over you ever since. I made Thomas hire you to find me—hoping, with all my heart, you would remember me. I didn't know all of your secret life, but I saw enough to know we could count on you to make our abusers suffer the way we always wanted. Thomas' creativity in regard to Rollins, aside." Jimmy finished his story, exhausted.

Jamie sat in stunned silence, unsure what to say or whether to say anything. She came here a couple of hours ago with the intention of making both of these men suffer. Now, hearing Jimmy's story—her story—she wasn't sure what to do. She knew Thomas and Jimmy were accomplished killers, as was she. But she never expected one of them to be her brother. The recurring nightmares made such perfect sense now. It didn't take a psychiatrist to figure out her dreams were a deeply suppressed memory, especially when coupled with her compulsion of head collecting. Didn't psychiatrists always relate everything back to Mommy or Daddy issues? The thought almost made her laugh. Almost. Was her headhunting a search for her parents, or her mind's way of leading her back to the truth? It made no difference either way. They say knowledge is power, yet at this moment, she felt completely powerless.

Jimmy spoke softly, breaking the long silence. "Melissa—I mean, Jamie? Are you alright?"

Soft though it was, his voice brought her back to reality. "Alright? You're fucking kidding me, right?" She laughed humorlessly. "Alright? I just found out I have a serial killer for a brother and my very first memory is of my parents being hacked into itty-bitty bits with machetes. Oh, and that same brother—instead of stopping in to say, 'Hey, this is crazy but I'm your long lost brother'—parades around my fucking neighborhood as a half-wit and stalked me. Then there's the best part, the crème de la fucking crème! This same secret brother has been leaving body parts with some weird message carved into them in my fucking kitchen! Am I alright? How's this for an answer? Go fuck yourself!" Jamie white-knuckled her stinger in her hand looking at the men in utter astonishment. "What in the holy fucking hell was that message, anyway? *Aesop's Fables* for serial fucking killers?" She felt herself on the verge of hysterics and letting her stinger fly recklessly again, but stopped herself.

"I didn't think you'd believe any of this without some extreme jogging of your memory, Executioner. Did you know that's what they call you? The cops, I mean?" It was Jimmy's turn. He wanted some information of his own.

"I do. I kinda like it." She smacked him with the stinger. "No changing subjects—this is my show. What's with the fucked-up messages?"

"Fine!" Angry himself, now, his eyes burned into her. "After those bastards finished, I told you they cleaned up and left. True, but not complete. The leader came to me before they left. He looked like a giant to me, though I doubt he was much taller than you, sis. And he was thick with muscle, like a wrestler or weightlifter. He reminded me of this wrestler from back then, one of those pro-wrestler guys, Ivan Putski. The leader could have been his twin. Remember that guy?"

Jamie shook her head no.

"Well, Putski was this short, Polish bodybuilder turned wrestler with arms like anacondas—the guy was the definition of brick shithouse. Anyway that's what he looked like. So he squats down in front of me and he says, 'I am not your enemy. Your father was a rat. We had to teach him a lesson and remind all of our other friends what loyalty means. One day when you're older you'll make your own blood oath, your *omerta*. One day you'll be bigger and stronger, you'll want your revenge for what happened here today. I would, if I were in your shoes. From now until then, I want you to think about these words and when you understand what they mean, you'll be ready. *Krew zapamiętać, Obłęd przychodzi, Obłęd odchodzi, Krew zapamiętać, Krew być płynąć.* That's Polish for *Blood remembers, Madness comes, Madness goes, Blood remembers, Blood will flow.* When you're ready, come find me.'" Jimmy took in a breath. "I don't believe he knew it was your blood that needed to remember, Melissa. He seemed smart, but I don't think he was that smart. After they left I sat rocking you, repeating it over and over. You're the blood that needed to remember. Thomas and I were the madness. Can you see that?"

"You should have come to me sooner without this damn game. I have contacts, connections. Maybe I could have found these guys a long time ago. But no, you had to play this stupid fucking game. You stalked me. You broke into my house. You desecrated my sanctuary with your presence. You ruined everything, *brother*." She spit the last word out. "So now I'm left with what to do with the two of you? I hate both of you right now!"

Jamie Windstein had never felt more angry or lost. She sat in silence, trying to make sense of it all. How could she kill her own brother? She still saw lovable Leon when she looked at him, though Leon was a farce, a parody of the man her brother really was. She was still furious over the deception. She felt like all she'd been was a pawn in their game. She was furious over the violation of her privacy. How long would she look over her shoulder now, before she felt at ease? Most of all she was furious because she faced the uncertainty of her next action. She hated uncertainty more than unsolved mysteries. She couldn't simply leave them for the police. It pissed her off having to admit to herself that Keane had been right. It wasn't Jimmy's name that mattered—the important part had been who he really was. She stood to pace, weighing her options. Her buzzing cell phone broke the silence.

She pulled her phone from her pocket knowing who it was without looking. "Hey, Care Bear! What's up?" Jimmy could have received an Oscar Award for his acting, but she topped even him.

Thomas looked to Jimmy with a knowing grin. Jamie's stinger left blood dripping from both of their faces in thin rivulets. The cuts burned, though the pain was bearable. They braced for the worst, fearing the end of Jamie's call.

"Calm down, girlfriend! What do you mean, he's missing?...Uh huh...Okay...He was doing what?...I see. Don't worry, we'll get him back in your arms...I know, I know...I'm on it...What was his new partner's name again?...Got it...Sit tight. I'll check some things out then head over...Uh huh...Please don't worry, hun. I'll get to the bottom of this one way or another. Trust me?...Try to relax, I'll be there soon. I promise." She ended the call.

Jamie stood in front of the men so irate she couldn't breathe for a moment. At the very least, she suspected her new-found brother knew exactly what that call had been about. Thomas likely did, also. She had considered letting the two men go, despite their deceptions. She disagreed with their method, but their reasons were legitimate. She was in no danger of them going to the police with what they knew about her. But Carrie's frantic call told her they had crossed an uncrossable line. Eddie hadn't come home or called and she was pretty sure the two people responsible were sitting tied up in front of her. It was a mistake she'd have to make them regret.

Jamie sat back down in her chair, her steely emerald gaze burning into Jimmy. "Is he alive?" She leaned down, rummaging through her duffle bag.

"Yes." Jimmy answered, prepared for whatever came next.

She continued to sift through her bag without looking up. "Where is he? Where can I find Officer Edward Washington?" An icy cold had overcome her. She was calm, too calm.

"I'd have to take you there, sister."

Jamie's head shot up like someone had yanked her by the hair. "No! You don't get to call me that! We may share blood, but we ain't fuckin' family!" Her eyes shot fiery daggers into Jimmy. "Eddie is *family*. You tell me where he is, and you best tell me now." A little of the fear she'd felt earlier came creeping back.

Jimmy's head lowered. "I'm afraid I want to live, Jamie, so I can't tell you. I'll take you there—that's the deal. He's alive for now. but I can't guarantee for how long."

Jamie sat back, holding a roll of duct tape. "Do you know where Eddie is, Thomas?"

"No. I only know that he's still alive."

"That true, *brother*? You didn't tell your partner what you did with him?"

"He's telling you the truth. He only knows what I told him," Jimmy answered.

Jamie stood without saying a word and pulled the end of the duct tape. The sound like music to her ears. She wrapped it around Thomas' head three times, covering his mouth.

"I don't need to hear anything more from him then." She smiled as she returned to her chair. "I need you to tell me where Eddie is, *brother*. Before I go and do something permanent."

"What time is it?" Jimmy asked nonchalantly, as if he were relaxing with a nice glass of iced tea with his sister.

"About seven. Why? Time doesn't matter for you right now."

"It's important."

"Jimmy, I'm done playing your fucking games!" Jamie could feel the little patience she still had ebbing away. "Where is Eddie?"

Jimmy took his time, enjoying the fact that he had her obviously sweating. "I didn't expect him to pop up today. You shouldn't have sent him in my direction. So, one could say his fate was always in your hands. I expected him and that Columbo looking partner of his to puzzle over my message all day, but no. You, little sister, you told him to find poor ol', Invinctigator Leon." Jimmy easily slipped back into Leon's parlance.

"What message?"

Jimmy smiled. "Technically, it was for you. Honestly, your police friend and his partner are too smart for their own good. They're hunting for you, by the way—though I suspect you know that."

"I do. I'm not worried."

"Perhaps you should be. I didn't expect them to get on my trail so quick. I think you, *Executioner*, inspired some extra determination from them. You should actually be thanking me."

"Why in the fuck would I do that?"

"The couple I—let's say liberated to leave my first message for you? I didn't expect anyone to come poking around until our business had concluded, but then your friend went and found one of your…um…scraps. They thought the missing couple was you, *The Executioner*. Gotta admit I'm a little jealous. That's an awesome nickname, little sister." He looked so proud. "So anyhow, I needed to let them know it wasn't you, so I thought I'd have a little fun with them. I found this line from an African poem that was just too good not to use. It's called '*The Executioner's Dream*' which is just too God damned funny, don't you think?" He was totally enjoying his game.

"Get the fuck on with it! Where the hell is Eddie? If he loses so much as a hair, I'll feed your fucking nuts to you." She was through being toyed with.

"You need to learn how to relax. Ever consider yoga?" Jimmy winked in her direction and she glared in response. "Alright, alright. But you only prove my point." His sarcasm wasn't winning her over. "So the poor young lady whose torso I left for you was next. I, well…I guess I can skip that part. I left the message, '*What horrors of human sacrifice have you seen, Executioner?*' along with my initials—my *real* initials. I figured that'd keeping them chasing their tails for a few days so we could conclude our business. I wasn't sure if they had figured out that the first poor couple wasn't your doing and so I wanted to make it clear to them. I have to say your friend and his partner are really quite good. You may want to be extra careful or stop for a time—if it's an option for you." Jimmy almost winked again then thought better of it.

"I'm always extra careful." She couldn't help the pride that leaked into her voice. "You still haven't told me where Eddie is. Aside from your message, I knew the rest. So you're just wasting fucking time. I have two friends on this whole big blue planet, and if you take one of them from me, even *I* don't know what I'm capable of."

"Threats are pointless, little sister. I want to live, but I'm ready to embrace death—with open arms even—if the price is pain. Pain is my oldest, dearest friend. You see, sister, threats only work when you hold leverage. You have none, because there is none to be had. I'll happily take you to Officer Washington, but that's the final and only offer on the table." His voice dripped superiority. "Tick Tock. He doesn't have time for you to dilly dally."

Jamie wanted more than anything to slam her fist right into his throat. His sarcastic arrogance pissed her off all the more now that she recognized it. She had used it herself, on many occasions—most recently with Keane. It was another thing they shared, aside from their proclivity for killing. She wasn't about to set Jimmy loose, even if it meant Eddie must die. She knew what that would do to Carrie, yet she wasn't sure she had a choice. She needed to somehow force Jimmy give up the location. She saw only one option, which she gave a 50/50 chance, at best. She reached into her bag again, palming one particular tool she could keep out of sight until the time was right.

"What time is it now, little sister?" Jimmy inquired.

Jamie pulled out her phone. "Seven thirty-five."

"We're running out of time. Better take me to him now, or else at the strike of eight poor, Carrie Washington will be a widow. You don't want her finding out it was your fault, do you? Could you live with yourself? Could you look her in the eye everyday knowing you could have prevented the death of her beloved husband?" Jimmy braced for the blow he assumed would follow.

Jamie let the cold numbness seep back through her. She calmly stood up and walked behind Thomas. Gripping him by the forehead, she pulled back hard.

Thomas' eyes went wild as he loudly tried to suck air in through his nose.

Jamie kept her eyes on Jimmy, making sure he missed nothing. She spun the blade she had hiding in her free hand, the light glimmering off the freshly stoned edge. Grinning wickedly, she promptly removed Thomas' ear, where it fell to the carpet like discarded rubbish. The man strained, trying to scream to no avail.

"Location." Coldly, Jamie stared at her brother, barely giving him any time to reply before slicing off Thomas' other ear. "Location."

"Wait, damn it!"

"If *my* family dies then so does yours, *brother*." Again, she spit out the last word before moving the blade under Thomas' nose. "Location."

Jimmy saw the fear in Thomas' eyes. A look he hadn't seen since his friend's first trip to the broom closet at Mormont. He had to stop this.

"Too long!" Jamie quickly sliced through cartilage, removing Thomas' nose without so much as a hesitation. "Location." She moved the blade to Thomas' eye.

"Damn it! Wait!"

"3…2…" Jamie began a count down.

"Stop!" Jimmy begged.

"Location."

"Fine! Just put the blade down."

"When you tell me the location!" She demanded.

"Alright! He's in your garage!" Jimmy looked down, defeated. "You truly are my sister." He'd never broken—regardless of the torture used against him. Until now. He felt sick to his stomach, but what could he do? Thomas was his only true friend. Their bond was stronger than steel. They took a blood oath. Their *omerta* was their lives. He couldn't let his brother die for a game. Even if it meant both their lives were forfeit.

"Thank you, *brother*." She looked at her new-found brother, a profound sadness filling her. He'd saved her. In his way, deep down, he'd always loved her. He left her with the Windsteins all those years ago—stable loving parents—while he grew up in hell. If DeLong and her Goon Squad hadn't entered his life, he may not have ended up the monster he was. *They* had ensured that the devil took permanent residence in his soul. She no longer felt anger at her brother or Thomas for the lies and deception. It was replaced instead, with a tremendous pity. Jimmy had never had a chance to be anything other than what he was now. He wasn't born evil. It had taken years of evil being mercilessly visited upon him to turn him that way. Unfortunately, the circumstances no longer mattered. Brother or not, one-time savior or not—he'd violated her trust, her home, and now the only family she knew.

Jamie Windstein had no more patience for games, and time was running out. She needed to quell the rage Jimmy and Thomas had stirred within her.

A tear spilled down her cheek as she locked gazes with her brother and pulled her blade across Thomas' throat.

Jimmy cried out helplessly, unable to do more than watch his brother die. Blood shot across the room from Thomas' gaping wound, slowing to a crimson waterfall down his neck within a second.

Jamie released her hold on his forehead. He flopped forward, dead within seconds.

"You knew all along it would end this way," she said quietly, without a hint of malice. "Didn't you, brother?"

Taking a good long look at her brother, she was conflicted. There was part of her that wanted to let him go, after everything he'd suffered through. Maybe he was a monster, but wasn't she one too? Their life paths were both altered—turned upside down—by the same event. She wanted to ask him so many questions about their parents, but she was running out of time. With a sad smile, she looked at him, wishing he had stayed the lovable Leon, instead of this murdering liar before her. Jimmy had ruined that, and now she needed to hurry before he ruined everything else. She took a deep breath, knowing what she needed to do.

"It's okay, sister." Jimmy knew it too and was ready. "I'm glad I found you. I love you, Melissa." A tear burned its way down his face, the salt stinging the bloody mess she'd left behind.

Melissa Angela Keenan leaned down and took her big brother's head in her hands. She kissed his forehead gently, then slid around behind him. He leaned his head back, making it easier for her.

"You're free, big brother," she whispered then slit his throat.

6

The world remained black even after Officer Edward Washington regained consciousness. His head hung like a rag doll as if no muscle or vertebrae attached it to his body. For one long panicked second, he thought he might actually be dead already. He blinked over and over, yet still nothing but darkness filled his vision. His heart began to race and his breathing accelerated while his brain frantically tried to assess his situation. Slowly he realized a blindfold covered his eyes. Yelling into the void, he heard nothing but his own voice echoing back.

It took Eddie another moment to realize his hands were tied behind his back and his ankles were bound to the legs of the chair he sat on. Something was wrapped loosely around his neck. He could glean nothing else of his situation or location. The blindfold prevented from determining whether he was buried underground, sitting in some basement or sitting out in the middle of the street.

Think, damn it! he ordered himself.

Eddie took a few deep breaths and tried to quell his panic. He didn't need to do anything stupid, like hyperventilate.

His first thought had been of Carrie on their wedding day. She was so young and beautiful. Still was. That day, she'd looked at him with a smile like he was the only person on the planet. It had been love at first sight for them, though the overwhelming love he'd felt for her on their wedding day was something he could never explain in mere words. He was sure he'd seen straight through to her soul, as he'd stared at his bride to be. She was the most beautiful thing he had ever seen. It felt like all the answers to every question in the universe were right there in her eyes.

Recalling that day, he felt his heart slow, his breathing moderate—the impending panic attack evaporated.

Leon! He suddenly remembered. He had been speaking to Leon! The scene played out in his mind like watching a movie. Leon had said he didn't have any information and had then started to turned away. *The waste paper sticker!* He'd seen the long thin pole strapped to Leon's back. Why didn't he pull his weapon? He'd froze like some fucking—"on the job two hours"—rookie. If he had drawn his service revolver, he'd be home with his beautiful wife getting ready to settle down for a delightfully boring evening of television. Maybe some popcorn, and if the stars aligned properly, a nightcap between the sheets. A nice thought, for sure.

Eddie's mind couldn't comprehend how the slow-witted, Leon could be the new killer in town. What had made the simpleton snap? Leon was just the damn lawnmower guy! Had been for years. Had he just snapped one day because the Osbournes treated him like crap? Jamie had told him that almost everyone in the neighborhood treated the guy poorly, so why now?

Then he remembered the look Leon had given him. Right before nearly crushing him like a child's toy. He remembered realizing Leon's slow-witted persona had been an act. A complete sham. Before Eddie had blacked out, he'd swear he'd seen the devil in Leon's eyes. Whoever Leon really was, didn't matter. Eddie now knew that Leon was a dangerous killer. Had Leon been killing all along? Could he be *The Executioner*? But, then why leave a message to *The Executioner*? His head began to spin with the possibilities, implications, and unanswerable questions.

Eddie struggled against his restraints, trying to distract himself from the mounting questions now racing through his brain. He quickly found freeing himself wasn't happening. For a second, he thought about rocking the chair over on its side, though quickly shoved the notion away, not wanting to hang himself. Someone had to have noticed he was missing by now. It was his only chance at freedom.

In the hope that someone might be able to hear him, Eddie let out a bellow for help every few minutes. He had no idea where he was, so there was no way to know if it was useless or not. His cop's brain kicked in, and tried to decipher any clues as to his location. His voice made a slight echo, and the place smelled slightly musty—though less than most basements he had been in.

Relax and concentrate! he commanded himself.

He caught a faint whiff of some old oil or gasoline, yet there was something else also. He couldn't quite place it. Concentrating on it, he forced the other odors to fade into the background. It was sweet, yet pungent.

"Pickles!" The word burst from his throat. "It smells like somebody spilled a jar of pickles in here." He frowned, confused.

He decided it wasn't exactly pickle juice, but something similar. Where had he smelled it before? It was familiar, though he couldn't quite place it.

He decided he'd talk himself through it, hoping to jar his memories. "I'm not locked in someone's pantry, or I'd smell spices or flour or cereal—something. I can smell oil and gas, so I've got to be in a garage or tool shed, something like that." He tilted his head. "What the hell is that odd smell and where do I know it from?" Eddie continued pondering the odor, unable to decipher where he could have encountered it before.

It hit him suddenly that he had no idea what time it was, or even how long he had been unconscious—it was impossible to guess with no visual cues. It felt like evening, but after being knocked out he couldn't trust his internal clock. If it was late afternoon, then someone would be looking for him by now. Barker wasn't the friendliest person he'd ever met, but the man would notice his partner missing. Carrie would be worried also, and making calls if it was well into the evening. Rescue was the only hope he had at the moment.

Eddie tried calming himself by playing the day out in his mind again. He'd left the Peterson woman's home to look for Leon around ten thirty in the morning and had expected to meet back up with Barker about noon, maybe one at the latest. So if his internal clock was telling him it was evening, then Barker should be looking for him. Doubt crept into his mind. Barker didn't know him well. Would he think Eddie just failed to check in? It didn't seem likely. He *had* let Leon get the jump on him, however he was known for being "by the book" when it came to procedure.

The way he figured it, if he hadn't checked in with Barker by at least two in the afternoon, the man would be suspicious. He'd probably be pissed when Eddie didn't answer calls, but that would have turned to suspicion fairly quick. He'd at least send a patrol car, Eddie thought. Carrie would have gotten a call by then, and by now, everyone would be looking for him. Or so he hoped.

Panic began to creep its way into his mind again. How long before Leon came back for the kill? Why had he left him alive in the first place? Obviously, Leon was a stone cold killer, so why wait? Eddie wanted to think the reason was that he was a cop, though he doubted a killer really cared. Even the worst criminals were often reluctant to become a cop killer, due to the enormous heat which followed such an action. Nothing motivates an entire police force like one of their own being injured or killed in the line of duty. Right now his colleagues didn't know his status, which would put the whole force on edge. He certainly hoped it provided some extra motivation for them to find him.

Eddie wasn't a religious man but he began to pray. "God if you're up there, please don't make my wife a widow. I don't care about my life. Please don't do this to her. She may not be a saint, but she's a good person. If something happens to me, she'd be destroyed. Please—I beg you—don't make her attend my funeral. I took an oath as an officer, and I'm willing to lay down my life for a good cause but, please, not like this. Not at the hands of some madman. Get me out of this and I swear I'll work harder every day to bring justice to the wronged. I'll find this Executioner and make sure he faces justice before his judgement day with you. Please, just don't make Carrie a widow. Hear this prayer for her, in Jesus' name, Amen." Eddie couldn't stop the tears from welling up and soaking through his blindfold.

As soon as Eddie finished his prayer, he heard a click behind him.

"Hello!"

No reply came.

Eddie sat still as a statue, straining his ears for any other sound. A faint ticking began from behind him, making his heart race. The word *Bomb* was exploding in his brain. Sweat broke out on his brow while his heart jackhammered in his chest. The panic attack he held at bay threatened to unleash at any second.

So much for prayer, he thought.

He listened to the ticking, sure that each tick brought him one step closer to the end. In his mind, he saw a gigantic fireball that would light up the entire city to witness the demise of Officer Edward Washington. There was nothing left for him to do. Eddie accepted his fate with an eerie calmness and waited for the explosion that would take him out in a literal blaze of glory.

7

Jamie sprinted from the elevator to her car in the parking garage, wishing she had found some place else to park. She peeled out and raced for the exit, wanting to slam through the barrier out onto the street. Unfortunately, the gate arm and spike strip made the Hollywood move impossible. She screamed at the infernal machine to take her money as she slammed the gas pedal to the floor the second the arm lifted enough for her to get through. Squealing tires sounded all the way to the highway entrance around the opposite side of the hotel.

"Hang on, Eddie!" She frantically looked to the clock on her dash, praying it was at least a few minutes fast, otherwise she wouldn't get there in time. Having opportunity to stop whatever Jimmy had set in motion was a problem for after she got there. She floored it up the onramp to the highway and nearly clipped the cement barrier trying to navigate the sharp curve. She merged into the highway, already ten miles over the posted speed limit. She sent up a silent prayer to avoid any of Eddie's colleagues while she pushed her car's engine to its limit.

It was nearly impossible to concentrate on the road and not stare at the glowing green digital numbers on her dash. The clock kept ticking as the lights of the city blurred past. She hadn't yet caught the attention of any of the boys in blue, though it was likely some do-gooder would call 911, reporting a car flying by them at a million miles an hour. Not that she had much choice, saving Eddie before he lost his head became her sole purpose in life. It wasn't a head she wanted in her collection and her best friend didn't deserve to be a widow.

"I'm coming, Eddie!" She was even more frenzied as her clock ticked down to five minutes left.

Jamie took her exit at over a hundred miles an hour, nearly flipping her car right over the side rail, yet somehow, the wheels stayed on the road. She had two minutes to go, according to her clock—which she desperately hoped was wrong. She raced toward her street, breathing a sigh of relief that traffic was dead as she blew through three red lights.

The seconds started to tick by in slow motion when she slammed on her brakes to make the turn onto Crown Drive. She had less than one minute to drive the final three blocks and then get inside to figure out how to even save Eddie. She had no idea what Jimmy had planned.

Soaring into her driveway, she barely stopped before bursting through her own garage door. She slammed the car into park without even coming to a complete stop and the transmission growled loudly, but there was little time to worry about it. She rushed out of the car to her front door, thankfully not hearing any sirens blaring in the distance, trying to catch up with her. Turning the doorknob, she found it unlocked—a peculiar thing—she never left it unlocked.

Jamie made a beeline for the side door in the kitchen that lead to the garage. She flicked on the light switch, pausing to carefully open the door, looking for trip wires and finding none. Pushing the door wide, she revealed Jimmy's contingency plan. If circumstances had been different, she would've taken time to admire the handiwork.

She could see Eddie was still alive, and she quickly thanked god that her car's clock had been slightly fast after all. Still, there was no time to dawdle.

Eddie heard the slight squeak of the door opening and a shriek tore from his throat. "Help!"

Racing down the stairs, she saw the evil simplicity of what Jimmy rigged up. Eddie sat bound to a wooden chair with a length of steel razor-wire around his neck and through the base of an electric weed whacker. The trigger was from a lawn tool compressed with duct tape, its cord plugged into a timer generally used for Christmas lights. She could see all she needed to do was get to the plug before the timer counted down. Eddie's last few precious seconds were ticking away fast.

Unable to move fast enough, Jamie nearly took a header down the steps. She braced herself on the railing and leapt over it, hitting the concrete floor with bone jarring impact she felt all the way up her spine.

"Please! Help me!" The sound of Eddie's pleas killed her.

She couldn't risk giving herself away, even to comfort her friend. Sprinting to the timer, she was aware that it could go off at any moment. Eddie continued pleading for help while time slowed to super slow motion. She willed her feet to move faster as visions of Eddie's head being sliced off and the sounds of his wife's screams played like a horror movie in her mind. Only a few more feet to go.

After what seemed an eternity, her hand gripped the timer and she ripped it from the outlet with so much force it flew off into the wall and smashed to pieces. She let out a heavy sigh. Eddie was safe. Carrie wouldn't be a widow today and that's all that mattered.

She gently lifted the razor wire over Eddie's head, careful not to hurt him now that the main threat had been removed. She cut the duct tape that held the weed whacker to the back of the chair and then tossed it aside to deal with later. She had thwarted Jimmy's plan, but her troubles weren't over yet.

"Hello? Who's there? Please help!"

Jamie froze for a moment like a deer in the headlights. She needed to let Eddie know he was safe now, without him recognizing her voice. She had purchased a voice distorter long ago in the event she ever needed it. She reached into one of the many pockets on her specially made cargo pants, hoping the device still worked.

Jamie took a deep breath and depressed the button, "You're safe now, Edward." A wave of relief rushed through her gut at the sound of the deep mechanical voice.

"Leon?" Eddie twisted his face in confusion.

"No. Leon can't hurt you now. He'll never hurt anyone again. I'm going to get you back home now." Tears of joy welled up in Jamie's eyes at the thought of giving Carrie and Eddie a happy ending.

"Why are you disguising your voice? Who are you?" Eddie was even more confused now.

"I'm a friend. That's all I can tell you. I'm sorry for all of this, Edward."

Jamie pulled a hypodermic needle from another pocket. She injected him with her custom sedative and instantly put him to sleep. Moving quickly to untie Eddie's hands and ankles, she left his blindfold on, just in case. To be sure no one lurked outside, she peeked out the window, then hit the automatic opener. She backed her car inside, loaded Eddie into the trunk and out of sight. She needed to get him moved quickly, before the sedative wore off.

She drove several blocks away—as far as she dared— then pulled into the vacant parking lot of an Elementary School, carefully looking around to make sure no one could see her. Removing Eddie from her trunk, she set him gently against the building and then dug into his front pocket, hoping her recently departed brother hadn't broken his cell phone. When she pulled it out, she used his finger to unlock it and quickly located his partner's number.

"Eddie? Where the hell are you?" Barker's voice was a combination of concerned and annoyance.

"Come to Willard Fillmore Elementary on Bradbury." Jamie spoke through the voice distorter. "Eddie is alive and well." She hung up without waiting for any reply.

***

Ten minutes later, Jamie knocked on Carrie's door. She hoped her friend had already received the good news.

"What took you so long?" Carrie grabbed ahold of Jamie, hugging her so tight she could barely breathe.

"Sorry, I came as fast as I could. Heard anything yet?"

Carrie pulled back, tears in her eyes. "Eddie just called! He's alright! Jams, my baby is alive!"

"Oh, thank God!" Jamie hugged her best friend back just as tight.

Jamie had never saved anyone before. A first time for everything, she thought. The feeling was bittersweet, because Eddie had only been put in danger because of her. It made her feel hollow, despite the relief that the situation had ended well.

Jamie couldn't help further contemplating the whole situation. Her brother was responsible for putting Eddie's life in peril. He'd saved her all those years ago, and tonight she turned savior to thwart him. She'd murdered her brother less than an hour ago. She had always felt like a broken woman, even before she ever knew James Xavier Keenan existed. Now, he was dead, filling her—Jamie Windstein, Melissa Angela Keenan— with equal amounts of joy and sorrow. Tonight left her more broken than before, and truly alone for the first time ever. She wished James had never revealed himself to her. That knowledge became her burden to bear for the rest of her days, and no one to talk to about it. She hated Jimmy for leaving her with no other choice.

Chapter Thirteen: God's Law In The Devil's Land

1: Sometime in the '80s

Jeremiah Brixton was a cruel boy even by the low standards of those he bullied into being his friends. He often found himself alone on the long weekends that separated the school week, due to his nature. None of the other kids willingly hung out with him. If they saw him coming, they'd quickly go inside or hide, hoping he didn't see them. He was mean, foul-mouthed and always seemed to be swathed in a repulsive odor, like he'd just been rolled in a dead animal or a septic tank. He knew the other kids hated him, yet he seemed to revel in their discomfort. His low social status only served to fuel his cruelty.

It was a warm Saturday morning in late May when Jeremiah stepped out his back door, shooed out by his mother. She didn't seem to like him any more than his peers, though she'd never admit it. Jeremiah—never Jerry unless you wanted to eat a fresh knuckle sandwich—wandered around his backyard, getting more bored by the second. He whipped a stick around and pretended it was a sword, while he wandered his way toward the wooded area at the back of his parents' property. In the woods, he could let his imagination run wild with no one watching. For most children, that meant acting weird out of sight to avoid embarrassment, but for Jeremiah Brixton it usually meant finding small animals to torture without anyone stopping him. Being alone in the woods made him feel like a king, the lord of his own domain.

He walked deeper and deeper into trees that towered over him, his head down as he searched for good throwin' stones. When both of his pockets were full, he went on lookout, crouching beside an old maple tree, a rock poised in his hand for any critter with the misfortune to cross his path.

He did have one hell of an arm on him. The rocks leaving his hand were deadly missiles. Fortunately, a blind man had better aim, and led to him missing his target about ninety percent of the time. Jeremiah lacked the two things that could have improved his aim—patience and the will to practice. However, his inertia benefitted any poor creature who happened to cross his path whenever he entered the woods with a pocketful of death.

Jeremiah threw some of his stones at squirrels that scampered up and down nearby trees. He didn't know why he wasted his time on them, aside from boredom. They were far too quick. When he managed to aim true, the little tree rats—as his mother referred to them—were too quick. They saw the stone coming a mile away and jumped. He found better luck with birds, since they tended to sit still long enough for him to get off multiple shots.

He wanted a BB gun more than anything. In his mind he saw himself laying waste to countless scores of squirrels, rabbits, skunks and more. His mother told him he had to wait until he was twelve and only then if he proved she could trust him with one. Jeremiah, being slow, didn't have a clue what that meant. All he knew was he wanted a gun. However, being only eight, twelve seemed an eternity away.

Jeremiah alternated crouching and standing next to an old maple for over an hour, throwing his stones without coming anywhere near hitting anything. He had to replenish his ammunition between throws several times. Thankfully, stones were never in short supply. He crouched beside the tree, waiting for another critter and getting more and more frustrated with every miss. He rubbed his thumb over the smooth surface of the stone, poised for his next throw.

About a minute later—an eternity for a boy with no patience—a large grey rabbit speckled with blotches of black fur came hoping along, only a few feet away. Jeremiah stood up slowly, trying not to spook such a fat target. The rabbit was so close he was tempted to reach out and strangle it instead, but he couldn't possibly miss this one. He cocked back his arm, hurling it with all his might. The stone left his hand and whizzed through the air with tremendous speed. The thought of the rabbit hopping out of the way to mock his poor aim crossed his mind. He watched the stone fly straight and true, smacking the unsuspecting bunny in the eye. Jeremiah leapt back in surprise, nearly crapping his pants. Joy filled him almost instantly, though it came with a slight twinge of guilt. He laughed as the rabbit's hind legs kicked in its final death throes. The poor creature had met Jeremiah Brixton—it never hopped again.

Jeremiah's heart leapt into his throat, knowing his mother would not approve. If she found out what he did out here he'd never hear the end of it, and he could kiss his hope for a BB gun goodbye forever. He instinctively looked around to check for any prying eyes and relaxed, seeing no one. Walking up to his kill like a brave hunter—a dragon slayer—he smiled, watching the rabbit's legs, twitching still. He stared at the animal, filled with pride over what he had done.

Looking around again, he was suddenly suspicious although he saw nothing. He picked the dead rabbit up by its ears, lifting it to eye level. He stared with morbid fascination at the spot his stone hit. The eye bulged out, nearly exploding out of the socket. The stone had struck the critter square in the orbital bone above its eye, crushing it instantly. The bone had been driven down into the skull, forcing the eyeball to nearly pop from the socket. The damage he'd caused brought even more joy to Jeremiah and he couldn't stop smiling. The only sad part, for him, was that the rabbit died so quickly. He took great pleasure playing with stunned or nearly dead critters. He wanted to hear the rabbit scream. He found it so much more fun.

Jeremiah believed his cruelty to be safe from prying, judgmental eyes, yet he was not alone.

Little Jamie Windstein, much to the dismay of her parents, also delighted in playing alone in the woods, often wandering farther than her parents found comfortable. At the age of six, she had an independent streak that her parents both admired and detested. The more they scolded her for wandering too far off, the further she went. They scolded her to make their unhappiness known, though she always returned home unscathed, easing their worry.

While the dew still clung to the grass, soaking her shoes, Jamie set out that morning, into the woods that surrounded her parents' new home. The cool morning would soon burn away into a beautifully warm afternoon. She didn't think the country would be for her when her parents first announced they were leaving the city. However, she fell in love with the tranquility of the trees almost immediately. Her parents weren't fond of her long excursions into the woods, though they knew it was infinitely safer than her wandering off in the city. Her mother often quipped that if they didn't leave the city she'd one day be putting up missing posters with Jamie's picture on them. Sheila Windstein originally hailed from Quebec, thus dubbing her daughter: *L' Enfant Sauvage*, Wild Child in French, usually followed by the colloquialism "I swear you're going to be the death of me!"

She had been exploring the woods for a couple of hours when, off in the distance, she saw the schoolyard bully, Jeremiah Brixton. She didn't realize he lived so close or she would have insisted her parents move again, no matter how much she liked the woods. Walking through the trees with critters scampering about everywhere was the only place she felt peace. She may have only been six years old, but the chaos in her head—the nightmares—had already begun. She loved laying in the leaves and staring up at the tree tops bathed in sunlight. It warmed her to her core, to her soul. Her mind was a million miles away when she caught movement from the corner of her eye. She immediately saw red at having her peace disturbed. Seeing Jeremiah Brixton as the culprit did nothing to quell her anger.

Silent as a ninja, Jamie moved through the woods, following the bully. She went easily from tree to tree, remaining out of his sight. Staying hidden wasn't hard. Making sure not to giggle while watching him miss one critter after another with his little stones, now that was more difficult. She heard his stones whizzing through the air with amazing speed, however, he had less accuracy than a blindfolded blind man. She didn't think he could hit the broad side of a barn if it was an arm's reach away. She stifled her laughter, watching him miss one squirrel after another along with a few missed birds in between. She already hated the boy, and seeing him attempt to hurt defenseless animals wasn't helping, despite his poor aim. She felt more connected to animals than people—her parents included—which only fueled her hatred of the Brixton boy. She was irritated by what he was doing, but as long as he hit nothing, her anger remained on hold.

Jamie watched the cute bunny hop along way too close to the bully. She held her breath, seeing that it would take a small miracle for him to miss it, despite his terrible aim. She nearly called out to scare the rabbit off, however, it would leave her alone to defend herself against an angry boy almost twice her size. She wasn't afraid of him, she simply doubted she could stop the beating he would put on her. She wasn't concerned with the physical damage, but when she came home bloodied and bruised it would mean the end of her solitude among the trees. She covered her mouth as he reared his arm back and hoped she was still holding laughter back once he missed again.

With her hand tight over her mouth, she watched Jeremiah launch his stone at the unsuspecting rabbit. Her big green eyes widened in fascination, quickly turning to horror as the stone actually hit its mark. She managed not to scream at the sickening crunch. Tears welled up in her eyes when the bully picked the rabbit up by the ears and the limp body instantly told her what she already knew. She loathed Jeremiah Brixton before he killed the rabbit, and in that moment her feelings twisted to a deep-seated hatred. Her first thought was avenging the poor creature who did nothing other than coming too close to a piece of pure human filth.

Jamie's anger didn't improve as she watched what he did next. The fire of hate behind her eyes grew to rage as he swung the dead bunny, smacking it into the maple tree for no reason. Why he did it didn't matter, she just knew it was sick and wrong. She continued to watch, while desperately thinking of a way to avenge the poor bunny.

Jamie reached into her pocket and found the small jackknife she had secretly stolen from her father. She knew the knife alone wasn't a good enough weapon. She needed to find a way to give herself the upper hand. She crouched and watched him smack the dead rabbit over and over again into the tree trunk until finally a light bulb went off in her head.

Jeremiah pulled a jackknife from his pocket and lay the dead rabbit on the ground in front of him. Jamie took the opportunity to creep closer, with him distracting himself. He stabbed into the animal a few times, getting no satisfaction from it at all. He wanted to hear it squeal or scream for him. Flipping the rabbit on its back, he splayed its legs out, feeling a desperate need to see the bunny's insides and what made it tick. He held his small blade in a white-knuckled grip, ready to plunge it through the rabbit's fur, while Jamie crept closer and closer.

The Windsteins, in an attempt to assimilate Jamie into their new community, had begun taking her to church on Sundays. They weren't religious people; however, they knew it was the easiest way to meet some of their new neighbors. Visiting the local tavern would have been better to them, though it wouldn't help young Jamie find new friends. Their daughter's introverted nature seemed anti-social, and that was concerning for them. They wanted her to have some playmates. Jamie wouldn't protest going through these motions for a couple more years. For now, she went along because it made her parents happy.

The only thing she'd managed to learn so far in her Sunday bible studies, was how to gain the ire of old

Mrs. Higgins who wasn't fond of having "the word of God" questioned. One passage did stick in little Jamie's head, the only one worth anything, as far as she was concerned. The words swirled in her head now, while she crept up behind the little son of a bitch, Jeremiah Brixton.

Jeremiah leaned over his kill and struggled to drag his dull blade through the rabbit's fur to get at its guts. Jamie held her breath while creeping the last few steps, careful to avoid dry twigs or leaves that would alert him to her presence. She removed her cotton t-shirt from under her overalls and wrapped the ends tightly around her tiny fists.

Jeremiah was so preoccupied trying to see the guts of his kill, he never noticed little Jamie creeping up behind him. He wouldn't have seen her as a threat if he had.

Jamie paused with Jeremiah crouched right in front of her, doubting her plan for a fraction of a second. She knew there was no turning back for her now.

In order for her plan to work, she needed to get her shirt around his neck on the first try. If she failed, he would easily overpower her and beat her to a bloody pulp. She silently sucked in a deep breath and let out a blood curdling scream as she leapt forward onto the bully's back. She quickly looped her shirt around his head. It worked perfectly! The shirt slid under his chin just like she imagined. She started to squeeze. She hoped she could hold on through his struggles.

Jeremiah yelled in surprise, being caught completely off guard. His confusion quickly gave way to anger when his brain caught up to his situation. He sprang up with ease, twisting back and forth to try and throw off whoever his attacker was. Jamie let loose a warrior's howl and pulled even harder, squeezing with all her might to choke him before she flew off of him like a rag doll. He twisted and turned with no success. Jamie held on for dear life, hoping her strength would hold longer than his breath.

Jeremiah began swinging his fists wildly back over his shoulders, still clutching his pocketknife in his right hand. She easily dodged the blows. However, Jeremiah wasn't so lucky, managing to stab himself multiple times in his neck and shoulder. The seconds felt like days until finally the bully's face turned from red to white and finally purple, at which point he collapsed to the ground. Jamie refused to let go out of fear the boy might be faking it, so she silently counted to twenty before she felt comfortable letting go. She waited for her arms to stop shaking and then secured the unconscious bully.

A few minutes later Jeremiah's eyes popped open and he loudly gulped in air, trying to breathe. For several seconds he failed to see how dire his predicament was, so frantic to catch his breath. While the boy was unconscious, Jamie had dragged him to a young tree whose trunk couldn't have been more than about six inches in diameter. She removed his shirt and used it to tie him to the small tree, wrapping him around the midsection with his arms tightly secured at his sides. She used his belt to bind his hands behind his back. The position was awkward and painful and the knot she made in the belt was weak. Luckily, he couldn't move well enough to test it. She smiled, glad that she didn't need much time to dole out the punishment she had in mind.

Jeremiah looked at the little girl, who he called "Jamie Lamey," with a mixture of fear, anger, and confusion while struggling against his bindings.

"Do you go to Sunday school, Jerry?" She smiled knowing how much he hated the name.

"You better let me go!" He intended a tough demand, but his fear only produced a high-pitched whine.

Jamie moved closer. "No one can hear you out here, dipshit."

"You better start running Whiney Windstein!"

Jamie laughed. "Why? Is there a bear behind me? Hey Yogi! You out here?" Jamie cupped her hands to her mouth for extra volume.

"I swear you're gonna pay for this! Jamie Lamey!"

"Oh, shut up!" Jamie pulled the little knife from her pocket and opened it slowly in front of Jeremiah's face, then held the flat side of the blade to his cheek. "I asked you if you ever went to Sunday school." Coldly, she pressed the blade a little harder into his cheek.

Jeremiah's eyes nearly shot from their sockets. "No! Sunday school is for pussies!" He tried to stay defiant, even though his fear came through loud and clear.

Jamie tapped the blade against his cheek and smiled. "See if you had, you would have learned some of God's laws. Now, I guess I'm gonna need to teach you."

Jeremiah knew the devil when he came across it, despite never seeing the inside of a church. It stood before him now, in the form of tiny, Jamie Windstein. Fear gripped him tight though he wasn't able to hold his bowels so firmly.

"Ewww!" Jamie backed away, covering her mouth and nose. "Some bully you are." She reveled in his embarrassment. "Glad I can stand over here for this part." She retreated a few feet to where she set the stones she found in his pockets. "It's time for you to learn God's most important law. Ever heard of 'an eye for an eye,' Jerry? Let's see how you like it."

Jamie took her time whipping the stones at him. Unfortunately for Jeremiah Brixton, little Jamie Lamey possessed a solid fast ball arm and, more importantly, deadly accurate aim. He screamed as the stones whistled through the air, hitting him one bruise inducing smack at a time. When Jamie's arm finally tired, Jeremiah's face ran red with blood. Both of his eyes were already turning a deep purple, his nose was broken in several places and he sat trying to spit out the remains of his teeth. He also sobbed uncontrollably while she laughed and rubbed the dirt from her hands. However, Jamie wasn't through with the bully yet.

"You shouldn't hurt helpless little animals, Jerry." She paused with a devilish grin. "You enjoy hurting things, don't you?" Retrieving her knife from her pocket again she tapped it against his bloody cheek. "Best answer me, Jerry."

"Yes," Jeremiah blubbered the word.

"Guess what, Jerry? I do too. Not cute cuddly bunnies though. I enjoy hurting you. An eye for an eye, Jerry." She winked at him, only convincing him that she was in fact, the devil in disguise.

Jeremiah screamed bloody murder as she shoved the short blade deep into his left eye. A mix of blood and ocular fluid ran down his cheek, the blade and finally her hand. She flicked it away, wiping her hand on Jeremiah's pant leg.

"Yuck! Now, let's see if the other one does that!"

Jamie laughed while Jeremiah screamed. He protested but he was powerless to stop the little girl who was avenging a bunny. A bunny he killed as much by accident as intent. In Jeremiah Brixton's final moments, he began to repent his many sins. His penitence came too late.

Jamie Windstein stood over Jeremiah Brixton and looked down at her handiwork. She felt no sympathy, no pity, and, certainly, no mercy. She cared about animals with all of her heart—but people…all she saw in people was cruelty wrapped in flesh. People were shit.

Killing Jeremiah taught her something she hadn't known. She really hated the sound of crying. She walked around behind the tree, behind her victim. She couldn't take his blithering cries any longer. She put the blade to his throat, sinking it deep and pulling her hand hard across. His crying ceased immediately. She felt no guilt from his death, only happiness that the wretched sound ended. The quick burst of arterial spray made her laugh with joy, but it ended too quickly. She wiped the blade and her hands off on his shirt and then walked away, like nothing happened.

Jamie whistled happily, skipping all the way home. A few days later the body of Jeremiah Brixton was discovered tied to the tree where she left him. The small town was in a panic, though Jamie didn't care. The only unfortunate part for her was her parents never allowed her in the woods alone again. She lamented the fact, though she harbored no regret over her first kill. It served as a valuable lesson: always hide the body.

2: Present Day

Detective Stephen Barker paced back and forth across the room, practically wearing a hole in the carpet. He wasn't worried or anxious. However, he had never been more pissed off. He knew it would be nearly impossible to keep the mess out of the papers. The press was the least of his worries. But he saw no way to keep the feds away now. Their quiet little secret investigation was about to blow up. If that wasn't bad enough, the murderer he had been hunting for over five years would likely go underground until the heat died down. He could feel *The Executioner* slipping through his hands.

Officer Eddie Washington stood alongside Dr. Clive Ketchum, in the center of the room trying to make any sense of the scene, while Barker paced and grumbled behind them. Eddie had only ever been to the Adam's Mark once for a Christmas party years ago. Now, he stood in one of the most lavish suites in the hotel—

possibly the entire city—looking over a crime scene so gruesome that he'd never even seen anything like it in a movie.

"That one is Leon? The same Leon who attacked you, Edward?" Dr. Ketchum broke the silence, though he knew the answer.

Eddie looked down at the man tied to the chair on their right. "Yeah, that one is Leon. Leon was nothing more than an act. I'll never forget the way he looked at me before he attacked. I've never seen anyone look more evil, Doc." The thought sent a shiver up his spine.

"Well, it looks like he won't be hurting anyone ever again. I'm sorry, Edward. I'm glad you came out fairly unscathed. Dr. Butler cleared you for duty already? His psyche assessments usually take forever."

"Yeah. I know he's not known for his speediness. They call him Doc Shlomo around the station." Eddie smiled. "To answer your question, doc, I'm not 'officially' here. Barker told me I needed to see this. I can't say I disagree. Hope he doesn't get in any trouble for it." Eddie glanced back over his shoulder to see if Barker was listening.

Barker continued his pacing, oblivious to everyone and everything around him.

"You're gonna drop straight down to the next floor if you don't stop, Stephen. Why don't you come over here while I show Edward the letter?" Ketchum frowned seeing Barker ignored him completely.

"Letter?"

"Yes, it's why he's pacing back there. We're probably gonna have company soon, Edward. The kind with suits, mirrored Ray-Bans and black SUVs." Ketchum frowned.

The news didn't surprise Eddie. He looked at the two dead men bound to their chairs. The man on the left was missing both ears and his nose, all of which laid at his feet covered in the blood from his slit throat. The man on the right, Leon, had numerous small, deep lacerations on his face, chest and shoulders along with his throat being cut ear to ear. Evidence markers expanded a few feet in front of each man, indicating the pattern of arterial spray, leading back to a pool of blood at each man's feet, soaking into the carpet.

"I assume we haven't found a fingerprint, thread of hair or anything else indicating who did this?" Eddie knew the answer but asked anyway.

"Nothing other than the letter, Edward." Dr. Ketchum handed Eddie a piece of hotel stationery.

Eddie wore rubber gloves, yet still held the page gently by the upper corner. He frowned, seeing even a handwriting analysis would be useless. The words were printed in block style letters, most likely with the hotel pen sitting beside the stationery. He wasn't surprised by that. However, the letter itself made his jaw drop to the floor. It was addressed to him personally. No wonder Barker insisted he be there.

To Officer Edward Washington,

The two men before you killed Karen and David Osbourne and Abigail Peterson. My apologies, I cannot point you to the bodies so their families may gain closure from a proper funeral. I was unable to learn the whereabouts of the remains. The man missing a few pieces is Thomas Combs. The man you knew as Leon has gone by many names but his real name is James Xavier Keenan. Both men have murdered many, though I do not know their victims' names nor exactly how many, I apologize. I know you will continue to do your job but I implore you to stop looking for me. You owe me that much now. Your life for my life. That is the only warning I can give. I have seen a multitude of horrors, but in my experience an existence that does not hide a great madness is of no value whatsoever.

P.S. I didn't want their heads and, btw, thanx for the nickname.

- The Xecutioner

Eddie looked up at Ketchum in stunned silence.

"You know what it means?" Barker grumbled from behind them.

Eddie didn't hesitate. "It means *The Xecutioner* saved my life."

"Exactly." Ketchum chimed in.

"This place has surveillance cameras?" Eddie's eyes glimmered with hope.

"All over the place—and guess what?" Barker sneered.

"They were miraculously turned off during the murders?" Eddie took a stab at it.

"Even better! Somehow all the footage from the entire day is missing. No tape backup." Barker snarled.

"Helluva coincidence." Eddie shook his head.

The shock of all the information left Eddie silent and stunned. The room swam out of focus on him and then a light went off in his mind. Thomas Combs, the earless, noseless victim also happened to be the new wealthy client of Jamie Windstein. Was someone targeting her clients? It was the only conclusion his mind allowed. Jamie was far too small to be *The Xecutioner*. He didn't think of himself as sexist, however, he couldn't fathom a female doing this. A conversation about the new coincidence would have to wait for later. He thought it best to keep the connection to himself—Barker may jump to conclusions. It gave him a head start on the FBI, who would likely swoop in any second. He had no intention of ceasing the investigation, and he knew Barker and Ketchum felt the same way.

3

Eva DeLong opened her eyes, surprised to see the sun shining through her window but happy to feel its warmth on her face. The blinds covering it had never been open before. Concern filled her for a moment, then she remembered it was Sunday. The sweet little aide, Melissa, must be on duty today since big darky occasionally took a weekend off. She didn't get many reprieves from her primary tormentor, so she tried to enjoy it while it lasted. She actually smiled for once— his petty torments and snide remarks would be gone for a day. It was the closest she got to a vacation in her current physical state.

Eva closed her eyes to the sun, simply enjoying the warmth creeping through her wrinkled skin to her old bones beneath. She decided to have a good day right then and there. Maybe she'd even go play bingo with the other residents, she thought. Her joy only increased when she reopened her eyes to see a hummingbird buzzing around the yellow petals of the sunflowers poking up from below her window. She couldn't remember the last time she woke up feeling so good— then, of course, it all came to a screeching halt.

"Well good morning to my most favoritest patient in the whole wide world!" Kirk Sheidt's voice boomed from the doorway.

She groaned loudly, recognizing the voice without even looking up. She wanted to pretend to be asleep but it was too late. Her good day was shot to hell before it even started. A tear spilled from the corner of her eye. She peered back to the window, finding the pretty little hummingbird was gone too. She longed for the days when she'd shackled this dark skinned son of a bitch to a wall and beat him until he was welted, raw, and bleeding.

"Why, Miss DeLong, you don't seem happy to see me at all! Was you expecting that cute young thing to take care of you today? I'm so sorry, ma'am." The sarcasm dripped from Kirk's tongue. "She wanted to spend the day with her fiancé, so I told her I'd happily take care of you. I guess it's your lucky day!" Kirk shot her the biggest dumb smile he could muster, knowing how much she hated it.

"Fuck yourself, blackie!" DeLong grumbled under her breath.

Kirk made no reply while shutting the blinds. He knew Melissa always opened the blinds for the residents when the sun was shining. She thought a little sunshine made everyone feel better, which Kirk conceded was true. But DeLong didn't deserve to feel better. He loved getting her hopes up right before crushing her with the reality of his presence. It made him happier than it should.

Kirk pulled back the blanket that covered DeLong, enjoying how she flinched and shrunk away from him. He picked her up, dropping her into her wheelchair even harder than usual. Something in the old bitch snapped loudly. He thought her hip possibly popped out of place, which made him even happier. It didn't matter now if he did permanent damage.

He leaned down to whisper in DeLong's ear. "You should really be more careful, bitch. Wanna know why I'm so happy today?"

DeLong remained silent.

"Your visitor is coming to see you today. I know she's a little late, but she has good news and bad news for you. I'll leave it for her to tell you, though. And that's only part of why I'm so damn happy today.

Wanna guess the rest? Go on! Guess why I'm so happy, you wrinkled up, old twat."

"Finally figure out who your daddy is? Fucking mongrel." DeLong snarled back.

"Any other day, I'd make you pay for a dumbass remark like that, but today is your lucky day!" He gripped her shoulders painfully hard. "You see, I'm happy today because it's my last day here. Doesn't that make you happy too?" Kirk relished his final moments with his nemesis.

DeLong knew his reason couldn't be good for her, so she saw no reason to be polite. "Certainly! Glad they finally wised up and decided to get rid of a worthless nigger like you." DeLong sat back with a self-satisfied grin. "Take me to breakfast, boy."

Kirk squeezed her neck until she teared up. "Good one. You can't bring me down today, cunt. Eva, it's been a real pleasure watching you wither away and suffer in this place, but I'm afraid I've seen enough. It's my last day here because it's yours too. You'll see. It's going to be so much fun! Sorry no one will be throwing you a goodbye party. No one likes you." Kirk put on his own self-satisfied smile. "Oh and if you think opening your mouth for help will save you, then think again. Everyone here thinks you have dementia. Or was it Alzheimer's disease I put in your chart? I don't remember. Doesn't matter. Ain't none of your powerful friends left to help you now, so keep your mouth shut. It'll all be over soon."

Kirk wheeled Eva DeLong down the hall to the cafeteria for her last meal. As last meals go, people on death row probably had it better than reconstituted eggs, lukewarm oatmeal, dry wheat toast, two pathetic greasy sausage links, three ounces of orange juice and black coffee. Kirk wished it was even worse. He remained glued to her as promised, the entire time, only moving from her side twice to help out another resident. DeLong, for her part, ate her breakfast in silence and wished for the strength to stand up and stab the black bastard in the throat with her fork.

Once DeLong finished her breakfast, Kirk wheeled her into the common area until her special visitor arrived. The call from Jamie Windstein surprised him the previous evening, only to be stunned into silence by what she had to say. The news of Tommy's and Jimmy's death brought an odd mix of grief, anger, relief, and joy. He was upset. However, it meant their nightmare was over. He knew Al would feel the same way. A part of him expected their ordeal to end this way. Jimmy warned him at the beginning it might. They played a dangerous game and it had caught up to them. He wasn't sure he'd actually believed it would.

Jamie left out the gory details, merely relaying his former friends were now at peace. Stunned by the news, he nearly fell over when she explained the deaths weren't the main reason for her call. She wanted his help. They decided Sunday was perfect for Jamie's plan, since the home's staff would be at a minimum. When she finished, he immediately called his colleague, Melissa, to see if he could take her shift. She happily agreed. Then he made the hard call to the only friend he had left, Al Jourgensen.

Eva Delong sat in the common area, becoming increasingly annoyed by the blithering idiot preaching his form of righteousness from the television screen, lacking the strength to roll herself away. She refused to cry, despite the tremendous pain. The big bastard displaced her hip when he dropped her into her chair. She didn't want to give him the satisfaction.

To take her mind off the pain, she tried thinking about who her mystery visitor might be. Jimmy had warned her days ago, though she never showed. She couldn't understand why he didn't come back to gloat one last time. She knew her end was imminent. She wasn't afraid. She wanted it over and done. She had sinned. *So what*, she thought. If they were going to kill her, she wished they'd get on with it. She wished she had killed the whole gang years ago, a mistake they made her regret daily. She couldn't see how they could possibly want her old broken-down body at this point. Wasn't her current life worse than death? She considered herself dead already, yet her body simply hadn't received the message.

A short time later, Jamie Windstein walked through the doors of Lake View Manor Nursing Home. She nearly skipped in, she was so happy. No one sat at the front desk to make her sign in, just as Kirk told her. She abruptly stopped after turning the corner and seeing a dark-skinned giant waiting for her. The man was nearly seven feet tall, in her estimation and solid.

"Kirk Scheidt, I hope?"

"Expecting someone a little more…uh…normal?" Kirk smiled at the tiny woman who looked like someone he could crush with one hand.

"You could have mentioned it on the phone." Jamie said dryly.

"What fun is that?" They laughed. "This way, Jamie." Kirk motioned her ahead of him down the hallway.

Kirk didn't show it, but he was no less surprised by Jamie's appearance. How did such a tiny woman overpower and kill both Tommy and Jimmy. He also felt an instant attraction. She was quite stunning, a fact Jimmy left out. She looked like a dwarf next to him, but then again, most people did. He walked behind, admiring her petite figure. Her long black hair combined with her sexy emerald eyes captivated him. She was the most beautiful woman he'd ever seen. He never considered himself the sappy sort, however, he had a stomach full of butterflies at the moment. He shook his head, trying to focus on the task at hand.

"Grandma!" Jamie rushed to DeLong, making a big show of it.

DeLong looked at her with a blank expression. "Who the fuck are you?"

"Grandma!" Jamie scolded DeLong. "That isn't proper language. It's me. Melissa! You remember!" Jamie put on the biggest, friendliest smile she could muster, embracing Delong in what looked like a loving hug. "Keep your mouth shut, bitch, or I'll let my big friend tear you in half," She whispered in DeLong's ear and then stood back up. "Let's go back to your room so we can visit without disturbing these nice people. Kirk, was it? Would you mind?"

Kirk wheeled DeLong back to her room with Jamie walking astride the chair. He had a burning desire to grab Jamie's hand for the walk, which he fought off. The butterflies continued to flutter in his stomach all the way to DeLong's room. Once inside he shut the door behind them.

Jamie took a seat on the edge of the bed. "I'm afraid I come the bearer of bad news, you crusty old cunt. Your favorite visitors James and Thomas won't be coming to see you anymore. I killed them." Jamie leaned in, absorbing DeLong's reaction.

DeLong unexpectedly burst out laughing. "Honey, that's the best damn news I've heard in years! I think I could learn to like you, whoever you are. I sure as hell know you ain't Melissa. Do tell me it was slow and painful." Delong continued to laugh.

Jamie slapped her hard across the cheek, putting an end to her cackling. "There's also bad news, I'm afraid, so shut the fuck up and listen. I know who you are. I know who you were. I know all the nasty, dirty things you've done. Let me tell you, none of your powerful friends are around to save your ass anymore. You're mine." The fire of vengeance relit in Jamie's eyes. "Jimmy was my brother. Yes, I killed him. I did it for my own reasons. Make no mistake, cunt, it doesn't mean for one single solitary second that I forgive or forgot what you did to him. Here's a little more news for you. Your old pals—your Goon Squad, Keane and Rollins—I killed them too. Their deaths were extremely slow and painful." Jamie stated with a satisfied grin.

DeLong looked Jamie in the eye with feigned apathy. "Honey, I don't know why you're here, but that ain't exactly bad news either. Those two were useful idiots a whole lifetime ago. I could care less if they're alive, dead, or hanging by their balls from your shower rod. Wanna get on with it, because the only bad news you gave me was the fact you were related to that rotten little bastard, James. My sincere condolences on that."

Jamie raised her hand then stopped herself, knowing that DeLong was trying to bait her into a quick death. "I really didn't expect you to be such a daft cunt. I've played with all your friends and now I'm here. Guess who's next, dumbass?" Jamie stared coldly into DeLong's eyes. "You think you've suffered? I came to let you know you don't even know the meaning of the word. The bad news? I'm an excellent teacher. So I'm taking you on a little trip down memory lane for today's lesson. The good news? Well…you never have to see this place again. Don't get too excited though, I guarantee you'll beg to come back here very soon." Jamie hopped off the bed and addressed the giant. "Shall we, Kirk?"

Jamie took Kirk's arm once they exited the room. Her touch had him floating on air while she practically skipped with joy all the way to the exit. The trio wound their way through the halls of Lake View Manor calmly and slowly, like nothing was out of the ordinary. They made it outside without anyone asking questions. To them, it was just a granddaughter taking nice ol' granny out to lunch, or maybe shopping. They walked to Jamie's car without incident, where Kirk loaded DeLong in the back seat. Jamie slammed the door closed with great satisfaction.

"Can I ask you something?" Kirk bashfully looked down.

"Anything, big man." Jamie smiled up at him.

"Why did you tell her your name was Melissa?"

"Apparently, it's my given name. Jimmy told me what happened to us, who we were, and how we were separated. My real name is Melissa Angela Keenan. I'm sorry. I know he never told you our story. Thomas didn't know either until…well, just before."

Kirk was suddenly suspicious. "Did he tell you anything about me? Obviously, he left out my handsome good looks." Kirk smirked.

"Honestly, nothing. I found you in his phone so I looked you up and saw where you worked. I naturally assumed if you worked at the home you were working with them. I took a chance that you'd help me."

"They were my best friends, along with Al. I knew they were out of control and it might end this way. I'm glad it was you and not some anonymous stranger or the cops."

"Jimmy tried to kill one of the only friends I have. I couldn't let it slide. I am sorry." Jamie sincerely reached up to put a hand on the big man's arm.

"I don't blame you." There was an awkward silence. "Guess I better get back before someone misses me. Meet you after my shift?" He felt like a nerd asking the hot, popular girl to the prom.

"You have more right to be there than I do. What are your plans now?"

"I planned to quit at the end of my shift. I only worked here for her. No reason to put up with it now. No one likes me here."

"Why not quit now and come with me? Maybe, work with me after this. In my line of work I could use someone as physically intimidating as you. My brains, your muscle?" Jamie smiled at him with sincerity.

"You don't have to tell me twice! I do have to ask. Umm, what do you do?" She could tell him she worked in raw sewage and he'd still say yes.

"I'm a private investigator. Long hours, shit pay. We can work out the details later."

"Sounds great! Count me in! I'll meet you there. I know the way." He was so filled with joy he felt like he may burst.

"It's a date. See you soon." Jamie turned to get in her car and Kirk went back inside.

Jamie took her time making her way to the remains of the Mormont Home. She was in no hurry for this journey to end. She wanted to savor every second of such a beautiful day. She thought about the events of the last week—one which felt like a full lifetime—while she drove. She thought about how Thomas came into her office, beginning the journey. She actually felt a twinge of sadness, not over the death of Thomas or Jimmy, but that the mystery was solved. She found all the answers to all the unanswered questions, including the why about everything. DeLong was the final chapter of the whole sordid story. The entire incident would be in her rearview very soon.

The bodies of Thomas and James, along with her note, may bring trouble to her doorstep, but it was nothing she couldn't easily handle. She saved her best friend's husband, thereby saving Carrie as well, in the nick of time. All in all, everything was right with the world in her eyes. The only worry for her was Eddie's curiosity in the coincidences surrounding the connections to her. For now, that was a down the road problem. Now, it looked like she found a new friend in Kirk Scheidt, who would come in extremely handy. Then there was little Albert Jourgensen who owed her too—big time. She didn't think having a set of eyes inside Sandy the Shark's office was a bad thing. Ending DeLong would be the end of a chapter and then tomorrow another story would begin. She was glad to have a new friend to add to her short list in the next one. Jamie Windstein was truly happy, the first time in a very long time.

She pulled around the back of Mormont to keep her car out of sight and opened the back door for DeLong, telling her to walk or be dragged—Jamie didn't really care which. DeLong grumbled reluctance, recognizing their destination despite its current dilapidated state. She drew in a deep breath, deciding to meet her fate with all the dignity she could summon. Jamie marched her slowly over the rugged terrain. She didn't care if DeLong fell, but she didn't want to have to pick her up every two feet the whole way.

DeLong cringed at the smell of her old kingdom—the faint musty aroma was drowned out by the overpowering stench of urine from the homeless taking up residence at night. There was also the stink of ammonia from the hordes of rodents who called the abandoned building home. Jamie held DeLong steady, marching her along the scattered garbage further into the old building along the path familiar to both of them. Jamie was surprised DeLong put up no resistance, seeming to accept her fate. It made the journey to their final destination easier, although Jamie didn't care if the old bitch accepted her coming death or not.

A few minutes later they rounded the final corner in their journey together. DeLong froze at the sight of the red door. The door seemed to bring the reality of the pain waiting for her into focus. The rush of memories, perhaps, held her stiff. Jamie let her pause a second, hoping the old woman would make her drag her by the hair the final few feet.

"Keep going. You knew where we were headed." Jamie spat the words at her.

DeLong hesitated. "I can't. I won't."

Jamie wondered if the fear she heard was the first the old bitch had ever felt. It made her smile. "Walk or be dragged by the last few wisps of grey you have up there, bitch. I told you we were taking a trip down memory lane. It's your choice. Decide now." Jamie had no mercy for DeLong.

"No. I won't go in there." DeLong's eyes filled with tears and fear.

Jamie didn't give her any longer to think about it. She pulled her along by the arm. DeLong's slippered feet slid along the filthy old tile until she hit some debris on the floor. She pulled back, unwilling to go any further. She remembered the red door, although she didn't expect it to have such an effect on her.

She once taught every child, who had the misfortune of arriving at Mormont Home for Children, to fear this door. Now, the door stared at her. Sobbing, she felt the pain, hate, and fear of each of those children as she crossed the threshold. Their scared little faces shuffled through her mind in a slide show from hell. They all wished for revenge in life. She felt them all here waiting to get it. The weight of her sins crashed down on her with terminal velocity.

Jamie smiled. "Once upon a time, this door led to your kingdom of sorrow. Now, you face something worse. This is my kingdom now, your sorrow will be legendary."

A wicked smile crossed Jamie's lips while she dragged a screaming, crying Eva Delong across the threshold of the red door, then into the secret dungeon. She had put all the pieces back together to forever close this chapter of the story.

END

ABOUT THE AUTHOR

Feind Gottes [Fee-nd Gotz] is a horror nut, metal lover and an award winning horror author. Feind currently resides near Omaha, NE with his girlfriend, son, and two crazy cats.

Feind has short stories and flash fiction appearing in over a dozen anthologies with more slated for release including his first ever published poem. His novella, **Essence Asunder**, unleashed by **HellBound Books** in 2018 was his first solo release. Feind also gained his first editing credit by co-editing the anthology, **Blood From A Tombstone**, with Don Smith Jr in 2019.

The first draft of Feind's debut novel, **Piece It All Back Together**, won the 2016 Dark Chapter Press Prize followed in 2017 by a Top Ten finish in The Next Great Horror Writer Contest and winning the Vincent Price Scariest Writer Award from Tell-Tale Publishing.

<u>Feind on the Web</u>

Feind Gottes

Amazon   Feind Gottes

Website   Feind's Fiends

Facebook @FeindGotteshorrorwriter

Twitter   @FeindGottes

Other HellBound Books Titles
Available at: www.hellboundbookspublishing.com

ReIncarnate

Cil Franklen wasn't good. He wasn't nice, liked, or thin. Hell, he wasn't even handsome!
And soon, he wouldn't even be HIM!
Some people get the chance to do good things: Bill Gates, Al Pacino, Einstein, Mother Teresa, Martin Luther King. Given a little magic, people can be magical, but not Cil. He just wanted to kill.
All life's fog built up in him to the point of leaking out... but it wasn't the pleasant puffy fog - it was dark and sickening.
Cil found a way to live again. And again, and again and again.
And he killed again. And again, and again, and, again.
REINCARNATION!

The Dead Room

A week before Christmas, terrorists detonate dozens of dirty bombs throughout Britain and release a man-made contagion, leading Nicola Allen to begin a frantic hunt for her husband and daughter while a nation burns. Fleeing from a horrendous event she refuses to speak of and desperate to find shelter in a dying country, Nicola's sister-in-law, Cate, takes cover in a partly destroyed hospital. Terrorised by visions of mutilated bodies and the screams of phantom children, Cate joins a group of survivors, all of whom are under attack by ruthless scavengers and looters. If Nicola is to have any chance of finding her family and if Cate is to escape from the siege, they must reunite and then descend into the belly of the ruined hospital where the horrific truth of what truly connects the two women is waiting for them. Waiting for them down in the dead room.

The Toilet Zone

RESTROOM READING AT ITS MOST FRIGHTENING!

Compiled and edited by the grand master of 80's

schlock horror, Bret McCormick, each one of this collection of 32 terrifying tales is just the perfect length for a visit to the smallest room.... At the very boundaries of human imagination dwells one single, solitary place of solitude, of peace and quiet, a place in which your regular human being spends, on average, 10 to 15 minutes - at least once every single day of their lives.

Now, consider a typical, everyday reading speed of 200 to 250 words per minute - that means your average visitor has the time to read between 2,500 to 4,000 words, which makes each and every one of these 32 tales of terror - from some of the best contemporary independent authors - within this anthology of horror the perfect, meticulously calculated length. Dare you take a walk to the small room from where inky shadows creep out to smother the light and solitude's siren call beckons you?

Dare you take a quiet, lonely walk into… The Toilet Zone

Invasive Species

A monster has come to Maldus, Arkansas, and the residents of the small mountain town are too busy to notice. With the monster comes something even more terrifying and threatening than gnashing teeth or razor-sharp claws.

The monster has brought change. The residents of the small mountain town are too busy to notice at first. Busy with things such as addiction, racism, work, or land deals. Unnoticed, the change the monster brings in its insidious wake spreads like wildfire.

Unnoticed, the town of Maldus falls prey to an Invasive Species.

Tremble

Widow and single mother, Rebecca Noland, wants nothing more than to rekindle the passion with her overworked fiancé, Detective Dan Slaviche. Expecting to surprise him by slipping into his apartment before he comes home from work, her curiosity gets the best of her when she discovers the key to unlock his desktop. What she finds there is a nightmare that sends her, along with her seven-year-old son, running for their lives.

Terrified and broke, her only option is to flee to her family's estate in Tremble, Tennessee where memories of her mother's violent death still haunt her childhood home.

But bad memories aren't the only thing that await her. As Dan abandons all morals in his attempt to locate his bride-to-be, Rebecca struggles to make the house a home for her son while growing closer to her next-door neighbors.

Her sanity comes into question when she realizes the entity responsible for her mother's murder is lying in wait, intent on destroying anyone who tries to come between it and the object of its deadly obsession… her.

**A HellBound Books LLC
Publication**

http://www.hellboundbookspublishing.com

Printed in the United States of America